**Praise for Harriet Fox, w̶**

'A delicious Art Deco novel ̶
heroine . . . Lovely ̶
**Marius G̶**

'What a page-turner! A bookshop in wartime Lisbon
is the gateway to a thrilling world of mystery,
espionage, adventure and romance.'
**Daisy Wood**

'Original and immersive. If you read one
Second World War novel in 2025 – make it this one.'
**Eva Glyn**

'A lively trip up the vertiginous backstreets of wartime
Lisbon . . . I lapped it up!'
**Eliza Graham**

'A must-read for historical fiction fans and for me,
Kerry Barrett's best book yet.'
**Annie Lyons**

'Heart-breaking but so uplifting – Kerry really is a
hugely talented voice.'
**Nicola Cornick**

'Wonderful . . . Both heart-warming and heart-
breaking . . . Unputdownable.'
**Kathleen McGurl**

'A gripping "what if" tale with a larger-than-life
heroine at its heart.'
**Tessa Harris**

**HARRIET FOX** is a writer and journalist who writes dark and twisty crime novels bringing women's stories out of the shadows of history. Harriet is obsessed with crime fiction, horror films and ghost stories as well as history podcasts and cryptic crosswords.

She also writes historical fiction as Kerry Barrett.

# THE WOMEN IN THE SHADOWS

## HARRIET FOX

ONE PLACE. MANY STORIES

HQ
An imprint of HarperCollins*Publishers* Ltd
1 London Bridge Street
London SE1 9GF

www.harpercollins.co.uk

HarperCollins*Publishers*
Macken House, 39/40 Mayor Street Upper
Dublin 1 D01 C9W8, Ireland

This edition 2025

1
First published in Great Britain by HQ,
an imprint of HarperCollins*Publishers* Ltd 2025

PB ISBN: 9780008744182
TPB ISBN: 9780008801878

Set in Sabon LT Std by HarperCollins*Publishers* India

Printed and bound in the UK using 100% Renewable
Electricity by CPI Group (UK) Ltd

*For my brilliant cousin Caroline who shares two of my passions: the Jack the Ripper mystery and* Dirty Dancing.

# Chapter 1

## Martha

Martha was so bored she thought she might fall asleep right here where she sat, in the front bar at the White Swan. She rested her chin on her hand and tried to look interested in what the chap sitting in front of her was saying. Something about how quick he was with something. Some sort of weapon, she assumed, as he was in a soldier's uniform. She didn't much care. She was only here because her friend Peg had dragged her in for a drink when she'd clocked the soldiers inside. She had always been weak for a fella in uniform, had Peg. And judging by the way she was all over the fella who'd caught her eye, she was just as weak now.

'What do you think?' the soldier was saying. Martha couldn't remember his name. Jack, was it? James? She smiled at him and fluttered her eyelashes.

'I think you sound awful brave,' she lied. 'Keeping us all safe in our beds at night.'

Jack or James nodded modestly. 'We do our best,' he said. He reached out and stroked Martha's hand. 'Talking of beds . . .' He winked at her. 'I'd like to keep you safe in yours.'

There was no doubting his meaning. Martha stifled a sigh. She knew it would come to this.

'Well,' she said, leaning forward slightly so he got the benefit of a glimpse of her bosom. 'The room I rent is strictly women only.'

That was another lie. She'd not had a proper room since she'd left Mrs Basfield's place last month. It had broken her heart to leave there – it was nicer than other places she'd stayed and it had really been women only, so it felt much safer. And a lot less smelly. But the rent was higher, and Martha knew when she had the choice between a safe, clean bed for the night and a drink, she'd always choose the drink. It was the way she'd always been.

She tilted her head slightly and let her fingers trail down her long neck. Her Henry always said she had a lovely neck. The soldier's eyes darkened as he watched her hand brush her collarbone, and Martha knew she was winning.

'I know a place we can go,' she said. 'No questions asked.'

'Sounds good,' said the soldier, his voice gruff.

'It's a bit pricier, mind.'

'How much?'

Martha thought about it. 'Five pence,' she said.

The soldier laughed. 'Cheap at half the price.'

Martha could have kicked herself. She should have asked for more. Next to them, Peg was virtually in the other chap's lap, his hand halfway up her skirt.

'We're going to go,' the other soldier said to Jack or James. 'We've got business to attend to.'

*Sod you, Peg*, Martha thought. *Don't give it up too easy.*

Giggling, Peg got up. The soldier with her was practically drooling. It made Martha feel a little queasy.

'I'll see you tomorrow,' Peg said cheerfully. Martha glowered at her, and Peg pretended not to notice. She watched them leave the pub. Peg paused to speak to a young woman who was just coming in. She looked a little familiar, but

Martha couldn't place her. Then the woman disappeared into a group of drinkers, and Peg's chap practically dragged her outside. There was no doubting what he was after, and it looked like he wasn't going to wait to get it.

Martha turned her attention back to her own soldier. He was, after all, the only way she was going to afford a bed for the night.

'Shall we go, too?' the soldier said, draining his glass.

'Let's have another drink first, shall we?' Martha said. Under the table she put her hand on his thigh and squeezed gently. She leaned over and spoke in his ear. 'We've got all night.'

He nuzzled her neck and she made a little throaty moan only he could hear. Then she pulled away and pushed her empty glass towards him.

'Large one,' she said.

The soldier's eyes flashed with annoyance and Martha felt a flare of irritation of her own. These bloody men, with one thing on their mind, so quick to anger if they didn't get it. But this lad didn't scare her, no matter how fast he was with his weapon, or how firm his thighs. And she wasn't about to give up now. She leaned over the table and kissed him, giving him just enough to leave him wanting.

'Large one,' she said again. This time he got up from the table and headed to the bar. Martha leaned back in her chair, exhausted. She was too old for this nonsense.

'Martha?'

She turned to see the young woman she'd seen coming in and realised it was Bet Palmer, the daughter of her old friend Jane.

'Oh, Bet, I saw you come in but I didn't recognise you straightaway.' She'd known Bet since she was a little girl and now here she was, grown up. Martha felt even older than she had done two minutes ago.

'I saw Peg,' Bet said. 'She looked like she had her hands full.'

Martha rolled her eyes. 'Are you here on your own?' She frowned. The White Swan was no place for a pretty young woman like Bet.

Bet shrugged. 'Looking for my dad,' she said. 'You ain't seen him, have you?'

'Not for about ten years,' Martha said. 'Thought he was in jail.'

'Well, he was, last we heard. But someone told Mum they'd seen him, and you know what she's like with her nerves, so I wanted to put her mind at rest.'

'She still bad?'

Bet gave Martha a small smile. 'Actually, no she ain't. Not really. She's got a good job now, sewing down Spitalfields. She's not like she was when he was first put away.'

'That's good news.'

'I don't want her going back there,' Bet said.

Martha put her hand on Bet's arm. 'Course you don't. Listen, tell her you saw me and if he was back, I'd know.'

Bet's shoulders relaxed. 'You know everyone.'

'I do,' Martha said, feeling a bit brighter for helping. 'I'll keep an eye out, but I reckon that waster's still behind bars, or long dead, or worse.'

'Worse than death?' said Bet with a grin. 'What's that then?'

'Oh, you'd be surprised.' Martha chuckled and she was pleased when Bet joined in. She liked making people laugh.

'You on your own?' Bet asked. 'Not like you.'

'Cheeky,' said Martha, but she didn't mind, not really. 'I was with Peg and a couple of fellas. Mine's at the bar,' she said vaguely. 'But tell me about you – you look good.'

Bet grinned. 'Got a job, ain't I? A proper one, with proper pay. At the police station.'

Martha laughed again. 'You a copper? Your old man wouldn't like that.'

'Cleaning,' Bet said. 'Sometimes I reckon I could do a better job than those men, though. They think they know how things work round here, but they don't. Not really.'

'You're not wrong,' Martha said. 'I've done a bit of work here and there for a private investigator. Divorce stuff, you know?'

Bet looked impressed, and Martha preened. 'Mrs Cameron – that's the woman who runs the agency – she says she could solve double the crimes in Whitechapel in half the time the police take.'

'I reckon she's right,' Bet said. 'I'll let the fellas at the station know who to call if they need help.'

The women laughed again. 'I have to go,' Bet said. 'Will you find me if you happen to see my dad? Mum and me are down in Spitalfields now.'

'I'll find you.' Out of the corner of her eye Martha could see the soldier coming back. 'Good luck.'

'And to you,' Bet said. She melted away into the drinkers crowded by the bar and Martha turned her attentions back to Jack. Or James.

'Large one for the lady,' he said, handing her the glass and sitting down.

Martha grinned at him. 'Oh, don't worry,' she said, draining the drink in one. 'I ain't no lady.' She stood up and held out her hand. 'Shall we?'

With the soldier gripping her fingers tightly, she waved to Bet across the pub and nodded to the barmaid.

Outside, the street was wet and it was starting to rain again, which was good news for Martha because it meant she had a proper reason to resist heading down an alley somewhere with this fella. She had no intention of giving him what he wanted. None at all. She was planning to take his money and do a runner, and she knew the perfect place for it.

'Come on,' she said to him now. But he pulled her arm, bringing her closer to him, and kissed her hard, pushing her up against the wall. Martha, realising he wasn't going to be as easy as she thought, let him slide his hand up her leg under her skirt, until thunder crashed overhead.

'It's going to piss it down,' she said into his ear. 'Let's get out of the rain, eh?'

Looking a little dishevelled, the soldier grabbed her hand and the pair of them ran through the dark empty streets as the rain hammered round. When they got to George Yard, she paused. 'It's down here,' she said.

The soldier looked unimpressed, peering down the narrow lane. As well he might. Everyone local knew George Yard wasn't a place to be after dark. But he wasn't local, and Martha knew these lanes like the back of her hand. She wasn't afraid.

He went to walk ahead of her and Martha pulled him back.

'Give me the money and I'll go first,' she said. She gave him another lingering kiss. 'I'll sort the room. I know the woman who runs it – she'll be fine. But we can't go in together in case she ain't there tonight.'

The soldier dug in his pockets and dropped some coins into Martha's open hand. 'Be quick,' he growled.

'I will,' she said. 'It's that house there, on the left.'

She walked away from him, into the gloom of the yard, knowing that as soon as she was a few feet away she'd have vanished from view. She didn't want to run, not yet, because he'd hear her footsteps echoing off the buildings either side, but she hastened her walk, past the house on the left she'd pointed to. It wasn't a boarding house as far as she knew, and she definitely didn't know anyone who worked there.

But she did know that in the corner of George Yard was a cut-through – a narrow alleyway, only wide enough for one person – that led to the street behind, and that was where she was headed. Out the back to freedom, with the pennies in her pocket.

Blimey, it was dark, though. She could barely see her hand in front of her face. The lights were all turned off now and the rain had stopped again but the night was thick with cloud. Letting her hand trail along the wall to her right, keeping her on track, Martha headed towards the alleyway as movement caught her eye.

Was someone there? For the first time that night, Martha felt a cold trickle of fear. Had the soldier followed her down here?

'Stop messing about,' she hissed into the darkness. 'I said I'll sort it.'

The alley was just a few steps ahead, but she couldn't see any light at the end. Something – or someone – was blocking it.

'Stop it,' she hissed again, just as hands grabbed her shoulders. She felt a hot, sharp pain on her lovely neck. She put her hands to her throat, where warm sticky blood soaked her skin, but she couldn't speak. Couldn't scream for help. Couldn't do anything as the pain came again, and again. And then, nothing.

# Chapter 2

## Bet

'It's supposed to be summer,' I muttered as I walked home, hunching my shoulders against the rain. 'The sun is supposed to be shining.'

I let myself into our room. Though the hour was late, my mother was still awake, sitting beside the lamp sewing. She looked up at me as she came in and her worried expression nearly broke my heart.

'He ain't here,' I said, taking off her hat. 'Don't know who saw what, but it wasn't Dad.'

'You sure?' My mother looked desperate. 'You're definitely sure?'

'Sure as I can be. I went to all his old haunts. No one's seen him. He's gone, Mum.'

Mum nodded. 'I hope he's still inside.' I watched as, almost unconsciously, she rubbed her ankle, still misshapen from the break my father had inflicted. My mother was covered in scars from her years at the end of his fists. And I'd not got off scot-free. I had suffered beatings and slaps until I learned to stay out of his way.

'I hope he's dead,' I said with venom in my voice.

'Bet,' my mother chastened. But mildly. Which made me hopeful she was over this brief return to her worries.

'Feeling a bit better?' I asked, looking carefully at her.

Like I'd told Martha, my mother had been a martyr to her nerves when Dad first got sent to jail. She had been jumpy – scared of her own shadow. Hadn't wanted to go out to work because she thought everyone was talking about her and her crook of a husband. But she was a good dressmaker, and she began doing mending and alterations for some of the nicely spoken women who lived round Spitalfields, while I took care of her – reassured her when she worried, and calmed her nerves when it all got too much.

Gradually, she'd got bolder and, when word spread about how good she was with a needle, she was offered a job with a tailor in Spitalfields. I'd been delighted when she accepted and grew more like her old self. Now I didn't have to look after her anymore. Which was taking some getting used to.

'Ready to go back to work?' Mum hadn't worked these past two days since she'd heard the rumour that Dad was back, and I'd been worried. 'Mr Segal will be pleased to see you.'

Mum's cheeks reddened. I thought she had a liking for Mr Segal. He was a lovely man – that was true – but friendship was one thing and money was another. If Mum missed more work, then no matter how friendly she and Mr Segal were, he'd replace her as soon as he could. Though my wages from the police station were better than she'd earned doing mending, it wasn't enough to pay the rent on this room, and I didn't want to lose it. Not now. Not when we were just getting ourselves back on our feet. I took a deep breath, calming my own nerves, and smiled at Mum.

'Dad's not coming back,' I said now, convincing myself as much as I did my mother. 'He's still in jail, or he's dead.' I chuckled. 'Or worse.'

'What's worse than death?' my mother said. 'You're talking nonsense, Bet.'

'It's something Martha said. Remember Martha? Turner, I think she is now? Used to be Tabram. I saw her in the White Swan.'

'Course I remember Martha,' Mum said with a grin. 'Still hanging about the White Swan, is she? Never changes, that one.'

'She's a character, all right.'

'Martha Tabram has always been the sort of woman who attracts trouble,' Mum said fondly. 'It follows her wherever she goes.' She sighed. 'Good heart, though. Loves those boys of hers. Men they'd be now, I suppose.'

'She's got a job working for some detective,' I told her, beginning to struggle out of my clothes, which were horribly damp after the rainy walk home. I examined the hem of my skirt and saw with dismay it was speckled with mud. That was going to need washing. 'So perhaps she's getting herself out of trouble now.'

'Is that skirt mucky, Bet?' Mum said. 'Put it by the door and I'll take it to work tomorrow. Mr Segal never minds if I put a couple of extra bits through the laundry.'

Relieved that she was talking about going back to work, I nodded, and balled my skirt up ready for washing.

'I've heard about those detectives,' Mum went on. 'They're not like the chaps you work for at the police station. This is different. It's for divorces.'

'What do you know about divorces?' I was surprised; I didn't know anyone who was divorced. In our world, if you didn't want to be with your husband or wife anymore, you just left. As far as I knew, Martha hadn't married William Turner, but she'd gone by his name, and called herself his wife.

'If you want to get divorced, you need to catch your fella in the act,' Mum said. 'So they use women like Martha to hang about and watch.'

I frowned, remembering. 'She was with a soldier. I saw him at the bar when I was leaving.'

'Well, there you go. Probably trying to trap him.'

'Most soldiers ain't married, though,' I pointed out. 'Married to the job.'

'Perhaps Martha found one that was.' Mum chuckled. 'Wouldn't surprise me.'

'I'm going to turn in.' I gave a yawn. 'I'm done in.'

'Early start in the morning,' Mum agreed, and I felt again a swell of relief that she was back to her old self.

I slept like the dead that night, listening to the rain lashing against the window. I saw my mother off to work, waving her goodbye at the crossroads where we parted ways, then I headed to Leman Street where the police station sat, squat in the middle of the street.

At this time in the morning – before most of the world woke and when the sun was trying its best to peek out from behind the clouds – the station was usually quiet. But not today. Today, the front door was open and there was a sense of urgent activity inside. Curious, I went round the back and in the side door, where I tied on my pinny and swapped my hat for a mob cap, then I picked up my broom, and went into the station, ready to start dusting and sweeping for the day ahead.

Except where there were usually empty offices, quiet rooms, and closed doors, today there were policemen everywhere.

'What's happened?' I asked a young constable, who looked rather like he should still be in school. I had seen him around, but I wasn't sure of his name – I was still learning who everyone was. 'Why is everyone here so early?'

'Been here all night,' he said. 'There's been another murder.' His eyes gleamed. 'A bad one.'

'All murders are bad,' I pointed out. 'There's hardly a good way to do it, is there?'

He half snorted, half laughed. 'Yeah, but this one was brutal,' he said. 'She had forty stab wounds.'

I felt a bit queasy.

'It's a woman then?' I asked. 'The victim? Do you know who she is?'

The constable shrugged. 'Some prostitute.'

'Ah, Bet, there you are.' Inspector Abberline appeared at the door of his office and I smiled. He was a nice man. Never talked down to me. 'Could you give my office a going-over when you're done elsewhere? I've got a feeling I'll be spending a lot of time in there over the coming days.'

He rubbed his hands together like a man ready to take on the task in hand, and I nodded.

Abberline turned his attention to the young constable.

'Percival? Why are you loitering in a corridor? Find something to do, won't you?'

Percival hurried off and with a glare at his retreating back, I went to find my mop and bucket.

The good thing about being a young woman in a police station full of men was that I was, to all intents and purposes, invisible. Oh, the conversations I'd overheard when I was cleaning. My mother always said I was a dreadful one for sticking my nose into everyone else's business, but I couldn't help myself. I was interested in everything, and working here was wonderful because there was so much to listen to and see.

Today was no different, though it was mostly snatches of chat that I heard, because everyone was dashing about, and talking while they were walking.

'No one knows,' I heard Percival say at one point. 'They're doing a photo.' He'd tilted his head towards the end of the corridor where the morgue was and I had averted my gaze. I didn't like going down that end of the

12

police station where my footsteps echoed on the tiled floor and the air was cold.

Now though, I was in Abberline's office, tidying up the mess he'd made since I'd last ventured in here. He was an untidy beggar, Abberline. There were empty teacups with brown rings in the bottom because they'd been left so long, papers scattered on the floor, and books stacked higgledy-piggledy in the shelves. He was a clever man – any fool could see that – but I often wondered if his mind was better organised than his office.

The room was empty when I went in – Abberline obviously occupied elsewhere. It was a large room, lined with shelves, and a map of the east side of London on one wall. There was a large sturdy wooden desk at one end and a big window – the sill covered in empty cups. I stood at the door and let myself sigh for a moment, then busied myself picking up all the paperwork from the floor and stacking it on Abberline's desk – I couldn't begin to mop or dust if there was stuff everywhere.

While I was rearranging the books on the shelf, Abberline came in, followed by more men. Percival was there, along with another chap I had seen around, who I knew was called Green. He had a spark of mischief – or was it insolence? – in his eyes that I rather liked. I'd always been drawn to folk who bent the rules – I blamed my dad for that, just like I blamed him for everything else. But I wasn't alone in liking the look in Green's eyes; Percival seemed to like it too. I'd seen him hanging on Green's every word. I glanced at him. And if I wasn't mistaken, he seemed to be growing himself a straggly moustache, just like Green's. Silly sod.

There was an older man in the room, too, with impressive epaulets on his uniform. He was the commissioner, I thought. I'd heard him talked about but I hadn't ever seen him in Whitechapel before.

Abberline nodded at me, and so did Green, but the other two ignored me. Perhaps they didn't see me at all. Lots of them didn't.

They all sat down except Abberline, who stood looking out of the window.

'Someone must know her,' he said.

'These women are ten-a-penny,' Percival said. Across the room, I stiffened. 'They're all alike. It's hard to tell one from another – isn't that the case?'

'In my experience, that is true,' said the older man with a guffaw that made my hackles rise. 'But nevertheless, we need to know who this unfortunate woman is. Or was. Do we have the photograph?'

'It's just being done now, sir,' said Abberline. He rubbed his forehead. 'We are no strangers to murder here, but this one . . .' He trailed off.

'Brutal, sir,' said Percival, echoing what he'd said to me but this time less gleefully because, I assumed, he was talking to his boss. 'Angry.'

'Indeed,' Abberline said. 'And frightening for the local people.' He thought for a moment, as I watched from the other side of the room. 'Can we keep the lights on later? All night if needs be? George Yard is blacker than hell in the dead of night.'

I shuddered. Was that where this woman had been killed? I wouldn't go into George Yard in the daytime, let alone at night.

'That would look good,' said the older man. 'Something positive, right off the bat.'

I glanced up, just in time to catch a flicker of annoyance in Abberline's eyes. But he turned away, back to the window, as there was a knock at the door.

'Photograph, sir,' said Blake, who worked in the mortuary. 'The newspapers have copies in time for the evening editions.'

'Excellent,' said Abberline. 'Let's have it.'

I pretended to be concentrating on dusting as Blake passed the sheet of paper to the older officer and I caught a glimpse of a dim photograph.

Abberline shook his head. 'Let's hope this does the trick.' He finally sat down behind his desk and looked straight at me.

'Do you live locally, Bet?' he asked. The other men turned to look at me, seemingly surprised to see me there.

'Yes, sir,' I said. 'All my life.'

'Know George Yard?'

'Yes, sir.'

'Do you know many people roundabout Whitechapel?'

I allowed myself a small smile. 'Everyone knows everyone in Whitechapel.'

Abberline held out the photograph. 'Do you recognise this woman?'

I stepped forward and took the picture. I looked down at the photograph, and for a moment my legs went weak and I steadied myself on the arm of the chair Percival was sitting in.

'I do, sir,' I said with some difficulty because my mouth was suddenly very dry. 'It's Martha. Martha Turner.'

# Chapter 3

## Emma

I was watching the clock on the mantel, waiting for it to strike the hour. It felt odd, having nothing to do. I hadn't finished arranging all the rooms in the new house, but I had little motivation. So instead I'd reordered all the books that Fred had dumped on the shelves, and now I was rattling around with no real purpose.

I walked to the rain-splattered window and looked out at Commercial Street. I knew I would like living here – back in the East End, closer to where I'd grown up. I'd lived in a house just like this one, in fact. Except that house had been full of noise and shouts and laughter and hurly-burly because I'd had three brothers and a sister, and a father who loved to roughhouse with the boys.

This house was quiet.

Outside, though, it was not quiet. Down on the street was the hustle and bustle I loved – I could see carriages splashing through puddles and people hurrying along the road. If I turned my head I could see the crossroads with Whitechapel High Street, and just the other side, Leman Street, where Fred was at work. I couldn't quite see the police station, but I liked knowing he was nearby.

Our new house was solid, tall and narrow with large windows and high ceilings, and I had been delighted with it when I first saw it. I turned away from the view and perched on the wide window ledge, surveying the room. I thought the light here would be lovely in the summer, streaming in through the glass, and then I sighed. 'It is the blooming summer,' I muttered.

I thought about the packing crates that were stacked in the corner of the rooms upstairs. We'd been here for several months but there were some rooms I couldn't face. And there were so many rooms to fill. This was a family house. A family house for just two people.

Downstairs the doorbell rang, clanging through the empty rooms. I jumped up from the window ledge and ran down to the tiled hall, pleased to have a distraction.

On the doorstep was a lad, his cap in his hand. I rolled my eyes; I knew what was coming.

'Message from Inspector Abberline, Mrs Abberline,' the boy said.

I nodded. 'He's been held up?'

'Yes, Mrs Abberline. He said . . .' The boy took a breath, ready to recite his message. 'He said to go ahead and eat because he would be late.'

'I will.' I looked at the lad carefully. He had deep, dark shadows under his eyes. 'Have you eaten today?'

'Yes, Mrs Abberline.'

'Enough?'

The boy dropped his gaze. 'A bit.'

'Wait here,' I said. I went into the kitchen and cut a few slices from the loaf of bread that was on the side. I added a lump of cheese and an apple, wrapped them all up in a cloth and tied it neatly at the top like a parcel. Then I went back out into the hall and handed the bundle to the lad.

'Here.'

He looked pleased. 'Ta, Mrs Abberline.' He raised the

parcel to his face and sniffed it appreciatively. 'Any reply for the inspector?'

'No reply,' I said. I gave the boy a coin and waved him off and then stood for a second on the doorstep, feeling disappointed that Fred wouldn't be home, and also silly for feeling disappointed.

'Goodness, Emma,' I muttered out loud. 'Pull yourself together.' I shut the door, and wandered back into the kitchen where I looked at the plates of food left by our temporary housekeeper – a sour-faced woman who had made it very clear she was doing us an enormous favour and only until we found proper help. I didn't even think I needed help – it wasn't as though I had my hands full with just Fred and me to think about – but my mother-in-law had scoffed at the idea of me looking after the house so thoroughly that I was nervous about disagreeing.

'If the mountain can't come to Mohammed,' I said, looking at the food. 'Then Mohammed will go to the police station herself.' I found a basket, put the plate of food at the bottom, covered it in a cloth, dropped in two apples and a bottle of beer and put on my hat and coat.

Outside, the rain had stopped but it was still gloomy and dark, with evening arriving much earlier than it should have. It was only a short walk, but I hurried along the road and down towards the police station, not wanting to get caught if the rain started again.

I went up the stairs and pushed open the doors. There was a policeman at the desk, who barely glanced at me as I went inside. I didn't recognise him, and he clearly didn't recognise me either.

'Yes?'

'Could I see Inspector Abberline, please?'

He didn't look up. 'No, 'fraid not. I'll have to do.'

I tutted. I was used to being ignored simply because I was a woman, but this chap was particularly rude.

'I think you'll find Inspector Abberline will want to see me.'

The man looked up properly this time, dragging his eyes from the newspaper he was reading. 'I'm sure your concerns are important,' he said, speaking slowly as if I were simple. 'But Inspector Abberline is a very busy man and there is an important case requiring his attention. Is there something I can help with?'

I gave him my best, most dazzling smile. 'You seem to be a most competent officer,' I said, an edge to my voice. 'But Inspector Abberline is my husband, so it's really him that I need. I'll be sure to tell him how . . .' I paused 'helpful you've been, Constable . . . ?'

The policeman got up from his chair, his insolence gone in an instant. 'Percival, madam. Constable Percival.'

'I'll go on through, shall I, Constable Percival?'

'Yes, madam. First door on the left.'

Feeling slightly triumphant, I walked past him without a second glance, and found Fred alone in his office, looking out of the window. I could see he looked worried and tired, but he turned as I entered and I smiled at the delight on his face when he saw me.

'Hello,' he said, wrapping his arms round me and giving me a kiss. 'What a lovely surprise.'

'Inspector, this is terribly unprofessional behaviour,' I said, kissing him back. 'What if one of your colleagues walks in.'

'I'll throw them in the cells,' said Fred good-naturedly.

'I brought you dinner.'

'You're an angel.'

I untangled myself from his arms and put the basket on a chair so I could unpack it.

'Why are you working late?' I asked. 'What's happened?'

Fred took the plate of food and sat down, indicating for me to do the same.

'Murder,' he said. 'Do you have time to sit and chat?'

'Of course.' Since the early days of our marriage, Fred had brought his investigations home to me, going over situations, asking my thoughts. It was one of the many reasons I loved him – the way he valued my opinion and listened to my ideas. Now I sat and looked at him as he picked up his sandwich and took a large bite. 'Tell me everything. Who's the victim?'

'Woman,' said Fred between bites. 'Early forties.'

I winced. 'Like me.'

'Bit younger than you, I'd say.'

'Cheeky.' I sat back in my chair. 'Do you know who she is?'

'Her name's Martha. Turner or Tabram depending on who you ask. Our cleaner knew her. She says she was a nice woman.' He sighed. 'Fun, was what she said.'

'Lord,' I said. 'How awful for it to be so close to home. Was she a prostitute?'

Fred shook his head and shrugged. 'Maybe,' he said. 'Maybe not. Maybe sometimes, if she needed to be. You know how it is.'

'I do.' I looked my husband's worried face and frowned. 'I hate to say this but it's not unusual to have a Whitechapel woman in your mortuary, Fred. What's vexing you about this one?'

Fred rubbed the bridge of his nose. 'It's so brutal,' he said. 'Vicious, even.'

'Aren't all murders that way?'

'Indeed. But this was . . .' He paused, looking up at the ceiling. 'It was frenzied.'

The word made me shiver. 'Frenzied?'

'Thirty-nine stab wounds altogether,' Fred said, pushing

the remaining part of his sandwich away. He opened a folder on his desk and found a photograph. He glanced at it and then held it out to me.

'Goodness,' I said, looking at the picture, which showed a close-up of a woman's face and shoulders. 'This is Martha? I've never seen a photograph like this before.'

'We put it in the evening paper because we didn't know who she was. Bet – that's the cleaner – recognised her as soon as she saw it, though.'

'Should have asked this Bet first,' I pointed out. 'Everyone knows everyone round here – you know that.'

'Lesson learned.' Fred handed me another photograph. This time it showed Martha's whole body – the dreadful wounds stark on her pale skin. I put my hand to my mouth, shocked at the sight.

'Take it away, Fred, that's awful. Poor woman.'

Fred tucked the picture back into his folder.

'Whoever did this was filled with hatred,' he said.

'Hatred for Martha? What could she have done to stir up such contempt?'

'Who knows?' Fred sounded weary. 'Perhaps just being in the wrong place at the wrong time was enough.'

'Now you know who she is, you'll be able to find out more about her,' I said, wanting to reassure him. I got up from my chair and went round to where Fred sat, putting my arm round his shoulders. 'You'll ask the right questions about who she was and where she went, and you'll narrow down the suspects and if poor Martha's killer isn't in your cells by the end of the week, I'll eat my hat.'

Still sitting down, Fred put his arms around my waist and leaned his head against me. 'I'm very lucky to have you,' he said.

'No.' I leaned back so I could see his face. 'The women of Whitechapel are lucky to have you. Just think, you could have still been stuck behind that desk at Scotland Yard, but here you are, back where you belong, and ready to find whoever committed this awful crime.'

A growl of thunder outside made us both look up.

'You should get home,' Fred said, sounding reluctant. 'The weather is awful, and you don't want to catch a cold.'

I kissed him firmly. 'You mean "go home, Emma, and stop distracting me from important police business".'

'That too.'

'You'll find whoever did this,' I said. 'You always do.'

'I hope so.'

'Don't stay too late, will you?'

'I'll be home by midnight.'

'I'll be waiting.'

I kissed him again, gathered my basket, hat and coat, and headed out of the office, the image of poor Martha's injuries etched in my mind.

# Chapter 4

## Bet

I was bone-tired. I'd been in Inspector Abberline's office for what seemed like hours, telling him everything I knew about Martha. Which wasn't much, really – she had been my mum's friend, not mine. But I knew the name of Martha's bloke – William. Abberline sent someone to try to track him down, but I knew it might take a couple of days to find him. He was slippery, was William Turner. That's what Mum always said, anyway. They might have more luck with Henry Tabram – Martha's actual husband – but he'd washed his hands of her long ago.

'You saw her?' Abberline said. 'You saw Martha on the night she died?'

I nodded. 'Not seen her for ages before that.' I paused, choosing my words carefully. 'I don't really go to the places she goes to, you know?'

'I do.'

'But I was looking for my dad – someone said he was out . . .' I paused. 'Someone said he was out and about and I wanted to make sure he wasn't.'

Percival opened his mouth ready to ask a question, but Abberline shot him a look and he shut up. I was pleased. I was shaken enough about Martha without talking about my stupid useless father too.

'I was in the White Swan,' I began. 'Martha was with a soldier.'

'Can you describe the soldier?'

I closed my eyes, thinking back to what I'd seen. But I'd only seen the soldier's back as he stood at the bar.

'I can't,' I admitted, opening my eyes again. 'I just saw him from a distance and from behind. He weren't there when I was talking to Martha.'

Percival sighed and I glared at him.

'Was he paying her?' he said. 'This soldier?'

'How would I know?' I snapped. I looked at Abberline. 'Martha was nice,' I said. 'She was fun.'

Abberline, his expression sympathetic, made a note on his paper.

'She had some bad luck,' I went on. I wanted them to know that Martha was just like any one of us. 'Made some bad choices.'

'Did she say anything else when you spoke to her?' Abberline asked.

'She said she was working for a private investigator,' I said. 'Mrs Campbell? No, Cartwright? Something like that. My mum said they do divorces.'

Abberline wrote that down, and I felt pleased that I was being helpful. Once more I closed my eyes, picturing the scene.

'She was with a mate,' I said, suddenly remembering the woman I'd seen on my way into the pub. 'She was just leaving but she was with a soldier 'n' all. There were two soldiers, one with Martha and one with her mate – Pearly Peg.'

'Pearly Peg?' Abberline said.

'It ain't her real name.'

Abberline gave a small smile. 'Shame.'

'What is her real name?' asked Percival from his spot at the window.

'I don't know,' I admitted. 'Everyone just calls her Peg.'

Percival snorted and Abberline put his pen down.

'Percival, could you go and relieve Green on the front desk, please?'

With a sulky glance at me, Percival slunk out of the office.

'I don't know what Peg's real name is,' I told Abberline as the door closed. 'But I can tell you where to find her.'

I listed a few places where Peg would be, most evenings, and Abberline wrote them down.

'If she ain't in one of those pubs I'd be surprised,' I said. 'And everyone round there knows her, so you'll find her with no trouble.'

'I should give you a job,' Abberline said. 'Constable Bet.'

'Palmer, sir.' I grinned at him. 'I'd be Constable Palmer.'

He wrote my name down, looking thoughtful.

'Why did you write Bet Palmer?' I asked looking over at his notes. His writing was almost as untidy as mine.

He glanced at me. 'Once I've written something down, I don't forget it.'

'Nice trick.'

'It's becoming quite a thing, you know,' Abberline said. 'Women being employed by the police. They call them searchers.'

'Searchers,' I repeated. 'I quite like that. My mum says I'm too interested in everyone's business, but I could tell her I'm not being nosy, I'm searching.'

He chuckled, his attention caught by something in his notes. He underlined something as I watched him.

'Are you good at this?' I asked abruptly, any rudeness in my tone dampened by the fact that my voice wobbled. 'I liked Martha, and it's not right, that someone's done this. Will you catch them?'

Abberline looked straight at me.

'I'm sorry that Martha was killed, and I know this is hard for you,' he said. 'I want you to know that I will do everything I can to find whoever was responsible for Martha's death. And that you have been very helpful.'

Feeling more reassured, I nodded. 'Thank you, sir.'

'Thank you, Bet.'

There was a moment of silence, and then I said: 'Can I get on, sir?'

'Of course,' Abberline said. 'If there's anything else, I'll come and find you.'

I nodded. I pushed my sleeves up and went to find my mop and bucket.

It was a good while later – much later than I usually finished because I'd spent so long talking to Abberline – that I went back through the front of the police station to collect my coat and hat.

Percival was at the front desk, reading a newspaper. Another constable was looking over his shoulder and they were both laughing.

As I walked past, Percival caught my arm.

'They printed the picture,' he told me. 'Though your mate's not looking her best.'

With a flourish he turned the paper round so I could see poor Martha on the front page. I knew he was trying to get a reaction out of me, like a schoolboy. So I averted my eyes and shook my arm out of his grip.

'Shut up,' I said.

Percival and the other constable exchanged an amused look.

'How many hours have we spent on this already, do you think?' Percival said in a conversational tone to his colleague.

'Green's out in the streets, speaking to all sorts. Abberline's in his office writing his notes . . .' the other man said.

'Bloody Abberline,' said Percival. 'I reckon any minute now he'll come out here and tell me to traipse off in search of . . .' He looked in my direction. I was putting on my hat and trying to ignore their loud chatter. 'What did you call her? Pongy Peg?'

'Pearly,' I muttered. 'Pearly Peg.'

Percival shrugged. 'It's just such a waste of time.'

'A massive waste of time,' agreed his mate.

'And money.'

'So much money.'

'All on some whore.'

I froze with one arm in my coat.

'Shut. Up,' I said again. 'Martha weren't a prostitute.'

'Course she was,' said Percival. 'She got mixed up with the wrong punter and she paid the price.'

'And now we're paying the price of all this extra work,' whined the other constable.

'You'll get paid for it, won't you?' I said in disgust. 'Thought you'd be pleased. Thought a murder like this would be good for bloody business.'

'Calm down,' said the constable, standing up straight and looking at me. 'There's no point getting yourself worked up about it.' He gestured at the photograph of Martha. 'She ain't worth it.'

I pulled on my coat and glowered at the two men. Then I pushed my way through the heavy front door of the police station. Outside, the sky was overcast – again – and in the distance I heard a rumble of thunder. As I went down the steps, a carriage trundled by. It splashed through a puddle and a wave of muddy water rose up and splattered all over my skirt.

Suddenly, everything seemed too much. I sat down heavily on the step, put my face in my hands and wept.

I'd been sitting there sobbing for a little while when I

became aware that there was someone next to me. I raised my head and the woman held out a handkerchief: 'Better?'

I took the hanky and wiped my eyes. 'A bit.'

'Are you Bet?'

'How do you know that?'

The woman tilted her head in the direction of the police station door behind us. 'I'm Emma Abberline,' she said. 'My husband told me you knew the woman who was murdered. Martha?'

I nodded, curious, despite my sadness, about the inspector's wife.

'I didn't know her well,' I said. 'She was a friend of my mum's really, and she wasn't always around. But she was nice.'

Mrs Abberline patted me on the shoulder. 'It's a shock.'

Her kindness made tears spring into my eyes again. 'It is.'

'They are doing their best to find whoever did this.'

I snorted. 'Your husband might be, but the rest of them ain't. They don't think Martha's worth the effort.'

'Fred won't stand for that.' Mrs Abberline looked bullish, which I quite liked. I studied her. She was older than me – more my mother's age. She was nicely dressed and her reddish hair was neat, and she was watching me with a sharp, knowing gaze that made me feel a little uncomfortable. 'I promise you, he'll do whatever he can. He said you were very helpful.'

'Right,' I said. I thought about Abberline saying the same and I gave a small smile. 'He said he'd give me a job,' I told Mrs Abberline. 'Maybe I'll catch the killer myself.'

Mrs Abberline grinned. 'Women are good at detective work,' she said. 'Fred often says that.'

'He said that to me too, but he weren't serious,' I said. 'Women can't be policemen.'

'Pity,' said Mrs Abberline.

There was a pause. I looked down at my muddy skirt.

'I can give you a job,' Mrs Abberline said suddenly.

'Pardon me?'

'I know you work here, of course, but if you need more work, I'm looking for some help at home.'

'At your home?' I said stupidly. 'Where you live with the inspector?'

'That's right. Just cleaning, mostly. Sorting laundry.'

'Like a char?'

'Exactly that.'

'And I can do it round my job here?'

'This is usually mornings, I believe?'

'Usually,' I said. 'When there ain't been a murder.'

'So you could come to me in the afternoons – we're just down on Commercial Street.'

I thought about the extra money that would bring in and I grinned.

'Sounds perfect,' I said. 'I'd like that.'

'Then it's settled.' Mrs Abberline stood up, so I did the same. 'It'll be nice to have someone else round the place. It's quite a large house for Fred and me.'

She patted my hand. 'Keep the handkerchief. Go home now and rest. I imagine it won't be much fun telling your mother what's happened to Martha.'

I shook my head. 'She might already know because it's on the front page of the paper. But she'll be upset.'

Mrs Abberline touched my arm briefly. 'It's sad.'

'It's really sad.' I took a breath. 'I could start work tomorrow, if you want?'

'Tomorrow would work very well.' Mrs Abberline held out her hand and, feeling faintly ridiculous, I shook it. 'I'll see you then.'

She walked off towards Commercial Street. I watched

her for a moment, then I turned and headed for home, wondering how I'd find the words to tell my mother that Martha was dead.

# Chapter 5

'Do you have a minute, Bet?' Inspector Abberline asked a few days later, putting his head round the door and looking out into the hallway where I was sweeping the floor.

'Yes, sir.' Still holding the broom, I followed him into the office. His desk was covered in papers and folders and he followed my gaze to the mess.

'I'm going to sort these out later,' he said, sounding like a naughty schoolboy.

I grinned at him. 'I don't know how you find anything.'

'Ah but I know exactly where everything is,' he said. 'It's only if something's moved that everything falls apart.'

'I believe you, but I'm not sure everyone would,' I joked.

As if to prove his point, Abberline leafed through one of his tottering piles and unearthed a page of notes.

'We're having trouble finding these soldiers, Bet,' he said. 'I wondered if we could go through the details again?'

'The soldiers with Martha?' I asked, frowning. 'I thought Percival was speaking to the lads at the barracks?'

'He did,' Abberline said with a sigh. 'He and Green went down there, but we have very little to go on. I just wondered if there was anything else you remembered?'

'Didn't Pearly Peg help?'

Abberline shook his head. 'Apparently she doesn't know who they were.'

'Did you speak to her yourself, sir?'

'No, unfortunately not. I've been up to my eyes with this other stuff for Commissioner Harrison.'

I raised an eyebrow. I didn't know Pearly Peg well, but I knew her sort, and I knew that if Percival had spoken to her the way he spoke to most women, she'd not have told him anything whatsoever. Abberline, with his kindly manner and jovial approach, would have been much more successful.

I took a deep breath. 'I could speak to her, sir, if you thought it might be useful.'

Abberline looked delighted. 'Would you really?'

'Course I would. Strikes me you need all the help you can get.'

'If we can find out more about these soldiers, then we'll be well on the way to finding whoever was responsible for Martha's death.'

'I'd be happy to help, sir.' I gave him a sideways glance. 'It's taking a while to find anything useful, ain't it?'

Abberline tapped his fingers on the desk. 'I've been looking into employing searchers.'

'Women? Like we talked about before?' I was intrigued. 'Do they search suspects?' I'd taken to deliberately lingering in a cell when a woman was being searched by one of the constables. Especially Percival, because I didn't trust him to treat the women like human beings.

'Yes, they search suspects, but they're also being used out on the streets – watching and listening.'

I felt a little shiver of excitement. 'I think I'd like that.'

'I imagine you'd be rather good at it.' Abberline smiled at me. 'As would my Emma.'

'She would be really good,' I said. 'Her mind is so quick and she sees patterns in stuff that other people don't notice.'

'You're right.' Abberline pointed his pen at me. 'And the fact that you've noticed that makes me think you'd make a good searcher.'

I preened, thrilled to bits with his praise.

There was a knock at the office door and Constable Green came in.

'Commissioner Harrison is just arriving,' he said. 'Shall I send him in?'

'Please do,' said Abberline. I noticed his shoulders slump, just a little and just for a second before he straightened up again. 'I imagine he's got another job for me to do regarding the Spitalfields thefts.'

Constable Green turned to go and caught my eye. He gave me a tiny wink and I smiled at him. He was a handsome man, and I was finding him more charming with every day that passed. Much more charming than Percival at any rate, who seemed like a silly boy to me. Green was a bit older than most of the constables – maybe ten or so years older than me, and he was new to the station. In fact, I'd heard he was new to London, but he already seemed at home in Whitechapel.

As Green left, the commissioner came in.

'Abberline,' he said, striding past without even noticing me. 'Quick chat about these Spitalfields thefts, if I may?'

'Certainly, sir,' said Abberline. I hid a smile. 'Bet, I'll let you know about Peg.'

'Yes, sir.'

'Who's Peg?' asked Harrison.

'The woman who was with Martha Turner the night she died. I thought Bet here might get more out of her than Green and Percival did.'

The commissioner looked horrified. 'I'm not sure that's the best course of action,' he said.

'Our colleagues in Hackney have been using female

searchers with some success . . .' Abberline began, but Harrison waved his hand.

'To catch petty thieves and pickpockets, perhaps, but this is completely different,' he said. 'Martha Turner was an unfortunate woman who met an unfortunate end. It's hardly worth introducing a whole new branch of policing.' He chuckled and I tightened my grip on the broom handle, wondering what would happen if I whacked him over the head.

'But I think if Bet can speak to Peg . . .'

'No,' said the commissioner firmly. 'Now about these thefts in Spitalfields. Mr Thorogood is an old friend of mine, and he's several pounds down, as are other jewellers in the area. They need to know we're taking this seriously . . .'

Frustrated, I backed out of the office, giving Abberline a sympathetic smile as I did, then I paused.

'Try the women's hair, sir,' I said.

Abberline and Harrison both looked at me, startled.

'Their hair?' Abberline said.

'The thefts in Spitalfields?' I had heard all the details of jewellery going missing from local businesses – vanishing into the ether.

'It's a way of hiding stolen trinkets – tucking them into their hair,' I explained. 'My mum told me about it – she's seen it happen loads of times.' I looked straight at Harrison. 'It's fancy women who do it because they ain't so suspicious. They'll ask to look at some jewellery, scratch their heads while they're at it and suddenly their hair's full of diamonds.' I gave him a sweet smile. 'You need to check their hair.'

Abberline gave me a little nod and a smile, while Harrison looked bemused and dubious. I rolled my eyes as I left the office, and went to the cupboard to put the brush away, giving the door a kick to close it.

'Oof,' said Constable Green, who was walking past. 'What's that door done to deserve a kicking like that?'

I turned round and made a face at him. 'I didn't see you there.'

Green smiled at me. 'Apparently not.'

Feeling silly, I groaned. 'I was just a bit frustrated, that's all.'

'With the door?'

'With Abberline. Well, not with him, with that old stick-in-the-mud Harrison.'

Green laughed loudly. 'Harrison? What's he done to you?'

'Underestimated me.'

'And you think he's made a mistake doing that?'

I sighed. 'Abberline wanted me to speak to Pearly Peg but Harrison said no.'

'We spoke to her,' Green said with a frown. 'She's not much use – she couldn't remember anything useful about that night.'

'Abberline thought she might talk more to me,' I explained. I leaned against the cupboard door and studied Green, who seemed genuinely interested. 'He wasn't saying you'd not done a good job – it's just that I know her, don't I? Well, sort of. We might find something we've got in common, and get chatting, and she might remember a name or a description.'

Green was still frowning. 'Maybe,' he said doubtfully. 'But this Pearly Peg's really not the chatty type.'

'You're not still fretting over Pearly bleeding Peg are you, Green?' Percival appeared in the hallway, holding his helmet under his arm. 'I thought you said she turned out to be a waste of space?'

'Waste of time,' said Green hurriedly. 'That's what I said.'

'Didn't you both speak to her?' I said, surprised. 'Abberline said you both went.'

Percival shrugged. 'We've been sharing out the jobs to get through them quicker – there's no point in us both being there when there's so much other stuff to do.'

He didn't say 'more important stuff' but the unspoken words hung in the air. Green looked slightly uncomfortable. He ran a finger round his collar.

'We're taking this seriously,' he said to me. 'We're investigating Martha's murder properly, I promise. You know, if Abberline asks you . . .'

Percival grinned. 'When we've got nothing else to do.' He nudged Green. 'Ain't that right.'

I closed my eyes briefly. Between the constables not asking the right questions, or speaking to the right people, and Abberline's attention being spread across too many crimes in the East End, I couldn't ever imagine them catching whoever had killed Martha.

'Right,' I said listlessly. 'Well, that's good to hear.'

Percival gave me a small, smug smile and I felt annoyance flare up inside me. He was so sure who held all the power. Well, he was wrong about that.

I straightened up. 'I'm off now,' I said. 'Off to my other job with Inspector Abberline's wife at their home.'

Green and Percival both looked gratifyingly surprised to hear I worked with Mrs Abberline. Surprised and, I thought, a little concerned. At least Percival did. Which was exactly what I had hoped. Constable Green just looked amused and, as I turned to go, he gave me that little wink again. I felt my cheeks flush and when I looked back, he was watching me go.

# Chapter 6

'Bet?'

I turned to see Constable Green hurrying along the corridor towards me and paused in sweeping the floor.

'You're here early.'

'It's busy.'

'Ain't it.' It was true I hadn't been working at the police station for long, but I'd never seen it so frantic – not even after Martha's murder, which was over a week ago now.

'I wanted to tell you something,' Green said. He looked pleased with himself, like an excited child on his birthday. His enthusiasm made me smile.

'What?'

'I went back to speak to her – to Pearly Peg. After we chatted yesterday.'

'You never did?'

'I did.' He nodded, looking serious. 'I thought about how disappointed you looked when I said she didn't give us any information. So I went back.'

'And did she say anything useful this time?' I was quite pleased that I'd influenced him, but I didn't say so.

His confidence faltered a tiny bit. 'Well, no not really.'

'No names?'

'No. All she remembers is the soldiers were a private and

a corporal, and they had white bands on their caps. And they said they were from Wellington Barracks.'

'Well, that's something to go on.'

Green made a face. 'It's not enough to identify them. But it was enough for me to get the inspector to agree to doing an identity parade.'

'What's that?'

'We'll get all the soldiers from the barracks to come outside and walk past Pearly Peg, and she can pick out the ones she recognises. Abberline said it was a good idea.'

He was so triumphant, I didn't want to ruin his excitement.

'That's a lot of soldiers,' I said.

'Yes.'

'All dressed the same.'

'Yes.'

'And Pearly Peg reckons she can pick them out?'

'Worth a go.'

'Yes,' I said thoughtfully. 'I suppose it is.' I desperately wanted to ask if I could come along but I remembered Harrison's firm dismissal of women working for the police and I knew it was out of the question. 'Will you let me know how you get on?'

'Course.' Green smiled at me and I smiled back.

'I'm glad you're putting the effort into this,' I said. 'Martha deserves this. And Abberline will be pleased about it.'

Green looked chuffed. 'I need to go and meet Pearly Peg.'

'Good luck.'

He headed off down the hall and I carried on sweeping, wondering if this harebrained identity-parade idea could possibly work with so many soldiers involved. Mind you, Pearly Peg was a clever woman. She had a quick mind and a sharp tongue, and I thought she could probably describe someone she'd met a year ago if she wanted to.

'Ah, Bet.' Inspector Abberline came along the corridor. 'I passed on your tip about checking the hair. We've got an officer there now. Undercover. He's going to keep an eye out.'

'Undercover?' I was learning a lot about policing today. I briefly wondered if one day I could be the one putting it into practice and then laughed inwardly. That would never happen.

'Farnworth's down there posing as a customer,' Abberline explained. 'He'll watch for any women playing with their hair.'

'Hope he catches the crooks,' I said. 'Though might be better if he was posing as a shop girl instead. Because then he'd have a reason to be there all day rather than hanging about in a shop all day and probably ending up looking a bit shifty himself.'

Abberline looked at me. 'Yes,' he said thoughtfully. 'Not sure he could pull off the skirt, though.'

I grinned, and the suggestion that I be the one to pose as a shop girl to catch the thief hung silently between us.

'I heard Green's doing an identity parade down at the barracks,' I said finally, taking pity on Abberline as he shifted awkwardly from foot to foot.

'Yes,' said Abberline, a bit too loudly, clearly relieved. 'He is. I believe I have you to thank for his new-found determination to catch Martha's killer.'

I ducked my head modestly. 'I don't know about that, sir.'

'Hmm.' Abberline studied me. 'Keep up the good work, won't you.'

'I will. You too.'

'Me too,' Abberline said with a chuckle. 'Right you are.'

He wandered off down the corridor and I ran through my mental list of chores. It was amazing really just how much mess the policemen made. There was always something to be done.

I spent a couple of hours sluicing down the cells – which were thankfully empty except for one very small, very drunk man, who was curled up on a bench, fast asleep and snoring loudly. Then I saw Abberline going out with Harrison somewhere, so I nipped into his office to give it a quick once-over. As I was straightening his desk, I took a peek at the notes he'd scrawled about Martha's murder. I wasn't the best at reading and his writing was a scrawl, but I could make out most of the words.

'Body removed from scene too soon,' he'd written. 'In future, police to be given the chance to see victim in situ.' He'd underlined the words 'in situ'.

'In situ,' I muttered. 'In. Situ.' I'd never heard those words before either – today was proving to be very educational – but I understood what it meant. It meant Abberline hadn't seen Martha where she was killed – only in the mortuary once she'd been moved.

'Another mistake,' I said out loud to the empty office. 'And they're supposed to be the experts.'

With the office tidy, I headed outside to sweep the stairs and polish the brass on the huge front door of the police station. I was almost finished when Green came back.

'How was it?' I asked eagerly, though by his heavy tread on the steps I was assuming it wasn't good. 'Did she recognise anyone?'

Green paused on the top step next to where Bet was standing. 'She did.'

I was pleased. 'And did you arrest him?'

'Briefly.' He looked annoyed.

'It weren't the killer?'

'It seems not.'

'How do you know?'

'Because he was in Windsor with at least twenty other soldiers on the night Martha was killed.'

'Ah.'

'Ah.'

'I'm sorry,' I said, wondering what was wrong with Pearly Peg's memory, because last I had seen of her, she'd been sharp as a tack and twice as prickly. Perhaps it was the drink. 'At least you tried, eh?'

'Yes, I suppose.' Green made a face. 'I really wanted to impress Inspector Abberline,' he admitted, lowering his voice a little. 'Show him I'm not just a run-of-the-mill policeman like Percival.'

'Oh I think he knows that already,' I said, thinking of the disdainful way Abberline looked at Percival. 'Here, I've got an idea.'

'What kind of idea?'

'A good one.'

Green took his hat off and rubbed his head. 'I'll try anything.'

'Abberline wanted to see Martha where she was killed,' I said. 'But he didn't get to see her there, because they brought her here first. Maybe you could go and have a look at where she was found.'

'It's been raining,' Green said. 'So any useful evidence like blood will have been washed away.'

I grimaced at the mention of Martha's blood. 'Maybe. But like you said, it's worth a go.' I smiled at him. 'Make sure you tell Abberline where you're going, though. Just so he knows.'

Green put his hat back on and straightened it. 'I'll tell him right now,' he said. 'See you later.'

And he was gone, barrelling through the door before I got a chance to tell him that Abberline wasn't there.

# Chapter 7

## Emma

*Two weeks later*

I could feel Bet's frustration from across the room.

'They did this identity parade, which is just a load of nonsense because all soldiers look the same in their uniforms. Green's trying but the rest of them ain't bothered one bit. I can't help thinking they've given up investigating Martha's death because they think she was just some unfortunate soul and she's not worth the bother,' she was saying, for the third – or was it the fourth? – time since she'd arrived. 'They think she was a prostitute. But even if she was a prostitute, which she could have been, I suppose – because, let's face it, they think we're all at it in some way or other – then why does that make her murder any less important?'

Wanting her to take a breath, I walked across the room and gently took the duster from Bet's hand. 'I think if you rub that mantelpiece any more, it'll fall apart,' I said. 'Why don't you have a sit-down and we can have a chat?'

Bet gave me a sheepish smile. 'Was I going on? My mum always says I don't know when to stop.'

'It's fine,' I said, steering her to one of the armchairs by the window. 'You've got a point.'

'I don't mean to criticise Inspector Abberline,' Bet said, sitting down heavily. 'He's such a nice man. But he's got it on both sides from that idiot Harrison loading him up with other work, and there aren't many of them really. They're all running round like headless chickens.'

She paused. 'And the worst thing is, it feels like it's passed now.'

'What has?' I sat down opposite her.

'Martha's death. They're all on to the next thing.'

'I'm sure that's not the case.'

'It is.' Bet nodded vigorously. 'First it was jewellery thefts in Spitalfields. Now it's some fight in a gentlemen's club in Ludgate Circus. That's taking up a lot of time, let me tell you.'

I sighed, knowing she was right. 'Fred said he was going to ask you for help with speaking to Martha's friend.'

'He did a while back but Harrison said no.'

'Lord, he really is an idiot.'

'Told you.' Bet sounded triumphant. 'And then Green was all eager for a while – like I said, he did that identity parade. And he went to the place where Martha was killed. But he didn't get nowhere.'

'And nothing came out at the inquest, I believe?' I said thoughtfully.

'Nothing useful.'

'It's disappointing.'

'It's baffling,' said Bet. 'Because I've met Pearly Peg a good few times and she is a clever woman. And maybe she's turned to drink since I last saw her . . .'

'It happens.'

'It does. But even so, that ain't Pearly Peg. And I don't understand how she'd pick out the wrong soldier. My mum says the same. We've been talking about it. And I know Harrison said no, but I've still got half a mind to go and chat to her myself.'

I knew I should tell her to steer clear but I didn't. 'Maybe you should go,' I said. 'I think that could be a good idea.'

'I don't want to get Inspector Abberline into trouble, mind.'

'I'll speak to him. I've got to take some papers down to the station for him later anyway. I'll see what he thinks about it. I don't see how he can object considering nothing's happened these last three weeks.'

Bet sat back in the chair, looking a bit happier. 'Thanks, Mrs Abberline.'

'Why don't you call me Emma?'

'Really?'

'Mrs Abberline makes me think of Fred's mother, the awful old battleaxe.'

Bet chuckled. 'All right then.'

'I will tell you one thing about Fred's mother, mind you,' I said. 'She's no one's fool.'

'What do you mean?' Bet narrowed her eyes.

'I mean no one tells her what to do.' I gave a little laugh, thinking of my mother-in-law. 'They might think they do. She might let them believe it. But she'll do what she wants in the end.'

'I quite like the sound of her.'

'Lord, she's a nightmare,' I admitted. 'But perhaps we could all learn a thing or two from her.'

There was a pause.

'I should get on,' Bet said. She looked a little awkward, and I felt bad for making her feel uncomfortable. Just because I was rattling round the house on my own, it didn't mean Bet and I were friends. 'Anything in particular you want me to do today?'

I looked round the very tidy lounge. 'Erm . . .'

'How about I unpack some of the boxes upstairs?' Bet said, standing up. 'Save you a job.'

'That would be good.' I nodded, glad the awkward moment had passed. 'Thank you.'

Bet bustled off and I went to find the paperwork I had to get Fred to sign. It was something about the house sale, and I knew unless I took it to him, and stood over it as he scrawled his signature, he'd never get round to it. It seemed nonsensical to me that I couldn't just sign it. But that was the way the world worked. A woman's signature was worth nothing while a man's bought houses and agreed deals and made things happen.

I found everything I needed, put the papers inside a folder, then I went upstairs to tell Bet I was going out. But she wasn't in the large bedroom at the back of the house where most of the boxes were and where I thought she'd be. She'd unpacked all the spare linen that had been stored away and stacked it neatly in the cupboard. And she'd hung up the winter coats, which had been draped across the bed. I was grateful.

'Bet?' I called.

'In here.'

My heart caught in my throat as I realised she was in the small bedroom at the front, next to our room. Rose's room.

Don't overreact, I told myself firmly. Be calm.

'I didn't mean this room . . .' I pushed open the door and found Bet sitting on the single bed, cradling Rose's doll like a baby.

'I had one just like this,' she said. 'I think my dad nicked it, but I loved it so much . . .'

'That's not yours.' My voice cracked.

Bet looked up at me, saw my horrified expression, and dropped the toy back into the box like it was hot.

'I'm sorry, I didn't mean to intrude. I'd finished in the other room, so I thought I'd check in here . . .' she began.

'Not this room,' I said. And then to my absolute embarrassment, I burst into tears.

Bet's eyes widened. 'Oh Lord, I'm so sorry,' she said again. She jumped to her feet, and put an arm round my shoulders, guiding me to sit down on the bed. 'I didn't realise you didn't want me in here.'

'No, I should have said.' My initial shock at seeing her with the doll was subsiding and I felt a little foolish. I took out my handkerchief and wiped my eyes. 'It's my fault.'

'You shouldn't ever apologise for being sad about something,' Bet said, sounding rather fierce. 'You can't change the way you feel.'

I sniffed. 'You're right.'

'I thought the doll was yours . . .' Bet began. 'But does it belong to someone else?'

I nodded.

'Your daughter?'

Again, I nodded.

'She died?'

Slowly I nodded once more.

'You don't have to tell me nothing,' Bet said. 'But if you want to talk, I'm a good listener.'

She sat down next to me and I looked at her.

'How old are you, Bet?' I asked.

'Nineteen.'

'You seem older.'

She shrugged. 'Had to grow up quick, didn't I? I looked after my mum. She fell apart for a bit after my dad . . .' She looked round as though she might be overheard. 'He went to jail.'

'I know,' I said. 'Fred told me when I offered you the job.'

'You don't mind?'

'You're not responsible for the sins of your father.'

46

'No,' Bet said with a note of caution. 'But not everyone thinks that way.'

I smiled at her, a little weakly because I was still shaken.

'Fred and I had a daughter,' I began. 'Her name was Rose. And when she was almost five, she died.'

'That's really sad,' Bet said. 'You must miss her.'

'Every day.'

I leaned forward and put my hand on the box, where Bet had found the doll. 'She had scarlet fever,' I said. 'We had to burn a lot of her things because of the infection. Everything I kept is in here. That's all we have left of her.'

Bet put her hand on my arm briefly. 'It's hard.'

'She'd have been eleven now,' I said. 'She never saw this house. This isn't really her bedroom even though I think of it that way. And she wouldn't be playing with dolls anymore.'

'I've still got my doll,' Bet said. 'Even though I'm an adult and even though she really wasn't even mine to begin with and my dad nicked her from some other little girl. She's under my bed.' She smiled at me. 'I reckon your Rose would be glad you kept her.'

The kindness of her words made tears spring into my eyes again.

'Fred doesn't like me looking at these things,' I admitted. 'That's why I've not unpacked anything.'

'He must miss her too.'

'So much.' I smiled as a memory came to me of tiny Rose scrambling up her father's legs for a cuddle when he came home from work. 'I didn't realise at first how hard it was for him. I sort of lost my way after Rose died. I was out of my mind with grief. Poor Fred had to look after me and himself.'

'That's why he changed his job?' Bet said. 'I've heard him talk about his years behind a desk.'

'He didn't enjoy it much.'

Bet made a face. 'I ain't surprised by that. I think he likes getting his hands dirty. Getting stuck in, you know?'

'He does.' I looked at her. 'You're a good judge of character.'

Bet smiled. 'Nosy.'

'Curious.'

She patted my arm again. 'We all have rotten things to deal with,' she said. 'And no one knows how they're going to react until it happens.'

I felt awkward again, as though I'd crossed a line between maid and mistress, though Bet seemed more relaxed about it than she'd done earlier. To hide my discomfort, I picked up Rose's doll, who had landed headfirst in the box when Bet dropped her, and straightened out her little dress. Then I stood up and sat her on one of the empty shelves, her cloth legs sticking out in front of her.

'She shouldn't be hidden away,' I said.

Bet nodded. She stood up too and brushed down her apron.

'I'm almost done,' she said. 'Are you going to the police station? I can make you some dinner and leave it in the kitchen if you like?'

I nodded, glad to have our proper relationship re-established once more.

'That would be helpful, thank you.'

Bet went to leave the room then she paused. 'And you'll speak to Inspector Abberline about me having a chat with Pearly Peg?'

'You really want to speak to her?'

'I do.' She looked determined.

'Then I'll ask him.'

She looked at me through narrowed eyes, sizing me up. 'You're bolder than you think you are, Mrs Abberline.'

'Emma.'

'Emma.'

Then she clattered down the stairs and I heard her go into the kitchen.

Absurdly pleased at being called bold, I set off to the police station later on. I thought I could gently suggest to Fred that Bet could speak to Pearly Peg on the quiet and maybe find out more about what happened at the identity parade. Harrison needn't know. I wasn't entirely sure Fred would agree – he was a stickler for the rules, was my Fred – but I thought it was worth a try.

But much to my disappointment, when I arrived at the police station, Fred was nowhere to be seen.

'I think he's gone down to Spitalfields,' said the constable at the desk. 'Something about jewellery thefts. I think they've had a breakthrough.' He chuckled. 'Farnworth's been dressing as a shop girl to catch the crook.'

I swallowed my frustration.

'Ah well,' I said. 'I'll see him at home later.'

'Green?' The insolent constable who'd been rude to me before appeared in the foyer to speak to the officer on the desk. He gave me a cursory glance that told me he didn't recognise me. Again. 'Can I get rid of the tart in the cell?'

Green shifted in his chair, looking slightly uncomfortable and avoiding my gaze. 'Has she sobered up, Percival?'

'Yes.' Percival shrugged. 'Pretty much.' He chuckled. 'For now. She'll probably be back here before long.'

'It's getting late,' I said, looking at the clock on the wall. 'Will she be all right if you let her go? Does she have somewhere to sleep?'

Percival screwed his nose up. 'I don't know,' he said. 'And I don't much care.'

'A young, vulnerable woman alone on the streets of Whitechapel?' I said sharply. 'With a killer on the loose.'

'Believe me, she ain't that young,' said Percival. 'And she definitely ain't vulnerable.'

'Not worth the bother?' I said sharply, echoing Bet's words from earlier.

'We'll let her go now, Mrs Abberline,' said Green quickly, clearly spotting my disgruntled expression and emphasising my name to remind Percival who I was. 'When it's still light and she'll be safer.'

Percival widened his eyes, then he disappeared off down the corridor towards the cells.

I nodded at Green. 'Thank you,' I said, albeit begrudgingly because I was sure he'd only acted because I was married to his boss. 'Please tell my husband I called.'

'Will do,' he said.

I pushed open the heavy door and paused on the steps outside, where I'd met Bet just a few weeks before. I knew the woman who'd been in the cells would come down the alleyway at the side of the police station and I wanted to check she was all right, with somewhere to stay, before she left.

Sure enough, a few minutes later, a woman came out of the little cut-through and out on to the main road.

'Excuse me?' I called. The woman paused, eyeing me with suspicion.

'I ain't got no money,' she said.

I shook my head. 'I don't want money.'

'I was going to say, nice-looking lady like you, pretty dress, smart bonnet, begging for coppers from a woman like me,' she said, giving a throaty laugh. 'Thought the world had been turned upside down for a second.'

'I just wanted to make sure you're all right,' I said. 'Those constables aren't always the nicest.'

The woman raised an eyebrow. 'Got that right.' She shuddered, looking shaken for a brief moment.

'So are you? All right?'

'I'm all right,' she said, pulling her shoulders back. 'I'm

always all right. After all, I'm Mary Ann Nichols. I get in scrapes and I get myself out again.' She leaned towards me. 'That's what I do.'

'Do you have somewhere to go tonight?' I asked. 'It's getting late.'

'I do.' Mary Ann's bravado wavered a tiny bit. 'Once I get the four pence I need for my bed.'

'I can help.' I put my hand into my bag and immediately realised I had left my coin purse on the sideboard where Bet had been polishing earlier. 'Damn and blast,' I muttered.

'No matter,' said Mary Ann, looking faintly amused. 'You don't need to give me nothing.'

But I was already pulling out my hat pins. 'Here,' I said, taking off my bonnet and holding it out to Mary Ann. 'Take this.'

'Oh no, miss,' she said. 'I can't do that. It's much too nice.'

'I want you to have it,' I urged. 'Keep it, sell it, do whatever you want. It might help.'

Seemingly delighted, Mary Ann rammed the bonnet on her head. I straightened it for her.

'That is lovely,' Mary Ann said, admiring her reflection in the police station window.

'Jolly,' I said.

'A jolly bonnet.'

She grinned at me, showing a missing tooth, and then she gestured with her thumb over her shoulder, along the road. 'I should go. Book my bed for the night.'

'Good luck, Mary Ann,' I said.

'My mates call me Polly.'

'Good luck, Polly.'

'Oh, I don't need luck,' Polly said. 'I've got a jolly bonnet.'

# Chapter 8

## Polly

In her darker moments, Polly thought she was her own worst enemy. All the bad things that had happened to her could be traced back to decisions she'd made. There was no one else to blame.

Tonight was no different. When she'd left the police station – sobered up and with a pounding headache – she'd been determined to go straight to Wilmott's and arrange a bed for the night. She liked it there, because it was a boarding house just for women. The White House, where she'd stayed a few times, had men too and an unsavoury smell. But Wilmott's was more expensive, and she already knew she would have to beg for the pennies she needed for a bed.

Even so, as she came out of the station, her chin lifted and her shoulders back, Wilmott's was her plan. And then she met that woman, a bit of a do-gooder, but nice all the same. When she handed over her bonnet, Polly felt like the luckiest woman in all of Whitechapel. She could sell it, she thought, but she'd rather keep it because didn't it make her look lovely?

So as she set off towards the boarding house, she was ready for the night ahead. She felt like something had changed. She would get the money for a bed, then tomorrow she would make a new start. Maybe get another position in a big house somewhere – because didn't she look the part now? And this time she'd do it right.

Maybe it was the smile on her face, or her pretty straw bonnet, or perhaps someone was just looking out for her, but it didn't take long for Polly to get the money she needed.

With her pockets jangling and her heart light, she set off towards Wilmott's, proud as punch that something had gone her way.

Overhead, thunder rumbled, and there was smoke in the air. People on the street were saying there was a fire down at one of the docks. Polly thought about going to see for herself, but no – she had a plan and she was going to stick to it.

She walked down Thrawl Street and past the Frying Pan – one of her favourite pubs – the coins clanking against her leg, just as the heavens opened and the rain began.

'That'll put the fire out,' she said to herself, adjusting her bonnet so it shielded her face. 'Lord have mercy, this rain is awful.'

She paused, glancing at the windows of the Frying Pan. It was warm and dry in there. Cosy, you might say. Her begging had been successful, and she had enough money for a bed tonight and for a drink. But just one. Just a quick one. She'd just stay long enough to shelter from the rain and to show off her new hat to anyone who might be there.

She went inside and immediately met an old mate of her husband's called Benny, who looked delighted to see her.

'Polly, my girl, you look like a fancy lady from the West End in that hat,' he said. 'What are you drinking?'

Polly ordered a beer, and then she had to buy one for Benny, and then a couple of women she knew from years back came in, and they were celebrating – well, she wasn't sure what they'd been celebrating – but they were in fine spirits.

And at some point Polly went out to use the privy and

took a moment in the cool night air, leaning against the wall because she was a bit unsteady on her feet.

'Oh, Polly,' she muttered to herself. 'Polly, what are you doing, you silly old cow?'

She put her hand in her pocket – she still had tuppence left.

'Right, that's enough,' she told herself sternly. 'No more drinks.'

She straightened up. The Frying Pan had a side gate that led out to the street and she made her way there, determined not to go back into the bar. But then the wind lifted her hair and she realised she'd left her hat – her pretty bonnet – on the table where she'd been sitting.

'Bloody stupid woman,' she hissed under her breath, considering leaving the hat where it was for someone else to pick up – if they hadn't already. But it was so pretty. And it was bound to rain again. And hadn't that do-gooder at the police station been kinder to her than anyone had been for a long while? She'd wanted Polly to have the hat.

And so she turned and went back inside the pub, and there was a drink on the bar for her, and it would have been rude to leave it, and Benny was wearing her hat and she had to wrestle him for it, and everyone laughed, and she felt so happy and full of life that she stayed for another, and another . . .

When Polly finally staggered out of the Frying Pan long after midnight, the streets were dark and her pockets were empty. She pulled her bonnet on, and tied it beneath her chin, and swayed off towards Wilmott's.

'Bad decisions,' she told herself as she went, the words keeping time with her footsteps as they echoed round the cobbles. 'Bad decisions.'

Willmott's stood at the end of the street, and she could see the silhouette of the keeper in the doorway. It was the deputy – she could tell from her shape. She was a grumpy woman whose name was Joanie. Polly's husband William often said the folk who wanted power shouldn't have it – Joanie always reminded Polly of that.

Thinking of William now made Polly's heart ache so sharply she almost gasped out loud. She shook her head, feeling the ribbons of her bonnet whip her chin. That was all so long ago, she thought. Her children wouldn't know her now. Walking away from them was one bad decision she'd regret until the end of her days.

She took a deep breath, pulled her shoulders back, and tried very hard to walk in a straight line down to the boarding house.

'Four pence,' said Joanie as she approached.

'About that,' Polly began.

'No.'

'I've not asked you anything yet.'

'No need,' said Joanie. 'No money, no bed.'

'I know you give credit,' Polly said. 'It's me – you know me.' She hoped Joanie would remember her from the last time she stayed. But she simply looked her up and down, and shook her head.

'No,' she said.

'I've been here before,' Polly said.

'I know.'

'So . . .'

'No. No credit. Not for you. Not tonight.'

Polly pushed away the flicker of annoyance that rose up inside her.

'I'll come back,' she said.

'You do that,' Joanie said, sounding bored.

'And you'll give me a bed?'

'If you get the money, I'll think about it. But I ain't promising.'

'I'll get the money.' Polly forced a smile. 'See what a jolly bonnet I've got?'

Joanie rolled her eyes and retreated inside. Polly swayed off along the street, wondering where to go next, until she came across another pub that was open, and went inside. And even though she had no money, she somehow found a drink or two, and then another, and time passed in a blur of men's voices, sharp bitter spirits, and sour beer.

When the pub closed, Polly found herself on Osborn Street. She wasn't sure where she was going. Nowhere and anywhere all at once. She was trailing her arm along the wall, using it as a guide in the darkness, and she knew her knuckles were grazed but she couldn't feel it.

'Polly?'

It took a minute to work out where the voice was coming from. Polly gazed around herself until she saw her friend Ellen, coming out of the darkness like a vision.

'Ellen,' she breathed. 'Hello, Ellen.'

'You're in a bad way, Polly,' said Ellen.

Polly leaned against the wall. 'No,' she said. 'I am fine.'

'Where you headed?'

Waving her arm wildly, Polly tried to gesture in the direction of somewhere. 'I am going to get some money,' she said, trying to speak clearly even though her tongue felt too big in her mouth. 'I have had my lodging money three times tonight and lost it.'

'Three times?' said Ellen, putting her hand on Polly's arm.

'Four times.' Polly leaned towards her friend. 'Or maybe five.'

'Are you going to Wilmott's? I'm going there now. Come with me?'

'No,' Polly snarled. 'That old cow won't let me in. I need to make up my money.'

Ellen looked doubtful, which rankled Polly.

'I will,' she said, jabbing her finger into Ellen's chest. 'I will make up my money.'

'Polly, I really think . . .'

'I am going this way,' Polly said firmly. 'And I will see you at Wilmott's later.'

She staggered away from Ellen. Just a few steps and she couldn't see her friend any longer, nor hear her footsteps.

'Bad decisions,' Polly muttered as she wended her way along the road. She'd lost her bearings in the darkness, not sure which direction she was going in. Her head throbbed and her eyes were heavy. Perhaps she could find somewhere to sit down. Rest. Just for a moment or two.

She stopped walking for a second. It was quiet now, with no one on the street, but just for a moment she thought she heard footsteps behind her. She listened to the sound of her own breathing in the silence, and then set off again. Beneath her hands she felt an alcove or a gate, and stumbled through. As she went, she tripped over a stone and, lurching towards the wall, hit the bricks heavily chest first. Winded, her legs gave way and slowly she crumpled to the ground.

Her eyelids closed for a second, then opened again. And looming over her was a figure. She put her hand on her straw bonnet.

'I have made some bad decisions,' she said. 'But I'm fine.'

And then she wasn't.

# Chapter 9

## Emma

I woke with a start, hearing a rap on the door and realising Fred was already getting out of bed.

'I'll get it,' he whispered. Still half-asleep, I heard him go downstairs, and then urgent voices. Just as I was wondering whether I should get up too, he came back into our room.

'Go back to sleep,' he said. 'Everything is all right.'

'What's happened? Are you going to the police station?'

Fred was picking up some clothes, starting to get dressed in the half-light. I felt a flicker of annoyance that he'd use his shirt and trousers being accessible in the dark as an excuse for him throwing clothes on the chair in our room, instead of putting them away. I found Fred's untidy nature very hard to live with and often told him how lucky he was that he had other positive attributes.

He saw me looking, and gestured towards the chair in triumph. I groaned good-naturedly.

His shirt on, if a little crumpled, Fred came over and kissed my forehead.

'I have to go,' he said quietly, fastening his buttons. 'But it's very early – stay in bed.'

I sat up, more awake now. 'Has there been another murder?'

'I'm not sure yet. Perhaps.'

'A woman?'

'Yes.' He paused. 'I don't know all the details yet.'

His face looked drawn in the dim light. Worried.

'Be careful,' I said. 'Please.'

'Always.'

He blew me a kiss from the door, and I heard his footsteps going downstairs. The rain was pattering against the windows again, though last night's storm had passed, thank goodness.

I yawned and stretched and thought about staying where I was because the weather was so awful, and it really was early; the light creeping round the curtains was grey. But even though I tried to snuggle back down under the bedclothes, my mind resisted sleep. Had there been another brutal attack like the killing of Martha? Whitechapel could be a dangerous place for men and women alike – I knew that – but the brutality of Martha's death had shocked even my world-weary husband.

I closed my eyes again but sleep still eluded me. I thought of Fred and the other members of his team, no doubt out and about somewhere in the rain, and I slid out of bed. I'd take them some food, I thought. Perhaps I'd bake some soda bread – that didn't take long – and it would be lovely for them with a mug of tea when they got back from wherever they'd been.

And if while I was in the police station, it happened that I found out more about this latest crime, then so be it.

So that's what I did. And a couple of hours later, when Whitechapel was still only just waking up, I was hurrying through the damp streets, bread and jam in my basket like Little Red Riding Hood off to see her grandmother.

The police station was full of people.

'He's busy,' warned the man on the front desk – an older

gent called Harvey who I had known for years. I held up the basket and he grinned. 'Go on through.'

I found Fred alone in his office, leaning back in his chair and looking up at the ceiling.

'Hello,' he said as I came in. 'I wondered how long it would take you to show up.'

'Am I that predictable?'

He smiled. 'Not to the average man, but I am a detective.'

'The best detective in all of London,' I declared. But Fred's smile faltered, just a little.

'Is it awful?' I said. 'Another murder?'

Fred nodded. 'She's in the mortuary.'

'Do you know who she is?'

He rubbed his nose. 'We've got a couple of leads, but she's not been identified officially. Green and Percival are out speaking to folk round the workhouses.'

I felt a wave of sadness. 'Poor woman.' I went to Fred's side and put my hand on his shoulder. 'Shall I go and make you a cup of tea? I brought some bread and jam.'

He gave me a tired smile. 'That sounds lovely.'

By the time I had found everything I needed in the tiny police-station kitchen and sliced the bread and spread it with jam, a little while had passed. I wondered where Bet was, and if she was working this morning – there was no sign of her.

I felt a little odd about the conversation we'd had yesterday when I'd told her about Rose and cried on her shoulder. Rose's life and death wasn't a secret, of course, but my friends in the West End were awkward and uncomfortable when I mentioned her. I'd liked how straightforward Bet was. Sympathetic without being mawkish. I liked Bet herself. She was good company around the house and I thought, in different circumstances, we could have been friends.

I desperately hoped Bet didn't know this murder victim – she was still so sad about Martha and the lack of progress on catching her killer – and she said her mother was distraught.

I put the teapot on a tray with some cups and a milk jug and a plate of bread and jam, then pushed out of the door backwards and went back to Fred's office.

Green and Percival were back, both sitting opposite Fred. And on the desk in between the men was a hat. A hat that looked so familiar to me that I almost dropped the heavy tray I was carrying. Green noticed me wobble and got to his feet, taking the tray from me and sliding it on to the desk.

'All right there, Mrs Abberline?' he said.

I reached towards the hat but didn't touch it. 'What is this?'

'That's a hat,' said Green, sitting down again. I noticed he glanced at Fred, obviously checking if he was all right to continue. Fred gave him a tiny nod and Green carried on. 'The victim was wearing it – we found it when we went to the scene. Must have fallen off her head when she was attacked.'

'It's my hat,' I said in dismay. 'This is my bonnet.'

Fred's eyes widened. 'It is similar to one of yours, isn't it? I thought it looked familiar.'

'Probably nicked,' said Percival. 'Ain't no way a woman like that could afford a hat like this.' I saw him glance at Green as he spoke, full of bravado, as though he wanted his approval.

Green nodded. 'Definitely nicked because she wasn't wearing it earlier in the day – that's what I've heard. Probably took it off some nice lady so she could attract a punter or two and make some quick cash.'

But I shook my head vigorously. 'It doesn't *look* like my

hat,' I said. 'It *is* my hat. I gave it to the woman who was here yesterday.' I turned to the younger police officers. 'The one you released from custody.'

Both men looked shocked, and slightly disbelieving.

'Her name is Mary Ann Nichols,' I said.

Fred looked at the others. His face was stern and his eyes steely. 'Did we have Mary Ann Nichols here yesterday?'

Percival glanced at Green, clearly hoping the older constable would take the lead. Green cleared his throat. 'Mary Ann Nichols?' He nodded. 'We did, sir. She was drunk and we brought her in. When she'd sobered up, we let her go.'

'So we have her details?' Fred wrote down the name.

'She said her friends call her Polly,' I told him. My voice sounded small and sad.

Fred nodded and wrote that down too.

'Is she married, do we know?' he asked the other men.

'I believe she was, but no longer,' Percival sounded a little less sure of himself than usual. 'I can find the name of her husband.'

'That would be useful.' Fred sounded calm but I knew he was furious. 'You've both seen her in the mortuary today, I believe?'

'Yes, sir,' said Green.

'And you didn't recognise her? Even though you saw her alive and well less than a day ago?'

They didn't recognise my hat, I thought. Even though I had been wearing it when I spoke to them yesterday. Men like this did not see women. Not properly.

'You didn't recognise her?' Fred repeated. Percival and Green didn't speak. Percival looked at his feet while Green stared straight ahead.

'No, sir,' he said eventually.

Percival looked shame-faced, which I was glad about.

Fred looked at them both for a long moment. 'I suggest

you both work on your observation skills,' he said. Then he turned to me. 'Is there anything else you can tell me about Mary Ann?'

I took a breath. 'She told me she gets in scrapes and gets herself out again,' I said in a voice that wavered, just a bit.

'Not this time,' Fred said. He looked straight at me, and I saw genuine sadness in his eyes.

'Not this time,' I echoed. Suddenly angry, I turned to the officers, annoyance overtaking sadness. 'I told you that it was the wrong time of day to be releasing a vulnerable woman. Didn't I say that to you? You let Polly go out into the streets without a care as to her welfare.'

'We had no cause to keep her,' said Percival. 'We can't keep innocent women in the cells, even if you want us to.'

'That's not what I meant,' I said. I pointed at them both. 'Her blood is on your hands.'

'Emma,' said Fred, putting a hand on my arm. 'I'm not sure this is the time . . .'

'Oh, it's the time,' I said, furious with Green and Percival, and with Fred too if I was honest. 'If you'd seen her right, she wouldn't be lying in your mortuary now with Dr Llewellyn cutting her into pieces.'

'That's quite enough, Emma,' said Fred firmly. 'We're all shocked and saddened by another murder happening on our doorstep, but the only person to blame for this is whoever killed Mary Ann. And I promise you, we will do everything we can to track him down.'

'Or her,' said Green. 'It might be a her.'

I shot him a fierce look.

'I'm just saying it could be a woman.'

There was a pause. Fred looked a little weary.

'Is Bet here?' I asked.

'She's around somewhere,' said Green. 'I saw her earlier.'

I nodded. I put my hand on my husband's shoulder again

and he leaned his head slightly, so I felt his beard tickling my fingers. 'Speak to Bet,' I said. 'She could be useful.'

Then, knowing it was petty but not caring one jot, I wrapped up the rest of the bread I had made and put it in my basket to take home and share with Bet later.

'I'll see you at home,' I said. And without a glance at the other men, I opened the door and left, letting it bang shut behind me.

# Chapter 10

## Bet

I hated being in the mortuary but I was in there all the same. Not the room itself but in the little anteroom next door. I'd been there, washing the floor, when Dr Llewellyn came in to examine the body. I usually went out of my way to avoid that part of the station, but I'd not liked to think of that poor woman lying in a dirty room, and so I'd come to clean up. Not that I had ventured into the actual mortuary – that would be a step too far for me and Dr Llewellyn alike, I suspected. But I'd cleaned the anteroom where the equipment was kept, and hung up some aprons, and generally made sure everything was ready. When Dr Llewellyn arrived, he'd put his arm round the door and plucked an apron from the hook and didn't even notice I was there, so I'd stayed put, curious to know what would happen next, though I'd firmly averted my eyes from the shrouded figure lying on the table in the centre of the room.

To my surprise, almost as soon as things began, I'd been so interested in what was going on, that I'd ended up pouring the dirty water out of the door into the gutter, turning over my bucket, and sitting there half the morning, listening.

Dr Llewellyn had carefully taken the sheet from over the victim. He and Blake – his assistant – had looked at the woman and I had heard a sharp intake of breath from one of them. Or perhaps both of them.

I heard Dr Llewellyn begin to talk through the woman's injuries – and it wasn't nice to hear. Her body had been mutilated. Slashed so violently that Dr Llewellyn had to pause for a moment to take it all in.

'This is monstrous,' I heard him mutter.

I heard the door to the mortuary open, and from my spot on the bucket, I leaned forward so I could peek out of the anteroom to see Inspector Abberline enter, ashen-faced.

'We have a name,' he said. 'Not confirmed, of course, but a step in the right direction.'

'Who is she?' Llewellyn asked.

'Mary Ann Nichols,' said Abberline. 'Friends called her Polly.'

The name meant nothing to me, but that didn't mean I hadn't crossed paths with the unfortunate woman at one time or another.

'Right,' said Abberline. 'Talk me through it.'

Llewellyn began listing the woman's injuries once more and I tried not to listen; hearing them once was enough. From my vantage point, I couldn't see Llewellyn or the victim, but I could see Abberline, who was scribbling notes. That gave me an idea. I found a piece of paper from a pile at the side of the room and dug about in my pocket for a pencil. Then, without really knowing why I was doing it, I scrawled Mary Ann Nichols along the top and began to write down everything Llewellyn was saying. I'd thought I'd heard it all before Abberline came in, but as it turned out, that was just the beginning. Mary Ann had suffered terribly and as Llewellyn carried on, it was obvious he was finding it hard. I felt sorry for him – what a job he had to do.

I tried to concentrate on my notes. I wasn't quick with a pencil – my spelling was, well, creative, and my handwriting was hard to read – so I wrote in a sort of code, hoping I'd remember what the notes all meant later. And when I got fed up with that, I drew a vague outline of a person and began adding the poor woman's injuries to my drawing. It made for horrific listening. I couldn't believe that anyone could be so cruel as to inflict such awful, gruesome wounds on an innocent woman.

'What a way to go,' I murmured. I hoped Mary Ann had died quickly. Abberline was clearly thinking the same as I was, because he interrupted Llewellyn.

'These wounds,' he said, waving his arm in the direction – I assumed – of Mary Ann's lower body. 'Were they inflicted after death?'

'I believe so,' said Llewellyn. 'The slashes to the throat would have killed her almost instantly. She was inebriated. Very much so. She wouldn't have fought back.'

I breathed out slowly, relieved that Mary Ann wouldn't have known anything about the injuries she'd suffered.

But Llewellyn was still talking. 'The slashes in her throat go from left to right, you see?' he was saying. 'I believe he approached the victim from the front . . .'

I frowned. I held my pencil in my fist like a weapon and pretended to be slashing at someone. 'Left to right,' I murmured.

'And the blood?' Abberline said. 'The chaps who found her said there wasn't as much blood as they'd expected, but I assume the rain had washed much of it away.'

'Due to the majority of the injuries being inflicted after death, I believe,' said Llewellyn.

There was a pause. 'In your opinion,' Abberline began. 'In your opinion was this woman murdered by the same person who killed Martha Tabram?'

There was no response, so I leaned forward again, straining to see Llewellyn. He was nodding, slowly.

'I believe so,' he said eventually. 'I think the brutality of the attack, and the pattern . . .' He coughed. 'And the positioning of the wounds, suggests the same killer.'

'I agree,' Abberline said. 'The way she was found is also similar.'

I closed my eyes briefly, trying to stem the rage that was building up inside me. If they'd investigated Martha's death properly, if Abberline hadn't been distracted by the jewellery thefts, then perhaps this Mary Ann would still be alive.

The door to the mortuary opened again and Green appeared.

'We've found the husband, Inspector,' he said. 'And there's a woman here from Lambeth Workhouse, says she knows Mary Ann Nichols.'

Abberline clapped his hands together. 'Right. I'll come. Thanks, Llewellyn.'

'We're pretty much done, here,' said Llewellyn. 'Anything else jumps out, I'll come and get you.'

Abberline followed Green out of the room and I stood up. I didn't want to be spotted lurking in the mortuary by Llewellyn, so I went out of the side door of the anteroom, into the courtyard. Then, stuffing my notes into the pocket of my skirt as I went, I hurried to gather my bits and pieces. My shift had ended ages ago, and I was eager to get to the Abberlines' house. I had a lot to tell Emma.

Outside, the rain had stopped and the sun – goodness me, the sun! – was shining on the wet pavements. I walked briskly, trying not to wonder if everyone I walked past was the murderer. Was it that man with the newspaper under his arm? Or that young chap with the bristly moustache? Or even the older gentleman tilting his head to the sunshine like a flower in spring?

Feeling a chill down my spine despite the warmth in the day, I almost galloped up the steps to the Abberlines' front door and rang the bell.

No one came. I waited a minute, and then rang again, hearing the clang echoing in the hallway. Strange. I'd asked Emma if she wanted me to use the back door – like most maids did – but Emma had laughed.

'Good heavens, no,' she'd said. She was a funny one, Mrs Abberline – Emma. She didn't talk to me like I was a maid. She talked to me like I was her equal. And I hadn't half felt sorry for her when she told me about her little girl dying. That was sad. The poor woman was probably a different person now, changed forever because she'd suffered such a sad loss. Just like how my mum had been changed by my dad being locked up. I liked Emma. And I liked Inspector Abberline, too. I was pleased to be working for them.

I rang the bell again, annoyed that I didn't have a key for the back door so I could let myself in instead of standing on the doorstep.

When once more there was no answer, I leaned over the iron handrail and peeked in the front window. And there, in a chair by the fire, was Emma. She was staring into space and she looked upset. I frowned. Had something happened? Was she upset about Rose again? I rapped on the window, quietly at first and then, when Emma didn't budge, more loudly. This time Emma jumped, startled out of her thoughts. I waved and Emma nodded and got to her feet. A few seconds later, the door opened.

'Are you poorly?' I asked as soon as I saw Emma's drawn, pale face. 'Shall I fetch a doctor? Or the inspector?'

'No, I'm not ill,' said Emma, standing back to let me enter. 'I'm just . . .'

I took off my hat and looked at her. 'What is it? You look all pale and clammy.'

'Clammy?'

'Sweaty.'

'I had a bit of a shock, that's all.'

'Got any brandy?'

'In the front room.'

'Have you had any?'

'It's three o'clock in the afternoon.'

'My mum swears by it for a shock.' I laughed. 'Though I've no idea where she'd get brandy from.'

Emma shrugged. 'Does it help?'

'She says so.'

'Come along then.'

I followed her into the front room and she uncorked a bottle from the sideboard. She poured two stiff measures of brandy and handed one to me.

'I've not had a shock,' I said, but I took it anyway. 'What's the matter with you? What's happened? Is it . . . Are you sad about Rose again?'

'No, it's not Rose.' Emma took a large swig of her drink and shivered as she swallowed. 'There's been another murder.'

'I know – I've just come from the station.'

Mrs Abberline sat down in one of the armchairs and I sat opposite her, feeling a little odd to be making myself so comfortable in such a nice house, and drinking brandy like a gentleman. I hoped my skirt wasn't dirty and wouldn't leave a mark on this fancy chair.

'I met the victim,' said Emma. 'She's called Polly.'

I frowned. 'No, her name's Mary Ann.'

'But her friends called her Polly.'

'That's what the inspector said . . .' I murmured, almost to myself. 'And she was your friend?' I was shocked. A woman with Lambeth Workhouse embroidered on her petticoats didn't seem the type to be friends with Emma.

'I met her yesterday.' Emma's voice wobbled. 'She was in the cells. But they let her out, and I was worried about her, because it was late and she said she'd get the money for a bed. And I didn't have my purse, so I gave her my hat instead. And now they're saying she was a prostitute and that's why she was killed, and they're only saying that because she was so proud of her jolly hat, and the only reason she had the bloody hat is because I gave it to her.'

She took another swig of her brandy.

'It's all my fault.'

I stared at her, trying to make sense of everything she'd just said.

'You gave her a hat?'

'A nice one.'

'But you didn't let her out of the cells late at night?'

'No.' Emma sounded uncertain.

'And you didn't get her drunk?'

Emma looked into her almost empty glass. 'No.'

'And you didn't kill her?'

'No.'

'Then it ain't your fault.'

Emma opened her mouth and I shook my head emphatically. 'No,' I said again. 'I saw Martha the night she died, so I know why you're thinking what you're thinking, but you're wrong. Should I have done something to help Martha? Taken her somewhere? Said something? But the truth is, nothing we did or didn't do could have changed this. We're not to blame, Emma.'

We looked at one another and Emma finally nodded.

'I know,' she said. 'You're right. It's just so sad. She was nice, you know? Funny. A bit cocky. I don't like to think of her suffering.'

I sighed. It really was sad. 'If it helps,' I said, 'I don't think she did suffer.'

'How do you know that?'

'I listened to Llewellyn.'

'Dr Llewellyn?'

'No, Mrs Llewellyn who does the laundry down

Spitalfields,' I said. And then when Emma widened her eyes I said: 'Of course Dr Llewellyn.'

I pulled my notes out of my pocket and thrust them at Emma. 'I wrote down what he said.'

Emma unfolded the notes and smoothed them out on her lap. 'Mary Ann Nichols,' she said.

I found the pencil and threw that at Emma. 'Write Polly there, too.'

Emma did as she was told, squinting at the paper.

'Bet, why did you write all this down?' she asked.

'I'm not sure exactly.' I drummed my fingers on the side of my brandy glass. I'd not taken a sip yet – I'd never tasted brandy and it smelled quite suspicious. 'I suppose I thought . . .'

Emma looked up at me. 'What did you think?'

'I thought that maybe it could help.'

'It would help more if I could read your writing,' Emma said, tapping the paper with the end of the pencil.

I felt my cheeks flush with embarrassment, because for all I was sitting with Emma in her lounge, suddenly the differences between us felt enormous. 'That's why I drew the person, see?' I muttered. 'I'm not quick at writing.'

'I was only teasing,' said Emma, putting her hand out and patting my knee. 'I can read it fine. I can read all of it.' She stopped talking for a moment as she scanned the paper, and winced. 'It's awful.'

'I know.'

We both fell silent for a second and then Emma spoke. 'Bet,' she said. 'Are we going to find out more about these murders?'

I pinched my lips together, then slowly I nodded. 'I think we are.'

# Chapter 11

## Emma

I stood up, suddenly full of purpose. 'We really could, couldn't we? Find out more.'

'Just to be sure. Are you saying we – me and you – could investigate the murders?' Bet frowned. 'Like the police are supposed to be doing.'

'Yes.'

'I thought you were joking.'

'I wasn't.' I clenched my fists at my sides, full of determination and anger and fight. 'Listen, I love my husband and I know he is an excellent detective but . . .'

'He's not being given a chance to be an excellent detective,' said Bet. 'Because there are too many other things going on, and not everyone thinks Martha and Polly are important enough.'

'Indeed.'

There was a pause.

'So you weren't joking?' Bet said.

'No.' I stood up straighter. 'I think we should do this.' I looked at Bet, suddenly desperate for her to agree to investigate these crimes, even though we didn't have a clue how to do it. 'Will you help me?'

Bet took too long to answer and for a second I thought she'd say no. But then, quite slowly, she nodded. 'I'll help you.'

Relieved, I let out my breath in a puff. 'We just need to think about the best place to start.'

'I think we've already started.'

'You've already started.' I flapped the notes at her. 'And when I met you outside the police station, after Martha, you said you'd catch the killer yourself.'

'Lord, I did, didn't I?' Bet chuckled, but I could see a gleam of determination in her eyes. 'But what about the inspector?'

'What about him?'

'Won't he be annoyed if we start sticking our beaks in where they're not meant to be?'

'We'll be helping him,' I said airily. 'He'll be grateful.'

'Will he?'

I thought that perhaps grateful wasn't the word, but I didn't say anything.

'Should we tell him?' Bet asked.

'He always asks for my opinion on cases,' I pointed out.

'So?'

'So, I think he'll be glad we're helping, but he won't want everyone to know.' I pushed away the little nagging voice that warned me that wasn't what Fred would think, and smiled at Bet. 'There are women detectives now; he told me that himself.'

'But Harrison doesn't approve. He didn't want me getting involved.'

'Harrison's an idiot.'

'He is but the inspector isn't,' Bet said. 'He really is taking this seriously, you know? When I was there – in the mortuary – with Llewellyn and the inspector and that other fella – Blake, I think his name is – they sounded . . .' She looked up at the ceiling, searching for the right word. 'They sounded shaken.'

I thought about how Fred had looked when he found out Polly had died – deflated by another brutal killing – and I nodded.

'They are taking it seriously today,' I said. 'Fred is a good policeman. But like you say, he is pulled this way and that, and the commissioner says one thing, and the officers say something else, and the people want something different.'

'He can't give these killings the attention they need, even though he wants to.'

I put my hands on my hips. 'I think that if something else happens to someone more important than Polly, then Fred will be told to focus on that instead.'

'Like a fight in a gentlemen's club in Ludgate Circus?'

'Exactly.' I breathed out slowly. 'And Martha and Polly will never be as important as a fight in a gentlemen's club, no matter how brutal their deaths.'

'Like their lives weren't worth nothing because they were unfortunate.' Bet looked thoughtful. 'That ain't right.'

'No.'

'Llewellyn said he reckons it was the same killer, who did both.'

'I read that in your notes,' I said.

Bet gave me a small smile. 'We should start at the beginning,' she said. 'Before Martha died.'

I lifted my chin. 'Go on.'

'We need to find Pearly Peg and have a chat with her. Like I was going to do ages ago. Because I don't reckon there's any way she's not sure who those soldiers were. No way at all.'

'That sounds like a very good place to begin.' I felt my heart beat a bit quicker. 'Shall we go now?'

'Right now?' Bet sounded half pleased, half alarmed. 'Don't you have chores for me to do?'

'Nothing that can't wait.'

'Then let's go.'

It took a fair while to track down Pearly Peg. I saw parts of Whitechapel I'd never seen before and it was quite the eye opener. But eventually we found her, in what Bet called a dosshouse.

'She's working there now – that's what Bert at the White Swan said,' she explained as we went through the maze of little streets. Each one looked the same to me, with their cobbled paths and looming walls, but Bet knew the way without a second thought. She darted through alleyways, and across streets. 'So she'll always have a bed for the night. This is it, down the end here.'

I had lived in the East End for much of my life. I had been involved in many philanthropic projects and prided myself on helping people less fortunate than me. I was married to Fred, for heaven's sake, and I thought I knew about the dark side of the city in which I lived.

But I didn't know about this.

The dosshouse was a tall, narrow building, with dirty windows and an open front door. I was never one to lack confidence, but even so I felt my steps slowing as we walked towards it.

'Come on, Emma,' said Bet, taking my arm. 'It ain't as bad as it looks.'

'I'll reserve judgement until I'm inside,' I said, faking bravado though my knees were shaking.

Inside was just as bad as I'd feared. There was a strange, pungent smell that settled in the back of my throat and made me gag. The light was dim, because the windows were small and grubby, and through the gloom I thought I saw a rat scurrying along one of the walls. When I mentioned it to Bet, she simply shrugged and said 'probably'.

'There's rooms upstairs with beds,' Bet explained. 'Four pence a night, most likely. And a kitchen. Some people come and go. Some folk stay a while.' She looked round. 'This is men and women, but there are a few just for one or the other.'

'And anyone can come here?'

Bet shook her head. 'Nah, they won't let you in if you're drunk, or up to no good.'

'Who decides?'

'The keeper.'

'They turn people away into the night?'

Grim-faced, Bet nodded. 'Probably what happened to Polly.'

I bit my lip. And then a man appeared from a small room at the side of the hallway where we stood.

'Four pence,' he said.

'We don't want a room,' Bet told him. 'I'm looking for Pearly Peg. She here?'

He rolled his eyes. 'Everyone wants Pearly Peg.' But then he went to the bottom of the stairs and yelled: 'Peg! Someone here to see you!'

There was a pause and then footsteps and a woman came downstairs slowly. She was older than I had expected – or perhaps she just looked older; it was hard to tell. She had dark hair, speckled with grey, and a suspicious gaze.

'Christ, I thought it was those sodding policemen again,' she said to the man, clutching her chest dramatically. 'You could have said.'

He laughed. 'Where's the fun in that?'

Peg turned to Bet and looked at her carefully. 'You're Jane's girl?'

'That's right.'

'What do you want with me?'

I was finding it hard to breathe in the stench, and I

swore I could hear scratching in the walls. 'Could we speak outside, perhaps?' I asked.

Peg looked at me and raised an eyebrow at Bet, who tilted her head towards the door.

'We won't go far. Just spare us five minutes.'

'Fine.'

We went outside and I resisted the urge to take deep gulping breaths of the air because it wasn't that much fresher outside than in.

Peg narrowed her eyes at Bet. 'I saw you that night in the White Swan. The night Martha was killed.'

'You did.'

'Did the police send you?'

Bet shook her head. 'They're useless.'

'So why are you here?'

'The police ain't doing enough to find out who killed Martha, and now there's been another murder . . .'

Peg's eyes widened. 'Another one? Who was it?'

'A woman named Mary Ann Nichols. She called herself Polly.'

'Rings a bell,' said Peg, her face stricken. 'I think I've seen her around.'

'Will you help us?' I asked. 'We've just got a couple of questions.'

'Who are you?'

'Emma.' I didn't add my surname in case she clammed up.

'Ain't seen you round here before.'

'I just moved here,' I said, honestly. 'But I grew up near the docks.'

'Right.' Peg gave me a curious look, but I obviously passed the test because she nodded. 'What do you want to know?'

'We know you picked out the wrong soldier at the

identity parade,' said Bet. 'He wasn't the one you were with that night. And I want to know why.'

'It's hard to remember,' Peg said.

Bet snorted. 'I've known you for years, Peg. And I know you never forget a debt, or a grudge . . .' She paused. 'Or a face.'

I held my breath. Peg glanced behind her at the door of the dosshouse and, for a second, I thought she was going to walk away. But then she sighed. 'You're right,' she admitted. 'You always was a sharp one, Bet Palmer.'

Bet sat down on the wide dosshouse window ledge and grinned. 'I still am.'

'Do you think the soldier could have been the one to hurt Martha?' I asked. 'The chap she was with that night?'

'Nah.' Peg shook her head. 'But I think it could have been the one who was with me.'

Both Bet and I gawped at her.

'Really?' Bet said. 'You really think he could be the one who did it?'

Suddenly I realised why Peg could have lied to the police. 'Are you scared?' I asked gently. 'Is that why you said you didn't know who the soldier was? Are you scared of him?'

Peg was a sturdy woman with broad shoulders. Her face told me that she'd seen a lot of life. But now her eyes filled with tears, and she suddenly looked much younger.

'Yes,' she whispered. 'I was scared of him that night, and I'm scared of him now.'

I felt a shiver down my spine. I looked at Bet, not sure what to say next.

'Why are you scared?' Bet said. 'What did he do to you?'

'We were in the pub,' Peg began. Her voice was small, and I had to lean closer to hear her over the noise in the street. 'And it was fun. We had a lot to drink. The soldiers were just cheeky enough. You know the type. Confident. Full of themselves. But funny with it.'

Bet nodded. 'Go on.'

'It was late when we left there. I'd had too much gin and I just wanted to get to bed. But I knew I had to pay for the drinks somehow. I knew what he expected.'

I understood what she was saying. I put my hand over my mouth to hide my shocked expression, not wanting Peg to think I was judging her. Or pitying her. I had a feeling she wouldn't welcome either emotion.

'Would Martha have thought the same?' Bet asked. 'She was taking her fella down George Yard for some privacy – to pay him for the drinks?'

Peg laughed. 'Martha was too clever for that.'

'What do you mean?' I was intrigued.

'I left the pub first – you saw me, right? But Martha stayed behind. She always liked to get as much drink as she could out of a fella.' Peg sounded affectionate and I felt my heart twist with sadness once more. 'We walked down the high street,' she went on. 'My soldier – he said he was called Bernie but I don't know if that was his real name – he pulled me into the shadows by the dairy.' She looked at Bet. 'Where it's set back from the road.'

'I know it. It's dark.'

'Black as your hat,' said Peg. 'And I felt a bit sick – you know, from the gin? My head was spinning. And he had me up against the wall, and he was undoing his breeches . . .'

I felt a bit sick myself.

'And I pushed him away.' Peg's voice shook. 'I was going to let him do it. Course I was. I ain't stupid. But just for that minute, I thought I might puke. So I gave him a shove to get him off me.'

'He didn't like it?' Bet said.

'One minute he was all charming, laughing and that,'

said Peg. 'And the next, his eyes were full of rage. Like he was possessed by the devil himself. He shoved me back – so hard that I stumbled on the cobbles and fell down. I banged my head. And he had a stick – Lord knows where he got that from – and he started beating me with it. Like I was a dog. It was whistling through the air as he hit me.'

'Oh God,' I said.

'And when he thought he'd hit me enough,' Peg went on, her tone so matter-of-fact that I wanted to weep, 'he took what I'd have given him anyway. Then he left me lying there on the cobbles, and he didn't even look back.'

Bet and I looked at one another. I saw my own shocked expression reflected back at me in Bet's eyes.

'Peg,' said Bet carefully after a second. 'Where was Martha when he was beating you? Do you know?'

Peg gave a small smile. 'I know, because I heard her, didn't I? When I was lying there in a puddle. I heard her laughing and I knew she'd left the pub.' She took a shuddering breath in. 'Martha used to take them down George Yard because there's a tiny cut-through down the end there.'

Bet looked startled. 'There is,' she said. 'But not many folk know about it.'

'Martha would make out she was going to get a bed for the night, at the boarding house there, and then leg it.' Peg sounded impressed. 'By the time the fella realised she weren't coming out, she'd be long gone with his money in her pocket.'

'So that's what she was planning to do that night?' asked Bet.

'Must be.' Peg closed her eyes briefly. 'That's where she was found, weren't it?' She breathed in. 'It was all really quick. That's what I keep thinking. How quick it all was. That fella did what he wanted with me, and off he went. And I lay there for a little while after – but not long, because it was cold and wet on them cobbles, and I was frightened he might come back. So I dragged myself up and out on to the street, and I saw him there – Martha's bloke. Waiting at the end of George Yard.' Her voice cracked. 'And I thought "good for you, Martha". But it weren't good for her, because that was when she was being killed.'

My mind was racing, trying to work out the logistics. 'So it couldn't have been Martha's soldier, because he was standing at the end of the street . . .'

'But it could have been Bernie,' said Bet. 'The one who attacked you.'

Peg nodded. 'If you'd seen his face, Bet. He was so angry. Like he didn't just hate me, he hated all women.'

I shivered. 'You really think it could have been him? That he was capable of such brutality?'

Peg pushed up her sleeves. 'It was three weeks ago now, but I've still got the bruises.'

Her arms were criss-crossed with fading purple stripes. I winced, exchanging a horrified glance with Bet and wondering just how bad it had looked three weeks earlier.

'You poor thing,' I said. 'I understand why you didn't want to pick him out. It must have been so frightening to see him again.'

'I didn't see him.'

'You didn't?' Bet sounded surprised.

'We went to Wellington Barracks, but he's based at the Tower Barracks. I told the police the wrong place.'

I was impressed with her ingenuity, despite it hampering the investigation.

'He knows where I live,' Peg said. 'I told him, didn't I? Like an idiot. If he'd seen me with the police, then I don't know what would have happened.'

'But the police would have arrested him,' I said. 'They'd have locked him in a cell.'

'Would they?'

The question hung between us all for a second, then Bet took Peg's hand.

'I think you did the right thing,' she said. 'Don't put yourself in the way of danger. There's already been another murder – we don't want any more.'

'What are you going to do?' Peg said, sounding scared. 'Don't tell the police what I said, will you?'

'Don't worry,' Bet said calmly. 'We'll find another way.'

# Chapter 12

Having assured Peg that we wouldn't be going straight to the police about what she'd told us, we asked her to give us a description of the man who'd attacked her. Sure enough, just as Bet had said, she reeled off a description so detailed, I wasn't sure I could describe my own face as well. The man – Bernie – had a dark, thick moustache, and dark hair, but his skin was fair and his eyes a blue-grey.

'They darkened when he was angry,' she said. I was scribbling notes, writing down everything she said.

'What about his height?'

'He weren't tall, but he weren't small neither,' she said thoughtfully. She put her hand up to show how tall Bernie stood.

'About five foot seven,' I estimated. I wrote that down too.

'One thing I did notice,' Peg said with a grimace. 'When I was lying on the ground . . .'

'Yes?' Bet gave her arm a little, sympathetic pat.

'He had absolutely tiny feet.'

'How tiny?' I said.

'About the same as mine, I reckon. I remember thinking it was a wonder he could kick so bleeding hard with those tiny toes.'

'Lord,' Bet said. 'You've really been through it.'

Peg lifted her chin. 'What will you do, if you find him?'

'Well, then we'll have to tell the police,' Bet admitted. 'But we'll keep your name out of it.'

'Just be careful – he ain't a nice man, that's for sure.'

Feeling slightly awkward, I gave her some coins, which I thought she might refuse, but she pocketed them quickly. Bet gave her a hug.

'You're so brave,' she told her. 'You've done Martha proud.'

'I've read that a vinegar poultice is good for bruising,' I said. 'That might help?'

'Cheers.' Peg was already heading back inside the doss-house. 'I'll try it.'

We waved her goodbye and hurried off down the street. When we got round the corner, Bet clutched my arm in excitement.

'Oh my God,' she said. 'Have we found him? Could it really have been so easy?'

'Well, we've got a name and a description, but no actual man,' I pointed out.

'Not yet.'

'What should we do?' I asked. 'Should we take these notes to Fred?'

Bet raised an eyebrow. 'Do exactly what we promised Peg we wouldn't do, you mean?'

'Then what?'

'I think we should go to the barracks.'

I felt a lurch of fear that was swiftly followed by a little thrill of excitement. 'The barracks?'

'Yes, why not?'

'What would we do there?'

Bet shrugged. 'Speak to soldiers? See if we can find this Bernie?'

'Ask to see their feet?' I teased.

'Worked for Prince Charming,' Bet pointed out. 'But he ain't no Cinderella, that's for sure.'

'We'd need a reason to be there,' I said. 'They won't just let anyone in, I'm sure.'

She looked at me, narrowing her eyes. 'You've come to tell your son some bad news,' she said.

'My son.'

'Yes.'

'I'm not old enough to have a son who's a soldier.'

'Well, you are.' Bet frowned, suddenly uncertain. 'Ain't you? How old are you?'

'I'm 44.' I was a little put out, but she was right so I couldn't really argue.

She grinned. 'See?'

'What about you? Why will you be at the barracks?'

'I'm your daughter.'

I studied her. 'You're nineteen?'

'I am.' She winked at me. 'Ma.'

'Oh, stop it,' I said. 'So we'll just stroll up to the entrance gate and ask for Bernie?'

'No,' said Bet. 'We'll ask for someone else. Then we can have a good look at the soldiers there while we're at it.'

'Do you really think this will work?'

'We may as well try.'

I chuckled. Martha and Polly's deaths were weighing heavily on each of us, there was no question; but despite that, I found I was rather enjoying myself. 'Come along, then, daughter of mine. Let's go to the Tower.'

We walked along Aldgate High Street, then down Minories towards Tower Hill. The castle loomed up before us, and we could see the Waterloo Barracks standing tall at the back.

'How do we get in?' I said. I couldn't see any gates.

'No idea.' Bet looked a bit deflated. 'I must have walked round here a hundred times, and I've never thought about how to get inside. Maybe round the front?'

We crossed the road, and looked left and right at the high wall and dry moat that surrounded the Tower.

'Perhaps we need to go along the river,' I suggested, only half-joking. 'Like Anne bleeding Boleyn.'

But then Bet nudged me. 'Look, down there.' She pointed to our right where an omnibus was pulling away, giving us a proper view of the side of the Tower. 'There's a gatehouse.'

Sure enough, through the gloom we could see a large, black structure where the road rose up a bit higher.

'Oh thank goodness,' I said in relief. 'No boat needed.'

Pleased with ourselves, we hurried along the road, to where two soldiers in white hats stood, staring straight ahead. They didn't acknowledge us as we drew closer. We both slowed our footsteps. These men were tall and broad, and their uniforms made them look imposing and rather frightening. We both stared at them, then Bet pinched me, hard, on the arm above my elbow.

'Ouch,' I whispered. 'What did you do that for?'

'Cry.'

'What?'

'Cry.' She shoved a grubby handkerchief at me and pinched me again. 'You've got bad news, remember?'

I buried my face in the hanky and Bet put her arm over my shoulders.

'Sir?' she said to the soldier closest to us. Grudgingly he dragged his gaze towards us.

'Sir, can you help us?'

He muttered something to the soldier next to him, who nodded, his eyes still front. Then he turned to Bet and me.

'What?'

'Good manners cost nothing,' I muttered to Bet from

behind my hanky. She trod on my foot, telling me to be quiet.

'We're looking for my brother,' Bet said. 'He's a soldier here.'

'What's his name?'

'His name?' She looked at me, her eyes wide. We'd not thought of a name.

'Yes, his name?' said the soldier with a tut.

'Name of . . .' She paused and I could see she was thinking of a name, casting her gaze about desperately 'River. Erm, Rivers.'

'Does he have a first name?' The soldier's tone was mocking.

Bet's gaze dropped to a pile of bricks beside the entrance where something was being constructed.

'Brick,' she said vaguely.

I nudged her hard.

'Rick,' she corrected. 'Rick Rivers. Richard.'

The soldier looked exasperated. 'You can't just come here asking to speak to men.'

Bet was still looking a little like a rabbit being eyed by a fox. 'Of course not . . .' she said weakly. 'Ordinarily we wouldn't, but you see we've had some bad news.'

'It's my husband,' I wailed. 'He's dead.'

'It was very sudden,' said Bet. 'I need to tell my brother that our father has died.'

'He's died,' I sobbed into my handkerchief. 'And I am alone in this world.'

Now the soldier looked less exasperated and more alarmed. He spoke in a low voice to the other soldier and Bet pulled me into a hug.

'There, there, Mother,' she said, patting my back. Then into my ear she hissed: 'Don't ham it up so much. They'll be putting you on stage at the music hall at this rate.'

'Wait here, please,' said the soldier. He turned and walked away and Bet loosened her grip on me. We both edged closer to the entrance. The other soldier didn't move or look at us. We inched a little further and now we could see into the courtyard. There were a few soldiers here and there, and on one side, a group of about twenty, all in rows. They were all in uniform, all of them had hats on, most of them had moustaches and it was impossible to see them in any detail.

'We need to get inside,' Bet said quietly. 'This is useless.'

'Can you see their feet?' I asked, peering round the wall. 'Do any of them look particularly tiny?'

Bet stifled a laugh and made it sound like a sob.

The soldier didn't move his head, but his eyes twitched in our direction.

'This isn't going to work,' Bet whispered. 'We can't tell them apart.'

'And this is only a fraction of the soldiers in here,' I pointed out. 'There are hundreds.'

Bet's shoulders slumped. 'We didn't plan this properly.'

'It could still work. If we get inside.'

But the other soldier was coming towards us now, shaking his head.

'We don't have a Richard Rivers,' he said. 'What are you pair up to, eh?'

Unsure what to do next, I buried my face in my hanky and watched through my fingers as Bet scratched her head. 'Well, I don't understand that at all, do you, Ma? Because he definitely said he was stationed at Wellington Barracks.'

The soldier's expression cleared. 'Ah, you've got muddled,' he said in a tone that suggested he felt enormous sympathy at just how stupid we were. 'This isn't Wellington Barracks, it's Waterloo.'

'We're in the wrong place?' Bet was wide-eyed. 'Ohhh, Ma. We're in the wrong place.'

'You need to go to Pimlico,' the soldier said kindly. 'You can take the omnibus.'

'Thank you so much,' Bet said sweetly. 'What would we do without men like you?'

'Thank you,' I said.

Bet looped her arm through mine, and we walked quickly along the street and round the corner, narrowly avoiding being drenched as a horse plodded through a puddle.

Then we stopped and looked at one another.

'Brick?' I said, the corners of my mouth twitching. 'Brick? What kind of a name is Brick?'

Bet began to laugh. 'Every name I'd ever heard in my life vanished out of my head as soon as he asked me.'

'River was bad enough, but Brick?' I leaned against the wall, as more laughter bubbled up.

Bet clutched her midriff, her whole body shaking as she chuckled. 'I was thinking on my feet!' she protested.

'Can you imagine the parents?' I said, wiping away a tear. 'What a beautiful baby boy. Let's name him Brick . . .'

'I know, I know!' Bet said between guffaws. 'At least I tried.'

Our laughter subsided for a second.

'I could have been called River,' I said. 'My parents' house was right by the Thames and my mother could see the water from the bedroom.'

Bet looked at me straight-faced for a second, but it was no good. Our giggles bubbled up again and we were both helpless for a few minutes more.

When we'd finally composed ourselves, I dabbed my eyes with my handkerchief and looked at Bet, who was smoothing down her hair.

'It was funny but it was also a disaster,' I said as we began walking again. 'What are we going to do now?'

'I bet Green just sauntered in and got them to do what he wanted,' said Bet. 'We need a uniform. Maybe we should nick one out of the cupboard at the station.'

'We don't need a uniform, we need a man.' I sighed. 'Perhaps we should have just gone to Fred after all.'

'Why don't we sleep on it, and make another plan in the morning?' Bet suggested, as we turned on to Whitechapel Road.

As if I'd summoned him, Fred suddenly appeared up ahead, walking along the street. He was with Green and Percival and he looked stern. But when he glanced over and saw me, his face lit up. I smiled. We'd been married a long time now and he was still always so pleased to see me.

'Should we mention it?' Bet asked as we walked over to the men. 'Should we mention Peg?'

'Leave it to me,' I said. 'Hello, darling.'

'Hello, ladies,' Fred said, looking at us closely. 'Out for a stroll? On this . . .' he glanced up at the threatening sky 'this overcast and slightly chilly evening.'

I gave him a nudge. 'We wanted some fresh air. Bet's been working all day.'

'I hate being stuck indoors,' Bet agreed and Fred nodded. I was pleased he accepted our explanation. Bet was beginning to feel more like a friend than a servant, after me telling her about Rose, and our laughing fit, but it was still a little odd for me to be spending time with her.

'What are you up to?' I asked Fred. 'More enquiries?'

'We've been speaking to Polly's friend, Ellen,' Fred told us. 'She said she was in quite a state.'

'Drunk?'

'Couldn't hardly stand up, she said,' said Percival. 'She must have got stuck into the booze again after she left us.

Made her an easy target. She probably went into the shadows with him and didn't come out again.'

'God, poor woman.' I shuddered, but inwardly I was wondering how a woman so drunk she couldn't stand up would be selling herself on the street.

'I need to call in at the house for some notes,' said Fred. 'Shall I walk along with you while Percival and Green go back to the station?'

He offered me his arm and I took it.

'Bet, go home,' I said. 'You must be tired after such a long day.'

'Sure?' she said.

'Go ahead.' I gave her a nod, signalling that I'd talk to Fred alone. 'I'll see you tomorrow.'

'Right you are.' Bet hurried off towards Spitalfields. Percival and Green wandered along ahead of us, in the direction of the station, and arm in arm, Fred and I walked home.

'Where have you really been?' Fred asked as we walked.

'Where have I really been?' I was startled, though I shouldn't have been – Fred noticed everything.

'Oh come on, Emma.' He sounded amused. 'Coming from Aldgate with Bet? It's not as though you've been for tea together, is it?'

I looked at him. 'We've just been speaking to a few people,' I said carefully.

'A few people connected to Polly's death?'

I squeezed my lips together, not wanting to lie, but not wanting to tell the truth either.

'Emma, darling,' he said, as we approached the house and he felt in his pocket for the key. 'I think you're a clever woman. A very clever woman.' He snorted. 'You're worth ten of Percival or Green.'

I smiled.

'But . . .' he began. 'But remember what happened after Rose?'

'This is nothing like what happened after Rose,' I said.

'Isn't it?' Fred turned the key in the door and pushed it open, standing aside to let me enter first.

'No,' I said firmly. 'It's not.'

'Darling, you had a shock, knowing you had met Polly and she was wearing your hat when she was murdered. It's possible this could set you back again.'

'It's sweet that you're worried, but I really am fine now.' I went to him and put my hands on his arms. 'I know that after Rose I got a bit . . . obsessive.'

Obsessive was putting it mildly. I'd spent months – more than a year really – reading book and journals about infections and illness. Sneaking into lectures at hospitals. Speaking to doctors. And then as my knowledge had grown, I'd become increasingly worried that there was no avoiding disease. That it was in the very air we breathed, the food we ate, and the water we drank. I'd become a shadow of myself and that was when Fred had taken the desk job at Scotland Yard, because he wanted to look after me.

Now I looked at Fred. 'I know how hard that time was for you, managing your own grief and my behaviour, and I will be grateful as long as I live. But I promise I'm not going to get obsessed with this.'

Fred didn't seem convinced. 'Murders are not out of the ordinary, but these ones do feel personal,' he said thoughtfully. 'Bet's connection to Martha, and your meeting with Polly, however brief, has made them feel different. But that is no reason for you to take it upon yourself to investigate these crimes.'

'I know, but . . .' I began.

'Let me finish.'

Chastened, I nodded, beginning to unbutton my coat.

He brushed a strand of hair away from my face. 'I can't tell you what to do and I wouldn't try.'

He could tell me what to do, I thought. Hadn't I stood in church and promised to obey him? But Fred had never been one for laying down the law – away from his work, of course – and I was glad.

'Just please be careful and if you feel like it could all be starting up again, the obsessive behaviour, then please just stop.'

He looked so worried that I felt a huge wave of guilt.

'I really am fine now,' I said. 'And I know that is all thanks to you and your patience and your care. Another man might have thrown me in an asylum.'

'Yes,' said Fred with a small, wry smile. 'Well, that's still a possibility.'

'I promise you, it won't happen again.'

'You need to understand that I am investigating these murders and I will do my best to catch whoever is responsible.'

'I do.' I felt we'd come to an unspoken agreement that as long as I kept my wits, and didn't make it too obvious what I was doing, I could continue to investigate.

He looked at me carefully. 'Lord, what I wouldn't give to have you on my team.'

'Maybe one day.'

I held out my hand for Fred's coat and went to hang it up with mine on the stand.

'My concerns about you aside, Harrison does not want female detectives working for H Division,' said Fred. 'He is an odious man, but I don't want to annoy him and end up back behind a desk in the Yard. Or worse, put out to pasture before my time.'

He took off his hat and handed that to me too.

'In fact, he is being very stubborn about this altogether. I believe there are some excellent female detectives working in London. There are a few women running their own agencies now. And didn't Bet solve the jewellery thefts simply by thinking about it for less than five minutes?'

'Bet's a sharp girl,' I said slowly. 'What did you say about the agencies?'

He frowned at me. 'There are women running agencies.'

'That's right.' I pointed at him in delight. 'There are women running agencies. Fred, you're marvellous.' I gave him a kiss. 'Do you need me for anything at the moment?'

Fred looked a little startled. 'No . . .'

'Then if you'll excuse me, I need to do some, erm, correspondence.'

Fred raised an eyebrow. 'Correspondence?'

'Yes.'

'Emma?'

'Yes?'

'Please be careful.'

'I will.'

I pushed open the door to the study, feeling his eyes on me. I had a lot of notes to make.

# Chapter 13

## Bet

When I reached the top of the steps up to the Abberlines' house the next day, the front door was thrown open. Emma stood there, looking eager.

'At last,' she said. 'What kept you?'

I looked over my shoulder at the clock on the church across the road. 'I'm not late.'

'Well, no, but I've been waiting. I've got so much to show you.'

I couldn't help laughing as she took my hand and dragged me inside. 'Let me take my coat and hat off first, won't you.'

Once I'd hung up my coat, Emma herded me into the study, which was a small room next to the lounge. I'd dusted in there a few times but hadn't paid much attention – it was obvious the inspector didn't spend much time in there, mostly because it was tidy. Or at least it had been tidy. Now it was . . . I looked around in surprise . . . well, busy was the word that came to mind.

One wall was lined with bookshelves, and on the other Emma had pinned sheets of paper – one reading MARTHA and the other POLLY.

Underneath each she had stuck up another page where

she had drawn a line and added times and what each woman was doing, when.

On the desk was a brown folder, open wide and showing a sheaf of more papers, covered in writing.

'Emma?' I breathed. 'What is this?'

'Fred has some concerns about what we're doing.'

'Investigating?'

'Yes.'

'What kind of concerns?'

Emma bit her lip. 'Do you remember me saying that after Rose died I lost my mind for a little while?'

I nodded.

'It was hard for Fred.'

'I'm sure.' I thought about looking after my mother all those years. 'But how is that related to this?'

Emma screwed her face up. 'I became a little stuck on how Rose had died.' She swallowed. 'On infections.'

I looked at her. 'When you say stuck?'

'It was all I thought about.' Emma looked down at her feet. 'When it was at its worst, I couldn't leave the house. Some days I couldn't eat. I couldn't see anyone or do anything. Fred looked after me.'

'And now he's worried because . . .'

'Because he thinks I might get stuck on this instead.'

'Do you feel like you might get stuck?'

Emma thought about it for a long second. 'No. I honestly don't feel that way.'

'My mum was very bad with her nerves for a long while after my dad went to jail,' I said. 'I had to look after her, because she couldn't always go to work. Couldn't go to the shop or the market, couldn't cook anything. She was too sad.'

Emma reached out and touched my arm softly. 'It was like you were her mother, not the other way round.'

Her unexpected kindness made tears prick my eyelids. 'Yes,' I said. I took a breath to gather myself. 'But she's fine now. Really fine. She loves her job. She's back to how she was when I was little. Better, in fact, because my dad ain't around to cause her trouble.'

'That's good news.'

'It is,' I said. I made a face. 'Though I can't say it isn't a bit odd now she can look after herself. I've had to think about her so long, I don't really know how to think about myself.'

Emma nodded vigorously. 'That's why I wanted Fred to come back to Whitechapel. He's been looking after me and now it's his turn to live his life again and get back to doing the job he loves.'

'That was a good thing to do,' I said. 'And I can see why he's worried. But I know better than most that people can get well again.'

'With a bit of help,' Emma pointed out. 'I'd have been lost without Fred, and it sounds like your mum would have been the same without you, even though you were just a little girl.'

I nodded again, feeling teary once more. 'If you think you're better, then your husband should believe you.'

'I think he does.' Emma looked thoughtful. 'But here's the thing. He is also worried he'll be pushed back to a desk in Scotland Yard if Harrison gets wind of us sniffing round. And that makes me worried, Bet, because he hates that. I really think it would kill him.' Her voice wobbled. 'But he said he can't stop us, as long as he doesn't know anything about what we're up to.'

'He lives here,' I pointed out, still looking in wonder at the notes on the wall. 'How can he not know?'

'Well, yes, but he never comes in this room really. All his work is at the station. And I can keep the door locked.'

'Gosh, you've thought of everything.' I shook my head in disbelief. 'You think you're up to it? It's not going to make you poorly again?'

'If anything, it's going to stop me being poorly again,' said Emma adamantly. 'Yesterday, when we were talking to Pearly Peg, I felt like we were making a difference. Doing something important. I felt like I had a purpose again.'

'I felt the same,' I admitted. 'It was . . . satisfying.'

I sat down on the chair behind the desk and leaned my elbows on the shiny wooden surface. 'I know I ain't worked at the police station that long, but I can't help feeling they don't always go about stuff the right way. Some of them had never been to Whitechapel before they started working here. None of them understand how women think or why we do the things we do – especially round here.'

'I agree,' Emma said.

'I don't mean the inspector,' I assured her. 'He's worth more than the rest of them put together. But I just think we've got something a bit different. Different knowledge.'

'Different abilities,' said Emma.

'And if they don't want to use that, then fine. Let's do it ourselves.'

'Exactly.' Emma nodded vigorously. 'Except . . .'

'What?'

'I think we need to understand that, yes, I've been married to Fred for a long time, and you've been around detectives and seen how they work, but when it comes to it, we're really very new to this.'

'Yes,' I said, not sure what she was leading up to.

'And I thought perhaps we should speak to someone who knows what they're doing.'

'Like the inspector? But I thought . . .'

'No, not Fred. Like Mrs Cameron.'

'Who's Mrs Cameron?'

Emma leaned over the desk next to me and leafed through the folder. 'Mrs Cameron is the private investigator Martha was working for.'

I stared at her. 'How do you know that?'

'Because you told me.'

'But I couldn't remember her name.'

Emma shrugged. 'But you knew it began with a C. It wasn't hard to find someone who fitted the bill.'

'How hard?'

'Well, I thought she was bound to be advertising in the newspaper and Fred is a terrible one for never throwing his papers away, so I just went through them all and looked at all the ads.' She shrugged. 'It took a few hours.'

I laughed. 'Blimey, Emma.'

'We need to speak to her.'

'You think she could help?'

'Maybe.'

My mind was racing. 'We've been fixed on this soldier bloke, but what if Martha bumped into someone else that night? Perhaps someone she was working for?'

'Or someone she'd annoyed,' Emma suggested. 'A disgruntled spouse, or a vengeful mistress.'

I shook my head. 'No way was she killed by a woman.'

'Well, a vengeful husband.'

'We definitely need to think about every possibility, so you're right, it's worth visiting this Cameron woman.' I was impressed with Emma's diligence and slightly annoyed with myself for not thinking of it first.

'Also, I thought, while we're with Mrs Cameron, we can see what sort of woman she is. And, if she seems a trustworthy, hard-working type, we could perhaps ask her to help us in our investigation.'

'Because she'll have the experience we're lacking?'

'Exactly.'

I made a face. 'I like it being the two of us, though.'

Emma looked quite touched and she put her hand on my arm. 'Me too,' she said. 'But Fred always says it's important to know your limits.'

'All right, then,' I said. 'But if we don't like her, we won't ask.'

'Agreed.'

'When should we go?'

'Well . . .' Emma started shuffling the papers on the desk into the folder. 'I made an appointment with her for this afternoon.' She looked at the clock. 'In three-quarters of an hour, in fact.'

'You are quite something.'

She frowned. 'Is that a compliment?'

'Yes.'

'Then, thank you.'

'Are you taking that folder?'

'I thought I might.'

I nodded. 'In case we want to show her?'

'Exactly.'

'Take some paper too, so we can write notes.' I grinned. 'Well, you should write them.'

Emma put the folder, some paper and some pens into her bag. We put on our coats and hats, amid the usual grumbles about how summer was almost over and we'd not seen the sun, and off we went.

'My mum says women work for these investigators to help with divorces,' I said as we walked.

'She's right. I did some reading last night.'

I felt a small tinge of envy that Emma had all this knowledge available to her because she was good at reading. She probably didn't even think about it – just did it. Read the words on the page like it was as natural as breathing. I wondered if she'd help me get better, but the thought of asking her, admitting how slow I was at reading and writing, made me wither with shame.

'What did you read about?' I asked. 'How do they investigate divorces?'

'It's before the divorce that the investigators get involved,' Emma said. 'A man can divorce his wife if there is evidence of adultery, but a woman needs evidence of adultery and more.'

'Like what?'

'Incest, bigamy, cruelty or desertion,' Emma said, reeling off the list.

'Adultery is going with someone else, right?'

'Right.'

'And bigamy is being married to two people at once?'

'That's it.'

'A man has to be doing all that for their missus to divorce them?'

'He does.'

'Well, that don't seem fair.'

'No.' Emma sighed. 'And of course no one will take a woman's word for it. They won't believe her that her husband is being cruel, or that he's scarpered and left her with nothing. So, that's where Mrs Cameron comes in. She and other investigators get the evidence the women need.'

'It sounds very exciting.'

'Yes, but as far as I can tell, it seems to involve a lot of sitting about, watching and listening.'

'Martha would have been good at that. She knew everything about everyone. She was so nosy.'

Emma laughed.

'No one gets divorced round our way,' I said. 'You don't want to be together no more, you just move on. Martha wasn't married to William Turner, not officially, but she used his name anyway.'

'That sounds much more sensible,' Emma said. She pulled the newspaper advert out of her bag and studied it. 'I think the office is just here on the corner.'

We went to cross the road but as we waited for a cart to go by, Emma clutched my arm. 'There are those insufferable constables.'

I looked round to where she was pointing, subtly. There were Percival and Green, speaking to a woman on the other side of the street – not far from the door to the agency. The woman was a little familiar to me – young and pretty with striking red hair – but she looked rather annoyed with them both. She was leaning against the wall, arms folded, not meeting their eyes.

'I don't think they're both insufferable,' I said. 'Green is quite sweet.'

Emma raised an eyebrow at me and I flushed. 'Sometimes.'

'We can't let them see us going into Mrs Cameron's office,' she said. 'What if they tell Fred? Or Harrison?'

'Shall we just walk on by?' I suggested. 'We can stroll to the end of the street and wait for them to finish – it doesn't look like she's being very helpful.'

Emma put her hand through my arm and we walked past, without the constables seeing us, then tucked into an alleyway a bit further on and waited for them to move.

It didn't take very long. The woman, whose name I couldn't remember – it was on the tip of my tongue but not quite there, rolled her eyes and went to walk away. Quick as a flash, Percival stuck his arm out and stopped her, pushing her up against the wall.

Watching from our vantage point, Emma and I both gasped. Percival put his face right up close to the woman's and spoke to her, his mouth twisted in anger. She turned her face away and he put his fingers either side of her chin and turned it back. Then, just as fast as he'd shoved the woman, he let her go. She hurried away, pulling her shawl round her shoulders as she scurried past the entrance to where we stood.

'See,' I said as the police constables began to walk in the opposite direction. 'That was all Percival.'

'Hmm,' said Emma. 'Didn't see Green try to stop him, though. Did you?'

Prickly at the criticism, I ignored the comment. 'They've gone,' I said. 'Let's go and see Mrs Cameron.'

# Chapter 14

## Maggie

Sometimes, when I was between clients, I liked to watch people from my office window. I was fortunate to be on the corner, which gave me a good view of the main road and the side street where there was always lots happening. I liked to test myself; see what I could glean about the people I watched. Not that I could ever find out if I'd got it right, of course. But I assumed I probably had.

It was quiet today, I thought, peering down at the street. Probably because rain threatened again and the puddles were already making it difficult to walk along the road without suffering sodden feet.

Down below I could see two police constables – one young, one older, both with moustaches, talking to a pretty woman with dark red hair the colour of autumn leaves. They seemed jovial at first but she was clearly reluctant to speak. As I watched, she folded her arms, making a barrier between her and them. I wondered if they were going to arrest her and thought she was probably wondering the same thing.

The jacket-potato seller wheeled his cart past the group, splashing through a puddle and earning himself a glare from the younger of the constables. And then my eye was caught by two women walking arm in arm along the opposite side of the road. They could be mother and daughter – I guessed that one was in her forties, while the other didn't look more than 20. And yet, the older one wore quality clothing. Her hat was shapely and her skirt well fitting. Her coat was an expensive shade of dark green. The younger one was neatly dressed but even from this distance I could see her skirt was faded around the bottom and her coat had patches on the elbows. Her hat was slightly askew. What kind of a mother wore quality clothes while her daughter wore a scruffy skirt?

'Interesting,' I mumbled to myself. 'Not mother and daughter, then, but what?'

I watched them hurry past. 'Strange friends, perhaps?' I wondered aloud, curious. 'Or could the younger one be a maid? But they are familiar with one another. What could have brought them together?'

And then, even more intriguing, the women darted down an alcove, a little way along the street, and stayed there. If I hadn't seen them hide there I wouldn't have known, or I might have thought they'd walked on down the alley-way. But as it was, I could see their shadows on the wall, and I caught a glimpse of the younger woman's hat as she peeked out. They were watching the policemen – and that also interested me. Were they criminals? But then why not simply walk on by? What were they watching?

Suddenly, down below me, one constable grabbed the red-headed woman's face. I rolled my eyes. I often doubted the skills of our London bobbies and this one wasn't doing much to change my opinion. The copper gripping the woman's face glanced at the other one, seemingly seeking his approval and I stood to attention, ready to shout at them from my window if it were needed.

A sudden draught blew through the office, making me curse the rattling windows in the frames that I couldn't afford to replace. A sheaf of papers blew on to the floor, and I picked them up, stacking them back on the desk. And when I looked down into the street again, the police constables, the redhead they'd been talking to, and the mother and daughter who weren't, had all gone.

Disappointed not to have got to the bottom of it all, I sat down at my desk and was rearranging the papers that had been on the floor, when there was a knock on the office door. I kept the main door downstairs open during my office hours, with a rather fine brass plaque on the wall announcing that this was where you could find Mrs Cameron, Investigator.

'Come in,' I called. I glanced at the appointment book to remind me of my next client. I was expecting a Mrs Abberline. Abberline – the name was familiar. I frowned as the door opened and in came the two women I'd been spying on from my window.

I was so surprised to see them that I let out an involuntary and most unprofessional 'oh!'

'I'm so sorry – are we early?' The older, better-dressed woman stepped forward, holding out her hand. 'I did make an appointment.'

I recovered my composure and smiled at her as I stood up and shook her hand. 'Not early at all,' I said. 'Please take a seat.'

The women sat down and I put my palms on my desk, trying to look business-like after my initial outburst. 'I'm very pleased to meet you both,' I said. 'My name is Margaret Cameron.'

'I'm Emma Abberline,' said the older woman. 'And this is my . . .' She paused. 'My friend, Miss Bet Palmer.'

'Nice to meet you,' Miss Palmer said. She was less well turned out than Mrs Abberline, there was no doubt, but I could see she was sharp. Her eyes were alert, taking in the room, scanning my bookshelves and me. And she had looked pleased when Mrs Abberline called her 'friend'.

'Mrs Abberline,' I began, suddenly remembering where I'd heard the unusual name before. 'Is it a divorce I can help you with? Because I'm afraid, I believe I have met your husband?'

'I thought you might have,' she said. 'He's a detective, down Leman Street.'

'In that case, yes I have – more than once.' I eyed her carefully. 'I can't take this case if you are planning to divorce him.'

Mrs Abberline laughed. 'Heavens no, that's not why we're here.'

I was relieved because, as far as I recalled, I'd rather liked Inspector Abberline on the occasions our paths had crossed. And I was intrigued, because I wanted to know why these women had hidden from two police constables outside my office. I opened my notebook to a fresh sheet of paper and picked up a pen.

'How can I help?'

The women exchanged a look. Then Miss Palmer spoke.

'We want to catch a murderer.'

My spectacles had slipped down my nose. Now I pushed them up so I could see more clearly. 'A murderer?'

Mrs Abberline nodded. 'You heard what happened to Martha Turner?'

My stomach lurched. 'I did, awful business,' I said carefully. Martha had been one of my girls – not that any of them were girls. They were all street-smart women with their wits about them. And though Martha hadn't been on a job for me when she died, the news had hit me hard. I'd been waiting for the police to come and talk to me, but they had not.

'And now there's been another killing,' Miss Palmer said. 'Polly Nichols.'

'Polly? I thought . . .'

'Her name was Mary Ann, but her friends called her Polly,' Mrs Abberline said. 'You read about her murder, then? I'm not surprised; it's been all over the papers.'

'Yes, I did.' I frowned. 'But surely the police are investigating these crimes? Your husband, Mrs Abberline. He's the one in charge?'

'They think they are investigating,' Miss Palmer agreed. 'But they ain't investigating properly.'

I raised an eyebrow. 'Far be it for me to criticise your husband's colleagues, Mrs Abberline, but that news does not surprise me one jot.'

Mrs Abberline smiled. 'Please, call me Emma.' She laced her fingers together and leaned her chin on her fists. 'We knew them, you see? Martha and Polly. We saw them before they died.' Her words were coming out fast, tumbling over each other. 'Bet saw Martha in the pub, and I met Polly.' She breathed in sharply. 'I gave her my bonnet.'

'And,' said Bet casually, like it was an afterthought, 'we know you knew Martha too.'

There was a moment of silence as we all looked at one another.

'Martha worked for me,' I admitted. 'But she wasn't working the night she died.'

'I know that,' Bet said. 'I saw her.' She gave a small, unhappy laugh. 'She was too grogged to be working. Probably why the killer chose her.'

Emma put a hand on her arm in comfort and I wondered again how they knew each other.

'What is the relation between you two?' I asked, unable to work it out.

'I work at the police station,' said Bet. 'And I work for Emma now, too.'

'Ah.' I leaned back in my chair, pleased that I'd got that bit right at least. Then I leaned forward again.

'And tell me, why were you hiding from those policeman down there?'

Both women looked gratifyingly surprised to have been spotted, and it took a moment before Emma spoke. 'My husband wanted Bet to work for him, as a searcher, you know?'

I nodded and Emma carried on: 'He wasn't allowed; the commissioner said no. But she's clever and she knows Whitechapel and I have helped Fred with his work over the years. We can help. But Fred's nervous . . .'

She trailed off and Bet jumped in. 'He's nervous about being shifted back to desk work at Scotland Yard,' she said.

I looked from her to Emma, thinking there was something they weren't telling me.

'He doesn't know you're looking into these crimes?'

'Well,' said Emma. 'He pretty much said we could ask around a bit, as long as we kept it quiet. Not in so many words, but that was what he meant.'

I tapped my notebook with the end of my pencil. 'You didn't want the constables to see you visiting me in case they told Inspector Abberline?'

'Well, no,' Emma admitted. 'It would make things awkward, wouldn't it?'

I wrote that on my notepad. Then I put my pencil down.

'So, tell me what you think I can do to help.'

'We need someone with experience and . . .' Bet thought about the word she needed, and gave up.

'Clout,' said Emma. 'We tried to trick our way in somewhere but it didn't work. We need someone with credentials.'

I was flattered. And more than that, I felt this could be

110

a way of calming the guilt I felt about Martha's death. But I didn't want to show these women that – it seemed like a weakness.

'Why should I help you?' I arranged my face into a steely expression and stared them down.

Emma stared back at me.

'Because you owe it to Martha?' she said, hitting me right where it hurt.

I caved immediately, spreading my hands out wide. 'All right,' I said. 'I'll help.'

I felt that excitement again. I loved my job. I was curious to a fault. Endlessly fascinated by people and their lives. But there was only so much satisfaction one could get from divorce after divorce. This was something different. Something meaty. Somewhere I could really prove my investigative skills.

'Tell me everything you know.'

As it turned out, they knew a lot. They had notes from the Nichols post-mortem, they'd spoken to Pearly Peg – one of the last people to see Martha alive – and they had a theory that the killer was a soldier.

Bet got to her feet as she was telling me about the soldier.

'Pearly Peg said his eyes were black when he was hitting her,' she said. She mimed raising her arm and bringing down an invisible stick. 'She's black and blue, still now, three weeks on. He done a real number on her, bless her. She's a mess. He knocked one of her teeth out.'

I knew Pearly Peg and I was surprised she had any teeth left to knock out, but I still felt sick at the thought of her getting such a beating.

'This soldier,' I said thoughtfully.

'Bernie,' said Emma. 'That's the name he gave Peg.'

'Bernie definitely sounds capable of brutality, but I have some questions.'

Bet and Emma both looked a little disappointed.

'If he had a knife, why not use it on Peg?' I asked. 'Why beat her with a stick and then slash poor Martha just a few minutes later? Why not just kill Peg?'

'Peg was by the old dairy,' said Emma, her brow furrowed. 'It's not as dark down there as it is in George Yard. Maybe he didn't want to be seen?'

'But he didn't mind being seen beating Peg?'

Bet held my gaze steadily. 'Many's a man who's beaten a woman in public,' she said. 'And many's a man who saw it happen and walked on by.'

I couldn't argue with that.

'But what of Nichols?' I asked. 'Do we know if she came across a soldier?'

Bet made a face. 'Not exactly.'

'Not exactly or no?'

'No,' admitted Bet.

'But we don't know that she didn't come across a soldier,' Emma pointed out.

I sighed. 'I'm afraid this soldier theory is as leaky as my roof.' I nodded to the corner of the room where a bucket was collecting drips.

Emma deflated. 'So you don't think we should investigate?' She groaned. 'We're not detectives, are we? Have we been deluding ourselves?'

'Nonsense,' I said. 'I must admit, when you first arrived I thought you were simply playing games, but you've proved me wrong there. I'm impressed with what you've found out so far.'

'But . . .' said Emma.

'But the mistake you've made is following one theory at the expense of everything else.'

The other women both grimaced and I clapped my hands together. 'Never mind, we'll soon put that right.'

Bet, who'd looked downcast a second ago, now beamed at me. 'So we're doing this?'

'We are.'

'Where will we start?' asked Emma.

'I think we start . . . where you finished,' I said thoughtfully. 'With this soldier.'

# Chapter 15

## Bet

I thought Mrs Cameron – Maggie – was absolutely wonderful. I'd never met anyone like her before.

She was older than I'd thought she'd be. Older than Emma, older than my mother – I guessed she was probably well into her fifties because her hair was more grey than brown, and she had a feathering of wrinkles around her eyes. But she was full of energy, and I liked how she was very sure of herself. I'd grown up around women who were mouthy and who stood up for themselves. Emma was self-assured and clever. But Maggie was confident in a different way. It was like she spoke and expected people to listen.

Which, of course, we did. Emma and I hung off her every word – even when she picked holes in our theory. And when she said we'd start with the soldier, I couldn't wait to get going.

'Are we going now?' I asked. 'Are we going to the barracks?'

Maggie chuckled. 'There's some more I want to ask you first.'

Disappointed, I folded my arms. 'I have to work first thing tomorrow. What if I miss you doing something good?'

'That's the chance you'll have to take.'

'What will we do in the meantime?' asked Emma.

'Tell me about those policemen you hid from,' said Maggie. 'Who's the younger one?'

'His name is Arthur Percival,' Emma told her. 'He's arrogant and lazy. Fred doesn't like him much.'

Maggie wrote that down. 'And the other one?'

'He's called Green,' I said. 'Silas Green. He's much nicer than Percival. He went back to the barracks because I was annoyed they hadn't chatted to the soldiers properly.'

Maggie's sharp eyes roamed across my face, and I felt my cheeks flush under her scrutiny.

'You think quite highly of him?'

'He isn't rude like Percival,' I said. 'He doesn't dismiss Polly and Martha like Percival does.'

'Hmm,' said Emma.

'What does that mean?' Maggie asked.

'I think he might be just as rude as Percival but he hides it better,' Emma said. I tutted because I thought that was rather unfair but she ignored me.

'What does Fred think of him?' Maggie asked.

'Green by name, green by nature,' said Emma with a shrug. 'He's new to London, I think, so Fred's not known him long.'

I felt a little like we were the ones being questioned by the police, although I admired Maggie's attention to detail. I shifted on my chair.

'They were talking to a woman down there,' Maggie went on, pointing to the window with her pen. 'I've seen her round here before, but I don't know her name.'

She drummed on her chin with her fingertips.

'I have to be honest with you,' she said. 'The girls I use here have often been making money in other ways.'

I looked at Emma, and she nodded.

'Fred said as much. You'll get no judgement from us – isn't that right, Bet?'

'That's right.'

'They're streetwise,' Maggie explained. 'Good at reading people.'

'All very fine talents to have,' Emma said. I thought she was overdoing it a little, but I just smiled.

'I hope that by providing one or two with a regular income, they can stop selling themselves and perhaps get a proper place to stay.' Maggie looked over the top of our heads as she was talking, as though she was really speaking to herself and she'd forgotten we were there. 'Because once you get that, it becomes easier to get more work, and to have some pride. And if you have pride in yourself, then you can do anything.'

Emma was nodding. I was wondering if Maggie herself had once been in some unsavoury situations. She certainly sounded like she knew what she was talking about.

'Anyway,' Maggie said, looking at us once again. 'Sometimes the girls come in groups because they all look out for one another, and let's face it – I could be anyone. They need to be careful.' She chuckled. 'Perhaps that's where I've seen her before. Her hair is very striking.'

'Do you think she's a prostitute?' Emma said. The word sounded harsh coming from her mouth.

Maggie nodded. 'I do. Perhaps that's why the policemen were talking to her.'

'Martha weren't selling herself when she was killed,' I said, frowning. 'Not strictly speaking. Polly might have been, I suppose, but she was very drunk. Too drunk to stand up straight . . .'

'The police think she was selling herself because she was wearing my bonnet,' Emma said.

'I've seen the redhead before too,' I said. I closed my eyes, trying to remember where I'd seen her. 'I think she goes by a nickname?' I said slowly. In my mind, I could hear someone calling her across a crowded pub. 'Ginger.'

I opened my eyes and watched Maggie write it down. 'I'm pretty sure she's called Ginger.'

'That's an interesting way of remembering,' Maggie commented. 'What are you doing when you close your eyes like that?'

I thought about it. 'Picturing myself back where I was.'

'Clever,' Maggie said. I beamed with pride.

'Why do you want to know about Ginger and the police?' Emma asked.

Maggie shrugged. 'I like to know everything.'

'Soldiers visit prostitutes,' I said suddenly. 'Don't they?'

'Indeed they do,' Maggie said. 'And they deny it most of the time.'

'Maybe the constables came up with the same idea as us,' I suggested. 'Maybe they were asking Ginger if she knew any soldiers? So maybe we should speak to her too?'

'And maybe we could be a lot less aggressive than Percival and Green were?' Emma said, her voice barbed.

'Percival,' I corrected. 'Not Green.'

I saw Emma and Maggie catch one another's eye and felt my cheeks flush again. 'I just think he's nice, that's all.'

'Nicer,' Emma said. 'Possibly. But not nice.'

'We'll see.'

'Shall we go and find her, then? This Ginger?' Maggie stood up. 'We can speak to some of my girls, too. If there is a soldier out there who's best avoided, you can be sure they'll know about it.'

'Let's go,' I said.

We went to a brothel. Maggie didn't call it that, but it was clear that was what it was. There were three women living there – all around my own age. Their names were Ruby, Kitty and Min, though later Maggie said they weren't their real names. Kitty and Min vanished into their rooms when we arrived, but Ruby greeted Maggie like a long-lost friend and stayed behind to chat. We sat in the lounge – Emma perched on the edge of her seat like she was about to take to her heels and run away. Which, I supposed, she might have been.

Maggie and Ruby made small talk for a few minutes and then Ruby smiled – it was a smile with a bit of an edge to it.

'Why are you here, Mrs Cameron?' She was speaking to Maggie, but she was looking at us.

'You heard about the murders?' Maggie said bluntly.

'Course.' Ruby's face twisted in sadness. 'Martha was one of yours, weren't she?'

'She was.'

'And the other one? Nichols?'

'Not mine, but a crying shame,' Maggie said.

'Min knew her. Said she was a dreadful one for the drink. Sort of girl who'd always choose a glass of ale instead of a cup of tea.'

'It wasn't her fault.' Emma sounded sharp, and I wasn't surprised.

'No, I wasn't saying it was her fault,' Ruby said, sounding more sympathetic now. 'I meant she put herself in situations where someone could take advantage.' She shrugged. 'But who hasn't?'

Maggie nodded. 'We're having a look into the murders,' she said. 'Because the police aren't doing it right.'

Ruby rolled her eyes, showing us exactly what she thought of the police. Emma looked even crosser, and I put my hand on her arm to calm her.

'Martha might have crossed paths with a soldier,' Maggie was saying. 'The wrong soldier.'

'Her wounds could even have been made by a bayonet,' I added.

Ruby had gone very pale. I was watching her carefully.

'Her mate Pearly Peg took a beating from a soldier that very night,' Maggie added. 'She said his eyes were black with rage against women and she reckons it was him that killed Martha.'

Ruby was listening to Maggie, gnawing her lip. She looked, I thought, very worried.

'Do you know him?' I asked.

There was a pause. We all stared at Ruby, waiting for her to speak.

'He will do this again,' said Maggie. 'I have no doubt.'

With another wince, Ruby nodded. 'Maybe,' she said. 'We get soldiers here – quite a lot of them, as it happens.'

'Go on,' Emma prompted, leaning forwards.

'We've got regulars. Nice lads. They look out for us. And a couple of them have told us to steer clear of one bloke.'

'What have they said?'

'That his mood can turn on a sixpence.' Ruby got up and began pacing the room. 'That he gets into a rage, and he don't even know himself. They said he almost killed a man who overcharged him for ale. And they said that he hates women.'

I felt a chill down my back. 'Have you met him? Has he been here?'

Ruby paused in her pacing and shook her head. 'We're lucky here, ain't we? We don't have to let them in if we don't like the look of them.' She gave me a sudden grin, making her look so much younger that my heart lurched at the thought of what she did night after night. 'And we charge for it.'

She started walking again. 'He don't like to pay – he just takes it. And the girls out on the streets, they don't have much choice. I've heard if they say no, he pummels them to a pulp and then does it anyway.'

It was so exactly what had happened to Pearly Peg that

119

Emma and I both gasped out loud. Maggie looked grimly satisfied.

'Do you know his name?' she asked. 'This soldier?'

'Calls himself Bernie, I heard,' said Ruby. 'But Mack – he's one of our regulars – he said his proper name's Bernard.'

'Last name?' asked Maggie.

Ruby shrugged. 'Don't know.'

Maggie looked at Emma and me and we both nodded.

'Do you know what he looks like?'

'Nah. But Min does.' She went to the door and bellowed: 'Min!' into the hallway. 'Min!'

Min appeared, her face made up now and her hair half done. 'What?'

'Tell Mrs Cameron about that soldier fella. The nasty one Jack warned us about.'

Min looked wary. 'What about him?'

'Have you met him?' I asked. 'This Bernie?'

'Once.' She was eyeing us all cautiously.

'Did he hurt you, darling?' asked Maggie softly.

'No.' Min sat down on the couch. 'Not really. But I thought he was going to.'

'But he frightened you?' Emma said.

Min nodded.

'Can you describe him?'

She thought about it for a second or two. 'I don't think so,' she said. 'I ain't so good with words.'

I was disappointed, but Min wasn't finished. 'I could draw him.'

Maggie gave her a piece of paper and some chalk. Min crouched on the floor so she could rest on the little table by the window and hunched over, concentrating.

'What about a girl called Ginger?' Maggie asked Ruby as Min drew. 'Bright red hair.'

'Yeah I know her,' Ruby said. 'She's all right, she is.

Funny. She works outside the Ten Bells sometimes and she's fierce with it. Everyone remembers her because of her hair. But she ain't working now – she's got a bloke.'

'Good for her,' said Maggie firmly.

'Why do you want to know?' Ruby asked. 'She's not . . . ?'

'She's fine,' Maggie reassured her. 'I saw her earlier today, talking to some policemen.'

'They always talk to her when they need one of us.' Ruby tutted. 'It's because she stands out. They can't even tell the rest of us apart, but anyone who looks a bit different – they're the ones they remember.' She grinned again. 'But she won't talk to them. Tells them she won't say nothing, even when there's nothing to say.'

I quite liked the sound of Ginger.

'There,' Min said, standing up and rubbing her knees like an old lady even though she was only young. 'That's Bernie.'

We all huddled round and stared at the picture she'd drawn. The soldier had a dark bristly moustache just as Pearly Peg had described, and dark hair.

'His eyes were lighter,' said Min, pointing to the picture. 'But when he got angry, they went dark.'

'This is definitely the same man Pearly Peg met,' I said.

Min looked at each of us in turn. 'If you find him, you be careful,' she said.

'We will.'

With a little nod, Min vanished off back to her room.

Maggie gave Ruby some money, and then she put her hands on the other woman's shoulders and looked at her right in the eyes.

'Stay safe,' she said, sounding stern. 'Is there someone you can put on the door? A big burly bloke?'

Ruby nodded. 'Bram, from the corner. He helps us when we need him.'

'Every night,' said Maggie. 'I mean it.'

Looking faintly alarmed, Ruby nodded.

We called goodbye to Min and Kitty and trooped out-side again. As soon as Ruby shut the door behind us, Emma leaned against the wall and pretended to fan herself.

'A brothel!' she said in a mock-shocked voice. 'Thank goodness Fred doesn't know what I'm up to.'

'I bet your Fred's been in a few himself,' I said. Then, seeing Emma's face change from mock shock to genuine horror, I quickly added: 'As a policeman, I mean! Not as a punter. He's much too nice for any of that.'

Emma laughed in relief. 'I feel like a real detective now,' she said. 'What do we do next, Maggie?'

Maggie had been studying the picture Min had drawn, but now she looked up at the darkening sky. 'I have a rather tasty slice of pie for my dinner that I've been looking for-ward to all day.'

'What about the barracks?' I said, disappointed but feel-ing my own stomach grumble at the mention of pie. 'Ain't we going there?'

Emma nodded vigorously. 'We can't leave it until tomor-row, Maggie. We can't. What if he kills someone else?'

There was a pause. Maggie looked into the distance as though she could see her pie vanishing off into the night. Then she sighed. 'I've got a mate down at the Tower,' she said. 'Let's go and have a word.'

# Chapter 16

## Emma

Maggie explained she had a friend called Amos who worked at the barracks. He wasn't a soldier – more a dogsbody who did odd jobs around the place.

'In my experience,' she said as we walked through the darkening streets towards the Tower, 'it's the servants you always need to talk to. They see everything, and they hear conversations, and to all intents and purposes, they're invisible.'

'I heard all about Martha's death when I was rearranging the shelves in Inspector Abberline's office,' Bet said. 'No one even thought about not talking because I was there.'

'Exactly.' Maggie grinned at us both, her eyes glinting in the dark. 'Amos works on the gate at night-time. He decides who's coming and going.'

Overhead, thunder rumbled and we all groaned.

'Not more rain,' I said. 'How can there be more rain in the sky?'

We trudged on, hats pulled down over our ears.

'So will your friend Amos let us into the barracks?' I asked. 'Because those soldiers on the gate when Bet and I went were not budging.'

'Amos owes me a few favours,' Maggie said. 'A few big favours, as it happens.'

Bet looked amused. 'What did you do for him?'

'Gave him an alibi,' Maggie said.

'He's a crook?' I was a little shocked.

'Nah, not really,' Maggie said. 'He was desperate, and he was easily led and he got in too deep with some blokes who knew they could manipulate him. Got mixed up in a few robberies. He didn't do the robbing, mind. He was a look-out.'

'What happened to the blokes?' Bet asked.

'They're in jail.'

'And Amos got off?'

Maggie gave a small smile. 'Not entirely,' she said. 'I gave him his alibi and I put in a word for him at the Tower. And I didn't tell his wife anything either. So now he owes me.'

Bet gaped at Maggie. 'Emma said we needed someone with clout and you've definitely got that all right.'

Maggie looked rather pleased with the praise.

'So your plan is to get inside and find Bernard?' I asked before we went entirely off course.

'Well, I thought we'd let him bring Bernard to us,' said Maggie. Ahead of us, the Tower loomed out of the darkness and she paused. Bet and I slowed too as Maggie studied us both.

'What do we know about Bernard?' she asked.

'He's a nasty piece of work,' Bet said.

'Well, yes, but that's us making a judgement on his behaviour, isn't it? It's not a fact.'

Bet looked a little put out, which made me chuckle.

'We know he likes . . .' I began, feeling a bit embarrassed. I lowered my voice. 'He likes sex.'

This time Maggie chuckled. 'Likes sex, hates women,' she said.

'That's a judgement,' Bet pointed out.

'Guilty as charged.' Maggie looked quite pleased with

Bet's interruption. 'He sleeps with a lot of women, by the sounds of things. So let's use that to get him to talk to us.' She pulled off her coat and handed it to me to hold. Underneath she was wearing a thick shirt and she took that off and gave it to me as well, then she put her coat back on.

'What are you doing?' Bet asked as Maggie began balling up her shirt.

'What you're doing,' she said, handing it to Bet, 'is pretending to be expecting old Bernard's baby. Stick this up your dress.'

Bet's eyes widened. 'Really?'

'It'll be fine – it's dark and rainy. No one will look too closely. And we need to give Amos a reason to fetch Bernard for us.'

Bet shrugged and, turning away from us, she pushed the balled-up shirt underneath her skirts and rearranged her jacket over the top.

'What do you think?' she said, smoothing her hand over the bulge.

'Not bad,' said Maggie appraisingly. 'Now, when you walk, make sure you waddle slightly.'

'Oh for heaven's sake,' said Bet. 'What else?'

'Emma, give Bet your hat.'

'Why?' I asked, slightly affronted.

'Because you're going to pose as Bet's mother, and your clothes are nicer than hers – any fool can see that. Bet, just put your own bonnet into your pocket.'

Bet and I exchanged glances, but we did as we were told.

'Amos has a hut round the side,' Maggie said. 'Let me do the talking.'

We all nodded and set off again, but we'd only gone a few yards when a thought struck me.

'Wait,' I said, stopping suddenly. 'What will we say to Bernard when we find him?'

'Oh, Lord, I'd not thought of that,' said Bet. 'We can't hardly say "oh excuse me, Private Bernard, but would you be so kind as to tell us whether you killed Martha and Polly?" can we?'

'Well, no, I suppose not,' Maggie said. 'We'll just talk to him, see if he can account for his whereabouts on the nights of the murders.'

'We know his whereabouts on the night Martha was killed,' I pointed out. 'He was right there, on the spot.'

'Yes, yes.' Maggie sounded impatient. 'We'll have to play it by ear. Let's just have a chat with him, and see how he reacts.'

'Have a chat with the man who attacked Pearly Peg?' Bet sounded dubious and I couldn't blame her. I was feeling nervous about this whole thing.

'We'll be in a barracks,' said Maggie. 'Surrounded by soldiers. And Amos. We'll be perfectly safe.'

Under the brim of my bonnet, Bet raised an eyebrow.

'I won't let anything happen to you,' Maggie said. 'But if you want to go home, then I don't mind. I can talk to Bernard alone.'

'Absolutely not,' I said, just as Bet said: 'Not on your nelly.'

'Listen, I think the best thing to do is treat him as a witness, not a suspect,' I suggested, thinking back to cases Fred had told me about in the past. 'Get his trust, pretend he's ever so clever and we really need his help. Maybe say someone saw him nearby or something.'

'Oh that's clever,' said Maggie. 'Good idea.'

'And then, if he seems shifty or suspicious in any way, tomorrow we can go to the police station and tell Fred what we've found out.' I folded my arms, hoping to show Maggie that, experienced as she was, I knew what I was doing too. Well, almost.

Maggie took a breath and then she nodded. 'Fine.'

It was properly dark now, though the rain was more a fine drizzle than the downpour that had threatened.

'Come on then,' I said. 'Let's go and talk to Bernard.'

We walked on, past a ballad singer who was crooning her song from a dry spot under an overhanging roof.

I clutched Bet's arm, making her stop walking. 'Listen,' I said. Maggie turned back too, and we stood in the little group of people who were swaying to the singer's clear, pretty voice.

'*Poor Mary Ann she did no wrong, but now she's dead and now she's gone . . .*'

'She's singing about Polly,' I said in a quiet voice. Bet's eyes widened as she listened to the words.

'*Be wary, women, he hunts you too,*' the singer continued. '*What dreadful evil will this man do . . .*'

Maggie had been listening intently and now she shuddered. 'I don't want to hear any more,' she said. 'Let's go.'

Maggie led us towards a small hut at the side of the Tower – round the corner from where Bet and I had gone last time.

She rapped on the wooden side of the little gatehouse and, beyond the railings, a door opened and out Amos came, eating a chunk of bread and cheese. He looked delighted to see Maggie and gave her a big smack of a kiss on her cheek through the bars.

'Margaret Cameron,' he said. 'Where you been, girl?'

'Here and there,' she said. 'It's good to see you, Amos. Family all keeping well?'

'Thriving,' he said. 'Our Gertie's expecting.'

'Aww that's lovely news,' Maggie said. 'I'm sure Nan is pleased as punch.'

'She can't wait to be a grandmother,' said Amos, beaming with pride. 'She loves little ones.'

'Well, that's fortunate, the number of children you've given her.' Maggie chuckled.

I watched closely, thinking how clever Maggie was to remind Amos of what he owed her – his family life – without saying the words.

'You after a soldier?' Amos asked.

'Course.' Maggie reached into her pocket and pulled out the picture Min had drawn. She passed it to him. 'This bugger. He might be called Bernard but we don't have a surname.'

Amos took the paper and turned so he could see the picture in the gaslight from his hut. 'Yeah, I know the one.'

'What's his name?'

'Bernard Hill.'

The name sounded so ordinary for a man I'd built up to a demon in my mind that I almost gasped.

'He here?' asked Maggie.

'He is.' He frowned. 'What do you want with him? He's a right sod.'

Maggie put her hand on Bet's arm and pulled her into the light. 'He's responsible for this unfortunate young woman.'

With a resigned sigh, Amos nodded. 'Well, you ain't the first to turn up here looking like that,' he said. He reached into his pocket and pulled out a jangling keyring, then he opened a gate in the railings that I'd not even noticed, and let us through. He looked surprised as I appeared from the shadows.

'This is another grandmother-to-be,' said Maggie wryly. 'And I can assure you, she's not nearly as pleased about it as your Nan is.'

Amos tutted. 'I'll tell Hill that someone's come to repay a debt,' he said. 'That's what I always say, else they won't come. Wait down there.' He gestured towards the river. 'By Traitor's Gate. It's quiet that way and when the guards do their rounds they won't see you.'

'Righto,' said Maggie cheerfully.

Amos vanished into the shadows and we all stood where we were for a second. The only sounds we could hear were the slapping of the river on the wall of the Tower and the distant wail of the ballad singer.

'It's very quiet,' I said.

'Too quiet.' Maggie glanced round. 'Maybe we should come back when it's light?'

'No,' Bet said. 'We're here now.' Her voice shook a little as she spoke but she sounded determined. 'He won't hurt us here.'

'We need to all agree,' Maggie said. 'Are we doing this now or will we come back in the morning? Emma?'

I took a breath. 'Now,' I said.

'Then let's go.'

Maggie led the way and we followed the path in the direction Amos had pointed us. My heart was hammering in my chest and I could hear Bet's gasping breaths like she'd been running.

'Do you think Bernard will come?' Bet whispered.

'Hope so.' I reached out in the dark and found her hand, and squeezed her fingers. She squeezed back and I felt braver.

'Here we are,' Maggie said. 'Traitor's Gate.'

There were torches on the walls here, one either side of the gate, so we could see better. But now there was light the shadows were darker.

I'd only seen Traitor's Gate from the river, shivering as I imagined the prisoners being taken through it to their doom. We were higher up than the water, looking down over the gate, and from here it looked less frightening, though the tide was in and the river was black and swollen from all the rain.

'Christ,' said Maggie, peering over the edge and down to the water below. 'Imagine being one of those poor buggers come to have your head chopped off.'

Bet shuddered. 'The stories that gate could tell if it could talk, eh?'

The sound of footsteps made us all freeze.

'He's coming,' hissed Maggie. 'Let me do the talking.'

'Remember we have to gain his trust,' I said quickly. 'Be nice.'

Bet slipped her hand into mine as a figure appeared out of the gloom, the white stripe on his hat glistening in the light.

'Is that you, Hengist?' said a man's voice, sounding smug and self-satisfied. 'I knew you'd admit you owed me in the end, you tight bastard.'

He was almost right upon us before he could see us clearly and for a second we all looked shocked as we stared at each other. It was Bernard all right – Min's picture had been accurate. His dark eyes and pale skin were exactly as she'd shown us. I glanced down at his feet – tiny, just as Pearly Peg had said. He was staring at us with as much surprise as we looked at him.

'What's this?' he said. 'Who are you?'

'Mr Hill,' Maggie began.

'Private Hill,' he snarled. But he wasn't looking at her, because he was looking at Bet. 'Who are you?' he said again.

'Private Hill, sir,' I said, forgetting that Maggie had said she'd do the talking. 'We wanted to speak to you about something that happened a few nights ago . . .'

Bernard was still looking at Bet. 'I've never seen you before,' he said. 'This . . .' He pointed to her belly, stuffed with Maggie's shirt. 'This is nothing to do with me.' He put his head to one side, and I could almost see his mind working. 'Is this a plan to extort money from me for some snivelling brat of a whore?'

'No,' Bet began. 'That's not why we're here . . .'

Before she had time to finish and before any of us had time to react, Bernard shot out his arm and punched Bet hard in the stomach. She cried out in pain and shock and doubled over. Bernard, shaking out his fingers, looked triumphant. 'It ain't real,' he said. 'You're a bloody load of swindlers.'

I rushed to Bet's side, trying to comfort her. She was crying soundlessly, the tears on her cheeks catching the flickering light of the torches.

Maggie stepped in between Bet and me, and Bernard.

'We simply want to talk to you about Martha Turner,' she said. 'You might know her as Martha Tabram?'

'That another one of your whores?' Bernard hissed at her. 'Another woman you're using to get poor buggers like me to cough up?'

'If you'd just listen,' Maggie said.

'You bloody listen.' Bernard raised his fist again and I thought he was going to hit Maggie this time. Quick as a flash, with my two hands out in front of me, I shoved him away. It was a trick Fred had taught me when I'd shown an interest in his training, and I'd never imagined it would work so efficiently. Bernard stumbled backwards, away from us, only just managing to stay on his feet.

He came towards us again almost immediately, silhouetted in the light from the Tower. He reached down into his boot and to my absolute terror, I could see something in his hand – a stick, like a skinny policeman's truncheon. *Oh, that's where he kept his stick*, I thought wildly. My stomach lurched in fear, thinking of Pearly Peg's bruises. Bet's sobs weren't soundless now – she was crying properly.

'You can't come here and accuse me of all sorts,' Bernard said, brandishing the stick. 'And attack me.'

'I'm sorry,' I jabbered wildly. 'I really didn't mean it.'

'Sir, if we could just all calm down.' Maggie held her hands out in a conciliatory gesture and crack! Bernard brought the stick down on her palm like a vindictive schoolmaster. She yelped in pain. And before I could even look at her, Bernard was coming towards me. He looked almost as though he was enjoying this, which made his strange smiling sneer even more frightening. He launched himself at me, hitting my shoulder hard with the stick. Red-hot pain shot through me as he came for me again.

'Stop it!' Bet cried. She dragged me out of the way, just as Bernard hurled himself towards me. Thrown off balance because I wasn't where he expected to be, he stumbled near Maggie, who scurried round to stand with Bet and me.

'We need to run,' she said in a low voice, as Bernard righted himself again. In the flickering candlelight, with his shadow lengthening, he looked 10-feet tall as he took a step towards us.

'Run!' bellowed Maggie. But as we made to flee, Bernard was too fast. He made a grab for us – any of us. As if time itself had slowed down, I saw Maggie shove him just as I'd done, firmly in the chest, throwing him backwards, and I brought my knee up into his groin as he flailed, and then Bet stuck out her foot to slow his progress, causing him to lose his balance, and the railing was right there, waist high, and he slammed into it and, aghast, all three of us stood stock-still and watched as he tipped over and fell head first down, down, down towards Traitor's Gate and the murky water beyond.

There was a thud as he hit something and then a soft splash that roused us all from our frozen shock. We leapt for the railings and leaned over but, other than a smear of something that could have been blood on a rock and some ripples on the surface of the black water, there was no sign of Bernard.

'Oh lawks,' breathed Bet. 'We've bleeding well killed a man.'

# Chapter 17

## Maggie

As we took in what had just happened, there was silence except the soft sounds of the river lapping against Traitor's Gate. I took a moment to thank my lucky stars that Bernard had landed on the river side of the gate and not the Tower side where he'd have been stuck until someone found him – probably as soon as it got light. At least now his corpse would join the legions of others thrown in the Thames, on a morose final journey downriver towards the sea. Maybe no one would ever find him. Certainly no one would miss him.

As I watched, the water splashed on to the rock where blood was smeared and washed it clean. There was no trace of Bernard now. A sudden memory of my husband Ralph lying broken at the bottom of the stairs made me dizzy. I'd looked over a railing that day too, just as I was doing now.

'Maggie?'

I turned my gaze from the water to the frightened faces of Bet and Emma.

'What are we going to do?' Emma said, her voice shrill. 'Should we get help? We need to get help.'

She turned to run, and Bet shot out her arm to stop her.

'Stay,' she said. She spoke quietly but her voice had an authority that made Emma stop. 'It's too late to help him.'

I nodded. 'She's right,' I said.

Emma gasped, putting her hand over her mouth. 'But we killed him,' she said. 'We killed a man.'

I looked straight at her. 'Did we?'

'Of course we did . . .'

'He fell,' said Bet. 'He was attacking us, and he fell.'

Emma frowned. 'I kicked him in the groin.'

'You did,' I agreed. 'That didn't kill him.'

'And Bet tripped him up.'

'I did,' Bet said. 'He weren't nowhere near the barrier when I did that, though.'

'He was off balance because he was full of rage,' I added. 'And he fell.'

'But he wouldn't have fallen if we hadn't been here,' Emma said.

'And if he hadn't been in the White Swan that night, then Pearly Peg wouldn't be covered in bruises and Martha might still be alive.' I spoke more sharply than I'd intended but I couldn't help it – I was finding it hard to muster up any sympathy for Bernard. Just as I'd not had any for Ralph.

There was silence again. From the street, we heard the ballad singer wailing about poor Mary Ann.

'She's singing about Polly,' I reminded the others. 'That's who she is now – a victim in a song. That's who she'll be forever.'

'They'll write songs about us soon,' Emma said tearfully. 'They'll call us wicked women.'

'The wicked women of Whitechapel,' said Bet. She sounded slightly gleeful. 'I rather like that. I think it suits us.'

*Angry, rather than wicked*, I thought. But I didn't say that. Instead, realising she was about to break down, I turned to Emma.

'Bernard was a nasty, brutal, evil man,' I said. I stuck my hands out to show her the welts glistening on my palm.

'He did this, and he hurt you even worse, and Pearly Peg, and now I've looked into those dark eyes, I'm positive he's the one who killed Martha, and probably poor Mary Ann, too.'

'Polly,' Emma muttered.

'Polly,' I agreed. 'I'll admit this is . . .' I paused, thinking of the best word. 'Less than ideal.'

Bet snorted. 'That's true enough.'

'It's not ideal, but I've faced worse problems than this before and got through them. We can get out of this one.'

Emma looked to be less on the verge of hysteria and more simply worried.

'I could go and get Fred . . .'

'No!' Bet and I shouted in unison. Emma looked alarmed.

'If we get the police here, who knows what would happen,' I said. 'You said yourself, your Fred told us not to investigate and yet we're here. He'll get into all sorts of trouble. Lord, it wasn't that long ago that a wife was seen simply as an extension of her husband, like another limb or a belonging. Many still think husbands are responsible for their wife's behaviour. If we tell Fred what happened here, he will pay the price.'

Emma nodded sombrely. She looked a little sick.

'He worries,' she said quietly.

Bet put her hand on Emma's arm, calming her. 'He's got a lot on his plate at the moment and this is a distraction, ain't it?' Bet added. 'They'll have to come down here and deal with this, rather than looking for the killer.'

'The killer's down there at the bottom of the river,' Emma pointed out, not unreasonably.

'Well, then they should be investigating other crimes,' said Bet. 'Not this one.'

'We can't just leave.' Emma threw her hands up in despair and then winced.

'Is it hurting?' I asked. 'Where he hit you? Let's have a look.' I turned her round and Bet helped slide her dress off her shoulder, revealing livid red welts, stark in the dim gaslight and far worse than anything on my hands. 'Lord, Emma. We should get something on these.'

'Vinegar poultice, weren't it?' Bet said. 'That's what you told Pearly Peg to use.'

'Yes,' Emma said. 'I'll need to hide these wounds from Fred.' She looked like she might burst into tears. 'I hate lying to him.'

'It's not lying, it's just not telling the truth,' I said, as – very gently – I covered her wounds back up and she fastened her dress.

Somewhere a clock chimed the hour and I stood up a bit straighter as an idea struck me. 'We ain't been here that long.'

'It all happened so fast,' Bet said. 'One minute he was here and then he'd gone.'

Emma shivered and I pulled her coat up tighter round her neck like she was a little girl. 'It's cold and it's bound to start raining again any minute,' I said. 'Let's go home, shall we?'

'But what will we say to Amos?' Emma asked.

'Leave that to me.' I turned to look at Bet whose no-longer-swollen belly had dropped so far down that one sleeve of my shirt was dangling beneath the hem of her skirt. 'Put that back, else Amos will be wondering where the baby's gone,' I said. Bet pulled it out, rolled up the shirt, and repositioned it. I stood back so I could see it properly, then nodded my approval. 'Come on.'

We retraced our steps back to the side gate. Amos was reading the *Illustrated Police News* – on the front page was a story about Polly's death. I averted my eyes.

'Get it sorted, did you?' he asked, without taking his gaze from the salacious story on the page.

'Did we, heck,' I said, sounding disgruntled. 'The cowardly sod took one look at poor Molly here and he legged it.'

Amos chuckled, which irritated me because how dare he think it was funny for a soldier with a steady income to wriggle out of his responsibilities? Fictional as those responsibilities were.

But I dampened down my annoyance and instead I said: 'Unfortunately not everyone is as reliable as you are, Amos.'

He preened a little. 'So he's gone, has he?'

'We waited for him to come back but he was nowhere to be seen.'

'I think he was drunk,' Bet added. I shot her a glance, warning her not to say too much, but Amos nodded.

'He was drunk,' he said, glancing down at the newspaper as though he wanted to get back to the stories. 'He was on the ale when I found him.'

'He could barely stand up straight,' Bet said.

'Sounds about right.'

'Then we shall return at a later date to speak to him when he is sober,' I said. 'Could you let us out, please?'

Amos put down the newspaper. 'It's good to see you, Maggie,' he said.

'You too.' I smiled, but fixed him with a steely glare. 'I hope things go well for your Gertie and her littl'un. They're lucky to have you around for them.'

Amos gave a tiny nod of understanding, then he opened the gate.

'It's been a quiet night,' he said, as though he was talking to himself. 'Not one person's come through this way.'

'Thank you,' I said, herding Bet and Emma through the railings.

'Always a pleasure,' Amos said. He pulled the gate closed

behind us with a clang that put me in mind of a prison cell slamming shut and I was suddenly desperate to get away.

'Come along, Molly, and you, erm, Dolly.'

I linked arms with the others to hurry them along and half bustled, half dragged them across the street.

'Molly?' said Bet as we went. 'I don't look like a Molly.'

'What do you look like?' I asked.

'A wicked woman of Whitechapel,' she said with a chuckle.

Emma tutted. 'A man is dead,' she said. 'This is no time for jokes.'

'I weren't joking,' said Bet. 'However wicked we are, that Bernard was a hundred times worse. I ain't sorry he's gone, and I don't feel guilty neither.'

Emma stopped walking suddenly. Bet and I turned to look at her.

'Neither do I,' she said, sounding surprised. 'I saw that picture of Polly on the front page of the newspaper, and I thought about how lively she was when I met her and I suddenly didn't feel bad anymore.'

'Exactly,' said Bet. 'And when someone misses Bernard – because they will eventually – or if he washes up down at the docks or further, they won't think about us.'

'If the police speak to Amos – and that's a big if . . .' I began.

'They won't,' said Bet. 'They ain't that quick.' Emma gave her a little shove.

'If they speak to Amos, he won't say anything. He's got too much to lose and, I've got to be honest, he's not a fan of the police at the best of times.' I pulled my shoulders back. 'So there will be no reason for them to think Bernard's death had anything to do with us. A man like that must have enemies all over London.'

We started walking again. 'I won't say anything to Fred,'

139

Emma said, sounding as though she'd been turning it all over in her mind and had reached a decision.

'No, best not to say anything at all,' I said. 'It's not lying.'

'No,' said Emma, a little uncertainly. 'It's not lying.'

Bet gave Emma a little comforting pat again. 'It's the right thing to do,' she said. 'You know he'll worry.'

Emma lifted her chin a little. 'Yes,' she said. 'This is the right thing to do.'

We reached the junction where we had to separate to make our different ways home and paused. Feeling a little emotional suddenly, I took the other women's hands in mine, so we were in a circle like children playing 'Ring a Ring o' Roses'.

'Despite the circumstances, which were . . . odd, it was lovely to meet you both,' I said. 'I enjoyed being the wicked women of Whitechapel with you for one night. Stay wicked, won't you?'

'We will,' said Bet with a grin. She reached under her skirt and pulled out the bundled-up shirt. 'Almost forgot to give you back my baby.'

I took it from her outstretched hand. 'Thank you.'

'You stay wicked,' said Emma, giving me a quick kiss on my cheek. 'Maybe we'll see you again one day?'

'I sincerely hope not,' I said with a wry smile. 'Your husband's much too nice for you to be in need of my services.'

I gave them both a cheery wave, and walked away, back to my empty rooms below my empty office, trying to ignore the crushing feeling of disappointment washing over me.

# Chapter 18

## Bet

I thought maybe I'd find it hard to sleep after our confrontation with Bernard but I didn't. I slept like a baby. It was the same the night after that and the one after that. And when I went to work early each morning, I was full of energy. I felt as though I'd achieved something.

I mopped the floors and dusted and tidied Inspector Abberline's study because it was, once more, in chaos. I felt a pang of guilt as I straightened the papers on his desk, thinking of the time he was spending tracking down the man who'd killed Martha and Polly, when that man was currently floating down the river towards Essex.

But it was only a little pang of guilt.

I'd almost finished at the police station a few days after the confrontation with Bernard, when the clock on the wall in the foyer chimed ten. It was quiet here today – just the usual coppers coming in and out. I'd not seen hide nor hair of the inspector, nor Green or Percival. I hoped they weren't down at the Tower.

I'd been so quick with my chores that I was too early to go to Emma's. So I was thinking about what I might do with my unexpected free time, as I put on my hat and pushed through the doors into the street. And there, coming up the steps, was Emma. Her face was pale, but her eyes were bright.

'Bet,' she said, trotting up the stairs to where I stood. 'I'm so glad I caught you.'

I studied her. 'Are you all right? How's your shoulder?'

'It's painful,' she admitted. 'I've not been sleeping well.'

I glanced round, making sure we were alone.

'Was that the only reason you're not sleeping?'

She looked thoughtful, then she nodded. 'I meant what I said. I'm not sorry about it.'

'Me neither.'

We smiled at one another, bonded by our secret.

'Fred hasn't noticed your wounds?'

'I've barely seen him. He comes home when I'm asleep, and he leaves early each morning.'

'That's a relief.'

'That's why I'm here.' She pulled a note out of her skirt pocket. 'Fred left me this. It's the details of Polly's funeral.'

'Oh my,' I breathed. 'When is it?'

'Today.' Emma looked determined. 'I think we should go. Pay our respects.'

'Of course we should go.'

She smiled. 'I knew you'd agree.'

'Where is she being laid to rest?'

'City of London cemetery but they're taking the coffin from the undertakers on Hanbury Street.' She waved the note. 'Fred said her husband and children are accompanying the hearse.'

'That's nice of them,' I said, saddened at the thought of them making such a grim journey. 'I suppose she wasn't the ideal wife or the best mother.'

'Apparently, when her husband came to see the body he said he forgave her on account of what she'd once been to him.' Emma's eyes filled with tears. 'It's just so sad, isn't it?'

Gently, because I knew she was still sore after Bernard's beating, I squeezed her arm. 'So sad.'

'I thought perhaps we should go and see her off?' Emma said, wiping her nose with a handkerchief that had lace around the edges. 'Fred said in his note that they were trying to keep it a bit quiet, but I think someone should be there.'

'Lead the way.'

We walked along Brick Lane, chatting about something and nothing for a while, until eventually I said: 'What did you make of Maggie?'

Emma thought for a moment. 'I thought she was very clever. She reminded me a little of my Fred.'

I chuckled. 'Her desk was much tidier than your Fred's.'

'You know what I mean.' Emma laughed, too.

'I thought the same, actually,' I said. 'I was thinking how much use a woman with a sharp mind like that could be to the Metropolitan Police. And what a waste it is that she's not allowed to serve.'

'You're right, of course.' Emma nodded vigorously. 'I'm glad we got to meet her and solve our own crime, even if it didn't end as it should have.'

'I'm glad too.' I looked at her. 'And I'm glad Bernard is gone. Now we can say goodbye to Polly and know we did right by her.'

We turned the corner on to Hanbury Street, and stopped stock-still in astonishment at the sight that greeted us.

'Oh my days,' said Emma. 'I've never seen anything like this.'

The street was always busy, but today throngs of people lined the pavements around the undertakers. Some of them were holding tiny posies of flowers. The houses nearby had their blinds and curtains closed.

'Is this all for her?' I asked, looking round at the people gathering. 'Is it all for Polly?'

A woman walking past overheard. 'She deserves a good

send-off,' she said. 'Way I see it, she could have been any one of us.'

'It's a horrible thought, ain't it?' I said.

'Don't bear thinking about.' She nodded towards the other side of the street where there were fewer people. 'I'm heading that way. It's a bit less crowded.'

Emma and I were about to follow when Emma tugged my sleeve. 'Look, it's Fred and some others,' she said. 'Over beside the undertakers.'

I followed her gaze. There was Abberline, Green, Percival, and some others. They all looked splendidly sombre in their uniforms. Dr Llewellyn was there too, which I found rather touching.

We weaved through the crowd and my eye was caught by another man. He had clambered up on to the low, flat roof of a building opposite and now he sat with a sketchbook open on his lap, drawing the scene. There was something about the way he was lounging there that put my hackles up. He looked disrespectful. Like he was watching the scene for entertainment rather than sending Polly on her final journey. I scowled at him and Emma frowned.

'What's wrong?'

'Look at him up there,' I said. 'Nosy bugger.'

'Perhaps he's come to pay his respects.' She studied him across the street and screwed her face up. 'Or perhaps not.'

'Maybe he's from a newspaper?' I suggested. 'Though he don't look much like he's working. He looks like he's enjoying himself.'

Emma grimaced. 'Let's just concentrate on Polly. Look, here's Fred.'

We reached the men and Abberline looked pleased to see Emma.

'I hoped you'd come,' he said. 'Though I rather thought we'd be the only ones here. Isn't this astonishing?'

She tucked in beside him and looped her arm through his. 'It's horrible that we're here at all, but I'm glad people are paying their respects.'

I watched them together, feeling a pang of loneliness. My mum had been married off to my dad by the time she was my age, and she'd had me on the way. Mind you, that hadn't worked out so well, so perhaps I was better on my own.

'This is really something, isn't it?' Green was standing beside me.

'It's very sad.'

He shifted in his heavy boots, looking a little out of place. 'There's so many people.'

'I was surprised to see it when we came round the corner.'

People kept walking past, stopping to shake Abberline's hand or wish him luck. He was smiling and thanking them. Green and I watched as another couple told him to 'find the bugger who did this'. Abberline assured them he would do his best, then he leaned into us and spoke quietly.

'All these people here today – they're sad and they're scared. We're bringing them hope and reassurance at the moment, and when we find whoever did this, we'll be the heroes. But if we don't arrest someone soon, it's us they'll blame. Don't you forget that.'

The constables all nodded and murmured among themselves. Percival looked mildly alarmed while Green looked determined. I caught Emma's eye, feeling a mixture of guilt that Abberline wouldn't be able to arrest anyone because the man he sought was at the bottom of the Thames, and smug, that we were the heroes the police thought themselves to be. Emma made a face at me, signifying she was feeling the same way.

'I didn't know so many people cared,' Green said. I turned my attention back to him.

'Whitechapel's a funny place. It's like a village inside a city – a mish-mash of families and people, all intertwined in some way. If you don't know someone, you know someone who does.'

Green looked at me intently. 'Did you know Polly?'

I shook my head. 'But I knew Martha.' I looked round at the crowds. 'Some folk round here have never been past Piccadilly Circus; some have come from Wales or Scotland or Ireland. Others have come from faraway lands, across the sea.' I smiled at him. 'Like you.'

'I've not come from across the sea.'

'But you're not a Londoner?'

'No.' He paused. 'I'm from Surrey.'

'Why did you come up here?'

'I'd been in the police there for ten years and . . .' He stopped, looking thoughtful. 'Well, it was time for me to move on.'

I opened my mouth to ask what he meant, but he hadn't finished.

'I've got family here in London. An aunt and uncle. So I thought I'd give it a try.' He gave me a small, boyish smile and I felt a tug of attraction towards him. Like he was a magnet, pulling me closer. 'I didn't like London much at first, but I'm beginning to see its good side.'

I gazed at him, wanting to hear more about his life before he came to Whitechapel.

'Did you . . .' I began, then I stopped as a hubbub of voices rose up around us and fell silent. The undertakers were bringing out Polly.

We all turned to look as they carried the casket to the carriage. The police officers took their helmets off, and Dr Llewellyn removed his hat. Emma and I bowed our heads.

Following behind the coffin were Polly's children – her grown-up son looking handsome but sad in his smart clothes, protecting his younger siblings, and the little ones holding tight to their dad's hands. They made a sorry group, and I felt tears prickling my eyelids.

The undertakers slid the casket into the carriage, and the family got into the carriages behind, and off they went, the feathers on the horses' heads bobbing up and down.

I felt Emma's hand touch mine.

'Look,' she said. 'There's Maggie.'

Across the road Maggie stood in an impressive black hat. She lifted her head, clearly feeling our eyes on her, and nodded in greeting. We nodded back.

'I'm glad we did what we did,' Emma said in a quiet voice right in my ear. 'God bless poor Polly and thank goodness no other women will suffer the same way.'

I watched two little children throw flowers under the horses' feet as they passed.

'Thank goodness,' I said.

# Chapter 19

## Annie

Annie was feeling sorry for herself after a horrible day.

She was not long back from the infirmary. She'd taken herself there this morning when she'd been so breathless and weak that she could barely stand. But after a few hours, a sombre-faced nurse had told her there was nothing else they could do for her now. She hadn't exactly told Annie to go here and die, but Annie knew that was what she had meant.

Except she didn't have a home – not anymore – so she'd come back to Crossingham's, because it was one of the cheapest dosshouses around and because they knew her here. She wouldn't have to answer questions about her cough or pretend to be less ill than she was.

And now she was sitting at the table in the Crossingham's kitchen, surrounded by strangers, feeling sorry for herself.

Annie had always been prone to morose thoughts. Her sister, who thought she knew everything and liked to tell everyone what she thought, said it was the drink. Perhaps she was right. Did Annie drink because she was miserable, or was she miserable because she drank? It was hard to tell now – she couldn't remember which had come first.

Another coughing fit caught her, each hack sending

pain through her chest. For a second, she couldn't catch her breath, and she tried not to panic, before the coughing eased again. Her handkerchief was speckled with bright red blood. She crumpled it up in her hand to hide the evidence of her disease, but she wasn't fast enough. Across the kitchen, a man was watching her with thinly veiled disgust.

'Ain't as bad as it looks,' Annie told him. He didn't reply. Instead, he addressed the other people in the kitchen.

'I'm going to buy ale,' he said. 'Who wants?'

There was a hubbub of activity as everyone handed over their money. Annie slipped her hand into her pocket, counting the coins as she felt them. She had enough for her bed, or she had enough for some ale. Not both.

Turning the coins over and over with her fingertips, she thought for a second, then she scooped them out and threw them all on the table.

'And for me,' she said.

The man looked at her, his expression unreadable. Then he took two of the coins and left the rest. Annie put them back in her pocket, grateful for his generosity.

He wasn't gone long. Annie reached for the bottle of ale he offered her, as eagerly as a baby bird asking for food. She took a long swig and felt the warmth begin to spread inside, soothing her aches and pains, and numbing her worries.

She already felt better than she had all day. She took another swig, and as someone began to sing, she joined in. She didn't know the words, but it didn't matter. When she finished her bottle, another appeared in her hand.

More people were gathering in the kitchen now, drawn by the warmth of the fire and the jolly atmosphere. There were bottles being handed round, the singer was still crooning. Annie felt safe and warm. She moved into one of the tatty armchairs beside the fire and let her head rest – listening to the words of the ballad, and swaying slightly where she sat in time to the music. Her eyelids heavy and her pain eased, she remembered the nurse saying there was nothing else to be done, and thought that perhaps it didn't matter so much. Perhaps she'd just stay here, warm and content, and see what happened.

And she did, for a while. Until the music stopped and someone knocked the chair she was sitting in and startled her out of her contented dozing. The kitchen was emptying out. The man who'd bought the ale had gone – so had the singer. There were two women sitting at the table, talking urgently and quietly to each other, and a man asleep in the corner. Annie got up from her chair and shook some of the bottles that were on the table. All empty.

'Any more ale?' she asked.

One of the women glanced up at her. 'All gone.'

Annie felt a headache beginning to pound at her temples. 'All of it?'

The woman gave an impatient sigh. 'I said it's all gone.'

Disappointed, Annie put her hand in her pocket and found the coins.

'I'm going to the pub,' she said. 'Coming?'

'Ain't you had enough?' the woman said with a tut. Annie ignored her. She put on a coat that was hanging on a hook in the kitchen. It wasn't hers – it was much too big and came down almost to her ankles – but she quite liked it. Then she marched out of Crossingham's and on to the street. Or at least she tried to. She felt slightly light-headed – like she was dreaming – and unsteady on her feet, and she wasn't sure if it was the ale that had made her feel that way or her illness. She focused on the lights in the window of the pub on the corner, the Britannia, aware of people around her but not seeing them.

Inside the pub was warm. Annie bought a pint of beer

and settled down in the corner. No one bothered her. No one really noticed her at all. She drank her beer, and then another. And then another, until her belly was full and her pockets were empty, and the landlord of the pub was helping her to her feet and locking the door behind her.

Annie stood for a moment on the corner of Dorset Street. She could see Crossingham's from where she stood, but now it seemed very far away. No matter, what choice did she have? She knew Donovan – the keeper – and he looked out for her.

Swaying from side to side, she made her way slowly down the road, stopping to cough every few steps. When she made it into the kitchen, Donovan was there. He was arguing with the man who'd been asleep in the corner, who was trying to pay for a four-penny bed with a penny.

'I'll come back,' the man said. He lurched towards the empty coat hooks and looked puzzled, then he shrugged and carried on down the corridor and out on to the street.

Annie took the coat off and hung it up on the hook as Donovan watched her.

'That ain't yours,' he said.

'Borrowed it.' Annie slumped into the chair by the fire, which was now smouldering in the grate and hardly giving out any warmth. 'Can I have my usual bed?'

Donovan nodded. 'Four pence.'

Annie put her hand in her pocket and found it empty. She looked up at Donovan and he looked back at her.

'Annie,' he said, his voice carrying a warning. 'I can't. Not again. Not when I've just kicked old Seth out.'

'Just tonight,' she begged. 'I'll pay double tomorrow. You promised Ted you'd look out for me.'

'Yeah, well Ted ain't here.' Donovan looked bullish. 'And fond as I am of you, Annie Chapman, you're not worth me losing my job over.'

'Please . . .' Annie said. She got up from the chair, with some difficulty, and slung her arm around Donovan's neck. 'Please.'

He recoiled as she breathed on him.

'You're drunk.'

'So? That ain't a crime.'

'You can find money for beer, but you can't find money for your bed,' Donovan said. His lip curled in disgust and Annie felt ashamed for a second, and then defiant.

'Who are you to judge me, Charlie Donovan?'

He gave her a tiny, tight smile and threw her arm off his shoulder. 'I'm the man who decides whether you get a bed for the night.'

Annie stared at him, lifting her chin in insolence. 'Yeah? Well, you keep that bed for me, Donovan.'

She reached for the coat, and Donovan stopped her hand. 'I said that ain't yours,' he growled.

Undaunted, Annie tossed her hair back. 'I shan't be long,' she said.

Outside the night air was cold and Annie felt the effects of the beer she'd drunk wearing off quicker than she liked. Shivering, she considered her options and found them lacking. The streets were quiet, she was weak and ill. She had no way of making a quick penny.

She could go back to St Bart's but they'd just send her away again, no doubt. Her best bet was to find a nook or alleyway somewhere to settle down for the night. She thought briefly and longingly of the thick coat that she'd left behind, which would have done for a blanket, and then set off, wandering through the churchyard at Christ Church, but the grass was wet and the ground boggy and she didn't want to settle there. She went up Brick Lane towards the brewery and then along Hanbury Street, where she knew there were houses with yards that were left unlocked.

She saw a woman called Enid who she'd had trouble with in the past, and crossed the street to avoid her. Enid was with a man and Annie felt a brief, outrageous flash of envy that Enid had a way to make money while she, Annie, no longer had that choice because she was so sick and so weak.

As she weaved her way along the cobbled street, her self-pity came back with a vengeance. London was a city with thousands of people. Why was she left to fend for herself with no one to lend a hand? Why did everyone just look after themselves with no thought for others? She ignored the memories of all the people who had helped her over the years. What use were they now?

The little gap between the stairs and the fence, tucked away from the wind, was empty. Annie breathed a sigh of relief. She would get a bit of rest and then tomorrow she'd get some money and this time she'd save it for her bed.

She tucked herself into the space, noting with slight alarm, how much easier it was to fit than the last time she'd slept there. There was nothing to her now – she was just skin and bone, which meant the ground felt harder than before on her behind, and her spine rubbed against the brick wall behind her. But she was here now. She felt her eyelids drooping. What a day she'd had.

Footsteps nearby made her stir, and she forced her eyes open again, looking up as a figure loomed over her, holding out a hand. At last – someone had come to help. She reached out to him and then she felt nothing more.

# Chapter 20

## Maggie

I had woken up with a thumping headache, and it was my own fault because I had stayed up far too late drinking brandy.

I'd been unsettled since the whole Bernard affair. The argument, as I'd taken to calling it in my head. It sounded less brutal that way.

I wasn't surprised it had unsettled me. Peering over the railing had brought back unhappy memories of Ralph, and sleep had been elusive these last few nights. Plus, and this was perhaps unsurprising, I was surprised how much I'd enjoyed being a 'wicked woman'. Suddenly, my work entrapping cheating men wasn't nearly as much fun as it once had been.

And so, last night, I'd ended up restlessly pacing my office, drinking brandy and wondering if I could perhaps become London's first female police detective. The thought had made me snort. But it wouldn't leave me alone. Of course, I knew it was out of the question, but could I somehow expand the business and take on cases more interesting, more dangerous even, than divorces and petty thefts?

Hadn't the women of Pinkerton's in America foiled an assassination attempt on none other than Abraham Lincoln himself?

Three – or was it four – brandies in, I'd sat in my chair and dreamed of being Queen Victoria's private investigator, foiling nefarious plots and keeping queen, country and empire safe from harm.

And that was where I'd woken now, with a thumping head, a cricked neck, a dry mouth and a pounding in my ears.

I sat up straighter. The pounding was not in my ears – it was downstairs at the door. Wincing as I stepped, but desperate for the noise to stop, I made my way down – slowly.

'Enough!' I rasped. 'What is this racket about?'

I threw open the door and there on the doorstep was Emma, looking tearful and dishevelled, and Bet, looking absolutely furious, her fist raised to pound again.

'What is this?' I said, surprised to see them.

Bet took a deep breath, her hand still in the air.

'There's been another murder,' she said.

'Same killer.' Emma sniffed. 'They're pretty sure.'

I put a hand on the doorframe to steady myself. 'Damn it,' I breathed.

'What are we going to do?' Bet demanded, hands on her hips now. 'We've killed an innocent man.'

Gathering myself, I bustled them inside, checking to make sure there had been no one walking past who might have heard her. 'Come in, come away from the street,' I said. 'We can't discuss this on the doorstep.'

We trooped upstairs, me bringing up the rear. But though my neck was still sore, and my head still ached, and I felt sick to my stomach about the thought of another dead woman, I felt a little shiver of excitement. This wasn't over.

Upstairs, Bet and Emma both talked at once and I couldn't make out what either of them was saying.

'One at a time,' I begged. 'From the beginning.'

'They found her this morning,' Bet said. 'Dr Llewellyn has already done the post-mortem.'

'Already?'

'Fred was furious,' Emma looked like she'd got dressed in a hurry – her usual neatness ruined by her blouse being askew and her hair loose. 'Because they moved her as soon as they found her.'

'He wasn't there? That's not like Abberline.'

She shook her head. 'He was at Scotland Yard first thing to speak to Harrison and some others. They sent him a telegram to call him back.'

I looked at the clock on the mantelpiece. It wasn't quite ten o'clock. 'And they've already done the post-mortem? How surprisingly efficient for the Whitechapel lot.'

Emma gave me a stern look.

'Poor woman,' I said, changing tack. 'Do they know who she was?'

'Her name was Annie Chapman.' Bet bit her lip. 'Riddled with consumption, apparently. Dr Llewellyn said she wouldn't have seen Christmas.'

'That's no comfort.' I sighed. 'Was she . . .'

'A prostitute?' Bet shrugged. 'Course that's what they think. Maybe she was once upon a time, but Dr L said she would barely have been able to walk without coughing up half a lung, let alone do much else.'

'Bet,' Emma tutted. 'Show some respect.'

'How do you know all this?' I asked Bet. 'Sounds like you were there at the post-mortem.'

'Oh, I was,' she said cheerfully. 'Not that they'd notice me – there's a little side room where I put myself.'

'Same as last time,' said Emma, sounding almost proud. 'Bet listened to the whole thing.'

'They've not done the whole thing yet,' Bet said. 'I'm going to go back later. Dr Llewellyn wanted some

156

other chap to be there, and he can't come until this afternoon.'

'And it was Dr Llewellyn who says it was the same killer?' I asked.

'He's certain.' Bet looked a bit sick.

I sat down at my desk, feeling my legs begin to shake.

'So that means Bernard weren't the murderer,' Bet went on, saying aloud what I was thinking. 'And we killed him.'

There was a pause as we all looked at one another.

'I was just about all right, knowing he was dead when I thought he'd killed Martha and Polly,' Emma said, beginning to pace about my office. 'But now I feel awful. We killed an innocent man, Maggie. A man is floating down the river because of us.' She took a deep breath. 'I think we should tell Fred.'

'No!' Bet and I both shouted at once. Emma looked alarmed.

I put my hands flat on my desk and took a deep breath. 'Let me tell you a story,' I said.

The women glanced at one another, but they both sat down without arguing.

'I was married,' I said. 'A long time ago, when I was young.'

Bet grinned at me. 'Get away with you, you ain't old now.'

'Blooming feel it.'

Emma was watching me intently. 'Go on,' she said. 'What happened to your husband?'

'Ralph,' I said. 'He was a bit older than me. And oh, I thought he was wonderful when he first took an interest.'

'Handsome?' asked Bet.

'Very. Good job, too. He was a coach driver. Always smartly dressed.'

Emma nodded in approval.

My mouth felt dry and I struggled to swallow. 'My dad died when I was young, and then almost as soon as we got wed, my mother followed him. It was like she was waiting for me to get off her hands before she died.'

It was years ago now, but I could picture my mother's face in the church at our wedding, clear as day. She'd been so happy. I was glad she never saw what happened next.

'We'd been married a month the first time he hit me,' I said. Emma looked shocked, but Bet looked resigned, as though she'd expected me to say that. 'The day of my mother's funeral, he kicked me down the stairs because I was sad and that annoyed him.'

'Was he a drinker?' Bet asked. 'My dad liked a drink.'

I looked at her carefully and she gave me a tiny nod, showing me she understood. I reached over the desk and touched her hand briefly. 'Ralph didn't drink. In fact, he prided himself on his abstinence. He said his standards were high and I was a disappointment to him.' I gave them both a thin smile. 'Took me years to realise that wasn't true.'

Leaning forward, I carried on. 'I worked in a hat shop, in the West End, before we were married. But I had to give it up, because I couldn't hide all the bruises. The day I left, I cried all the way home because I knew I was on my own.'

Bet and Emma both seemed saddened by my story but also confused.

'You're wondering why I'm telling you this?'

They nodded.

'There was a woman who came to the shop, whose husband was a solicitor's clerk,' I said. 'I went to see him. And I told him what Ralph did to me, how he beat me and forced himself on me, and how he broke my arm, and held my face under the water in the basin until I thought I would drown.' It had been a long time since I'd spoken of this, but it wasn't any easier.

'Did he help you?' Emma asked. She looked hopeful and I felt sorry that she had such faith in the way the world worked. I knew it would eventually disappoint her.

'He did not.' I breathed in deeply. 'He told me that I was married now and there was nothing to be done. Those were his exact words. "There is nothing to be done, Mrs Cameron." I heard them in my dreams for years.'

'That's why you do the job you do,' Bet said, realisation growing on her face. 'That's why you help women get divorced.'

'Yes.'

'Did you get divorced?'

'No. Ralph died.'

Emma looked at me sharply. 'He died, or . . .'

There was a pause. Outside we heard shouts as a coach rattled by, shaking the window. Emma and Bet were both watching me intently.

'I didn't kill him,' I said. 'But I didn't help him either.'

'What happened?' Bet breathed out slowly.

'He was shouting at me one day. I can't even remember why. But he was furious – I remember his face was red and there was a bit of spittle at the corner of his mouth. His eyes were wild and even his breath smelled sour. He used to do this thing where he'd sweep my legs out from under me with his foot – it caught me by surprise every time when I found myself thumping down on the floor.'

Emma winced. 'And this time?'

'He did the same, but on that day it happened that I was beside the newel post at the top of the stairs, and I grabbed it – almost wrenched my arm out of the socket – but it stopped me falling. But Ralph, he wasn't expecting that to happen. It threw him off balance, and he tumbled right down.'

'Down the stairs?' Bet said, her eyes wide.

I shook my head. 'Straight over the banister and down on to the floor in the hall.'

'Lord.'

'And I sat there for a while, at the top of the stairs, peering through the banister, watching his chest rise and fall. There was blood, too. He was at an odd angle – kind of crumpled against the wall. But he was alive. He was trying to speak, but I couldn't hear what he was saying.'

'What did you do?' Emma asked.

I pinched my lips together, knowing that if I told them the truth it would change the way they thought of me forever. Not to mention risk me being thrown in jail. But I looked at their worried faces and, though I had only just met these women, I knew I could trust them.

'I stayed there for a while,' I began. 'I could see he was still breathing, though it was ragged and uneven. There was a bubble of blood at the corner of his mouth and it was moving with his breath.'

I looked down at my hands.

'And then, I realised I should fetch help. It didn't look good, but there was a chance Ralph might survive. So I went downstairs, and I promise you at that stage I was still intending to help him. I went to him, and I crouched down, and I said his name . . .'

My voice wobbled. 'I said his name and he opened his eyes, and all I could see was rage. He reached out his hand and he grabbed me by my throat. I really believe that had he had the strength he'd have killed me.' I lifted my chin. 'But he was weak. I pulled his hand away and I realised that it was a straight choice – his life or mine.'

'And you chose yours,' Emma said.

I glanced at her. She was pale but she didn't look shocked.

'I stood up, then I stepped over him, and I went out of the back door, and I went to the shops.'

'You went to the shops?' Now Emma sounded shocked. But Bet looked almost impressed.

'Because you wanted to be seen. You made sure people saw you so you could say Ralph fell when he was at home alone.'

I nodded at her. 'When I went back to the house, I raised the alarm. I ran to my neighbour. But it was too late to save Ralph. He was dead.'

'No one thought you might have done it?' Bet asked.

'Just one neighbour.' I grimaced. 'He outright accused me of killing Ralph.'

'What did you say?'

'I laughed,' I said. 'I pointed out how much bigger and stronger Ralph was. He didn't go to the police but the damage was done – I saw the expressions on people's faces when I walked by.'

'What did you do?'

'I wasn't poorly afterwards, not physically. But I felt like I had been. As though I was recovering from a long illness. So I went to Broadstairs for a few months,' I said, remembering how weak and broken I'd felt. 'Lovely place. Nice people. And when I came back to London, I moved here.'

A heavy silence hung in the air. Emma's expression was unreadable, and for a second I felt panic fluttering in my chest – would she tell her husband what I'd done?

'He would have killed you,' Bet said after a moment. 'There were a few times when I thought my dad might kill my mum. And his drinking was getting worse when he was arrested – that's why he was making the sort of mistakes that put the police on to him. But he had such rages back then. I reckon if he'd not been sent to jail when he was, well, I'm not sure either me or my mum would be alive to tell the tale.'

I looked at her in astonishment. She was young, but she'd seen so much.

'Ralph would have killed you too,' she added.

'I have no doubt about that.' I clasped my hands together almost like I was praying and then let them go. 'I am alive today, because my husband is dead.'

Bet reached out across my desk and took my hand in hers. I felt absurdly moved by her show of support. And then Emma did the same with my other hand – the three of us linked again, Ring-o'-Roses style – and I felt tears flood my eyes.

'Bernard could have killed one of us,' Emma said. 'Or all of us.'

'He could have killed Pearly Peg, too,' Bet pointed out. 'And we know she weren't the first woman he'd beaten. Ruby told us that. And she weren't the last either – we've got the wounds to prove that.'

'But he didn't kill Martha or Polly. And he definitely didn't kill Annie Chapman,' I said.

'No,' Emma said. 'He didn't.'

'Someone did, though. And I don't know about you two, but I want to find out who that was,' Bet said. 'Will you help?'

I looked from her to Emma. 'I will.'

Emma sighed, like this was totally out of her hands. 'Fine,' she said. 'But I'm bringing everything here, all the notes and drawings, so Fred's not involved at all. I don't want him knowing anything about this.'

Bet looked at her. 'But you're all right?'

'Yes.' Emma nodded vigorously. 'I'm all right.' She let go of my hand and gestured round the office. 'This is our headquarters now.'

'Headquarters?' I said with a small smile. 'That sounds official.'

162

'If we're doing this, we're doing it properly,' she said. 'We can't risk making another mistake.'

'Agreed.' I pulled my handkerchief out of my pocket, dabbed my eyes and wiped my nose. 'Tell me everything you know about Annie Chapman.'

# Chapter 21

## Bet

It turned out, we didn't know a whole lot about Annie Chapman.

'Where was Annie found?' Maggie asked.

'Hanbury Street,' I said with a shiver. 'Where we were for the funeral.'

Emma looked pale. 'What if he was there then, watching? Getting some sort of odd thrill from seeing everyone mourning poor Polly?'

'Looking for dark alleys where he could commit his next crime?' Maggie said. 'Lord, that's horrible.'

'There is one thing that could be important,' I said, enjoying the drama just a little. 'This time there was a witness.'

'A witness to the murder?' Maggie put down her pen.

I shook my head. 'Not to the murder, but this woman called Enid said she saw Annie walking by.'

'She didn't speak to her?'

'Apparently they didn't get on. Enid was with a bloke and she was distracted.'

'Well, that's not much use,' Maggie said bluntly. 'Tell me exactly what the witness said.'

I squinted at my notes, cursing my terrible writing. 'There was a copper there early doors,' I said. 'He talked to this Enid.'

'What did she tell him?'

I began to read. 'She saw Annie go by, and a few moments later, she saw a man going the same way. He had a moustache and a cap. He wore a coat that was speckled black and white. He wasn't very tall – not much taller than Annie – and he looked foreign.'

I looked up at Maggie. 'That's it.'

Maggie frowned. 'Foreign?'

'That's what Dr L said she'd said.'

'It's helpful but not enormously so.'

'No.' I looked down at my notes again. 'And Annie and this man were on the street when Enid saw them anyway. Not down the dark alley where she was found.'

'I'm afraid we're the ones down a dark alley.' Maggie tapped her chin with her finger. 'I don't know where to begin with this.'

'We were so convinced Bernard was the killer that now we've got no one else to look at,' I said.

'Indeed.' Maggie sighed. 'We need to start from the beginning.'

'I'm going to go home and get all my notes, like we agreed,' Emma said. 'I'll bring everything back here and we can go through it all again.'

'I could go back to the police station and see what they're thinking,' I suggested. 'I heard one of the other officers mentioning they had a suspect this morning, though Abberline didn't seem too keen. I'll see what I can find out.'

'Good,' said Maggie. 'I might have another chat with Ruby – see if she knows anything. We can meet back here in a couple of hours.'

We all nodded. I felt like we should have a secret handshake or something, to seal our commitment. Emma clearly felt the same. She put her hand in the air, as though she was brandishing a sword.

'One for all and all for one,' she declared.

Maggie and I stared at her.

'It's from *The Three Musketeers*,' Emma said. 'It's a book about three French rebels.'

'I like the sound of rebels,' I said. 'But I like being a wicked woman of Whitechapel better than a musk . . . What was it?'

'Musketeer,' said Emma, amusement in her voice.

'I don't even know why you're still here, whether you're musketeers or wicked women,' said Maggie. She sounded stern but her eyes flashed with laughter. 'Go away and do what needs to be done. Go on.'

Emma gave a little flourish of her pretend sword and tucked it back in her pretend belt, and laughing properly now, I bustled her out of the office and down the stairs.

We walked along together a little way before we split to go to our separate destinations. I felt exhilarated. Sad, of course, that another woman had died, and angry, and despairing, but no longer so helpless. After Martha's death I'd felt like we women were just lining up to be the next victim and there was nothing we could do about it – not while the police weren't even taking things seriously, judging poor Martha, and asking the wrong questions of Pearly Peg.

But now I felt more in control.

'We're fighting back,' I said to Emma. 'I feel strong.'

'A little scared as well,' she admitted, looking at me as we walked. 'But strong.'

'And wicked.'

'That too.'

We reached the corner where she'd head home and I would turn down to the police station and said a quick goodbye.

'Find out everything you can,' she said.

'I will.'

I went in the side door of the station, not wanting to attract the attention of anyone who'd notice me being where I shouldn't be. I didn't want to see Green or Percival – or Abberline himself. But I needn't have worried – everyone was in Abberline's office, no doubt talking about Annie's murder. I desperately wanted to know what was being said, but I knew it wouldn't be easy. The room was on the large side, but it was full of men and I knew I couldn't sneak in without someone spotting me.

Luckily, the office next to Abberline's – belonging to Sergeant Thicke – was empty. I grabbed a duster and went inside, propping the door open. Abberline's door was ajar too, and I could clearly hear what they were talking about.

Not even pretending to dust, I leaned against the wall and listened.

'Left to right,' someone was saying. From the accent I knew it was Dr Llewellyn. 'And a similar size blade to the one that did for Nichols.'

I made a face, understanding he was talking about Annie's fatal wound. I found a piece of paper on Thicke's desk and a pencil and began taking notes again, just as I'd done when I'd listened to the post-mortems.

'There was blood splattered on the walls around,' said someone else whose voice I didn't recognise. I wrote that down too, stumbling slightly on the word 'splattered'.

'Then there is the mutilation,' Llewellyn continued. He reeled off a list of wounds so gruesome and inhumane that my legs went weak, and I sat down at Thicke's desk, hoping no one would walk by and notice me.

'This is surely the work of a madman?' said another voice. This one I recognised as being Harrison – older and gruffer. 'A lunatic.'

'I agree,' said Llewellyn. 'This brutality is something I've never encountered before unfortunate Martha Tabram was killed.'

'Martha Turner,' I whispered to myself. 'She called herself Turner.' It was just another way of proving to me that the men didn't know the women whose deaths they were investigating.

'There is the issue of the leather apron,' Abberline said. I sat up straighter, because this was new information to me. 'Though I don't believe the apron we found at the scene is linked with the case. Several local residents have said it belongs to someone from nearby.'

'That's as may be, but unfortunately the press are already drawing their own conclusions,' Harrison pointed out.

I wrote down 'apron', listening intently.

'The unfortunate women who Green and Percival have spoken to have told us of the man they call "Leather Apron" who extorts money from them, and now a leather apron has been found at the scene of a murder,' Harrison went on. 'You must admit, it's worth considering.'

'I have indeed been considering,' Abberline said. I could hear an edge to his voice. He didn't like Harrison – I was sure of it. 'And after such consideration, I have concluded that the apron found at the scene is not linked with the crime.'

I heard Harrison begin to speak again, but Abberline jumped in.

'But I have a name for the man known as Leather Apron,' he said.

There was a pause. I sat still, pencil ready to write the name.

'Well?' said Harrison.

'Well?'

'Well what is the name?'

'It's John Pizer,' said Green. It was the first time he'd

spoken and I hadn't known he was there until this moment. 'John Pizer, sir,' he added.

I scribbled the name on my paper.

'What do we know of this Pizer?' asked Harrison.

'He's a slipper maker, sir,' said Green. 'Used to handling knives sharp enough to cut through leather. And he wears shoes that don't make a sound on the street, so the girls don't know he's coming, and sometimes he wears a cap and at other times a deerstalker hat.'

'Like Sherlock Holmes,' said Harrison, chuckling. 'Did you read that, Abberline? I thought it was marvellous. Very well done.'

I pushed the pencil against the paper so hard the tip snapped off and I had to swap it for another from the pot on Thicke's desk.

Abberline obviously did not want to be drawn into a discussion on Sherlock Holmes. Instead, he said: 'According to our sources, Pizer has a moustache, and as you say he wears a leather apron – that's why the girls gave him the name. But he is taller than the man described by the witness and, as for the apron, I really think it's just a coincidence, sir. Why would he leave such a distinctive item at the scene?'

'Why would this madman do anything?' Harrison said. 'Pizer sounds like a nasty piece of work – there's no doubt about it.'

'The girls are scared of him, sir,' said Percival. 'I could tell by the way they spoke about him. He tells them he'll look after them, for a hefty fee. If they say no, bad things happen to them.'

'Hmm,' Harrison said thoughtfully. 'I think we should start with Pizer, don't you? Green? Percival? Bring this Leather Apron to the cells.'

I heard Abberline – I assumed it was Abberline – sigh, but he didn't argue. Then there was the sound of chairs being pushed back and of footsteps, and I got up from my seat at the desk and pretended to be dusting as the men – except Abberline – trooped past Thicke's office. When they'd all drifted away, I hurried back to my cupboard, put the duster away, dragged on my coat and headed outside again. I had to tell Emma and Maggie what I knew.

Back at the office, I found them pinning the notes from Emma's house to the wall. I paused for a second, admiring what we knew so far.

'We ain't doing so badly,' I said, taking off my coat. 'And now we have a suspect to put up there, too.'

'A suspect?' Maggie turned to look at me, and I basked in the glow of her approval.

'His name's . . .' I began, just as we heard a knock on the door downstairs.

Maggie went to the window, pushed it open and leaned out.

'It's open!' she bellowed to whoever was down on the street. 'Come on up.'

There were footsteps on the stairs and then in came Ruby – one of the women from the brothel. She was pink in the face and breathless.

'The police are sniffing round again,' she said, pulling her hat off. 'And guess who they've arrested?'

'Leather Apron,' I said.

Ruby deflated, her shoulders slumping. 'Oh, you know already.'

Taking pity on her, I shook my head. 'Only the name,' I said. 'And I'd not had a chance to tell these two yet.'

'Have you seen him?'

I shook my head again.

'He's massive,' she said, flinging her arms up above her head. 'Like a huge barrel of a bloke.'

We all looked at one another, remembering the

description the witness had given of a short man, just a bit taller than Annie. 'And he's mean and cruel. I don't know that other fella – Bernie . . .' Maggie, Emma and I all glanced at one another at the mention of Bernard's name, but Ruby either didn't notice our discomfort or didn't care. 'But everyone knows Leather Apron. He's got girls handing over most of their earnings because they're so frightened of him and what he'll do if they don't.'

'But not you?' Maggie said.

'Not yet.' Ruby's face was pale now, making her red cheeks stand out. 'But he's always around. It's only a matter of time.'

'You're safe now because he's in a prison cell,' said Emma.

'Yeah, for now, but how long will they keep him there?'

'Forever if he's the killer,' Emma reassured her.

'He ain't.' I shrugged. 'Sorry to disappoint you, but Abberline doesn't think he's the murderer. It was Harrison who sent the constables to arrest him.' I looked at Ruby. 'Harrison's an idiot.'

She grinned. 'I never thought it was him neither.'

'Why not?' asked Maggie, picking up her pen.

'Because he's making a lot of money from the girls on the streets,' said Ruby matter-of-factly. 'Why would he kill them?'

Maggie, Emma and I all looked at one another and then we looked at Ruby.

'You're right, there,' said Maggie.

'I've got to go.' Ruby put her hat on again. 'I've got places to be.'

Maggie gave her some money. 'Now,' she began. Ruby smiled at her.

'I know, be careful.' She nodded. 'We're all looking out for each other, don't worry.'

'Of course I worry,' said Maggie.

Ruby blew her a kiss and darted off. Her footsteps pounded down the stairs and then the door slammed shut.

'Pizer,' I said. 'His name's John Pizer but the girls call him Leather Apron.'

'And Fred doesn't think it's him?' Emma was writing the name on a piece of paper.

'He sounded pretty definite,' I said. 'And I think . . .'

Maggie was sitting on the edge of her desk. She turned to me. 'What do you think?'

'Harrison kept calling him a madman – whoever did all this. Llewellyn, too.'

'And?'

'And I think he ain't mad.' I rubbed my brow – this thought had been coming back to me since I'd listened to Polly's post-mortem. 'I think he's clever. I think . . .' I took a breath. 'I think he's learning.'

Emma pinned the name John Pizer to the wall then she stood back and looked at everything she'd arranged.

'I think you're right. Don't you agree, Maggie?'

Maggie nodded. 'I do.'

I breathed out slowly, relieved they hadn't laughed at me. Feeling bolder, I pointed to the picture of Martha.

'He attacked Martha from the front,' I said. 'He must have been covered in blood after – and I reckon it was only luck that he got away from the scene without no one noticing.'

'It was dark,' Maggie said. 'And perhaps he was wearing black clothes that didn't show the blood.'

'Right.' I nodded. 'But perhaps he realised he wouldn't always be so lucky. Because with Polly – Llewellyn said her throat was cut left to right.' I went to Emma and stood behind her. 'So, assuming the killer was right-handed . . .'

'Most people are,' said Maggie.

'Assuming that, then he got her from behind, didn't he?' I put my arm across Emma's chest and pretended to slit her throat from left to right. She let out a little squeal. 'So the blood wouldn't have got on him that time.'

'Clever,' said Emma putting her hand to her throat. 'And awful.'

'Oh, it gets worse.' I pulled out the notes I'd made about Annie. 'Llewellyn said Annie's face was swollen and her tongue was sticking out.'

'What does that mean?' Emma asked with a shudder.

'Apparently, it means she was strangled first.'

'Why would he do that?' Maggie was watching me carefully. 'What do you think, Bet?'

'I think . . .' I paused and Maggie gave me a little nod of encouragement. 'I think maybe Polly made a sound – no one said they heard anything but that don't mean she was quiet. Maybe she made a sound, like Emma did just now, and that spooked him. Because everywhere the women were killed, there were people sleeping just a few feet away, who didn't hear a peep. But again – maybe that was just lucky. And this time he was so close to where people live, he needed to make sure Annie didn't squeal, so he strangled her first.'

There was silence in the office. Outside in the street, a man shouted, and we all jumped.

'This man is no lunatic,' Maggie said. 'You're right, Bet. He's learning.'

'He's clever,' I said. 'And frightening. And we don't know who he is.'

'We know who he's not,' said Emma. She pointed to the names on the wall. 'He's not Bernard Hill, and he's not John Pizer.'

'Some detectives we are,' Maggie said with a tut. 'We don't have a clue who this killer is.'

'And until we know who he is,' I said, gazing up at the wall where Emma had pinned all the information, 'we've got no way of stopping him.'

# Chapter 22

## Emma

I had decided I was going to put my foot down. I'd barely seen Fred since Annie's murder. He'd come home so late that I'd been fast asleep, and when he'd left, the sun was only just up. So I'd sent a message to the police station, telling him in no uncertain terms to come home for dinner. He could go back afterwards but I wanted him to have a break, to eat some proper food, and well, maybe give me a quick account of what the latest thoughts on the murders were.

I'd been to the shops and bought some chops and potatoes and now I was cooking. I quite liked pottering round the kitchen, despite what my mother-in-law thought of me doing the domestic duties myself. I'd told Bet to take the day off because she was exhausted, poor girl. All three of us – the wicked women of Whitechapel, as Bet insisted on calling us – were tired and emotional and horribly aware we'd hit a dead end.

Even though I'd made myself very clear in the message, I was still pleased when I heard the front door open and Fred come inside.

'I wasn't sure you'd be able to get away,' I said as he came into the lounge.

'I will need to go back.' He came over to where I sat

beside the window and gave me a kiss. 'But I had a hanker-ing for chops.'

'Well, isn't that fortunate?' I said. 'Go and have a quick wash and I'll serve.'

I put the dinner on to plates and when I went into the dining room, Fred was already sitting at the table.

'I'm ravenous,' he said.

'Busy day?'

'Harrison is making things more difficult than they already are.' Fred cut a large piece of chop and chewed on it in delight. 'This is very tasty.'

'What's he doing?'

'Insisted on going after some chap called John Pizer.'

I sat up straighter. 'Why?'

Fred rolled his eyes. 'He's a nasty piece of work and no mistake, but he's not our killer.'

'How do you know?' I ate a bit of my own chop and nodded appreciatively. They were indeed tasty.

'He's got an alibi for the nights of the murders – well, for Nichols and Chapman, at any rate. Several alibis. It wasn't him.'

'Waste of a day?'

Fred rubbed his forehead wearily. 'That's not even the worst of it,' he said. 'Someone told someone else who told someone else that we had a suspect. They printed his name in the newspapers. And now everyone knows.'

'Was it a police officer who told the press?'

'I believe it must have been. Thicke has known Pizer for years, so I don't think it was him. But it could have been that weasel Percival or Green, the simpering fool.'

I was privately quite pleased that Fred clearly wasn't a fan of the constables either. 'So what happened next?'

'They went to arrest Pizer and found him locked inside

his own house – terrified – because people were waiting outside, baying for his blood.'

'Goodness.' I put my fork down. 'Will he be safe now you've let him go?'

'He can look after himself,' Fred said. 'He's no shrinking violet. He even says he's going to get some compensation from the newspapers.'

'Good luck to him,' I said. 'Though perhaps it might do him good to have been the one who is scared for a change. Perhaps he'll see the error of his ways, and stop frightening those unfortunate women.'

As soon as I spoke, I realised I'd said too much. Fred stared at me over the top of his fork, stopped on the way to his mouth, and his eyes narrowed.

'Stop frightening those women?'

I shut my mouth tightly. But it was too late. Fred was on me like a cat pouncing on a mouse.

'Which women?'

'Oh you know,' I said vaguely. 'Just women in general.'

Fred, infuriating man that he was, put a bit of chop in his mouth and chewed slowly. Then he said: 'Pizer extorts money from prostitutes.'

'Does he?' I said, trying to sound surprised.

'But you knew that?'

Lord help the criminals who were questioned by my husband – he had a way of getting the information he needed.

'Someone told me,' I said truthfully.

'But it wasn't me. I didn't tell you about the women.'

'No,' I admitted. 'You didn't.'

'What do you know, Emma?'

'Not much.'

'Not much?'

'A little.'

'Have you been doing some investigating on your own?'

'No,' I said, telling the truth once more. I definitely wasn't doing anything on my own.

Fred sighed. 'Emma . . .'

I put my knife and fork down. 'I know you worry,' I said. 'And I love you for it. But I promise you this is nothing like when Rose died.'

'Are you sure?'

'Didn't I tell you if I felt it was taking over, I'd stop?'

'Well, yes you did.' Fred's eyebrows were furrowed.

'This is just . . . well, it's like a hobby, isn't it? Like knitting.'

'Knitting?'

I nodded. 'Exactly.'

'Three women are dead,' Fred said. 'This is dangerous, Emma.'

A sudden image of Bernard disappearing into the murky black water of the Thames flashed into my head and I thought perhaps it was dangerous, but not in the way Fred meant.

'You don't need to worry about me,' I said. 'Do you want the rest of my chop?'

As a diversionary tactic, food always worked on Fred. Now he smiled and took my plate from my outstretched hand, putting it on top of his own clean one.

'You're not the only person to be interested in these murders,' he said. 'The public have taken this case to heart. We're being inundated with letters at the station. We read the first few, but we simply don't have the manpower to read them all and they just keep coming. Apparently the newspapers are getting them too.'

'What are the letters saying?'

'Ideas about who the killer could be. Pointing out mistakes we've made. Even telling us they think the murderer is their neighbour. Or their husband.'

'Gosh,' I said. 'Everyone's a detective.'

'It's a nightmare.'

'Do you want me to read them?' I said, suddenly thinking this could be a way to guide us out of our dead end. 'I can trawl through them and see if there's anything important, and discard the ones that are nonsense.' I smiled at him. 'Reading letters isn't dangerous.'

Fred looked extremely pleased at the suggestion. 'Would you?'

'Of course. I'm happy to help.'

'Perhaps you could come back with me in a little while and pick them up. I'll get one of the constables to walk you home again.'

I opened my mouth to say that wouldn't be necessary then thought better of it. The night was dark, and there was still a killer on the loose.

'It's quite a sobering thought, knowing how dangerous it is to be a woman,' I said as I cleared away our plates.

'You have no reason to be scared,' Fred said. 'I'll always protect you.'

I dropped a kiss on his head as I passed. 'I know and I love you for it. But some women are married to dangerous men. Often the biggest threat is inside their home.'

'Indeed.' Fred looked grave. 'What made you think of this? Is someone in trouble?'

'No.' I shook my head. 'You have no need to worry.'

Fred gave me a long stare. 'You know you can always come to me?'

'I know. Let me rinse these plates, then I'll walk with you to the police station.'

Of course, it was raining as we set off along the road towards Leman Street. The police station was quiet for once, with only a few constables milling about. Fred nodded to the chap at the front desk and I followed him through into his office. There on the desk was a pile of letters, six inches high and tied with string.

'Oh my,' I said in surprise, slightly regretting my offer.

'You can't go back on your word now,' Fred said, picking them up and thrusting them at me. 'You promised.'

I laughed. 'I know. I will read them, of course. I just wasn't expecting there to be so many.'

'Everyone's a detective,' he said wearily. 'Like you said.' He sat down at his desk heavily.

'Everyone's a detective but you are the only one who matters,' I said. I leaned over his desk and gave him a kiss. 'I'm going to go. Can I just pick a constable to walk with me?'

'Anyone you like.' He caught my hand as I straightened up and I looked at him. His expression was sombre. Strict, even.

'Emma, this is the hardest, most brutal case I have investigated, and it is made considerably harder by . . .' He paused, tilting his head sideways and glancing out of his office door to the empty hallway beyond. 'It's made harder by bloody Harrison sticking his nose in at every opportunity.'

'I know.' I tried to pull my hand away but he held on.

'Don't get too involved,' he warned. 'Just don't.'

I clutched the letters to my chest.

'I'm just doing this reading,' I said. 'That's all I'm doing.'

'Hmm,' Fred said.

'Hmm,' I repeated. We looked at one another across the desk like a pair of alley cats about to fight and then he let go of my hand.

'You're the most infuriating, strong-willed woman I've ever met,' he said. His words were harsh, but his voice was fond and it made me smile.

'Oh, come on,' I said. 'Your mother is surely a more infuriating woman than me?'

'I used to think so,' he said, shaking his head in bewilderment. 'But no longer.'

I hit him on the shoulder with the pile of letters. 'Now I really am going home. Don't stay here too late, will you? You need to sleep.'

I found a willing constable to walk me along the road – thankfully not Percival – and when I got home, I made some tea, then curled up in the big armchair beside the window to read the letters.

They were quite something. Some of them were scrawled on scraps of paper, spouting barely legible gibberish. Others were written in beautiful calligraphy, on expensive notelets, but still contained nothing but nonsense. There were a surprising – and disturbing – number of confessions, none of which were remotely convincing. I was beginning to despair that I'd never find anything interesting, when I reached for the next letter in the pile and noticed one sticking out, a little further down, on thick, creamy paper. Intrigued, I pulled it out and almost dropped it in shock as I noticed the royal seal on the envelope.

'What the blazes is this?' I murmured, slitting it open and carefully taking out the paper inside. I unfolded it, smoothing it on my lap, and as I scanned the writing, I noticed the flourish of the signature at the bottom: *Victoria R.*

'Oh dear God, it's from the queen,' I said aloud. I stood up, then I sat down again. 'It's from the queen.' I wished Bet was there with me, but I wasn't going to wait to see her tomorrow to read this.

I took a deep breath and, with slightly trembling hands, I lifted the page and began to read.

*Dear Inspector Abberline,*

*It is with great sorrow that I feel compelled to write to you regarding the tragic and most disturbing murders in Whitechapel.*

*I have read the reports on the case and have been kept apprised of developments by Commissioner Harrison.*

'Bloody Harrison,' I said.

*I am confident you are doing your utmost to catch this lunatic. However, I am curious as to one aspect of the killings and I wanted to draw your attention to this question.*

'Oh, good Lord,' I said, sitting back in the chair. 'Everyone's a detective. Even the queen.'

*These unfortunate women have been discovered soon after their demise, I believe, and yet their killer has disappeared into the night. And so I wondered if you had considered whether he could have made such a quick getaway by use of a carriage?*

'Your Majesty,' I breathed. 'That's rather clever.'

*I also wondered if the killer could be a medical man?* the queen continued. *He'd have sharp knives to hand and a knowledge of anatomy.*

I shuddered, but my mind was racing. A doctor? He'd have access to a carriage and, like Bet said, whoever had

182

killed these women had to be clever. Doctors were clever. I turned my attention back to the queen's letter.

*I trust you will find these musings useful,* she finished. *I would be grateful if you could communicate your next moves.*

I put the letter down on my lap. 'I think,' I said to the empty room. 'That we've just recruited a new member for the wicked women of Whitechapel.'

# Chapter 23

## Maggie

I was on edge. I couldn't settle at my desk. Couldn't concentrate on a job I had taken – a common-or-garden divorce that didn't interest me at all. And so I put on my coat and went for a walk. I was just getting some fresh air, I told myself. Just going for a quick plod around the streets for half an hour, going nowhere in particular.

But somehow my feet took me to Hanbury Street. I walked along the road, past the undertakers where Polly had made her final journey, and ended up outside number 29: the place where Annie Chapman's body had been discovered.

I stood outside and looked up at the narrow house. I knew it was a crowded building, with many occupants, but today it was quiet. Trying to look as though I belonged there, I slipped across the pavement and down the little passage that led to the yard where Annie had breathed her last.

Like so many other yards in Whitechapel, this one was grimy. It wasn't raining today but the ground was wet all the same and the water that pooled in the cobbles was dank and brown. An unpleasant smell in the air made my nostrils flare in distaste.

Because I'd pretended to myself that I wasn't coming

here, I'd not brought the notes Bet had made from the post-mortem. But I'd read them so many times already that I didn't need them. Annie had been found in between some stairs and the fence, I knew. Her head had been level with the bottom step and her feet pointing towards the shed at the back of the yard.

I walked slowly towards the stairs and baulked slightly as I noticed there was still a smear of blood on the fence. I wished it had been raining so I hadn't had to see such a grim reminder of what had happened here.

I wasn't sure what I was looking for, but it felt important that I was there, seeing these things with my own eyes. Annie's belongings – meagre as they were – had been scattered around her corpse. No, not scattered. Bet had used a different word. Arranged. Like a still-life painting.

I stood there a while, taking in the surroundings. It may have been quiet where I stood but it was just a few steps from Hanbury Street. The stairs in front of me led to a room where people would have been sleeping when Annie was killed. I stood stock-still and listened – I could hear the murmur of voices from the nearby rooms, and someone coughing. If Annie had screamed for help, surely someone would have heard? So perhaps Dr Llewellyn had been right and she had been strangled to keep her quiet. It was a horrible thought.

'Maggie Cameron, as I live and breathe.'

Startled out of my musings, I turned and – much to my utter surprise – I recognised my old neighbour, George Lusk.

He was older than the last time I'd seen him, but I had no trouble recognising him. He looked rather pleased to see me. I imagined my face showed the very opposite emotion.

'Mr Lusk?' I said politely but coldly. 'What are you doing here?'

'I could ask you the same question,' he said. He sounded jovial, though his good humour held an air of being forced. 'Wherever trouble is, Maggie Cameron isn't far behind, ain't that right?'

I gave him a thin smile. 'Do you live here now?'

'No, I don't. I'm still in Alderney Street, as well you know.'

I nodded slowly.

'You don't live here either?'

'No.'

We looked at one another for a moment and then realisation dawned for both of us.

'Oh Lord, are you investigating these murders?' I asked.

'Are you playing detective?' he said at the same time.

There was a pause. 'I am a detective,' I said. 'I run my own agency.'

He put his hands on his lapels and puffed out his chest. 'And I am the founding member of the Whitechapel Vigilance Committee.'

'Saints preserve us,' I muttered. 'You always were a nosy bugger.'

George looked vaguely sheepish.

'Did you not learn your lesson about meddling after my Ralph died?'

Dropping his gaze, George sighed. 'I believe I owe you an apology,' he said.

'For?' I wasn't going to make this easy for him.

He swallowed. 'For accusing you of having something to do with Ralph's death.'

'Thank you.' I tossed my head back.

'Though you must admit his death did look suspicious. What sort of man falls down the stairs like that? Especially one who doesn't take a drink.'

I held his gaze, challenging him. 'His death was suspicious, but my bruises weren't?'

He shifted from foot to foot, clearly uncomfortable. 'Well, you don't like to pry, do you? Who knows what goes on in a marriage.'

'You never heard my screams or Ralph's shouts?'

George ran his finger round his collar. 'It's hard to know for sure . . .'

'But you thought you'd accuse me of killing my husband, even though everyone knew I was at the butcher's shop when he died?' I knew I was being a little unfair, but I had been so hurt by George jumping to blame me, and I wanted him to know. 'I thought you were my friend but instead you set the gossips on me.'

George took his hat off and rubbed his forehead, looking wretched. 'I was wrong,' he said. 'So very wrong. I realised quite quickly how wrong I had been but by then you'd gone. Moved away. But I am sorry.'

I nodded. His apology sounded genuine and I wasn't one to bear a grudge. Not when so much water had passed under this bridge.

'Susannah was furious with me,' George admitted, sitting himself down on the stairs. 'I don't remember another time when she was so angry with me.'

I smiled. 'She was?'

'She said Ralph was a "piece of work". She never liked him.' He looked straight at me. 'She said that there were many women trapped in dangerous marriages and that if Ralph were to have met with an unfortunate accident, then perhaps that was just God making sure justice was done.'

'Wise woman, Susannah.'

George looked stricken for a second, then he cleared his throat. 'I realised she was right. And I did a lot of reading. Pamphlets and that. And I went to a few talks by folk who want things to be better. More equal. Social reformers, they're called. Clever bunch.'

'You went to talks?'

George seemed quite pleased with himself. 'Way I see it, there's no point sitting around complaining about the hand life's dealt you. You need to get on and change things.'

I wasn't often struck dumb but now I was astonished. I simply nodded.

'And just so you know,' George went on, 'I have learned my lesson, about meddling.' He grinned at me. 'I've learned to do more of it. Perhaps if I'd meddled more, then you'd have been spared those bruises.'

I smiled back, despite being so surprised. 'Perhaps.'

'I suppose we'll never know.'

I looked at him. His accusations had hurt me at a time when things were already hard. But he wasn't a bad man. And his interest in social reform had warmed my heart. 'So tell me, what is this committee all about?' I asked, hoping my tone made him understand I accepted his apology.

'I'm glad you asked,' said George, making me groan inwardly as I realised he was gearing up to give me chapter and verse. He wasn't a bad man, that was true, but he did like the sound of his own voice at times.

'We held our inaugural meeting last night in the Crown and we discussed these murders and agreed that they're bad for Whitechapel. Bad for business. I've already had jobs cancelled because the takings at the music halls are down – and that means no renovations. No carpentry work for me. And of course it's bad for women. The streets are quieter.'

'That's true,' I said grudgingly. 'People are scared.'

'And I don't blame them,' George said, pointing at me. 'The police investigation has been lacking.'

'Also true,' I agreed. 'So what are you doing about it? What's the plan of the Whitechapel Vigilance Committee?'

'Watching,' said George, widening his eyes.

'Vigilance,' I said with a chuckle.

'Indeed.'

'That's right up your street, George. Like I said, you always were a nosy bugger.'

He snorted. 'As if you've not made a career out of being nosy.'

'Curious,' I said.

'Whatever you say.'

We both chuckled.

'Anything else?' I asked. 'Apart from vigilance?'

'We're putting up posters, appealing for information.' He dug into his bag and produced a sheaf of papers, saying just that. I was impressed, though I didn't show it. 'And we're also talking about organising ourselves into patrols, to keep an eye on the streets. Do what the police should be doing.'

I nodded. 'That's good. It's a lot of work, though. Have you got many volunteers?'

'Enough. More than enough actually and more interested, by all accounts.'

'Is Susannah helping?'

His face twisted again as it had when I'd mentioned his wife before, and he breathed in sharply. 'Susannah died. Just short of a year ago.'

'Oh Lord, I am sorry. She was a nice woman. Always kind to me.' I put my hand on his arm, suddenly understanding why he was so determined to protect women and his own livelihood. 'How are the little ones doing?'

'Well, they're not all so little anymore. The boys are all grown. And the girls are managing.'

'You want to make sure they're looked after?' I said. 'Make sure there's enough money coming in.'

'That's right.' He nodded. 'But it's not just about the money.' He rested his forearms on his knees where he sat on the dirty step and looked round the grimy, smelly yard like he was the lord of the manor admiring his estate. 'This is our home,' he said. 'We deserve to live and work somewhere safe.'

'You're a good man, George.'

'Not always,' he said. 'But I try.'

There was a moment of quiet, then he stood up and regarded me with a slight tilt to his head. 'What are you doing here?' he said.

'Oh you know,' I said. 'Just being nosy.'

'Curious.'

'Right.'

He looked at me carefully for a minute.

'If I get any information because of these posters, should I pass it on to you?'

'Well,' I said. 'Me and the police, of course.'

'Of course.'

'Eventually.'

'And should I mention to the police that I've seen you . . .' he gave a small laugh 'being nosy?'

'Best not.'

'Righto,' he said.

'Thanks, George.' I smiled at him. 'Please let me know if there's anything I can do.'

'I am sorry, you know. About Ralph and that.'

'I know.'

'It was nice seeing you, Maggie Cameron.'

Waving his pile of posters at me, he walked out of the yard, pausing to pin a notice on the lintel of the entrance.

I watched him go, wondering how many other people were investigating these crimes, alongside the police.

A carriage pulled up close to where George had disappeared out on to the main road, and I saw a man get out. He was vaguely familiar with a long, thin face and an aloof air. Where had I seen him before? Without really knowing why, I shrank back into the shadows beside the stairs, near the door to one of the rooms. Just where Annie had lain.

The man came to the entrance of the yard and glanced round, as though he was looking for something. Then he pulled out a sketchpad and I remembered where I'd seen him before.

Pretending I'd come out of the room where I was lurking, I emerged from the shadows.

'Morning,' I called to him.

He started.

'Sorry, didn't mean to make you jump,' I said cheerfully. 'Was there someone you were looking for?'

'No,' he said, a note of caution in his voice. 'I'm here on police business.'

A tingle of suspicion ran down my neck. 'Police business?' I said. 'About that poor unfortunate woman?'

'I'm just here to draw the scene,' he said.

'You an artist, then?' I asked.

He looked disdainful as he brandished his sketchbook at me. 'Clearly.'

'And you draw pictures of crime scenes, do you?' I put similar disdain in my voice.

'Not always,' he said. 'Without intending to flatter myself, I am a painter of some repute.'

'Are you now?' I looked him up and down. 'What's your name?'

'Walter Gent,' he said. 'You will see my paintings in the Royal Academy.'

'Yeah, well I don't get there much.'

'If you'll excuse me, I need to get on,' he said.

'Oh don't let me hold you up.' I grinned at him. 'Walter Gent, you said?'

'That's right.'

'Working for the police?'

'Indeed.'

'You crack on,' I said. 'I've got things to do. Nice to meet you.'

'You too,' he said politely, his concentration already on his paper.

I left him to it, heading back out on to the street, absolutely convinced this man was lying, but not entirely sure why.

# Chapter 24

## Bet

It had been a long morning. There seemed to be more policemen than ever at the station, which wasn't surprising really, but they were all filthy sods and liked to leave a trail of mess in their wake.

I'd been picking up half-drunk cups of tea, crusts of bread, and discarded coats and hats since sparrow's fart this morning and I needed some air. So as I was heading to the cells to give them a mop-down, I instead dumped the bucket at the end of the bars, then I sneaked out the back of the station and leaned against the wall for a breather.

Out in the street I could hear raised voices and I stiffened for a minute. I was – though I hated to admit it – a little skittish after our confrontation with Bernard. But no, these were women's voices and, though they were arguing, it sounded good-natured.

'I'm just saying if you've got a knife, chances are it's going to end up being your skin that's cut,' said one voice, which sounded familiar. 'I've heard folks saying he's a doctor. They know what they're doing with a knife, ain't that a fact?'

'That American fella, he's handy with a blade, and no mistake. That's what I've heard.'

There was a murmur of agreement.

'Plus, if you keep it tucked away under your skirts, how are you even going to get to it if you need it?' said someone else.

There was a loud burst of laughter.

'Sorry, Mr Whitechapel Murderer Sir, would you mind waiting before you attack me so I can get my knife out of my petticoat?' said the first woman, her voice mockingly polite. 'If you'd be so kind.'

At the mention of the murderer, I straightened up, realising where I knew the voices from. I darted out into the street and saw Min, Ruby and Kitty from the brothel walking by arm in arm.

'Ruby?' I called. 'Remember me?'

The women turned and grinned at me.

'All right, cock?' said Ruby. 'You was Maggie's friend.'

'That's right. I'm Bet.'

'Bet.'

'I heard you talking,' I said. 'About the murderer.'

Min eyed me suspiciously. 'We weren't doing nothing.'

'Have you got a knife?'

'No.' She folded her arms, defensive.

'I heard you,' I said again.

Ruby nudged her. 'She's all right.'

Min patted her thigh. 'It's under here. I ain't taking no chances with that fella on the loose.'

'But I said she's more likely to end up slit by that knife herself than fighting anyone off,' said Ruby.

'I think you're right.' I nodded.

Kitty looked nervous. 'It feels like we're just waiting for him,' she said softly. 'At least this way, we're doing something about it.'

'I heard some girls have got themselves pistols,' said Min. 'Maybe that would be better than the knife.'

'You should learn to fight,' I said, thinking of the way

Emma had shoved Bernard away. 'My friend showed me something.' I tugged Min's sleeve. 'Come in here.'

I led them into the yard at the back of the station next to where the horses were kept. It was quiet in there.

''Ere, you ain't taking us to the police station?' said Min in alarm. 'Are you a copper?'

'Nah, I'm just a cleaner,' I said, chuckling, but quite pleased she'd asked. 'Look, if you put your hands out like this and sort of shove them hard, you can push a man away, even if he's bigger than you.'

I demonstrated. The women all watched me carefully. 'Put all your weight behind it,' I said. 'Have a go on me – go on, Min. You first.'

I stood in front of her. She was shorter than me, but stocky. I planted my feet wide on the cobbles, and said: 'Now, go on.'

Min shoved me hard in the chest and before I had time to even realise what was happening, I was on my backside in a puddle, trying to catch my breath. I looked up at the three women who were all looking down at me.

'Bloody hell,' said Ruby. 'It works.'

Kitty held out a hand to haul me to my feet. 'Can you teach us anything else?'

I took a deep breath in, feeling my ribs complain where Min had made contact. 'I've heard you can swipe someone's legs from under them,' I said. 'Make them lose their balance.'

'Like this?' Quick as a flash, Kitty stuck out one of her long limbs and I was back on the ground again.

'Yes,' I said, examining my dirty grazed hands and mucky skirt. 'Just like that.'

Min helped me up this time and I took a step away from the women who were all looking at me in expectation.

'Who was the chap you said looks out for you?' I asked, shaking my skirt out. 'Brandon?'

'Bram,' said Min.

'Ask him to help you. I bet he knows lots of moves like this. And then when he's told you, you can teach other girls, then get them to teach others.' I smiled at Kitty, who was looking serene and not remotely bothered by having sent me crashing to the ground. 'Then you're not sitting round waiting anymore, are you?'

The three of them all looked at me and I felt the warm glow of their admiration.

'Don't use the knife, though,' I added. 'It ain't safe.'

'Bet?' a voice called from inside the police station. 'We need one of these cells mopped out. There's been a bit of an accident.'

I groaned. 'I've got to go,' I said. 'Please be careful.'

The rest of the morning went by in a blur of mopping and sweeping. When I eventually left the police station after my shift, I found Emma pacing up and down on the pavement at the bottom of the stairs.

'At last!' she said as I came through the doors. 'Where have you been?'

'Work?'

'I've got something to tell you.'

'Me too,' I said, thinking of the girls from the brothel as I ran down the steps to where she stood. Her face was flushed and her eyes were bright.

'You first. What is it?'

'We have a new addition to the wicked women of Whitechapel,' she said.

'Oh we're calling ourselves that now, are we? I thought you didn't like it?'

Emma gave me a fierce stare. 'Don't you want to know who it is?'

'Yes, all right then.'

She tossed her head and gave me a triumphant smile. 'It's the queen.'

I laughed. 'Who is it really?'

'Queen Victoria.' She dug into her pocket and pulled out a letter bearing a fancy seal. 'She wrote to Fred and offered some ideas about the case.'

'What on earth . . .' Stunned, I took the letter from her, feeling the heavy paper and admiring the intricate writing on the envelope. 'Is this really from the queen?'

'It is,' Emma said. 'She thinks the killer could be someone with a carriage.'

My head still spinning about the queen getting involved, I nodded. 'That's a good idea, actually.'

'And she said it could be a doctor.'

'A doctor?' I was amazed. 'I've heard that – you're right.'

'It makes sense because of the injuries.' Emma screwed her face up.

'It does,' I said, thinking about it. 'Goodness, that's clever.'

'I know.' Emma bounced on her toes. 'Come on, we need to go and see Maggie and tell her all about it.'

'Now?'

'Yes, of course now. There's no time to spare.'

'Has Fred seen this letter?'

'Not yet.'

'Should we show him?'

There was a pause, then Emma took the envelope from me and put it in her pocket. 'Not yet.'

Smiling, I followed her as she took off along the road towards Maggie's.

'There is a doctor,' I said to her back as I hurried to catch up. 'I heard the girls from the brothel talking about him. I think he's American.'

'Let's ask Maggie about him.'

She dashed across the road, and I followed.

'Should we write back?' I said, panting slightly. 'Blimey, you're quick when you want to be.'

'To the queen?'

'Of course to the queen.'

'I don't know.' Emma came to a stop at the corner beside Maggie's office. I wondered if she was watching us out of the window as she had done that first day. I squinted upwards, but I couldn't see. 'I was actually thinking I'd just give the letter back to Fred. If we write back, she might tell Harrison what we're up to.'

'That's true.' I tried the door to Maggie's but it was locked. 'She's not here.'

'Well, where is she?' Emma looked affronted at the idea of Maggie being elsewhere. 'We need to speak to her.'

'Perhaps she's working,' I pointed out. 'Some of us have jobs, you know.'

Emma gave me a disappointed glance. 'Strictly speaking, you should be cleaning my kitchen about now.'

I grinned. 'Fair enough.'

'Ladies?'

We both turned to see Maggie marching down the street.

'Where have you been?' Emma demanded. 'We've been waiting ages.'

'Nonsense, I saw you as I turned the corner,' Maggie said. 'You've only just arrived.'

Emma huffed. 'Well, it felt like ages. We've got lots to tell you.'

'And I have lots to tell you. Come on in.'

We all trooped up the stairs to her office and settled down in the chairs. Maggie looked at us expectantly.

'You first.'

'We have a letter,' said Emma. She sounded calm then she let out a little squeal of excitement. 'From the queen.'

Maggie rolled her eyes. 'Everyone's a detective.'

I chuckled. 'Emma says the police are getting piles of letters every day.'

'But this one's different,' said Emma. 'Because it's from the queen. And she's got some good ideas.'

'Now Vicky wants in, does she?' Maggie sounded unimpressed. 'What's she got to say?'

Emma pulled out the letter and handed it to Maggie, who looked shocked. 'Oh good Lord, it's from the queen.'

'I just said that.' Emma frowned.

'Yes, but I thought it would be a hoax. You'd be astonished at how many oddballs there are out there who like to pretend to be someone else.'

'Oh, it's not a hoax,' I said. Then my confidence faltered because really, how did I know? 'Is it?'

Maggie was studying the envelope. 'No,' she said carefully. 'I don't believe so.'

Clearly impatient with Maggie taking too long to read the letter, Emma leaned forward. 'She says she thinks the killer might have a carriage.'

Maggie looked up from the page. 'Huh.'

'What does "huh" mean?' I asked.

'Let me read,' she muttered. 'Two ticks.'

Emma and I waited while Maggie read the letter, then we waited some more as she read it again.

Then she put it down on the desk and leaned back in her chair.

'Huh,' she said again.

'What do you know?' I asked. We may not have been working together for long, but already I was recognising a gleam in her eyes.

'I went to Hanbury Street today.'

'Where Annie was killed?' Emma said.

'Yes, indeed.'

'Did you find something?' I wasn't sure if there would

be any evidence left, given the police seemed to be working harder on these killings now, and the rain was still teeming down almost every day.

'Not something, someone,' said Maggie. 'Firstly, I met my old neighbour George Lusk. He was the chap who accused me of killing Ralph.'

'What a sod,' I muttered.

'I was furious at the time, but we cleared the air. Long while ago now.'

'You're a better woman than I am.'

'He's a terrible busybody but his heart's in the right place,' Maggie said. 'He's a carpenter – does music hall work usually. But he's worried about his trade, and he's worried about his daughters, and to be honest, he's worried about everyone, so he and a few others have formed a vigilance group.'

'What's that?' I wasn't sure I'd heard that word before. 'Vigilance?'

'They're going to patrol the streets and keep an eye out for suspicious behaviour.'

'Lord, Fred won't like that,' said Emma. 'He says things always get out of hand when the public get involved.'

'I shouldn't think they'll cause any problems,' said Maggie. 'But he said he'll let us know if they come across anything interesting.'

'What else?' I asked. 'You said "firstly" so there must have been something else?'

Maggie gave me a little approving nod. 'At Polly's funeral, did either of you see a chap who was drawing?'

'Yes!' Emma exclaimed. 'He was perched high up, hanging on to a lamp post?'

'That's the one.'

'We thought he must have been working for the newspapers,' I said. 'Why?'

'Because he was there, today, at the very place where Annie was killed.' Maggie got up and went to the wall where we'd pinned all the pictures and notes. 'He said he was an artist, but he was rather odd.'

'Odd how?' asked Emma. She got up too and stood next to Maggie, and I followed because I didn't want to miss anything.

'He was very interested in the scene of the crime,' Maggie began.

'So were you,' I pointed out. 'Perhaps he was investigating too. Everyone's a detective, after all.'

But Maggie shook her head. 'It didn't seem that way. He told me he was working for the police, but I didn't believe him.'

Emma screwed her face up. 'Fred's not mentioned any artist.'

'No,' said Maggie pointedly.

'And what would be the point of drawing the crime scene after everything had been cleared away?' Emma added. 'It makes no sense.'

'Indeed,' said Maggie.

'When Annie died, we wondered if the killer had been in the crowd at Polly's funeral, didn't we?' I said. 'Well, this artist – what was his name, Maggie?'

'Walter Gent.'

'This Walter Gent was there. We know that for sure because we all saw him.'

Emma looked disgusted. 'He was at Polly's funeral and at the place where Annie died? Like he was getting some sort of satisfaction from the murders?'

'I don't know much about the sort of man who kills a woman,' I said. 'But I reckon there's a difference, ain't there? Between someone like your Ralph or my dad, who lashes out in a rage and might kill someone if he ain't careful . . .' I took a breath. 'And someone like this, who plans his crimes and works it out and takes pleasure in it all.'

'I think you're right,' Emma said, her face pale. 'I think the killer's enjoying this. All the fuss. The big funeral. The newspaper stories . . .'

'When Gent first came into the yard, I ducked into the shadows because I wasn't sure who he was or if I should let myself be seen,' Maggie said, her eyes fixed on the picture of Annie we'd stuck to the wall. 'And I saw the expression on his face quite clearly.'

'What was it?' I asked. 'What was on his face?'

'Satisfaction.' She looked at Emma. 'Just like you said. He seemed satisfied.'

'Lawks,' I muttered. 'That ain't right.'

Maggie went back to her desk where the letter from the queen still lay. She picked it up.

'The queen suggests the murderer has a carriage,' she said. She waved the letter at Emma and me. 'Walter Gent arrived at Hanbury Street in a carriage.'

I felt a quiver in my stomach. Excitement mixed with nerves and fear.

'Do you think he could be the killer?' I asked.

'I think it's definitely worth finding out more, don't you?' Maggie looked from me to Emma, and we both nodded.

'I wonder . . .' Emma began. She rubbed her nose. 'There is a glove shop in Aldgate run by a woman called Veronica? No, Verity? Something like that. I believe she used to be a model for artists in her younger days and now she provides models – at a fee, of course. She might know where to find this Walter Gent.'

'Well then,' Maggie said. She had a gleam in her eye that I rather liked. 'Let's go and find this Verity, shall we?'

# Chapter 25

## Emma

The glove shop was just as I remembered, though I'd not been there for some time. It was down a little side street, with leaded windows and an impressively arranged display behind the glass.

'Very creative,' Maggie murmured as she admired the front of the shop. She nodded to the name painted along the top. 'Verity,' she said.

I was pleased I'd remembered correctly. 'I thought that was it.'

I pushed open the door, making the little bell tinkle. Verity was standing behind the counter and she looked up as we entered.

'Hello, Mrs Abberline,' she said, smiling. 'I've not seen you for a while. What are you after? Something pretty, no doubt, to flatter those long delicate fingers of yours. Piano player's fingers, I always think, though of course I've got no idea if you're a musical type. Anyway, it's waterproof gloves we all need in this weather, isn't it? Let me see what I've got under the counter. And introduce me to your friends while you're at it . . .'

She paused to breathe, and I jumped in.

'It's nice to see you again, Verity,' I said. 'This is Maggie and Bet.' I glanced round at them, both looking slightly startled by Verity's enthusiastic welcome. 'We're not actually here for gloves.'

Verity looked round at the counter and smiled. 'Then I'm afraid you might be disappointed because gloves is all I've got.'

She laughed loudly and, before she could carry on talking, I said: 'We're looking for an artist.'

'Urgh,' Verity said with tut. 'Waste of bloody space, the whole lot of them. Pretending to be penniless, wafting around the West End, drinking in taverns and spending hours on one brushstroke.' Despite the way she was talking, her voice was affectionate. 'I despair of them all, I really do. Fancy yourself as a model, do you? I'm joking, though lovely-looking as you are, you could be a wonderful artist's muse. I expect it's a painting you want, is it? I heard you'd moved house. Must have plenty of empty walls to fill.' She took a breath. 'Who is it that you're after?'

'Walter Gent,' I said.

The change in Verity was immediate. Where a second before she had been animated and smiling, now she was still and wary. She put the gloves she was holding down on the counter and stared at us, her expression stony.

'I don't know him.'

I looked at Maggie for guidance and she stepped forward.

'I think you do know him,' she said, putting her hands on the counter. 'But I think you're scared of him.'

Verity swallowed. 'Oh, look at your lovely hands,' she said. She reached out and took Maggie's wrists, turning them this way and that. She was trying to speak brightly, but her voice was weak. 'I've got a pair of fine-knit woollen gloves that would show them off to a tee . . .'

Maggie clasped Verity's wrists with her own hands and Verity stopped talking.

'Do you help the artists find models?' Maggie asked.

Verity nodded.

'And you take a fee?'

'I do.' Verity studied Maggie's hand clasped in her own. 'I was a model myself when I was younger. It was such a hoot. We had a laugh, and they treated us well. Most of the time. And when they didn't, it weren't malicious. It was more them getting lost in the moment – you know what those arty ones are like.' She looked up at us. 'I made good money.'

'And you put it to good use buying this shop,' said Maggie, extracting her hands from Verity's grip.

Verity nodded. 'First time in my life I'd ever been glad not to have married. I wanted to have something of my own and I could, because I didn't have a husband.'

'Good for you.' Maggie picked up the gloves Verity had put on the counter. 'These are lovely.'

Verity smiled. 'Fine stitching.'

'When you stopped modelling, you must have missed it?' Maggie prompted.

'So much. It was all I'd known really. I was 14 when I started. But finding models for the artists helped me stay in that world.' She leaned sideways and looked past Maggie, to Bet and me. 'You're a pretty one,' she said to Bet. 'Your hair's lovely. They'd make good use of you.' She gave a tiny laugh. 'It's fun, you know? Dressing up as shepherdesses, or characters from books, or the Bible. It's like playing. There are some nice chaps painting nearby. I can put you in touch.'

'It's really Walter Gent we need.' Maggie was firm.

Verity sighed. Then she came out from behind the counter, flicked the lock on the shop door, and turned the sign to closed.

'Walter Gent ain't a good man,' she said, leaning against

the door. 'I said I wasn't sending any more girls to him, and I meant it.'

'Why not?' asked Bet. 'What did he do to make you say that?'

There was a pause. I held my breath.

'Nasty things,' said Verity.

'He hurt the models?' Maggie's voice was gentle.

'At first he just wanted them to pose like they were hurt,' Verity said. 'It was odd but it wasn't doing anyone any harm. I didn't know about that at the time, though; they only told me later. When things got . . . worse.'

'What sort of poses?' I asked.

'Crying, like they were in pain. Holding their arms funny as though they were broken.' She scratched her head. 'Lying across the bed with their heads at an angle like they were dead.'

I gasped and, next to me, Bet put her hand on my arm.

'What did you mean when you said it got worse?' Maggie asked.

'If they weren't convincing enough, if their injuries didn't look real, then he'd hit them.' Verity looked sick. 'The day one girl came home with her face black and blue, and her arm broke for real, was the day I said he wasn't having no more models from me. And I told the others too. No one has been going to his studio to model for him – no one who works for me anyway.'

'How long ago was this?'

'About a year?' Verity frowned. 'We spread the word, telling other women to keep away, but sometimes the money is too tempting. Or the girls think it'll be different for them. That they can handle it.'

She came over to Bet and put her hand on her arm. 'But I meant it when I said I know some good artists,' she said urgently. 'I don't want you going to Gent.'

'I don't want to model,' Bet said. 'That's not why we're here.'

'Then why?' said Verity. She looked confused. 'Not gloves, and not modelling?' She turned back to the door and reached for the lock. 'Maybe it's time you went?'

'We think he might have hurt some other women.' Maggie said quickly. 'Emma is looking into some things for her husband – you know her husband, Inspector Abberline?' Verity nodded. 'I run a detective agency. And Bet here is my assistant.' Beside me, Bet looked delighted. 'We really need to speak to Gent, and we assure you we will not go alone.' She smiled at Verity. 'We will be safe.'

For a moment Verity didn't say anything, she simply studied us, her eyes flicking over each of us in turn.

'I felt awful when Dora came back like that,' she said eventually. 'Her arm hasn't been the same since.'

'Of course.' Maggie nodded.

'And I said to her, then, he won't stop. He's not going to stop hurting you. He's going to get worse. That's why I said no more.'

'You are a good woman,' said Maggie. 'I use some girls myself in my agency, and I feel the same about them. Protective.'

'That's right,' said Verity. 'But I like to give them independence.'

'Indeed,' Maggie agreed. 'In fact, perhaps I could send some girls your way if I think they're suitable? And if you have any you think could help in my divorce cases, maybe you would be so kind as to send them to me? I need street-smart women. Quick thinkers.'

Verity looked pleased. 'Course.'

'And I will take those gloves, please.'

I sighed inwardly, wondering when we would actually get to know where to find Gent. Bet glanced at me and raised a questioning eyebrow. I gave a tiny shrug.

Maggie paid for the gloves and as Verity was wrapping them, she said, almost like it was an afterthought: 'Where would we find Gent, then?'

'Finsbury Circus,' said Verity without hesitation. 'Number one.'

'Nice,' said Maggie.

'Yeah, well, he's got money, ain't he?' Verity sounded annoyed. 'He gets up late so if you wake him first thing in the morning, he might be a bit sleepy and less scary.' She handed Maggie her package and went to open the door so we could leave. 'Just be careful.'

'We're not really going to wait until tomorrow morning, are we?' I said as soon as we were back out on the street. I looked up at the clock on the church at the end of the street. It was still only afternoon.

'Not likely.' Bet was adamant.

'Absolutely not,' Maggie said at the same time. 'But we do need a proper plan. We don't want to jump in with both feet and have everything go wrong.'

'Again,' I said pointedly.

Maggie tutted. 'That was just bad luck.'

'For Bernard,' Bet said with a chuckle.

I glared at her. I had made peace with Bernard's death, but I wasn't ready to joke about it. 'Let's walk,' said Maggie, gesturing down the street with her parcel of gloves. 'Finsbury Circus isn't far.'

She set off with purpose, and obediently Bet and I trotted along beside her.

'Gent said he was a painter of some repute,' she told us. 'He was rather smug about having his paintings in the Royal Academy.'

'You're thinking we should flatter him,' I suggested. 'Like we were planning to do with Bernard.'

'Exactly,' said Maggie. 'In my experience, a little flattery goes a long way. The only question is, what do we say to get inside his studio?'

'Not "we",' I said. 'You can't go in.'

Maggie looked round at me as we walked. 'Why not?'

'You've met him, haven't you? Did you give him a reason for loitering round the scene of Annie's murder?'

'Not in as many words, but I pretended I'd come out of one of the rooms.' Maggie sighed. 'You're right. I'll have to stay out of sight. At first at least. Or he'll be on his guard straightaway.'

'Maybe I could pretend I want to buy a painting?' I suggested. 'Ask to see his work?'

'Maybe,' said Maggie. 'Or commission him, perhaps?'

Bet clutched my arm. 'We could use the letter,' she said in excitement. 'The letter from the queen.'

'Use it how?' I asked. We stopped talking for a moment as we passed a group of men outside a pub, then carried on as we crossed the road to walk past Liverpool Street station.

'Maggie said he lied and claimed that he was working for the police,' said Bet. 'Why don't we pretend we've come to sign him up on the request of the queen.'

'Oh that's clever,' breathed Maggie. 'Flattery and playing on his interest in the case.'

'We can just write a new letter and put it in the envelope,' said Bet. 'Well, not me. My writing's awful. But Emma could, or you. The envelope's addressed to Abberline, so we write the letter as though the queen's told the inspector to recruit him.'

'If he's as dangerous as Verity warned, we need to be careful,' said Maggie. 'So this is a good idea, to let him know we have links to the police.'

'That's settled then,' I said. 'But if we're going to write a convincing letter, we'll need to sit down somewhere.'

'There's a tearoom by the station,' said Maggie. 'We'll go there.'

Bet looked thrilled. 'A tearoom? Really?'

I put my hand through her arm, remembering once again that Bet led a very different life to me, and I was glad our paths had crossed. 'Perhaps there will be some cake.'

'Lead the way,' she said.

Maggie pointed a little way along the road. 'It's just up there, and then Finsbury Circus is at the end, where the trees are.'

'I see it,' I said. I felt nervous suddenly. 'Gosh, I hope he's there.'

'We'll go and see what's what, and then if we find anything at all that suggests he is the killer, we'll go straight to the police,' said Maggie firmly.

Bet looked disappointed. 'Really?'

'What else can we do?' Maggie said. 'We can't arrest him ourselves, or cart him off to the police station.'

'I suppose not.'

'We'll go to Fred,' I said. 'None of the others. Not Harrison, nor Green and Percival.'

'I really don't think Green's as bad as Percival,' said Bet. 'It doesn't seem fair to lump them all in together.'

'They come as a pair.' I looked at her, with her bright eyes and slightly flushed cheeks, and tutted. 'He's too old for you.'

'That's not what I meant.'

'Really?' Maggie raised an eyebrow and Bet gave a little girlish giggle.

'It's not.'

I jumped in. 'Even if Green is nice, and even if you are sweet on him, we need to be careful,' I said.

She opened her mouth to argue, then clearly changed

her mind. 'Fine.' She narrowed her eyes at me. 'As long as you buy me a slice of cake.'

'Agreed.'

'Come on then,' said Maggie. 'Let's get going.'

# Chapter 26

We went to the tearoom, which was rather nice, with tall windows.

'It's a good place to watch people from,' Maggie explained. 'I've spent a few hours here in my time.'

Bet sighed. 'I wish I really was your assistant, like you told Verity.'

'I don't have call for an assistant at the moment,' Maggie said, sounding genuinely regretful. 'But if things pick up, then you're first on my list.'

'If we catch the Whitechapel murderer, everyone will want to employ you and then you'll need to give me a job.' Bet poured some tea into her cup. 'And we can sit here all day and watch the people go by.'

'This all sounds very nice, but we do need to get on,' I pointed out, feeling a little affronted that Bet and Maggie were making plans that didn't include me. 'Let's write this letter, shall we?'

'Your writing is much nicer than mine,' said Maggie, pulling some notepaper out of her bag and sliding it across the table to me. 'You do it.'

I found the original letter from the queen in my own bag, and opened it out on the table. It still gave me a thrill to see the signature.

'What should I say?'

Bet leaned forward. 'Say you've heard about his talents and want him to help the police with their investigation.'

'And that you want to pay him for his time,' said Maggie.

'This feels a bit deceitful.' I paused with my pen over the paper.

'No more deceitful than him pretending to work for the police,' Maggie pointed out.

I shrugged. 'Right,' I said. In my neatest hand, I wrote a few lines, detailing what Bet and Maggie had said, and then I carefully copied the *Victoria R* signature from the original letter.

While we waited until the ink was dry, we drank our tea and ate our cake. Bet told us how she'd spoken to Ruby, Min and Kitty and they'd mentioned a doctor.

'Like the queen said in her letter,' she explained. 'They said he was American and that he was handy with a knife.'

I shivered at the thought of anyone being handy with a knife. 'Once we've spoken to Gent, perhaps we should track down this doctor?'

'I agree,' said Maggie. 'What else did the girls say, Bet?'

Bet grinned. 'They were talking about arming themselves – apparently lots of girls are doing it. But instead, I showed them how to defend themselves.'

'You did?' Maggie sounded surprised.

'And I said they should speak to that Bram – you know, the fella who looks out for them? I thought if he showed them some punches and that, then they could teach other girls, and the other girls could teach more . . .'

'Good Lord,' said Maggie. 'What an excellent idea.'

Bet beamed with pride and started to ask Maggie about how she got started as a detective while I tried not to bristle. Once more I felt excluded from their plans and that in turn made me worry that I was becoming too attached to

Bet. She was my maid, not my friend. But then she looked up at me and smiled and said, 'You must learn so much from Fred,' and I found myself telling her about some cases that Fred credited me with helping solve. Maggie nodded along and offered opinions and Bet seemed to be soaking it all up, and I thought perhaps we were friends, the three of us. Mismatched and unlikely companions that we were.

After a while, Maggie picked the page up and inspected it. 'It's good,' she said. 'Nice work, Emma.'

I took it from her, put it in the envelope and smoothed it out.

'Shall we go?'

Maggie reached out and took one of my hands and one of Bet's, so we were once again in our Ring-o'-Roses formation.

'Good luck,' she said.

'The wicked women of Whitechapel ride again,' said Bet with a grin.

I let go of her hand and put the envelope into my bag. 'I sincerely hope not.'

We put some coins on the table to pay for the tea and cake, and headed outside into the late afternoon. It wasn't raining for a change, and the sun was actually shining, so I hoped the good light meant Gent might be painting. I had to admit, I was vague on the exact details of what artists did all day – I'd not paid much attention to drawing lessons at school.

Suddenly nervous, I slipped my hand into Bet's.

'You'll come with me, won't you?'

Bet looked at Maggie, who nodded.

'I'm not letting you go in there alone.'

I breathed out slowly in relief. 'And Maggie, will you stay close by in case we need you?'

'Of course.'

'Then I think we're ready.' I squeezed Bet's fingers.

'Let's go,' she said.

We crossed the road, walked along to Finsbury Circus, and stood outside number one for a moment. Then I marched up the path, Bet following, and rang the bell before I could change my mind.

It took so long for anyone to answer that I was beginning to think Gent wasn't at home. But then the door was thrown open and there he was, wearing a paint-splattered smock and an irritated expression.

'Yes?'

I took a breath. 'Mr Gent?'

'Yes.'

'My name is Emma Abberline,' I began. 'And this is my companion, Bet Palmer. We're here on behalf of the police in Whitechapel . . .' I saw a glint of interest in his eye and that gave me courage to continue. 'And Queen Victoria. We have an important commission to discuss with you.'

He looked me up and down. 'Abberline?'

'Yes.'

'Your husband is Inspector Abberline?'

'Yes. He asked me to come and show you this.' I reached into my bag and brought out the letter. 'It's from the queen.'

Gent took the envelope and pulled out the paper inside, his little ratty eyes roaming over the page. 'This is from the queen.'

'That's what I just said.'

'She wants the police to commission me?'

He looked up at Bet and me, still standing on the doorstep.

'Could we come in, do you think?' I said. 'We have a lot to discuss.'

Gent smiled suddenly, a wolfish grin that made me shudder inwardly. Outwardly, I smiled back graciously.

'Of course, I was forgetting myself there, for a moment. Please, come in.'

I followed as he turned and walked down the hallway, and Bet paused for a second behind me. I turned to see her closing the front door, but leaving it slightly ajar. Clever. I gave her a tiny nod.

'Excuse my appearance, I have been taking advantage of the sunlight to paint,' Gent said.

'Do you have a studio here in your house?' I asked.

'At the back.' He pointed through to the end of the hall. 'I have an orangery so it gets good light.'

Gent led us into a sitting room with a low coffee table, a sofa and two high-backed chairs. He gestured for us to take a seat and we both sat on the sofa. He took one of the chairs, and turned his gaze once more, to the letter.

'I'm flattered the queen believes I can be of use,' he said, looking at the seal on the back of the envelope.

'Your reputation precedes you,' I told him. 'I believe you have work in the Royal Academy? And my husband said he saw you at Mary Ann Nichols' funeral.'

'Yes, I was there,' Gent said. 'The dark side of human life fascinates me.'

'The queen's letter made my husband realise that the sketches you made at that time would be of great use to the police,' I said, thinking on my feet. 'Perhaps you could let us have one of them?'

'Absolutely.' Gent looked thrilled. 'I'll fetch them from my studio.'

I made to stand up. 'I'll come with you.'

Gent's expression changed from jovial to – was it alarmed? – and then back again so quickly I almost thought I'd imagined it. 'No, no, you stay. I'll be two ticks.' He gave a little awkward laugh. 'I'm sorry I've not offered you a drink. My housekeeper has finished for the day, but I could . . .'

216

'No need,' I said, waving my hand. 'Please, fetch the sketches.'

Gent went off and I turned to Bet. 'He doesn't want us in the studio,' I said in a low voice.

'I saw that,' she agreed. 'Let me see if I can see Maggie.'

She got up and went to the window. The sash was open and Bet stuck her head out.

'Maggie?' she whispered.

Maggie appeared from behind a hedge.

'He doesn't want us to go in his studio,' Bet said quickly. 'He's hiding something. It's at the back of the house – the front door's open. We'll keep him talking in here and you go and find out what he's up to.'

'Righto,' said Maggie cheerfully. She shrank back into the shadow of the hedge, just as I heard Gent coming back along the hallway.

'Here we are,' he said. 'Admiring the view of the gardens?'

By the window, Bet nodded. 'It's nice. We don't have nothing like that in Whitechapel.'

'Show us the sketches,' I said quickly, not wanting him to walk over to the window and chance him seeing Maggie. Gent sat down next to me on the sofa, leaving Bet to take one of the chairs near the door, and handed me the pictures. As he did, his hand brushed mine and I almost shuddered at his touch.

'So you can see I had a good vantage point,' he said. 'The crowd was large and it was important to get high up.'

'You did well.' I wondered if Maggie was in the house now. 'Tell us more about why you decided to go to the funeral . . .'

# Maggie

Gent's house was nice. Nicer than I'd expected. His paintings were clearly making him a good living. Or he had family money. Or perhaps both. I stood for a moment in the hallway, my back to the front door, listening. I could hear Gent talking and Emma asking questions. *Well done, Emma*, I thought. Down the end of the hall I could see sunlight, which was clearly the studio. So quickly but quietly, I headed in that direction, past the kitchen. The whole back of the house opened out into a small orangery, with low brick walls, then tall windows at the back, and a glazed lantern roof. It smelled of paint, but it wasn't unpleasant. To one side was a small table stacked with pieces of wood – picture frames, I guessed pieces of canvas and a few tools. Across the room was another table loaded with paints and brushes.

The sunlight streaming in was glorious – somehow stronger there than it had been outside – and the room was warm. A cat lay on a low bench beside the window, and I thought how nice it would be to curl up there with a book and a cup of tea and spend the afternoon. What a beautiful spot Gent had created for himself here.

But then I looked properly. The walls on either side of the doorway where I stood were hung with paintings, more canvases were stacked on the floor, leaning against the walls, windows and furniture. A large, half-finished work was on an easel – clearly Gent had been painting when we interrupted him.

The work was well done – any fool could see that. I had very little interest in art, and even less knowledge, but even I could appreciate that he was good at what he did. Slowly, I studied the pictures on the wall. Gent was obviously talented, prolific and . . . I looked round, my stomach churning . . . he was twisted, sadistic and cruel.

My heart thumped as I saw a painting of a young woman crying. She was dressed in a torn blouse, showing bruises on her skin and her eyes were red. I wondered if the model for this painting had been one of Verity's girls. There were more pictures of young women in various states of undress, and various states of distress. There were paintings of rooms with no one in them, but Gent had done something odd with the perspective and the shadows, so looking at the work made you feel you were almost in the room, with someone watching just out of sight.

I walked round the easel to see what he had been working on and gasped. The half-painted work was of Annie Chapman. Except in this painting, the poor woman wasn't lying in the street. In fact, she wasn't actually dead. Or at least I didn't think she was dead. Instead, she lay artfully on a bed. If you didn't know about Annie's death, you wouldn't know the inspiration for the picture, but I knew Annie's injuries by heart because I had read the post-mortem notes over and over. I knew how she'd been lying when she was found and the gruesome, brutal wounds her killer had inflicted. And here I was, seeing those words I'd read in horror and disbelief, made real before my very eyes.

'Oh good Lord,' I breathed. My stomach lurched and for one moment I thought I might vomit, but with a huge effort I managed to calm my disgust, just enough. I looked at the canvas again. The woman – Annie – was lying on the bed, not wearing very much. She had a sort of loose nightgown on, which left little to the imagination, and the light from the window above her cast shadows on her body. Shadows which were in the places where Annie's worst wounds had been. Round her neck – where Annie had been slit – the woman was wearing a necklace, shining like drops of blood. The painting wasn't finished – the background was unpainted, and the woman's face was blurred – but the whole effect was accomplished, faintly erotic, and one of the most awful things I'd seen in my whole life.

'What is it?'

I tore my eyes from the painting to see Bet standing in the door of the studio.

'You're white as a sheet, Maggie. What have you seen?'

'You shouldn't be in here.'

'I slipped out while Gent was focused on Emma. He didn't even notice I'd gone.' Bet took a step towards me. 'What's on the easel?'

'Don't look,' I said.

But it was too late. Bet had ducked round my arm and now she was staring at the canvas too, just as horrified as me.

'It's Annie,' she said. 'But not.'

'It's horrific.'

Aghast, Bet raised her eyes from the painting, and I watched as she took in the other shocking works hanging on the walls.

'Oh my good God,' she breathed, putting her hand over her mouth. 'He's a monster.'

An awful thought suddenly struck me. 'And we've left Emma alone with him.'

Bet started in shock, flinging her hands up. As she did so, she knocked the easel where the canvas was propped. We watched as it teetered and then fell, bringing down a pile of paintings stacked nearby and a jug full of water, which smashed on the tiled floor. Loudly.

# Emma

Gent was hanging off my every word, soaking up the praise I was inventing from Fred and the queen.

Bet was sitting near the door, behind Gent. I could tell she was feeling twitchy, and I wasn't surprised when she stood up quietly and edged out into the hall. Gent didn't even notice.

'This is most impressive,' I said, studying the pictures he was showing me of the yard where Annie had been found. 'I imagine the inspector will be extremely grateful.'

'I have a keen eye for detail,' Gent said. He shifted along slightly so his thigh was touching mine. I shifted too, but he'd already done this twice and now I was right at the edge of the seat. Any more and I'd end up on the floor.

'I see that.' I nodded. Hoping to distract him, I turned the page to see the next picture and gasped aloud as I saw it was an image of a man and a woman engaged in a very intimate act. The woman was naked as the day she was born, and she stared straight out of the canvas, through half-closed eyes, meeting my shocked gaze.

'Oh dear,' said Gent mildly. 'I didn't mean to leave that in there.'

I felt my cheeks flame and I pushed the picture back towards him. But he didn't cover it up. Instead, he looked down at the image.

'I am proud of this one,' he said. His voice was gruff. 'Thinking of doing more like this.' He gave me a lascivious smile. 'There's a lot of money to be made from erotica. What do you think? She's beautiful, isn't she?'

He pointed towards the woman's ample breasts. Embarrassed and nervous, I averted my eyes, leaning back over the edge of the sofa. Gent was very close to me now. I could feel his breath on my cheek.

'I pay well,' he said. 'Very well.'

'I do not need money.' My voice was meek and I hated myself for being so intimidated. 'My husband . . .'

Gent smiled his wolfish smile. 'He could come too. I'll draw you together. Lots of married couples enjoy having an audience. They like to see the pictures later.'

I was frozen to the spot as he leaned over me.

'No?' he said. 'They all say no at first. But I soon get them warmed up.'

All I could do was shake my head. Gent laughed. He was almost lying on top of me now and, as I recoiled, he leaned forward and licked my cheek. I squealed in disgust and he laughed again.

'What about you, Miss Palmer?' he said, turning to where Bet had been sitting. 'You're a pretty girl.'

He moved off me and I leapt to my feet away from him just as he realised Bet had gone. 'Where is she?'

'I . . . I don't know,' I stammered. 'I didn't . . . I don't know . . .'

Gent turned back to me, looking furious. And then suddenly there was a huge clatter from elsewhere in the house and the sound of something smashing.

'That bloody bitch,' he growled.

# Maggie

As soon as Bet knocked over the easel, we heard a shout of angry surprise, and then footsteps. I grabbed Bet's arm. 'We need to leave,' I said.

But we were too late. There in the doorway stood Gent, with Emma – looking rather dishevelled – behind him.

'Why are you in here?' he snarled. He wasn't a large

man, but he was frightening in the same way a cornered rat would be. Bet, who was closest to him, looked terrified and I felt my legs begin to shake. All I could think about was running away. But then I looked at Emma, pale-faced with fear in the hall, and Bet, cowering next to me, and I felt somehow responsible for these women.

Drawing on every ounce of strength I had, I pulled my shoulders back and stared right at him.

'Looking at your work,' I said. 'It's very revealing.'

He turned to me, surprised. 'You?' he said, confusion flashing in his eyes. 'You were at Hanbury Street. Who are you? Why are you here? Get out!'

There was nothing I wanted to do more, but I dug my feet into the floor. 'We're investigating the Whitechapel murders. That's what I was doing at Hanbury Street and that is what we're doing now. And we've found out some very interesting information about you, Mr Gent.'

'You don't know anything about me.'

'I do,' said Emma from the hall. 'You are disgusting.'

She sounded tearful and I felt a little sick as Gent laughed.

'And I know what kind of man you are from your paintings,' I said. 'Sadistic. Evil.'

'Creative,' he said with a shrug. 'These are all works of imagination.'

'But they're not, are they? We know you hurt models so you can paint them.'

His face twisted, and I felt mildly triumphant.

'Did you kill Annie Chapman?' I said.

'No.'

'I don't believe you.' I gestured at the painting on the easel. 'This is exactly as she was found. How would you know that if you hadn't killed her?'

Gent narrowed his eyes at me. 'How do you know that?' He lifted his chin. 'Perhaps you killed her?'

'We're working with the police, ain't we?' Bet said boldly. 'That's how we know. And that's where we're going now – straight to the police station, to tell them about these disgusting paintings.'

Gent gave his horrible smile. 'Oh I don't think so,' he said. 'Because they will see these paintings and they'll think what you think – that I killed Annie, and the others.' He gave a small, mirthless chuckle. 'And I can see why they'd think that.' He smoothed out his moustache. 'It doesn't look good, does it?'

'Because you're a murderer,' I said. I wasn't frightened now. Just absolutely furious at this unapologetic, nasty piece of work.

'I'm not.' Gent almost sounded sorry about it. 'I can't deny I enjoy the thrill of these murders and I did find it . . .' He looked up the ceiling, searching for the word. 'I found it satisfying to recreate Annie's murder scene. But I didn't murder her.'

'How did you know what happened to her, if you didn't kill her?' Emma asked from behind him.

He turned to her. 'I have friends in the police, just like you do. They pass on information, for a small fee.'

'I don't believe you,' she said. 'They're good men. Honest men. Why would they do such a thing?'

'In my experience people will do anything for money.' He leaned towards her and she shrank back, making me wonder again what had gone on when they had been alone. 'I paid the woman in that painting you saw,' he said in a loud whisper. 'Not much, admittedly. She was quick to agree.'

He grinned, looking round at Bet and me. 'As was the little eager policeman.'

'Percival,' growled Bet in an undertone. 'It has to be.'

'We've heard enough,' I said, feeling sick to my stomach.

'We're going to the police right now. And even the reports of you hurting the models will be enough to throw you in jail.'

'I said no.' Gent turned and grabbed Emma's arm, yanking her forwards into the studio where we stood. Where before he had been sinister in his calmness, now he was showing real anger. 'You will stay here while I think about what to do.'

As Emma edged towards Bet and me, there was a flash of something in Gent's hand and I realised, to my horror, he'd picked up a knife – a blade that had been lying on the table with the tools and canvases. 'Stay still,' he said, threatening each of us with the knife. It was small, but even from where I stood I could see it was sharp. Very sharp. 'I need to think.'

Emma let out a little gasp of fright and I took a deep, shuddering breath, my mind racing as I tried to think about what to do next.

'Listen,' said Bet, sounding jovial even though I could see her entire body was shaking. 'We know men have their, erm . . .' She looked at me, desperate for help.

'Their preferences,' I put in.

'Yes, that's it,' Bet said. 'And frankly it is no business of ours what a grown man does in his own house. Is it, Maggie?'

'No it is not.' I shook my head vigorously. 'No business whatsoever.'

'And I can't see what good us telling the coppers would do.'

Gent was still holding out the little knife but he looked slightly less intimidating.

'You're right, Bet,' I lied. 'If you'll let us leave, Mr Gent, we can just go about our days and forget this ever happened.'

There was a pause. Gent slowly lowered the knife.

'But what about my commission?' he said. 'From the queen?'

Emma, Bet and I all gawped at him.

'You still think . . .' I began.

'As I have said before, I am an artist of some repute,' said Gent, puffing out his scrawny chest. 'I have been recognised by Her Majesty, and I will not let you three harlots stop my career progression. You said it yourself, a man's preferences are his own private business.'

Stunned, we all stood stock-still for a second. And then Emma stepped forward.

'You are a disgusting man,' she said. 'The queen would no more be interested in you and your work than she would be interested in the manure the horses leave on the streets.'

Gent's expression darkened.

'Emma,' I said, trying to warn her not to say any more when we were so close to leaving. 'Don't . . .'

'Do you know what he did to me?' she said. Her eyes were filling with tears but she sounded more angry than upset. 'He showed me a picture he'd drawn of a woman and a man having intercourse. He watched them and he drew a picture. He made sure to tell me that. And then . . .' Her voice was shrill. 'And then he asked if Fred and I would like him to draw us.'

I glanced at Gent, who looked unrepentant.

'And then he licked me,' said Emma.

'Urgh,' said Bet. 'You dirty sod.'

'And yet the queen still wants me to help the police and work on these murders,' said Gent with a shrug.

'Oh for heaven's sake, we made it all up,' said Emma, sounding infuriated. 'The queen wouldn't know you from Adam.'

Gent roared in anger and jabbed the knife towards

Emma. She darted back, letting out another shriek of fear. 'Maybe I am the Whitechapel murderer,' he said, waving the knife wildly. 'Maybe I'll kill you all and slash your throats from ear to ear.'

Bet grabbed my arm, but I wasn't scared; I'd had enough. How dare this man, this awful man, try to scare us. 'Oh stop it,' I said. 'If you really were the murderer, you'd have killed us by now.' I glanced round at Bet and Emma. 'Come on, ladies,' I said. 'We're leaving.'

I breathed in, and with my head held high and my hands on my hips, I made to march past Gent.

'Stay. There,' he hissed, slashing the air in front of himself with the knife.

'We will not do as you tell us,' I said. Without looking at him, I barged past, sending him crashing against the wall. Bet and Emma followed me and together we walked down the hall to the front door. Gent didn't come after us. He didn't even make a sound. Which was . . . odd.

As we reached the end of the hall, I looked back. He was slumped on the floor, against the wall, not moving.

'Gent?' I said.

'What's wrong with him?' Emma said, her voice shaky. 'Why isn't he moving?'

'Gent?' I said again, louder this time.

Bet was standing very still, looking down the hallway. 'Is he pretending?' she said. 'Because it don't look like he's pretending.'

'I'm going to look,' I said.

Emma pulled my arm. 'No don't,' she said. 'He's going to leap up and attack you as soon as you get close. He's sneaky.'

'Gent?' I shouted this time, making Bet flinch at the sound of my voice. But still he didn't move. I looked at Emma. 'I don't think he's going to leap up.'

She gave me a nudge. 'Go on then,' she said. I took a step down the hall. 'Careful!' she said. 'Careful.'

Slowly, I crept along the tiled floor until I reached the doorway to the studio. 'Gent?' I said again. I crouched down and reached out, intending to touch his shoulder, then pulled my arm back fast as I noticed a pool of blood spreading out around him. The front of his paint-splatted tunic was soaked through, and a puddle was gathering on the floor.

'Oh bugger,' I sighed.

'What is it?' Bet came up behind me. 'Oh you're joking?'

'What's happened?' asked Emma, hurrying up the hall too. 'Oh my God, is he dead?'

I stood up, peering over the top of Gent's thinning hair to where the knife he'd been brandishing at us was now wedged into his chest. 'He's stabbed himself with that knife,' I said. 'It must have happened when he fell against the wall.'

'Oh, for the love of God,' said Bet, sounding genuinely exasperated. 'We've gone and killed another bloody man.'

# Chapter 27

## Bet

I should have been shocked. Or perhaps felt fear? Or guilt even? But actually I just felt a bit annoyed. Like this was a complication we could do without.

I nudged Gent with my toe.

'He's definitely dead,' I said with a sigh. 'What should we do now?'

Maggie ran her fingers through her hair and made the front stand up. 'Lord only knows,' she said. 'At least with Bernard we didn't need to worry about getting rid of the corpse.'

I looked down at the blood pooling on the tiles. 'There's a lot of mess to clean up this time.' I thought about my mop and bucket back at the police station. 'And we don't have any equipment.'

Emma had been standing very still and quiet next to me but now she spoke. 'What was it you saw?' she said. 'In the studio?'

'It was bad,' I told her. 'Awful paintings of the women, like Verity told us about. And . . .' I trailed off, not wanting to describe the picture of the model laid out like Annie.

'And?' Emma said.

I pinched my lips.

'And?' she said again.

I said nothing, and she sighed. 'Fine.' She hitched her

skirt up, stepped over Gent, and went into the studio. Maggie watched her go, widening her eyes in shock, and then followed, and after a second, I too stepped over Gent's splayed legs and went back to the studio.

Emma was standing over the painting that had fallen from the easel. I thought she'd be upset, or sickened, or any of the emotions I'd felt when I'd seen it, but instead she seemed unsurprised. As though she'd been expecting this.

'Right,' she said matter-of-factly. 'Well, this seems to me to be proof that this odious little monster was, in fact, the Whitechapel murderer.'

'That's what I thought.' Maggie nodded. 'But he claimed he was just interested in the killings. And I meant what I said back there. If he was the murderer, why didn't he just kill us right there and then?'

'He was outnumbered,' I pointed out. 'We could have fought back, unlike poor Annie or Polly.'

Emma snorted. 'He was the killer all right. What a twisted, evil man he was.'

'Twisted and evil or not, we do need to decide what we're going to do about this,' I said, nodding towards Gent. 'Because currently we're stuck in a house with a corpse and a load of creepy paintings, and frankly, it don't look good for us.'

Maggie groaned. 'You're right. What are we going to do with him?'

'Nothing,' said Emma. She clapped her hands together. 'We're going to leave him exactly as he is.'

'What?' I said, but Maggie was looking at Emma thoughtfully, her head to one side.

'Mrs Abberline, I believe you're on to something here.'

'We can't just leave him,' I said. 'Can we?'

'Look at the studio,' said Emma. 'What do you see?'

'I see a load of sick pictures.'

'What else?'

I looked at her blankly.

'It's as though someone's fallen,' she said. 'Overbalanced.' She gestured towards the fallen picture, the spilled water and broken jug.

'Someone did overbalance,' I said. 'But it weren't Gent.'

'That doesn't matter. Someone coming in here would see the spilled water – no doubt making the floor slippery – the broken jug and the dead man who, by the way, is holding the knife that is stuck in his own chest, and see a chain of events they have no reason to question.'

'Gosh you're good,' said Maggie sounding slightly awestruck. 'I'm glad you're on our side.'

Emma flashed her a quick smile. 'Gent said he had a housekeeper who was done for the day. I assume she'll come in tomorrow. She'll find him, then I assume she'll fetch a policeman, and once they see these paintings they'll think the same as we do.'

'And we'll be off the hook,' I said.

'Indeed.' Emma nodded. 'Do you remember if there was anyone around when we arrived?'

'Do your thing, Bet.' Maggie looked at me and I felt proud. I closed my eyes and remembered the sun on my face, the sweet taste of the cake on my lips as we'd gone up the stairs to Gent's front door.

'A carriage went by,' I said. 'But that was before we went up the steps.'

'Good,' said Maggie. 'Anything else? I don't remember seeing anyone, but I've been wrong before.'

I doubted that very much, but still I squeezed my eyes even more tightly, and thought. 'No,' I said eventually. 'It was quiet. There was someone in the gardens, I could hear shouts – children playing, I think. But there was no one on the street.'

'Good,' Maggie said, satisfied.

'Now we just have to get out again without being seen,' said Emma.

'There's a back gate.' I pointed out of the windows of the orangery to where there was a wooden door in the garden wall. 'We could go out there.'

Maggie was thinking. 'It must lead to an alleyway or cut-through between Finsbury Circus and London Wall,' she said. 'This is good. We can go in different directions and meet back at mine tomorrow.'

'Excellent.' Emma glanced back at Gent. 'And we don't have to step over him again. The last thing we want is to accidentally tread blood all over the place.'

'Emma,' I gasped, shocked by how matter-of-fact she was being, but she looked unapologetic.

'I know I went a bit wobbly last time,' she said. 'After Bernard. But that was the shock, and I was frightened, and he'd hurt me, and it was all so unexpected . . . well, it didn't work out how we'd planned, did it?'

'Nor did this,' Maggie said wryly.

Emma scratched her forehead. 'Well, no.'

'I understand,' I said, touching Emma's arm briefly. 'I really do. The first time was awful. We'd killed a man. Taken a life.' I gave her a small, thin-lipped smile. 'But it turns out we're learning from it, too. Just like the killer did.'

'Like Gent did,' said Maggie firmly. 'But it's over. We've put an end to it.'

'And I'm glad,' Emma said.

We stood there for a second and then I said: 'Shall we go then?'

'Let's,' said Emma. 'Have we got everything? There's nothing left to suggest we've been here?'

'Do you have the letter? From the queen?'

Emma nodded.

'We didn't have a drink so there are no cups to worry about,' Maggie said. She walked slightly closer to Gent and looked down. 'No footprints.'

'Good.' I went to the French windows and tried the handle. It was locked but I turned the key and I was relieved when the door opened with no trouble. 'Come on.'

We all filed outside, and I shut the door behind us. It would have to stay unlocked. I thought a policeman like Abberline might notice that and think it was odd, but perhaps not everyone would. We crossed the garden quietly. I could feel my heart hammering in my chest as we reached the gate. But that was locked too and this time there was no key in the lock.

I sighed heavily.

'No matter,' said Emma. 'We can go out the front if we're careful.'

But Maggie simply reached up and felt above the frame and there was a key.

'Wonderful,' I breathed. She unlocked the gate, which was a little stiff, and peeked out into the alleyway.

'There's no one around,' she said. So one by one we slid through the gate. Then Maggie locked it again and with an impressive overarm, threw the key over the wall. We heard it drop softly into the garden.

'Knocked off the frame by a squirrel or a bird,' she said.

'Or a rat,' said Emma pointedly.

'I'll go that way,' Maggie said. 'You two go the other way and separate as soon as you can. Be seen. Talk to people, pop into a shop if you can.'

'It's becoming a habit, this, ain't it?' I said, only half joking.

'Let's hope not.'

We stood for a moment in the alley, looking at one another.

'So this is it,' I said sadly. 'Again.'

Maggie looked at me with consideration.

'Bet,' she said. 'I was thinking. Only if you're interested, of course, and I can't pay you, not at the moment, but perhaps one day . . .'

'What?' I asked. I had no idea what she was trying to say. 'Interested in what?'

'Would you like to come and work as my assistant?' Maggie said. 'When you have time. I can train you. Teach you everything I know about being a detective.'

I stared at her, so utterly thrilled I found I didn't have the words to accept. 'I . . .'

'Is that a yes?' Maggie said.

'Yes,' I said, finding my voice. 'Yes please. I'd love that. I really would.'

'That's settled then. I'll be in touch.'

Maggie gave Emma and me a brief nod, turned and headed off along the alley.

'Oh my,' I breathed in delight. Emma took my arm and squeezed it.

'Good things can come from bad,' she said.

'Who'd have thought it, eh?'

We walked along Houndsditch together, chatting about Maggie's offer and all the things she could teach me, then when we approached Whitechapel, we paused, ready to go our separate ways.

'Where are you going now?' I asked Emma.

'I'm going to go into the bakery, then I'll head home. Hopefully Fred will be back soon.'

'My mother should be home as well.' I gave her a small smile. 'We'll be seen.'

'Indeed.'

We hugged, and I thought how odd it was that we two women – more than twenty years apart in age, and worlds

234

apart in background – had been brought together by such an awful thing.

I walked away, giving Emma a wave, and headed south, past the police station. It would do no harm, I thought, if any constables happened to see me.

As I sauntered on, thinking about everything that had happened, a figure loomed out of the darkening evening in front of me and I shrieked in surprise.

'It's me,' he said, taking off his hat. 'Sorry to frighten you.'

'Oh, Constable Green.' I breathed out in relief. For a moment I'd thought I was about to be arrested, and I felt my heart pounding. 'I was away with the fairies there.'

He smiled at me and I thought how boyish he was, despite the fact that he had to be a decade older than I was.

'Please, call me Silas. What were you thinking about?'

*The men I've killed*, I thought. 'Just, life,' I said instead. *And death*.

'Are you going home?' Silas offered me his arm. 'Can I walk you there? It's getting dark and I don't like to think of you out here alone with a murderer still on the loose. It's not safe.'

*It's fine*, I thought. *The murderer is no more.*

'Thank you,' I said. I put my hand in the crook of his elbow, enjoying the feeling of his strong arm under the rough fabric of his uniform. 'It's not far.'

We walked past a newspaper vendor, and I saw the front page was still shouting about the murders.

'Silas,' I began. 'Do people ever ask you constables for information about the murders?'

'Journalists, you mean?'

'Well, yes, but there seem to be a lot of folk who are very interested in the crimes. Worryingly so, in my opinion.'

He looked at me either in amusement or bemusement, I couldn't tell.

'Worryingly?'

'Well, it ain't healthy, is it? To be so fascinated by poor women's gruesome deaths.'

'These killings have captured the imagination of the public, I'll grant you,' Silas said.

'And do people ask you about it?' I paused. 'Or even offer to pay you for information?'

Silas scoffed. 'No,' he said. 'Well, they don't ask me. But perhaps they ask others . . .'

The implication hung in the air, and I wondered if he meant Percival, but we were approaching my rooms. I thought for a second about pretending I lived elsewhere to extend our walk, but I was exhausted and my feet hurt and the lure of getting home and into bed was stronger than my desire to keep walking with Silas.

'This is me,' I said.

'Bet, I wondered if you might like to go out with me one evening,' Silas said. 'Perhaps to the music hall, if you like that?'

I had never been to the music hall, and I had no idea if I'd like it, but I did like Silas, so I smiled. 'Yes please.'

'Saturday night?'

'Yes please,' I said again. *Good things can come from bad*, I thought.

'Excellent.' He leaned forward and for a thrilling second I thought he might kiss me, and I felt a little dizzy just from the closeness of him. But he didn't. Instead, he simply said: 'I will see you tomorrow. Sleep well.'

'I will,' I said. 'You too.'

# Chapter 28

## Maggie

Once more, I was at a loose end. I was again lacking enthusiasm for divorces and petty thefts, though I'd resisted the urge to drink myself to sleep.

I got up at my usual time, ate some breakfast in lacklustre fashion, then sat at my desk and stared at the pile of papers I didn't want to read. Then I stared out of the window for a while. And then I got up and I looked at all the things we'd stuck up on the wall.

I thought about Gent, considering the awful, shocking nature of his pictures, the way he'd treated Emma, and his absolute protestations that he wasn't the killer. Then I went back to the window and looked out for a bit longer.

'Are you still out there?' I murmured to myself, peering down at the men and women walking by. 'Or did we get you?'

Realising I wasn't going to get anything done, I picked up my coat and hat.

I would go and see George, I thought. I'd see how he was doing with his patrols and his vigilance committee. If we'd got things right – I shuddered as the thought we might have got things wrong hit me once more – the murders would stop. But I hoped the vigilance committee would continue all the same. After all, if the experiences of we wicked women of Whitechapel had taught me anything, it was that these streets were teeming with bad men. We needed more chaps like George.

I plodded down the stairs, pulling on my coat as I went, and stepped outside into the chilly morning air. Autumn had definitely arrived now, though summer hadn't had a look-in really. I pulled my coat tighter and walked on.

George wasn't at home, but one of his children – a sandy-haired girl who eyed me suspiciously – told me he was working at the music hall on Commercial Street. So off I went. I found George round the back, watching a lad, with sandy hair just like the girl's, rounding off a piece of wood into a perfect sphere.

'That's it,' he was saying. 'You've got that now.'

The lad – well, he was a young man really – held up the ball and George looked impressed.

'Well done.' He ruffled the lad's hair – he had to reach up to do so – and, laughing, the young man ducked away.

'Morning,' I said.

'Hello there, Maggie.' He turned to the boy. 'Alf, do you remember Maggie? She used to live next door.'

'This is never your Alfred?'

'It's me,' said Alf. 'But I don't remember you, sorry.'

'It was a long time ago. You were only this big the last time I saw you.' I held my palm out flat, just below waist height.

He shook my hand. 'Well, it's nice to meet you.'

'You too.'

Alf turned to his dad. 'I'm going to go and measure up for that cabinet inside,' he said. 'You go and catch up with Maggie. You're on patrol soon anyway, ain't you?'

'I am.' George began taking off his apron. 'Thanks, son. I'll see you later.'

Alf nodded to me, then he took his ball of wood and went into the musical hall.

'What a charming lad he's turned out to be.'

'A credit to his mother,' George said, beaming with pride. 'Hard-working, polite . . . all the boys are the same.'

I thought that boys followed in their dad's footsteps and that if the lads were like that, it was probably a lot to do with George, but I simply smiled. 'You must be very proud of all of them. I hope they're coping with the loss of their mother.'

'Helping one another,' George said. 'That's another thing I'm proud of.'

He folded his apron up neatly and put it in his bag.

'What can I do for you, Maggie?'

I followed him round the side of the music hall and out into the street.

'I was just being nosy, really,' I said. 'I wanted to see how your vigilance committee was getting on.'

'It's going well.' He made a face. 'I wish it wasn't necessary, but we seem to be making a difference.'

'Good for you.' I walked round a puddle. 'I bet people – women – are pleased when they see your lot out and about.'

'I hope so.' He smiled at me. 'Are you busy today?'

'Not very.'

'Want to come to mine for a cuppa?'

'Yes, all right.'

'And then perhaps you can come along on my patrol this afternoon.'

'Really?'

He shrugged. 'Why not?'

I was pleased. 'Go on then.'

We walked back to his house and I met Edith – the girl I'd seen at the house earlier – who was much less suspicious when I turned up with her father. She had to go and collect the littlest child – Lil – from school.

'I want to be a teacher,' she told me. 'So I like to go and

chat with them there, help them out a bit, make myself useful, because I think they might offer me a job.'

'She's very clever, my Edith,' said George. 'Very quick with numbers, good with words, reads any book she can get her hands on. Susannah was determined that all the children should learn to read.'

'Susannah was a clever woman,' I said in approval, looking at Edith. 'You clearly take after your mother.'

Edith flushed, but she smiled. 'I'll be home later,' she said.

I watched her go, feeling a rare prickle of envy at a family. That was another thing Ralph had robbed me of. And now my chance to be a mother had passed. Not that I minded most of the time. I had my girls, and now my women of Whitechapel too; I was looking forward to Bet becoming my assistant. But George's family were so nice to one another. He was clearly very proud of all of them, and they seemingly thought the world of him too. I couldn't help wondering for a moment what it would be like to have such a thing.

'What are you thinking about?' George asked me, sounding amused. 'You were deep in thought there.'

'I was thinking about families,' I told him honestly. 'You have a lovely one.'

'I do.' He touched my hand very quickly. 'You and Ralph didn't ever . . .'

'No.'

I didn't tell him that the one time I did think I was expecting, Ralph punched me in the stomach so hard that when the bleeding started I wasn't even surprised. And things were never really the same after that, and I thought perhaps he'd done some damage inside that had stopped me ever falling pregnant again.

He looked at me for a second, and I thought he was

going to ask more, but then he drained his mug of tea. 'Shall we go and join the patrol?'

We met in a back room at the Crown – a group of four men and me.

'We do shifts,' George explained. 'I do the early ones because I like to be home in the evenings for the children. It's mostly the younger men who do the late ones.'

There were sticks – like policemen's truncheons – for the patrol to arm themselves with, and they had blue sashes they wore over their coats to make sure everyone knew who they were.

'The police ain't investigating properly,' said one of the patrol members, who George called Chip. He wasn't a big man, but his eyes were sharp and his muscles lean, and he bounced on his toes, like he was ready to run for miles. 'We want them to offer a reward.'

'Do you think that would help?'

'Someone must have seen something,' he said. 'But no one's talking. They might if they got a bit of cash for it.'

'True.' I thought about Gent saying the police gave him information about the killings for a price. 'Do you think someone's helping him? The killer.'

Chip shrugged. 'Perhaps. There's got to be more to it.'

George handed Chip a stick. 'You do south of Whitechapel High Street,' he said. 'Like yesterday. It's good that people are getting used to seeing you around.'

'Righto, guv,' said Chip. He looked at me. 'Who do you think it is?'

I was amused and impressed that he thought I would have a theory.

'I heard there's an artist . . .' I began.

Chip shook his head. 'Nah.'

'Nah?'

'It's the doctor.'

241

My ears pricked up. Hadn't the queen herself suggested the killer could be a doctor?

'Which doctor? Does he work at a hospital?'

'He ain't a real doctor.'

'A quack?'

'A monster,' Chip said. He sounded quite gleeful. 'Obsessed with women's insides, he is.'

'Chip,' George said in a warning tone. 'We don't know that for a fact.'

'Oh, I do know. Flo, my sister's mate, she went to see him and she was lucky to get out of there alive.'

I remembered Bet saying she'd heard people talk about a doctor when we'd been chatting in the tearoom – the girls from the brothel had told her.

'Is he American?' I asked.

Chip looked delighted. 'That's him.'

'Chip, it's getting dark,' said George. 'Go on.'

Chip waved his stick at us cheerfully and headed for the door. 'Nice to meet you, darling,' he said.

'You too.' I chuckled. 'He's a character,' I said, as George rummaged around in a cupboard and pulled out another sash.

'Isn't he just?' He handed me the sash. 'Put this on.'

Absurdly pleased, I looped it over my head. 'I'm one of you now,' I said.

'Lord help us.'

'Can I have a stick?'

'Really?'

'Yes.'

A little reluctantly, George found one of those too and I took it. It was pleasingly heavy in my hands and I gave it a few practice swipes through the air.

'Careful,' said George. 'We need to be responsible.'

'Oh, shush.'

He laughed. 'Maggie Cameron, you never change.'

'Where are we going?'

'North of the high street.'

'Near where Martha was found?'

'That's it. We won't go as far east as where Polly was, though. Philip's doing that section.'

'Right.' I thought about how far Polly's murder site was from where Gent lived, and once more I felt that tiny prickle of unease. I pushed it aside.

'Shall we go?'

It was rather fun being out on patrol with George. He knew everyone, and those he didn't, I knew. We strolled along, eyes and ears open, chatting with passers-by and listening to their worries. And when we reached Brick Lane, I saw Mildred, one of my girls, chatting to another – much younger – woman.

'Oh, Maggie, look at you, all official,' Mildred said. 'Are you a copper now?'

I laughed. 'No.'

'They'd be lucky to have you.'

'Wouldn't they just,' said George.

I gave him a quick smile, enjoying the praise.

'Are you arresting the bad men?' asked Mildred.

*Arresting them? No*, I thought. *Killing them? Yes.*

'We're hoping the bad men stay away,' I said.

The other woman tapped my arm. 'Who do you think it is?' she said. 'The killer.'

'Oh, I don't know,' I said vaguely. 'Could be anyone.'

'Or no one,' she said.

'It can't be no one.' Mildred frowned. 'That makes no sense.'

'Well, it's everyone then,' said the young woman. 'Loads of people. All copying each other. One does it, then another one thinks "oh that sounds like fun" and soon he's doing it too. And they're getting famous off it, ain't they? All over the newspapers. They're probably loving it.'

'And Lord knows there are enough horrible blokes round here,' added Mildred.

I stared at them both. That thought had never so much as crossed my mind. What if we weren't looking for one killer, but lots of them? What if it had been Gent? *And* Bernard? And more? I felt sick suddenly.

But then I thought about all the details of the post-mortems that had never made it into the newspapers, and the injuries that were the same on Martha's body and Annie's and Polly's, and I felt a bit calmer.

George nudged me. 'That's him,' he said into my ear.

I frowned. 'Who?'

He was nodding towards an older man – in his sixties, I guessed – with a handlebar moustache. He was wearing a dark coat, with speckles of a lighter colour, and a smart hat and he was coming out of a pharmacy carrying a parcel. He looked rich, and he looked like he was pleased about that.

'That's the American doctor Chip was talking about. Timothy, I think his name is.'

I watched as the man walked away from us. Despite his age, he was straight-backed and quick on his feet.

'He doesn't look like a monster,' I said.

'Well, that's the trouble, isn't it?' said George. 'The real monsters never look that way.'

'Indeed,' I said.

Mildred and her friend were still chatting.

'I've heard,' said the young woman, leaning in towards me and George. 'I've heard that some of the people who live in the posh parts of London didn't know what places like Whitechapel were like, 'fore they saw all them stories in the papers.'

Mildred nodded wisely. 'They ain't got a clue how we live round here.'

The young woman grinned. 'My mum's mate, she's a housekeeper for some posh family up the West End. She reckons they're all talking about the murders – they've all got theories about who did it. So they asked her if she'd give them a tour of Whitechapel – show her where the dead women were found.'

'Oh, Lord,' I said with a shudder. 'Did she?'

'Too right. She got her sister to charge them a pretty penny to have a nose round her rooms 'n' all. Now the whole street's at it – inviting the posh ones round. Charging them a fortune, they are.'

George chuckled. 'That's quite enterprising. Might try it myself.'

But I shuddered at the thought of people making money from women's misery, and well-to-do folk gawking at Whitechapel residents like we were there for their entertainment. 'Ain't right,' I muttered. Filled with rage suddenly, I brandished my stick. 'Come on, George. Let's go and find some bad men.'

# Chapter 29

## Emma

For once, Fred and I enjoyed breakfast together, chatting over our food like we used to do before the murders became all-consuming.

I felt proud that we'd helped him – taken some of the load from his back – and that now his brow might unfurrow. Though I was disappointed that I couldn't tell him what we'd done. Couldn't ever tell him. I pushed away the worry that keeping this huge secret might damage our marriage somehow. Fred and I were solid. We were lucky to have found one another and we had survived losing Rose, and my troubles afterwards. We were happy. Perhaps not as happy as we would have been if Rose was still with us. But we were content, just the two of us. Nothing would change that.

'Are you going to the police station now?' I asked as Fred got up from the table.

'I am,' he said. 'There is still so much to do.'

'Perhaps it's over,' I said vaguely. 'Perhaps the killer has had his fill.'

'Perhaps.' Fred looked doubtful. He gave me a kiss. 'I'll be home later, hopefully.'

*You will be*, I thought.

'Fingers crossed,' I said.

He headed off to work, and I pottered around, re-arranging some of the furniture, bundling up some laundry, picking up a book, reading one page, then putting it down again, until eventually I thought I would go for a walk. It was quite a nice day – though it looked chilly – and it would be a distraction. A way to keep my mind off Gent. Though I really hadn't been lying when I told Maggie and Bet that I wasn't bothered by his death. I could still feel the rasp of his tongue on my cheek, and I'd scrubbed my face until it glowed pink when I'd got home, trying to get rid of the smell of him. The paintings in his studio had been shocking and I was pretty sure they proved his guilt. London was a better place now he was gone.

I put on my coat and hat, and went outside. It was mild, almost warmer than it had been all summer, and I was soon feeling too hot in my winter clothes. I stopped on the corner to take off my shawl, and my eye was caught by a newspaper seller. He was shouting out the news and I heard him call 'Artist found dead!'

I stood still. Did he mean . . .

Quickly I fished a coin from my purse and bought a copy and yes, there on the front page of the *Post* was the headline *Artist Walter Gent found dead in strange accident at home.*

'Accident,' I murmured. This was good. I scanned the story. There was no mention of his paintings, nor any link to him being the Whitechapel murderer, but still.

I thought about going to see Maggie, then thought again. I was very close to the police station, so I thought I'd visit Fred first – see if he knew anything.

He was in his office, looking out of the window.

'This is a nice surprise,' he said as I entered.

'I was just passing,' I fibbed. I showed him the newspaper. 'And I saw this and wondered what it was all about?'

'Ah,' he said. 'I might have known you had an ulterior motive.'

'It just sounded . . . curious,' I said. 'A strange accident. Do you know anything about it?'

'I do, as it happens.'

'Did you go?'

He shook his head. 'Not our patch. At least, not at first. Harrison's been here this morning so he told us all about it. And he recruited Green to go and stand guard outside Gent's house.'

'I bet he loved that, looking all important to the passers-by.'

'Undoubtedly.' Fred reached for the newspaper and began to read the story. 'The newspapers don't know the details, then.'

'Details appear to be fairly thin on the ground.' I sat down at his desk. 'What happened?'

'His housekeeper found him this morning.' Fred looked sombre. 'But we think he died last night. It seemed he was cutting canvases and slipped on some spilled water. Somehow, as he fell, he stabbed himself with the blade.'

'Oh my,' I said. 'Goodness.'

'Just one of those things.'

'What did you mean when you said it wasn't on your patch at first?'

'Ah,' Fred said. He steepled his fingers and tapped them on his chin. 'Ah.'

'Fred,' I said in frustration. 'What does that mean?'

'Mr Gent was apparently very interested in the Whitechapel murders,' said Fred with a sigh. 'Unhealthily interested.'

'How do you know?'

'He had painted pictures of women in positions just like the victims were in when they were found.'

'Women?' I repeated. We'd only seen the painting of the one who looked like Annie. Were there more?

'Several of them.'

'Pictures of the murders?'

'In a way. Really, you'd only make the connection if you'd read the post-mortems or had seen the victims when they died.'

'Good Lord.' I was genuinely shocked that there were more of those awful pictures.

'The housekeeper is a little mousy woman herself. Clearly terrified half to death of him. She said she heard models crying and always made sure they were all right when she could.'

'But she didn't report the awful paintings?'

'Well, firstly she hadn't seen them – she said his studio was off limits to her. She wasn't allowed in. And she wasn't about to go against his word.'

'And secondly?'

'Even if she had seen the paintings, she wouldn't have made the link between the pictures and the murders.'

'Because she wouldn't have read the reports or seen the women when they died.'

'Exactly.' Fred rubbed his forehead.

'But Gent knew how the women looked when they were found?'

'Apparently so.'

'Does that mean Gent . . . was he . . .'

'The killer?'

'Yes.'

Fred took a breath. 'I think not.'

My stomach lurched. 'But you said yourself, the only way to know these women were posed like the victims were if you were there when they died . . .'

'According to the housekeeper, Gent has a wife in Paris.'

'A wife?' The man I'd met hadn't struck me as the domestic type.

'She is older than him – considerably so – and rich. I believe their arrangement suited both.'

'But him having a wife doesn't stop him being the murderer?'

'I'm afraid it does, because he was in Paris with the wife when both Martha and Mary Ann – Polly – were killed.'

The room swam before my eyes. 'And have you . . . will you . . . check? Do you have proof?'

'We have constables going through passenger manifests on the ships the housekeeper believes he took, and I have telegraphed the Parisian police.'

'He could have lied,' I pointed out. 'Told everyone he was going to Paris, only to stay in London and start his killing spree.'

Fred looked faintly amused. 'Yes, that had occurred to me. We'll find out either way. Are you all right, Emma?'

I gripped the edge of the desk. 'Yes,' I said faintly. 'Quite all right, thank you. What do you think?'

'I think you look rather pale.'

'I didn't mean what do you think about me,' I said, sounding more irritated than I'd intended. 'About Gent. Do you think he was the murderer?'

'I don't.' Fred tapped the end of his pen on the desk. 'I think he was an unpleasant man with an unhealthy interest in these killings, but I think he really was in France. But if he wasn't the murderer, then my question is, how did he come to have the information that enabled him to draw such horribly accurate depictions of the murder victims?'

I took a breath. 'Was Gent a wealthy man?'

'I believe he was a gentleman of considerable means, yes.'

I nodded. 'Someone told me that if you have enough money, then you can buy anything.'

Fred gave me a sharp look. 'That's very cynical for you, Emma.'

I shrugged. 'It's true.'

'Sadly, it is true. So you think Gent bought this information? But from whom?'

'Someone in this police station?'

'No,' Fred said. 'No one would do that.'

I raised an eyebrow. 'Are you sure?'

'What are you suggesting? Not Dr Llewellyn?'

'No,' I scoffed. 'Someone further down the ranks. A constable, perhaps?'

'Emma, you're out of line here,' Fred said. 'I am responsible for all my officers, and I trust them.'

'But how well do you know them?' I leaned forward across the desk. 'I mean, really know them? There are new policemen who have joined since you last worked here. This isn't your team, Fred. It's someone else's.'

'But just because I didn't recruit everyone personally it doesn't mean . . .'

'Bet said Percival speaks terribly about the women,' I blurted. 'She says he talks in very unpleasant ways, and he seems gleeful about their fate. What if he's been pocketing money from Gent and passing on information about the victims?'

Fred's expression hardened. 'Emma, this is too much.'

But I wasn't stopping now I'd started. 'He doesn't like women,' I said. 'He was rude to me, and I saw him with an unfortunate woman, shoving her up against a wall. I'm positive if anyone has been selling information to Gent, it's Percival.'

'Constable Percival . . .' Fred began, emphasising the Constable, 'has been away from the station for a few days.

Unfortunately, his mother is very ill and he has gone to be with her.'

'Well, that's convenient, isn't it?'

'Emma!' Fred sounded genuinely shocked. 'I think you should go. I've got a lot of work to do.'

I picked up my bag. 'Fine. I'll see you later.'

Fred didn't answer and when I glanced back, his head was bent over his notes.

'Fine,' I said again.

I tossed my hair back and marched out of the office and down the corridor. At the end was a larger room used for meetings. The door was open and as I walked by I could see several policemen all standing round the table in the middle, looking at something. Intrigued, I took a step closer to the open door. It looked like artwork piled on the table. Were they all peering at Gent's paintings? I stepped closer again.

'Emma?'

I jumped and looked round to see Fred standing in the doorway to his office, glaring at me.

'I thought you were going home?'

'I'm going.'

'Then go.'

Annoyed, I didn't respond, just marched on, through the entrance to the police station, out of the doors and down the stairs on to the street.

I felt cross and prickly and rather uneasy. Was Gent really innocent of the murders, or was his trip to Paris a cover for his actions? Was Percival's mother truly ill, or was that another convenient excuse? Having been so sure of both men's guilt, suddenly I had no idea anymore.

With my head spinning, I decided there was only one thing to do – go and see Maggie and see what she thought.

I headed off to her office, but she wasn't there. I was

cross about that too. So, disgruntled and grumpy, I turned on my heels, intending to go home to stew about everything that had happened.

As I walked, I gradually became aware that I was following two soldiers who were chatting loudly.

*Flaming men*, I thought to myself, irritated by the world. *Making their presence felt everywhere. Taking up too much room.*

'They dragged him out of the river,' one soldier was saying. 'But ain't no one sorry about it.'

I went cold, all my irritation suddenly forgotten. I hurried my steps so I would catch them up and hear them better.

'He won't be missed,' the other soldier agreed. 'Reckon he had a lot of enemies, the way he carried on – it's bound to be one of them that pushed him in.'

'Word is, he got drunk and slipped.'

'Don't matter, does it? Fact is, we're well rid of Private Hill.'

The soldiers walked on, but I stopped still. So they'd found Bernard at last. Perhaps our time was up. After all, we had killed two men. Two innocent men. Almost innocent. I screwed my face up. Not innocent exactly, but not guilty of the crimes we accused them of. Were we about to pay the price?

# Chapter 30

## Bet

It wasn't often I was lost for words, but when I stepped inside the music hall – Foresters, it was called – there was a good couple of minutes when I simply couldn't speak.

'You all right?' Silas said as we made our way through the lobby.

I didn't answer. I was too busy looking up at the huge, high ceiling with its ornate carvings, and the pretty painted walls.

'It's enormous,' I said in awe.

'You're going to hurt your neck, looking up like that,' Silas said, sounding amused. 'Come on. If you think this is good, wait until you see the main auditorium.'

'Auditorium,' I repeated, rolling the unfamiliar word around my mouth. 'Show me.'

Eager to see, I took Silas's hand to hurry him along and felt his fingers close round mine, as though they were meant to be there. It felt nice. I smiled at him and he smiled back and inside I felt warm and happy. Content, even.

I tugged his arm. 'Come on,' I said.

Inside it was even better. More ornate. There were seats in rows in the middle, and at the sides were tables with waitresses serving drinks.

'The show won't start for a while,' Silas said, pulling out his pocket watch. 'Shall we get a drink first?'

I nodded, still looking in wonder at my surroundings. 'I didn't know it would be like this,' I breathed.

'You've not been here before?'

I laughed. 'No. Music halls ain't for the likes of us.'

'But it's just normal people,' Silas said, with a frown that made him look much younger. 'Constables like me. Shop assistants. Clerks.'

'Now this is where I can see you're not a Londoner,' I teased. 'Because if you were, you'd know there's the well-to-do folk up here . . .' I held my arm up, level with my head, my hand flat. 'Then there's the ones like Inspector Abberline and his wife.' I dropped my hand, so it was level with my chin, then again to my chest. 'Then there's your shop assistants and constables . . .' Now my hand was down beside my stomach. 'And then there's us.'

Silas grabbed my hand. 'Well, you're here now,' he said. He brought my fingers to his lips and kissed them and my legs went weak. 'And I'm glad.'

'Evening, Constable.'

We both turned to see a large older gentleman with fading blond hair standing nearby.

'Hello, Mr Lusk.' Silas smiled but it wasn't his usual smile because it didn't quite reach his eyes. 'Bet, this is George Lusk. Mr Lusk, this is my friend, Bet Palmer.'

Mr Lusk shook my hand vigorously. 'Hello, there. Enjoying your evening?'

'Oh, it's wonderful,' I said. 'I've never been here before and I can't believe how beautiful it is. Look at the carvings on the walls.'

'I made those,' Mr Lusk said. 'Well, some of them.'

'You did?'

Mr Lusk held out his hands. 'I've got the callouses to prove it.'

I chuckled. 'It must be so difficult. It's a real skill.'

'I've been doing it a long time,' Mr Lusk said. 'Training my boy up now. He's already better than I am . . .'

'Shall I get us some drinks, Bet?' Silas interrupted us. He was holding his wallet and I could see there were several notes inside. It made me think I'd put constables on too low a footing in my rough description of London's class system.

'Yes please,' I said.

'Have a seat,' Silas nodded towards some tables. He didn't ask what I wanted to drink, which was a relief actually, because I didn't know what I wanted. Instead, he simply turned and headed towards the bar. Mr Lusk watched him go for a moment and then turned to me.

'If you look at the end of each bit of coving,' he said, 'you'll see a cat.'

'A cat?'

He nodded. 'Look, there at the end. See it?'

I gazed up and sure enough, now I knew it was there, I could see a carving of a sleeping cat, curled up like a spiral.

'Oh I see it!' I said in delight. 'Why is there a cat there?'

'It's my signature. I can't write George Lusk on there, obviously, so I put a cat on all my work.'

'That's lovely. And now I can look out for it all over London.'

'You can.' George smiled at me. 'And you can say "my friend George Lusk made that".'

'George Lusk,' I repeated. The name was familiar. 'George Lusk! You know my friend Maggie Cameron.'

George looked downcast suddenly. 'I do know Maggie,' he said. 'She's an impressive woman.'

'She is.' I looked at him. 'Why the sad face?'

'I'm afraid I let her down once, a long time ago.'

I put my hand on his arm. 'She told me you were a good man.'

'She said that?' He looked pleased.

'She did.'

'I was with her yesterday,' he told me. 'She came out on patrol.'

My eyes widened. 'She never did.'

'Oh, she did.'

'She must have loved that.'

'Every minute.'

I chuckled. 'Did you catch any bad men?'

'No,' he said, shaking his head. 'I think Maggie was a bit disappointed.'

'I've got the drinks.' Silas appeared next to us. 'I thought you were going to sit down.'

'I got chatting,' I said.

'I'm going to go and let you get on with your evening,' George said. 'It was lovely to meet you, Bet.' He glanced from me to Silas and then back to me. 'If you need anything, come and find me.'

'I will,' I said, slightly confused.

'Constable.' He nodded at Silas.

'Mr Lusk.'

I waited until George had melted away into the groups of people and we'd sat down before I said: 'You don't like him?'

'I don't dislike him,' Silas said. 'He's just a busybody who makes our lives harder.'

'He seemed nice.'

'Harrison can't stand him.' Silas took a mouthful of drink. 'Says he's interfering.'

Privately I thought that if Harrison disliked someone then that probably meant they were a good person, but Silas seemed to admire his superior officer greatly. So I kept my mouth shut.

'Let's finish these drinks and find a better seat in the

middle,' Silas said. 'There are some acrobats on tonight that I think you'll enjoy.'

We drained our glasses, chatting about this and that, and then made our way to the middle of the room and sat down just as the curtain went up.

I had never, in all my days, seen a spectacle like the music hall. It was glorious. The acrobats made me shriek in amazement as they threw one another around.

'I told you you'd enjoy them,' Silas whispered.

But it wasn't just the acrobats I loved. I enjoyed every minute of it. The singers were astonishing – their voices echoing round the huge room – the comic acts had me crying with laughter. Silas had to pass me his handkerchief to wipe my eyes. I handed it back and he said: 'Keep it.' So I tucked it into the pocket of my skirt.

There was an odd chap – small, with a neat moustache – who stuck his hands in his pockets and sang a very funny song about being rich and drinking champagne. He was a clever mimic and I watched him closely, thinking how talented he was. But there was something else about him . . .

'Silas?' I said towards the end of the song. 'Is that man . . . is he a girl?'

Silas laughed loudly. 'He is. Or rather she is. Her name is Matilda, I believe.'

My jaw dropped. 'Well, I never.'

'That moustache is a smudge of ash from the fire.' Silas chuckled. 'It's very clever.'

'Goodness me, what will they think of next,' I said, clapping wildly as Matilda finished her song.

I was sorry when the acts came to an end, and delighted when Silas said we could come back again.

'Have you been here a lot?' I asked him as we joined the crowds streaming towards the doors.

'Not a lot, but I come occasionally. It's always a fun night. We didn't have any music halls in Guildford.'

'You're getting to know the delights of London.' I tucked my arm into his, feeling bold, and he looked down at me.

'I certainly am,' he said.

We strolled back through Whitechapel.

'Want another drink?' Silas asked.

I shook my head. 'Early start in the morning. Are you working?'

'I am,' he said reluctantly. 'I'll walk you home – it's not safe on these streets at this hour.'

*It's safer than it was*, I thought. 'Yes please,' I said. I didn't want our evening to end just yet.

'You're safe with me.' Silas pulled me closer to him and my heart thumped. In my experience men were to be feared. Treated with caution. Avoided as much as possible. My dad had been attentive and fun when I was little – until he wasn't. He could change with the weather, going from jovial to frightening in a moment. And goodness me, hadn't we seen the worst of the men in Whitechapel these past few weeks? But Inspector Abberline was a good, kind, clever man. I felt safer knowing he was around. And perhaps, perhaps, Silas made me feel the same way.

'Anything new happening with the murders?' I asked casually, enjoying the feeling of Silas's warm body against mine. I was keen to know if anyone knew anything of Walter Gent's death.

'This artist – name of Gent – was found dead at home,' Silas said, sounding rather excited by it. 'It's really interesting, actually.'

'Was he a murder victim?' I asked, keeping my eyes on the road ahead and my voice level.

'No, Llewellyn doesn't reckon so. Just an accident. Silly sod slipped on some water while he was holding a knife.'

'So what does he have to do with the murders?' I asked.

'He was obsessed with the killings.' Silas slowed his steps as he spoke, really emphasising his words. 'Obsessed.'

'What does that mean?'

Now Silas stopped walking altogether. 'He painted women in the poses of the murder victims,' he said. 'Like they were when they died.'

'That's horrible.'

'He was an odd one all right.'

'Did you know him?'

'No,' Silas shook his head vigorously. 'No. Why would I know an artist? But I've seen the paintings. I went to the house – Harrison sent me.' He sounded proud.

'So you think this artist was the killer?' I said innocently. 'If he had a knife and he knew about the victims . . .'

'That's what I said,' Silas said. His expression darkened and for a moment, in the shadows from the street lamp, he looked older and angrier than usual. 'I said he had to be the killer. But Abberline says he isn't.'

'Abberline says he isn't?' I repeated in surprise, my voice shrill. My mouth went dry. 'Why would he think that?'

'According to Mr Gent's housekeeper, he had a wife in Paris and he was off visiting her when some of the women were killed.'

'And do you know that's true?'

'Yes, well, Abberline is checking.'

I gripped Silas's arm more tightly and we started walking again.

'So if Gent was in Paris, then he can't be the killer?'

'No.'

'And that means the real murderer is still lurking?'

'I suppose so.'

'And that means . . .' I began. But I didn't get to finish my sentence because Silas suddenly leaned down and kissed me firmly on the lips.

'Sorry,' he said. 'You just looked so beautiful, I couldn't resist.'

'Don't apologise.' I gazed up at him. 'It was lovely.'

He kissed me again, and I let myself melt into him, all thoughts of Gent forgotten.

# Chapter 31

## Liz

Sometimes Liz thought she had spent her whole life keeping secrets. *Lying* might be a better word for it. As a child, her mother had always scolded her when she lied. 'Don't tell tall tales,' she would say, often giving Liz a clip round the ear at the same time.

But Liz never learned not to lie. She just learned to get better at it.

She lied to her husband about being free of disease, to her friend Mary about being her long-lost sister, to the kind-hearted folk who gave her money after she lost her husband and two of their nine children in the *Princess Alice* riverboat accident . . . Not that Liz had ever had nine children, of course. And though she had once had a husband who was now six feet under, he hadn't been dead back then. And neither he nor Liz had been anywhere near the *Princess Alice* when it sank.

Her life had been one big tangle of lies and deceit. And now Liz's mind was increasingly foggy and sometimes it felt as though all of the things she claimed happened, really had, and they weren't tall tales at all. And sometimes she couldn't tell what was truth and what was lies.

Now it felt as though it was all beginning to unravel. Her memory was muddled. She had times when she wasn't sure what she'd been doing or where she'd been. It frightened her a little at first. Now she just let it happen. What else could she do?

She wasn't sure if her confusion was because of the disease she'd once had – though even her memories of that were faint now – or because of Michael.

Liz had loved Michael at first. He'd been everything her husband Jonah wasn't. He was younger than she was. Lean and muscled from his job at the docks. Jonah had been older, more brains than brawn, though his hands were calloused from carpentry and his arms sinewy.

But Michael was handy with his fists, and when he lost his temper, he lost it badly. More than once Liz had found herself sprawled on the floor, hours after he'd lashed out. Battered, bruised, her memories of what had happened hazy.

She tried to get away, but he always tracked her down and begged her to come back. Sometimes, Liz wanted to return. Sometimes she just didn't have anywhere else to go. But each time it would end the same way – with her crumpled and bleeding on the floor, turning to drink to numb the pain.

Not this time, though. This time Liz was determined to stay away. They'd had words, her and Michael, and so she'd gone. She'd taken her hymn book – the only possession she really treasured because it had come all the way from Sweden with her when she'd left – and given it to her old neighbour, Mrs Smith, to look after.

Then she'd lied to Mrs Smith about where she was going, in case Michael asked her, and gone to find rooms on Flower and Dean Street. It wasn't the nicest lodging house, but it was warm enough and clean enough and far enough away from Michael to be safe. She'd even helped sweep the rooms in exchange for sixpence, which she'd used to pay for her bed.

This was a new beginning, she thought, sitting in the kitchen. A new start. Michael was in her past now. She, Elizabeth Gustafsdotter, was never going to rely on a man again.

But when she said as much to Agnes – another woman who helped clean the rooms – Agnes laughed.

'Good luck,' she said, pouring herself some beer and offering it to Liz, who accepted. 'The world ain't set up for women to be on their own. 'What will you do for money?'

'I'll sell things,' Liz said. 'I've got this velvet, see?' She had a piece of beautiful green velvet, given to her by Mrs Smith when she dropped off the hymn book. 'Someone will pay for that.'

'Then what?' asked Agnes. She gave Liz a wicked smile. 'You'll make nothing more than a few pennies, and I know you will drink away the profits you make.'

Liz glared at her. 'Not all of them.'

Agnes shrugged. She leaned over the table. 'The only thing we've got that's worth selling is ourselves,' she said. 'And the only way we can survive is with a fella at our side. You know it and I know it.'

She swigged her beer and Liz thought she might be one of the most annoying people she'd ever met. Mostly because every word she said was true.

'Well then,' she said. 'Maybe I'll go out and find myself a fella. But a good one this time. One with money and ideas and a good heart.'

Agnes howled with laughter. 'Yeah? Where are you going to find one of those?'

Liz got up from the table and drained her glass. 'I don't know.'

She looked down at her skirt, which was dusty, then picked up a brush and gave it a good scrub.

'You ain't really going out?' Agnes said, watching her.

Liz smoothed out her skirt, which was looking much better, and straightened her jacket. 'I am.'

'Liz, it's not safe.'

'Why not?'

'Because of the murders.'

Liz vaguely remembered hearing something about murders, but it was hard for her to keep hold of information these days. So she waved away Agnes's concerns. 'That's nothing to do with me.'

On the wall was a mottled mirror. Liz peered at her reflection and tied her hair up more neatly.

'Not bad for someone of my age,' she said, feeling rather cheerful, though she knew the mirror was a flattering one and the light in the kitchen was dim.

'Stay here,' Agnes begged. Her previous jollity was gone now, and Liz could see worry lines etched in her forehead. 'Please, Liz.'

'You don't need to worry about me,' Liz said. 'I'm fierce.'

'That's true enough.' Agnes gave a small smile.

'I'll be back before too long.'

'Unless you find a man.'

'Maybe,' Liz said. Already her plans were twisting and turning in her head, and she couldn't quite remember where she was going, or why.

Agnes was rooting through her bag. 'Here,' she said. 'Take this.'

She pulled out a little nosegay, tied with fern.

'It's a rose, there, see? And that flower – that one there . . .' She pointed with a slightly grubby finger. 'That's heather. It's for protection.'

Liz was delighted. 'It's pretty.'

'It'll keep you safe.'

'Really?' Liz tried to pin it to her jacket, but her hands weren't doing as she told them. Agnes, seeing her struggling, stood up and took the nosegay from Liz. She pinned it neatly to her lapel. 'There,' she said. 'That'll see you right.'

'Where did you get it?' Liz asked, bending her neck so she could smell the scent of the rose.

'My sister's a florist,' Agnes said, standing up straighter and looking proud. 'She gave it to me.'

'Nice.' Liz frowned. 'I had a sister. Mary.'

'Where's Mary now?'

But Liz was shaking her head. 'She wasn't really my sister.'

Agnes looked confused, but Liz smiled at her. 'We're all sisters, really. Deep down.'

'Right,' said Agnes doubtfully. 'You be careful, sister.'

'I will.'

Without a hat or a coat, Liz made her way down the hall and out into the night. The rain was teeming down and just a few yards along the street, Liz paused, feeling the water running down her neck. Should she go back? She looked over her shoulder in the direction she'd come, but she couldn't quite remember where she'd been.

She walked on, pulling her collar up round her damp neck, and trusting her feet to take her where she wanted to go.

And it seemed where her feet wanted to go was the pub. Almost in a dream, Liz found herself outside the Bricklayer's Arms, and there – just coming out of the double doors at the front – was her Michael.

'Lizzie,' he said as she approached. 'I've been wondering where you were, girl.'

He took her in his arms and kissed her thoroughly.

Liz thought about wriggling free. She had a feeling she wasn't supposed to be there, but she couldn't quite remember why.

'Come on, Lizzie,' said Michael. 'Let's go home.'

Liz let him guide her along the road, leaning against him for some protection from the rain. They turned into Berner Street as the rain got heavier.

'Let's shelter there,' Michael said, pointing across the street at a doorway. He grabbed her hand and laughing they both dashed across out of the rain. Michael kissed her again, nuzzling her neck and sliding his hand under her jacket. Liz let him, though again something inside told her she shouldn't.

'I've missed you,' he said. His breathing was ragged and he was pushing himself up against her.

'Michael,' Liz said. Now he was pulling up her skirt, his hand exploring everywhere. 'Michael, this isn't the place . . .'

But he didn't stop. Instead, he unbuckled his belt and thrust inside her, moaning in pleasure, while Liz's head banged against the wall behind her. With his hand under her jacket, grabbing her breast hard, Michael grunted and then relaxed against Liz, pushing her up against the wall so heavily she felt her spine graze on the rough bricks.

Liz let him embrace her, wondering how she'd ended up there. And then Michael yelped in surprise, yanking his hand out from her jacket and examining his fingers.

'What's that?' he said. 'Something pricked me. Look, I'm bleeding.'

Liz, whose head was throbbing from hitting the wall and whose back was aching, tried to look concerned. 'It's from my posy,' she said. 'Look.'

She pointed to the flowers on her lapel. Michael's face changed from contentment to anger, and Liz felt a flicker of unease.

'Who gave you them?'

Liz thought hard. 'I don't remember,' she said. 'Someone kind.' She smiled.

'A fella?'

'No,' Liz said. 'A friend.'

Michael hit her hard across the face, sending her spinning into the wall. Too shocked to even gasp, Liz put her hand to her jaw, feeling it begin to swell.

'You've got another bloke,' he said.

'No, I haven't, I swear,' Liz said, hoping it was true.

'You would say anything but your prayers,' Michael said. He hit her again, and this time Liz slumped down to the floor. She thought she heard footsteps, maybe a shout, and she tried to open her eyes fully, but it was hard to focus. A man loomed over her. Was it Michael? Was it someone who could help her? She wasn't sure. Her head hurt and for a brief second, she saw her mother's face in her mind, as clearly as if she was standing in front of her. She reached out to the man and he leaned down. Liz felt sharp pressure on her throat. She closed her eyes.

# Chapter 32

## Bet

I was coming home late. I'd been helping out where my mother worked as they had a big order and needed extra hands. Mum was still there – she'd probably be there all night, but Mr Segal had said they could have the day off tomorrow. I had been enjoying watching him and my mother working together. Mr Segal was a widower, and Mum was – well, what was she? Still married to Dad, I supposed. But they worked like a team, knowing what the other was doing before they did it. Finishing each other's sentences when they talked. I liked seeing my mother so comfortable. So happy.

But I had to leave because I needed sleep. I was due at the police station for my usual cleaning shift first thing, so I was going home.

It was funny because I felt uneasy being out so late – the clock on the church was striking midnight as I passed. I knew Gent was dead and, despite what Silas had said about him being in Paris, I told myself he had to have been the murderer – no one who'd seen those grim pictures could think otherwise.

But still I felt uneasy. Unsure.

My route home from Mr Segal's took me close to Maggie's office, and out of habit I glanced up at the windows and saw a light on upstairs. Maggie had told me that when she'd taken over the building, she'd swapped round the areas designed for living and business – using downstairs as her home and upstairs as the office.

'It makes sense for a shop to be downstairs, with the flat above,' she'd said. 'But I'm not running a shop, and I like to be able to see out along the street.'

So I knew that the light being on in the office meant Maggie was working. And with Gent still in my mind, I paused for a moment under the window and then bent down and picked up a couple of small stones, which I lobbed at the glass.

There was a moment and then the curtain moved and Maggie appeared.

I waved and Maggie waved back, beckoning to see if I wanted to come in. I didn't hesitate – just nodded. Maggie dropped the curtain again and disappeared, so I went round the corner to the door and waited, and after a couple of minutes I heard the key in the lock.

'It's late,' Maggie said as she opened the door. She looked stern. 'Have you been out with Silas?' She said Silas in a slightly mocking tone, which almost made me wish I'd not come.

'No I haven't,' I said, defensive suddenly because I liked Silas even if she thought little of him. 'I've been working with my mum, but she's stayed behind to do more. Why are you up so late?'

'Working,' said Maggie. Then her shoulders slumped a little. 'And fretting.'

'About Gent?' I asked softly. It was late and the streets were quiet, but you never knew who was listening in Whitechapel.

Maggie nodded, putting her finger to her lips to quieten me, then bustling me inside and closing the door. We went up the stairs to the office and sat down in the armchairs.

'I'm not sure he was the killer,' Maggie blurted almost as soon as I'd sat down.

I looked at her carefully. 'He had a wife,' I said. 'In Paris.'

'So?'

'He was with her in Paris when the women were killed.'

Maggie nodded as though that was no surprise to her. 'Right.'

'You knew that?'

'No.'

'But you had doubts anyway?'

'Yes.'

'Why?'

'It just doesn't feel right. Gent didn't live round here. He didn't know these women or these streets – where there's light, where there isn't. He didn't know the dark corners and alleyways where victims could be found.'

I felt a squirming sensation in my stomach. 'You're right that the killer needs to have known Whitechapel, but we don't know that Gent didn't.'

'I suppose so,' Maggie said, but she didn't sound certain. 'He was definitely a nasty bloke, that's for sure. Sick in the head. Obsessed with the murders.'

'But you're not sure that makes him a killer?'

'No.' Maggie sounded a bit disappointed and I didn't blame her.

'Silas says . . .' Maggie sighed as soon as I said the name, but I ignored her. 'Silas says that Abberline doesn't think Gent was the killer.'

'Abberline doesn't think so?' Maggie rubbed her forehead. 'If Abberline has doubts . . . Oh dear.'

'You think highly of Inspector Abberline, I know.'

'I do.' She looked at me. 'What does Silas think about Gent?'

'He looked annoyed when he was telling me about it. He seemed to think Gent was guilty.'

'Hmm.' Maggie sat back in her chair.

'Have we done it again?' I asked, my voice trembling just a little as I realised the vastness of the question. 'Have we killed another innocent man?'

'Well, first of all, no.' Maggie looked bullish. 'Strictly speaking, we haven't killed anyone.'

I opened my mouth to argue and she jumped in before I could talk. 'We just happened to be there when they died, Bet. It was just bad luck.'

'For them.'

Maggie gave me a small smile. 'Second of all, they were not innocent men.'

'Well, some people might say it ain't up to us to decide.'

Maggie shrugged. 'No one else is doing it. Sometimes you just have to take the law into your own hands.'

'You've been out on patrol with George Lusk.'

'How did you know that?' She frowned.

'I met him. He's a nice man.'

'He is.' Maggie nodded. 'He's like Abberline, I think.'

I remembered Silas saying he didn't like George, but I pushed the thought aside.

'How was it?' I asked. I pulled my boots off and curled my legs underneath me. 'Was it like being a police officer?'

Maggie's eyes shone. 'It was a bit. We didn't do anything really, but it felt good, walking round, keeping an eye on things.' She paused. 'I saw that doctor.'

'The one we talked about before?' I bit my lip. 'The American?'

'Timothy,' said Maggie.

'Is that his first name or his second name?'

'No idea.' Maggie chuckled. 'He's smart. Nice clothes.' She looked at me pointedly. 'Carriage.'

'Oh Lord. You're not thinking . . .'

'I'm just saying it's an option. If Gent wasn't guilty, then the killer is still out there.'

'Gent might have been the murderer. He ain't been ruled out yet. Abberline's checking the records and he's hoping to speak to Gent's wife.'

There was a pause.

'Tell me more about this doctor, then,' I said.

'One of George's committee told me about him. Said a friend of his – his sister's mate or his wife's sister's mate – went to see him and was lucky to come out alive.'

I scoffed. 'That's not proper evidence. You should know better than that, Mrs Cameron. What sort of lady detective are you?'

'You're right.' Maggie rolled her eyes. 'I'm just fretting, that's all.'

I yawned widely. 'I should go. It's so late, and I'm working first thing.'

'Stay,' said Maggie immediately. 'Don't be walking round Whitechapel at this time.'

'Lord, you really don't think Gent was the Whitechapel murderer, do you?'

There was a pause and then Maggie shook her head. 'No. Do you?'

Slowly, and slightly reluctantly, I shook my head too. 'No.'

'Bugger and blast,' breathed Maggie.

'We ain't going to be found out,' I assured her. 'They reckon Gent was an accident.'

'It was an accident.'

'Well, yes, but they don't know anyone else was there.'

'That's something, I suppose.'

'And even if he weren't the killer, he was properly twisted. Think of all those models he hurt.'

'True.'

'We've not done anything wrong.'

Maggie met my gaze. 'No.'

A knock on the door downstairs made us both jump.

'Blimey,' said Maggie, getting up from her chair. 'Who's that?'

'Could be Abberline come to arrest us for killing Gent,' I said, only half joking.

Maggie glared at me. 'Could be someone in trouble.'

She went to the window, pulled back the curtain and peered out. 'It's a woman.'

I got up too, looking over her shoulder. 'Go and let her in, for pity's sake, whoever she is. She might need help.'

Just then the woman moved out of the shadows and looked up at the window and I realised with a start that it was Emma.

'What's she doing here?' Maggie said, waving.

'It's gone two,' I added. 'She shouldn't be walking around on her own.'

Maggie plodded downstairs and I heard her open the door, and then the sound of footsteps coming up again. Emma came into the room looking serious and sad. She was pale except for two red spots on her cheeks. I went to her and took her hands.

'What is it?' I asked, worried. 'What's happened?'

'There's been another murder.' Emma let go of my hands so she could take off her hat. 'Fred's just been called out.'

'Another woman?' Maggie asked. She went to her desk and sat down. 'Do we know where?'

'Mitre Square,' Emma said. 'I don't know who she is or anything like that. I just waited for Fred to leave, then I ran straight round.' She looked from me to Maggie. 'Gent wasn't the murderer.'

'No,' I said. 'He wasn't.'

'Fred was right.'

'Apparently so,' Maggie said.

'What are we going to do?' Emma wailed. 'Gent's not the murderer. And they've pulled Bernard out of the river.'

'They have?' I was surprised to hear that. 'How do you know?'

'I overheard some soldiers talking and put two and two together.' Emma ran her finger round her collar. 'Are we in trouble?' she said. Her face looked clammy. 'Will we hang for this?'

Maggie banged her palms on her desk, making both Emma and me start at the unexpected noise.

'We will not hang,' she said firmly. 'It is doing us no good to be panicking this way.'

'But Amos . . .' Emma said.

'Amos does not like the police. And more importantly, Amos is no one's fool.' Maggie looked stern. 'He knows that one word from me and his life is over. Either he'll end his days in prison, where the gang he betrayed will be waiting for him. Or his Nan will throw him out on the streets. She doesn't stand for any nonsense.' She gave a small, pinched smile. 'Formidable woman.'

'You're absolutely sure?' Emma said.

'I'm sure.' Maggie gave one firm nod. 'There is no need to be panicking.'

'Fretting,' I said, looking at her and remembering our earlier conversation. 'Fretting, not panicking.'

'Either way, it's doing us no good.'

'Then what should we do?' asked Emma. 'Because, the way I see it, another woman has been murdered, and we've got two deaths on our consciences.'

'First,' said Maggie slowly. 'We're all going to get some sleep. I've got enough space for all of us downstairs. Fred won't be home tonight by the sound of it, so he won't worry . . .' She glanced at Emma, who shrugged.

'I suppose not.

'And Bet, your mother is at work?'

I nodded.

'Fine, so you'll both stay here. Then Bet's going to work tomorrow as usual, and she can find out more about this murder in Mitre Square. Then we'll think about what to do next.'

I looked at Emma and she looked at me, then we both looked at Maggie. I felt a wave of relief that someone more capable than me was taking charge.

'Agreed?' Maggie asked.

'Agreed.'

# Chapter 33

## Kate

When Kate woke up, she wasn't sure where she was. There was a hard, cold surface beneath her and it was dark. Disorientated, she struggled to sit upright, feeling her head pounding.

'Oof,' she said. 'Blimey.'

Her eyes were adjusting to the dim light and she could see she was in a cell. Her heart sank. 'Oh, Kate,' she muttered. 'You bloody idiot.'

She leaned against the wall and thought about what she'd done to end up here. They'd been hop picking in Kent, she and Jed. Oh, the laughs they'd had. Jed was nicer away from London – she always thought as much. In London he was quick to temper, but away from the city he relaxed. Kate thought it might have been because he'd grown up on a farm, over in Ireland, and he liked the countryside – he'd even talked about staying there. Kate hadn't argued – she was used to being on the move. Hadn't she been moving her whole life? They were coming back to London to sort some things out, and then they'd go back to Kent. That was the plan.

Sitting in her cell, she began to sing quietly to herself, choosing a familiar tune and adding her own words about their journey back from Kent and the things they'd seen.

The little hole on the door opened and a pair of eyes peered through.

'You're awake, are you?' said a voice. 'Giving us a song.'

'Wish I weren't,' Kate said. 'My head's thumping.'

'Yeah, well, you deserve that.'

'Can I go home?'

'Not yet.'

'Why not?'

'Because you're still drunk.'

The door opened and Kate squinted in the light from the corridor. A young policeman stood there.

'Hello, Constable Hutt,' she said in delight.

'Hello, Nothing,' he said.

Kate chuckled. 'Is that the name I gave?'

'Again.' He sighed. 'I can't write nothing, and I can't just write Kate. You need to tell me the truth this time. What's your full name?'

'Mary,' said Kate.

'Kate ain't short for Mary.'

'Mary Margery Beth,' said Kate, reeling off names of women she'd been friendly with in Kent.

Hutt looked at her for a moment too long, and then he shrugged. 'Mary Margery Beth it is.'

'I ain't seen you in ages,' Kate said. 'I've been down in Kent.'

'Thought it had been quiet,' said Hutt. 'The poor coppers in Kent had to deal with you, did they?'

'Didn't get in trouble once.' Kate grinned at him. 'It's different down there. Easier.'

'Grass is always greener,' said Hutt. 'I'll give you half an hour to make sure you're sober, and then you can go, all right?'

'All right,' Kate said. Her head was still spinning and she

wasn't sure she was sober, despite what Hutt said. 'What time is it?'

'Midnight.'

'Lord.'

'Your fella will be wondering where you've got to.'

'I told him I was going to Bermondsey to see my daughter.'

'Yeah? Well you weren't in Bermondsey when they found you.'

Kate felt a huge wave of sadness. 'I don't know where she is,' she told Hutt. 'She don't speak to me no more.'

'And who can blame her?' said Hutt.

Kate felt a flicker of concern. 'Jed will be annoyed with me.'

'I expect so.'

'We're going back to Kent.'

'Is that right?'

'New life.'

'He might go without you,' Hutt said. He spoke jovially but Kate felt that flicker of worry again. Had she ruined everything? Jed had warned her about her drinking. He'd told her it sent her wild. Took away all her inhibitions. And Lord knows she didn't have many inhibitions to begin with.

'He won't go without me,' she said now, more sure than she felt. 'You'll see.'

Hutt smiled. 'Let's hope not, eh?'

He slammed the cell door shut and Kate was left in darkness again.

She sang softly to herself for a while, then she felt her eyelids drooping. Perhaps, she thought, it might be better to stay. It wasn't nice in this cell. There was a horrible smell and she could hear scratching in the walls. But it was dry and warm, and she could sleep. She lay down on the hard pallet and shut her eyes.

It felt like only a couple of minutes later that the door was opening again.

'Up you get then,' Hutt said.

Blearily, Kate sat up. 'I was asleep.'

'Time to go.'

'Is it morning?'

'Pretty much.'

Kate stood up – slightly wobbly – and Hutt took her arm. She eyed him with suspicion. 'It's the middle of the night.'

'It'll be morning soon enough.'

She let him lead her out into the main part of the police station.

'You got my things?' she asked. She'd been arrested enough times to know what was what.

'Constable Byfield's got them,' said Hutt. 'He's at the desk.'

Kate looked at the young constable at the desk. 'I ain't never seen you before.'

The constable didn't reply; he simply watched Kate stagger towards him.

'I know every copper from here to Aldgate,' Kate said. 'But I don't know you.'

'I'm not sure that's anything to boast about,' said Hutt. 'Byfield, this one's ready for release.'

'It's the middle of the night,' Byfield said to Hutt.

'That's what I said.' Kate looked at Hutt. 'Didn't I say that?'

'We need the space,' Hutt said.

But Byfield shook his head. 'We don't.'

'If we get rid of her now,' Hutt said in an undertone that Kate could hear perfectly. 'We can go home as soon as our shift's over.'

Byfield, though, wasn't budging. 'It's not safe.'

'I'll go back, shall I?' Kate offered. 'Back to my cell. I won't cause no trouble.'

'Yes,' said Byfield.

'No,' said Hutt.

'What's going on?' asked Kate. She began to sing again, a ballad about two battling brothers she'd not thought about for years. Wasn't it funny how she couldn't remember why she'd been arrested but she could remember this song?

'Fine,' said Byfield. 'What's your name?' He raised his voice to be heard over Kate's singing. 'What's your name?'

Kate stopped singing and looked at Hutt, because she couldn't remember that either.

'Mary Margery Beth,' he said.

'Yes!' Kate pointed at him and then at Byfield. 'Mary Margery Beth.' She smiled sweetly. 'That's me.'

Byfield wrote it down, and then gave Kate her things – a pitiful collection of belongings – that she stashed away in her pockets.

'Where are you going?' he asked her.

'I'm going to find Jed,' Kate said. It was only half a lie. She didn't know where Jed was, but she'd find him soon enough – she always did. 'He'll give me a damn fine hiding.'

'No more than you deserve,' said Hutt, but Byfield looked worried.

'Really?'

Kate shook her head vigorously then regretted it as she lost her balance. 'Nah,' she said. 'Not Jed. He ain't violent. Not like my Thomas was.'

'Just watch yourself.' Byfield sounded concerned. 'Find a safe place to sleep.'

'Righto,' Kate said cheerfully. She had no idea why Byfield was so worried. She'd be fine. She was no stranger to sleeping on the streets. She gave them both a mock salute. 'Goodnight, old cock.'

She headed out into the night, leaving the door open behind her, and heard Hutt's exasperated sigh. As he locked up, she heard Byfield say: 'We should have let her stay.' But she didn't hear Hutt's reply.

Undaunted, Kate wound her way down Houndsditch – the last place she'd seen Jed. She had an idea to ask anyone she came across who she recognised if they knew where he was. But though there were still people about, there was no one she knew. Everyone was scurrying away, hunched in their coats and hats. For the first time, London – Whitechapel – seemed unfamiliar to her.

'We ain't been gone that long,' she muttered as she tramped through Dukes Place. 'Why has everything changed?'

She reached the corner of Mitre Square and paused, knowing there were places to sleep there.

A man walked by, giving her barely a glance.

'Sir?' she called. 'Do you know Jed Kelly?'

He paused, just as three other men went past.

'Don't know him,' he said. He walked on.

Kate thought about going after the other men to ask them, but she was tired and her head was throbbing and it would be easier to find Jed when it was light. Glancing up at the church clock, she saw it was long past one o'clock now. Almost half past. She might get lucky and not be moved on until morning.

So she made her way into the square, and went towards the darkest corner, where she settled down on the damp ground, pulling her coat around her. As she got herself as comfortable as she could, a figure emerged from the shadows at the entrance to the square.

Kate squinted through the darkness. 'Jed?' she said. 'Is that you, my love? Come sit with me.'

The man approached and as he passed by the gas light, Kate saw that it wasn't Jed – he was much too short to be Jed. 'Jed?' she said again, less certain this time. And then she didn't speak anymore.

# Chapter 34

## Emma

I woke up to the sound of Maggie's front door slamming shut next to the room where I'd slept. I slid out of bed and went to the window, to see Bet hurrying along the road, obviously on her way to work.

She started her shift much earlier than I'd realised, which made me feel a pang of guilt. I'd never even asked her what time she worked at the police station, or thought about how early she'd have to get up. I just gave her chores to do when she got to my house in the afternoons. Mind you, those chores had mostly been linked with the murders recently. Still, I made a mental note to make sure Bet was not being burdened with too much.

I had borrowed a nightdress belonging to Maggie and it was enormous, billowing round my legs. So now I pulled it off over my head, had a quick wash using water from the jug on the stand, and got dressed.

Maggie's living quarters were surprisingly nice. Not that her office wasn't nice, but it was, well, lived-in. There were books piled higgledy-piggledy on the shelves, papers on the desk, notes scribbled here and there, and of course all the information about the murders pinned on one wall. But downstairs, there were three small bedrooms, a large living room with a table at one end, and a little kitchen. It was neat and tidy, very clean, and the kitchen was spick and span too. I got the impression that Maggie spent most of her time up in the office.

Once I was dressed, I made the bed, left my borrowed nightgown on the pillow, and went in search of a cup of tea. I found Maggie – and a pot of tea – sitting at the table in the living room.

'Bet's gone to work,' I said, sitting down.

'I heard her leave.' Maggie made a face as she reached for the teapot. 'She doesn't know how to shut a door quietly, that one.'

I laughed. 'I feel bad that I didn't realise how early she starts.'

'Before the sun's up.'

'Yes.' I took the cup of tea she'd poured me. 'I hope she finds out more about this murder in Mitre Square.'

'It's not in Whitechapel,' said Maggie. 'I've been looking at my map. It's over the border.'

I blinked at her. 'Pardon?'

'It's the City, isn't it? It won't be the Whitechapel police.'

I shrugged. 'Fred got called out to deal with it, though.'

'I suppose so,' Maggie said. 'Maybe they just wanted his expertise. He's making a name for himself as a murder detective of some note.'

'Lord, I hope not.'

'If this was the same killer then it's certain Gent wasn't the man,' Maggie said. She sipped her tea.

'Gent wasn't the man,' I said. 'Fred's sure of it and I trust his opinion.' I gave her a small smile over the top of my cup. 'He is, after all, a murder detective of some note.'

Maggie smiled back at me.

'And,' I said, 'there's more.'

'More?'

'Fred said Percival couldn't have been the one who sold

Gent all the information about the murders, because he's been away caring for his sick mother.'

'He has?' Maggie raised an eyebrow. 'That goes a small way towards changing my opinion of Constable Percival.'

'That's what I thought.'

'But if it wasn't him, then who was it?'

I shrugged. 'I suppose it doesn't matter now.'

'I suppose not.' She tapped her fingers on the table. 'And what of Bernard?'

'Fred's not mentioned it, so I'm assuming it's being considered an accident. He was drunk, after all. I think they can tell that from the post-mortem?' I had learned a great deal about post-mortems and what they revealed in the last few weeks.

'They can.' Maggie nodded.

There was a pause.

'So,' I began. 'What should we do?'

'Do?'

'Should we continue to investigate these crimes? Even though we've not been successful so far?'

Maggie got up from the table. 'How does one measure success?' she said. 'We have been instrumental in removing two very dangerous, unsavoury men from the streets of London. I'd say that was successful, wouldn't you?'

'I suppose.' I stood up too. 'Are you saying that we will continue investigating?'

'How about we go up to the office and make a plan?'

I nodded. 'Let's go.'

We'd only been upstairs for five minutes when there was a knock on the door. Maggie went to answer it and came back with a man of around her own age with a moustache and a kind face.

'Emma,' she said. 'This is my good friend George Lusk, from the Whitechapel Vigilance Committee.'

Did I imagine it or did George stand up a bit straighter when she called him her good friend?

'George, this is Emma Abberline.'

'Pleasure to meet you,' I said, shaking his hand.

'Abberline,' said George. 'Fred's wife?'

'I am indeed.'

'He's a good man.'

I smiled. 'I think so.'

'What brings you here, George?' asked Maggie, who was – I was beginning to understand – always impatient with pleasantries.

'There's been another murder,' he said, his expression grave. 'But it's different . . .'

Maggie nodded. 'Not within Whitechapel,' she said.

'It was in Whitechapel.' George frowned. 'Berner Street.'

'Mitre Square,' I said.

'Berner Street,' said George.

'My husband is Inspector Abberline,' I said, more than a little barbed. 'I hardly think he's got this wrong.'

George looked put out. 'I didn't say he was wrong, I just said I'd heard there's been a murder in Berner Street.'

'Mitre Square.'

'Berner Street is what I heard.'

I opened my mouth to argue again, and Maggie held her hand up.

'Is it possible there have been two murders in one night?'

I stared at her. 'Two?'

'What did Fred say exactly when he went to work?'

'I heard the lad at the door,' I said, remembering. 'Fred got up, and he told me to go back to sleep. So of course, I got out of bed and went on to the landing, then I leaned over the banister to listen. I definitely heard the lad say Mitre Square.' I closed my eyes like Bet did, remembering the feel of the smooth wood of the rail beneath my fingers and rerunning the conversation in my head. 'He said "more".' I opened my eyes and looked at Maggie and George. 'The lad said there had been "more".'

'Blimey,' said George. 'Two killings in one night?'

Maggie went to her desk and unfolded her map of Whitechapel. 'Those two places aren't very close to one another – it's a bit of a walk in between.'

'Imagine killing one woman and that not being enough,' I said, feeling sick. I sat down on one of Maggie's chairs, all my energy drained suddenly. 'Having to go and slaughter another poor girl to keep you satisfied.'

'Ah,' said George. 'Ah, perhaps . . .'

'What?' Maggie looked up from the map.

'This murder was different – the woman wasn't . . .' George winced. 'She wasn't mutilated like the others.'

'He stopped?' Maggie said.

'Or he was stopped,' I pointed out, sitting up straighter again. 'Perhaps someone walked by, or interrupted him, or spooked him in some way. He couldn't finish what he'd started, and so he went off hunting for another woman to kill.'

'That makes sense,' Maggie said, nodding. Then she frowned. 'Although, if this poor woman wasn't mutilated, why would they think she was a victim of the same killer? It's the viciousness of the attacks that links them, surely?'

'Ah,' said George again.

'Oh, for heaven's sake, George, just spit it out,' said Maggie.

George rolled his eyes at me and I decided I quite liked him.

'There was a witness,' he said, clearly enjoying the drama of drip-feeding us information.

'Oh good gracious.' I looked at Maggie, who was

studying the map again and pretending she wasn't interested. 'Tell us more, George.'

George gave me a tiny wink. 'He says he saw the victim on the street. And then he saw someone else.'

'Who?' I asked.

'A man, foreign-looking, moustache, cap with a peak.'

I frowned. 'That's similar to the description of the man someone saw with Annie Chapman.'

'Indeed, that's why they think it could be the same killer.'

'And half of the men in Whitechapel, including you, George,' said Maggie. 'Strikes me that anyone looking a bit foreign is to be regarded with suspicion.'

'There's more,' George said, almost gleeful. 'The chap walking along behind the Berner Street victim was wearing a jacket that the witness described as "salt and pepper coloured".'

Maggie went very still. She stared at George.

'Salt and pepper coloured? As in speckled black and white?'

'Sounds like it.'

I looked from her to him, bewildered.

'Why is that important?'

'Because when George and I saw the doctor – Timothy – he was wearing a jacket just like that,' Maggie said.

'What doctor?'

Maggie hit her forehead with the heel of her hand. 'Of course, I didn't tell you. There's a doctor, an awful quack. Remember Bet mentioned she'd heard Ruby and the others talk of him when we got the letter?'

I nodded. 'I remember.'

'What letter?' George asked.

Maggie and I both ignored him.

'I met some people who knew him, and they said he was a monster,' she said.

'In what way?'

Maggie looked pale. 'Obsessed with women's insides.'

I went cold. 'Maggie,' I said quietly. 'When we got that letter, we talked about how the killer could have been a doctor, because of the injuries those poor woman suffered.'

'We did.'

'And the actual queen suggested the killer could be a doctor.'

'She did.'

'The queen?' said George.

Again, we both ignored him.

'And we got sidetracked by Gent.'

'We did.' Maggie looked stricken. 'Have we made a terrible mistake?'

There was a moment of silence.

'I think . . .' I began. 'I think we should tell Fred about this doctor?'

'Absolutely,' said George.

'Absolutely not,' said Maggie.

'Maggie, we are out of our depth here,' I said. 'We need to tell the police what we know.'

'We agreed that we're doing this ourselves.' She looked bullish.

'Well, we're not by ourselves now, are we? George is involved.'

'I wouldn't say involved,' said George. 'Not involved, as such.'

'We are lady detectives,' Maggie said.

'We're not doing a very good job of it, though.'

Maggie's shoulders slumped. 'I suppose not.'

'And may I remind you that two men are . . .' I paused, glancing at George, who still looked thoroughly confused, and changed tack. 'Our first two suspects were innocent.'

'Innocent of the murders, perhaps,' said Maggie.

I tutted. 'I'm going to the police station.'

'Fine.' Maggie turned away from me, looking out of the window. 'Do what you want.'

'I will.'

She looked at me over her shoulder as I put on my coat. 'But come back here and tell me what you find out, won't you?'

'Of course.' I didn't smile at her, simply turned and left the room.

I hurried down the stairs and out into the street, then splashed along the wet road, still full of puddles from last night's downpour, towards the police station.

When I arrived, it was chaos. There were people everywhere. I could hear Harrison's booming voice from where I stood in the foyer, where there were two women and a man sitting, all looking fearful and sad.

'Is Fred available?' I asked the chap at the desk.

'Go on through,' he said. 'He'll be glad of the break.'

As I went towards the corridor, Dr Llewellyn came out in a clean white coat. His eyes were drooping with tiredness, and he nodded a greeting at me as he passed, heading for the man.

'Father Olsson?' he said. 'We're ready for you now. Could you come this way?'

I watched as the man got to his feet, noticing he was wearing a dog collar.

Dr Llewellyn turned his attention to the women. 'Mrs Frost, I'll be right back,' he said. His voice was soft and kind. 'Please wait here just a little longer.'

The woman nodded. She gripped the hand of the younger woman next to her so tightly I could see their knuckles were white.

I stood back to let Llewellyn and the priest go ahead

towards the mortuary, not envying them their grim chore. Then I went to find Fred.

He was, of course, in his office, looking harried as he stared at the map of Whitechapel on the wall. Green was with him.

'I'm just not sure it's possible,' he was saying.

'Harrison thinks it's possible.'

'Maybe he's wrong this time?' said Fred with a snort that made me think Harrison had been wrong many times, in Fred's opinion at least.

'Sorry to interrupt,' I said.

Fred turned to me and smiled. 'I'm glad of the distraction,' he said. 'Hello. You remember Constable Green?'

'I do.' I nodded at Green, without warmth. I thought he was too old to be wooing Bet and I didn't want to encourage him. 'I heard there's been two murders?'

'I'm afraid so.' Fred leaned against his bookcase.

'The same killer?'

'Harrison thinks so. I'm not so sure.'

'Elizabeth died just before one o'clock in Berner Street,' said Green, sounding a little like a frustrated teacher explaining a complicated sum to the class dunce. 'Catherine died between ten past one and quarter to two, in Mitre Square. It's a ten-minute walk between the two sites. It's possible.'

'Possible,' said Fred. 'But is it plausible?'

'Elizabeth and Catherine,' I said. 'Those are the victims?'

'They've not been officially identified yet, but we believe so.' Fred nodded.

'There are people with Llewellyn now,' I told him. 'I think they were going to the mortuary.'

'Good,' said Fred. He sat down at his desk with a heavy sigh. 'Good.'

'Fred,' I began cautiously, because I didn't want to add to his woes. 'I've heard something that might be useful.'

'Oh?'

I sat down too. 'There's a doctor,' I said. 'A quack, of course. Name of Timothy. Apparently, he's obsessed with women's insides.'

Fred's eyes flashed with interest. 'And you know this because?'

'I've got friendly with a woman called Maggie Cameron,' I said.

'I know Maggie,' said Fred. 'Sharp woman.'

'She is,' I agreed. I glanced at Green, wishing he wasn't there, because I didn't like talking in front of him. I didn't entirely trust him. 'And she knows George Lusk of the Whitechapel Vigilance Committee.'

Green gave a long, exaggerated groan. 'Officious little man,' he said.

'I think he's rather nice,' I said truthfully but not without satisfaction at disagreeing with Green. 'He's clever.'

'He's a good man,' Fred agreed and, smug, I smiled at Green.

'He told me about Timothy,' I said. 'Said he's a monster. There's lots of speculation he could be the killer.'

'That's just hearsay,' said Fred. 'If we listened to every bit of Whitechapel gossip . . .'

'He wears a jacket that Mr Lusk said is salt and pepper coloured.'

This time Fred looked more interested.

'Really?'

'Really.'

Green was rubbing his nose. 'Perhaps this is worth investigating, sir,' he said. 'A monster doesn't sound too good. Perhaps he could be our man.'

'He has a carriage,' I said. 'A carriage could travel quicker between the two murder locations.'

'See?' said Green. 'That sounds plausible to me.'

A flash of irritation flickered on Fred's face, and then it was gone. 'Yes,' he said. 'Fine. Go and ask around, Green. See what you can find out about this Timothy.'

Green looked delighted. 'I will,' he said. 'Thank you, sir.'

He left the office, and I reached across the desk for Fred's hand. 'You look so tired, darling.'

'I'm sickened,' he said. 'Sickened that another two women have lost their lives on my watch.'

'It's not your fault.'

'It feels like it was my fault.'

'Inspector Abberline?'

We both looked round to see the man from the front desk in the doorway with another chap – rotund and ruddy, but nervous. 'Yes?' said Fred.

'This is Mr Best, from the Central News Agency,' said the policeman. 'He's got something to show you.'

'Come in, Mr Best,' Fred said. *Journalist*, he mouthed at me, rolling his eyes.

I got up from the chair beside the desk, letting Mr Best sit, but I didn't leave. Instead, I loitered at the back of the office, hoping the men would forget I was there.

'What it is,' Mr Best began. 'What it is . . .' He dug into his pocket and took out an envelope, which he put on the desk.

'We got this a few days ago, and I was convinced it was just a hoax. Because we've been getting a lot of this sort of stuff, letters and whatnot.'

Fred looked a little bemused. 'Right.'

'But then I heard what happened, to poor Catherine,' said Best. 'Well, read it for yourself.'

He pushed the envelope towards Fred. He picked it up and took out a sheet of paper, covered in red writing.

I watched as Fred's face paled while he read, desperate

to know what was written there but not wanting to draw attention to myself in case Fred asked me to leave.

'You see?' said Best. 'You see he's said he'll clip the lady's ears off? And that's what happened to Catherine, ain't it? So I thought it could be genuine.'

I steadied myself on Fred's bookshelf.

'It is what happened to Catherine,' Fred said, sombre. He looked straight at me. '*They say I'm a doctor now, ha ha,*' he read.

My stomach lurched.

'Have you published this?' Fred asked.

'No,' said Best. 'But I might.'

'You won't,' said Fred.

Best glared at him. 'He's given himself a name,' he said.

'I can see that.' Fred sounded bleak.

'The readers will love it,' said Best. He sounded quite happy about it.

'What is it?' I asked, all thoughts of staying quiet abandoned. 'What's the name?'

Best turned in his chair and looked at me.

'Jack the Ripper,' he said.

# Chapter 35

## Bet

'Jack the Ripper?' I stared at Emma, who was taking off her coat. 'Jack the Ripper?'

'That's how the letter was signed. This journalist fellow was terribly excited by it. He said the readers would love it.'

I looked at Maggie, who was scowling. 'That's horrible.'

'I know,' Emma said. 'But we've all seen it all over the newspapers. People are interested in these murders, despite it being so awful.'

'But giving him a name makes him sound like a sort of hero. Like Robin Hood, or Dick Turpin.'

'I know,' Emma said with a shudder. 'Fred's furious about the whole thing.'

She sat down in a chair and looked at me and Maggie. 'Where's George?'

'He had to go to work,' Maggie said. 'He left before Bet came back.'

'George Lusk?' I said, remembering Silas's reaction to him and feeling slightly uncomfortable about it. 'He was here?'

'He came to tell us about the second murder,' Maggie said. 'The one in Berner Street.'

I shook my head. 'First murder.'

I'd sneaked into the mortuary again, hiding out in my usual spot. I had an inkling that Llewellyn knew I was there, but he didn't let on and I didn't make it obvious. I'd been there a long time, because today there had been two post-mortems for Llewellyn to do, and two families to identify the bodies.

'Tell us what you know,' said Maggie. She was sitting at her desk, so she pulled a piece of paper towards her and picked up a pencil.

'Two murders, two victims,' I said, looking at my own notes. 'First victim was Elizabeth Stride. She was found in Berner Street and she was killed with a slash to her throat. That was it – no other wounds.'

Maggie nodded, grim-faced.

'And the other?'

'Catherine Eddowes,' I said. 'But her family called her Kate.'

Emma shifted in her chair. 'Were her ears cut off?'

I looked at her, horrified. 'Why do you ask that?'

'That's what Jack the Ripper said he was going to do, in the letter.'

'One of her ears was cut,' I said, my mouth dry. 'But Llewellyn said it was because of the viciousness of the slash to her throat.'

Emma nodded. 'Right.'

'I can't read it aloud,' I said. 'I wrote down every word Llewellyn said as best I could, and I drew some diagrams. It's all here, but I can't read it aloud. It's too awful. Even worse than the others.' I heard my voice tremble.

Maggie and Emma were both very still.

'He took her kidney,' I said, almost whispering. 'He cut it out and he took it.'

Emma looked like she was going to cry. Maggie looked like she might vomit.

'So,' she said eventually. 'Can we assume that the killer could be a medical man?'

'That's what Llewellyn said.' I swallowed. 'He said the killer must have known where the organs were positioned in the abdomen.' I felt Llewellyn's words heavy in my mouth. 'That he must have some medical knowledge.'

Emma drew a sharp intake of breath. 'The American doctor,' she said.

'Timothy?' I looked at her. 'He's a quack. He ain't a real medical man.'

'He's obsessed with women's insides,' Maggie said.

'Obsessed how?'

She shrugged. 'I spoke to some women when I was out with George and that's what they said.'

'That don't sound good.' I looked at Emma. 'What does Fred say? Did you tell him about Timothy?'

'He was interested. He sent Silas Green to do some digging.'

I felt my cheeks flush. 'He sent Silas?' Inwardly I was pleased that Fred was trusting Silas with important jobs.

'Silas was very keen,' Emma said. She sounded a little spiky.

'You don't think that's a good thing?' I matched her irritable tone.

'I just . . .' she sighed. 'I'm not sure what I think of him, that's all.'

'He's a nice man.'

'I'm sure he is.'

'Well,' I began, but Maggie interrupted.

'Should we do some investigating of our own?' she said. 'Find out some more about Timothy?'

'I suppose so. What do you think, Emma?'

'I'm not sure. I think perhaps we should leave it to Fred.'

I tutted and she glared at me. 'What?'

'Leave it to Fred,' I said in a mocking voice. 'Except now four women are dead and the police don't seem to be doing anything about it.'

'Four women are dead and two men,' said Emma, getting to her feet. 'Two men who wouldn't be dead if we hadn't stuck our noses in.'

'I can't keep having this same conversation with you,' I said. 'Bernard and Gent were awful people, and they died because of their awful behaviour. It wasn't our fault, and I'm not sorry. And you ain't sorry, either – you're just in a bad mood because you're tired. And sad. And a bit scared. Because I know I am.'

I stopped talking because both Emma and Maggie were staring at me.

'Sorry,' I said.

'Don't be.' Emma shook her head. 'You're right. It's all just so awful, and I feel like we're not getting anywhere.'

'So let's do something about that, shall we?' said Maggie. 'Let's go and find out some more about Dr Timothy.'

Keen to lighten the mood, I quacked like a duck, and I was pleased when Emma laughed.

'Where will we start?' I asked.

Maggie got up from her desk and pinned the notes I'd taken at the post-mortems to the wall. 'There's a bloke called Chip, works with George on the vigilance committee,' she said thoughtfully. 'I think we'll start with him.'

Chip wasn't hard to track down. We found him in the pub – though he wasn't drinking, he was working. He was repairing the stairs up to the flat above the bar.

'Hello there, Maggie,' he said jovially as we came into the corridor. He didn't sound remotely surprised to see three women approaching him.

Maggie grinned. 'How are you, Chip?'

'Oh you know,' he said. He hammered in a nail and

turned so he was sitting on a step in the middle of the staircase looking down at us. He was older than Maggie, but lean and wiry with taut stringy muscles in his arms. 'Same old, same old.'

His bright eyes took us in. 'Who are your mates?'

'Emma and Bet,' said Maggie. 'We're actually working on an investigation.'

Chip raised an eyebrow. 'What kind of investigation?'

'Remember the doctor you mentioned?' Maggie stepped on to the bottom stair and leaned against the banister, looking casual.

'I do.' Chip rested his hammer on his knee. 'Timothy.'

'Who was it you said had seen him? Your Flo's sister?'

He shook his head. 'My Flo's sister's mate.'

'Know her mate's name?'

'Ettie.' He frowned. 'But she don't live in London now. She's gone up north with her fella.'

I felt absurdly disappointed. 'Have you heard anyone else mention him?'

Chip's brow furrowed as he considered. 'You know who might know? Ettie's mate. They lived together for a while, but now she's on her own in the room.'

'She rents a room on her own?' I was impressed.

But Chip looked uncomfortable. He looked round at the door to the bar, and lowered his voice.

'She's, erm, well. She's what you might call a fallen woman.'

'I wouldn't call her that,' Maggie said sharply.

'I ain't judging,' said Chip. 'She's a nice girl, by all accounts. I've heard now she's got the room to herself she's opening her doors to women, so they don't have to sleep on the streets while the killer's on the loose.'

'That's kind,' said Emma.

'Where does she live? This mate?' Maggie asked.

'Miller's Court, I believe.'

'And her name?'

'I don't know her real name,' Chip said. 'But I've heard people call her Ginger?'

'Red hair?' I asked. 'Bright red?'

'That's the one.' He nodded. 'Pretty girl. Always nicely dressed. No wonder—'

'Chip,' Maggie stopped him, a warning in her voice.

'I ain't judging,' he said again.

'Well make sure you don't,' Maggie said. She leaned forward and slapped him on the shoulder with affection. 'You've been really helpful.'

He regarded her, his head on one side.

'George was right about you,' he said.

'What's that?' Maggie lifted her chin.

'He said you're some woman.'

'He said that?' Maggie looked chuffed to bits.

'You've got that right,' I said. 'Thanks, Chip, you've been really helpful. Come on, Maggie.'

I tugged her sleeve and she followed me and Emma out of the back door of the pub and into the late-afternoon gloom.

'George thinks you're some woman,' Emma teased as we walked across the courtyard. 'What do you think of George?'

'I think he's a good man,' said Maggie firmly. 'No more, no less.'

But her cheeks were flushed and her eyes glittering as we walked. I caught Emma's eye and smiled, and she smiled back and I felt better again. We were working together once more, getting along like before.

'Are we going to Miller's Court?' I asked, trying to keep up with Maggie's long stride.

'We are.'

'Ginger's the one the girls at the brothel told us about, isn't she?' said Emma. 'The one we saw with Percival and Green?'

'That's right,' I said. 'Remember they said she didn't like talking to the police? I hope she talks to us.'

'She will,' Maggie said with confidence. 'Everyone talks to us.'

I chuckled. 'Let's hope you're right.'

Miller's Court was a little yard off Dorset Street with low, grubby buildings. It wasn't unlike the rooms I shared with my mum, which made me feel an affinity towards Ginger. I knew how small the rooms were inside, and her throwing open her doors and welcoming other women inside to keep them safe was admirable.

'What number did Chip say?' Emma asked as we paused in the yard.

'He didn't.' Maggie smiled. 'But I reckon everyone knows Ginger. We'll just knock on a few doors.'

But we didn't have to because, as we stood there, the door to the end house opened and out came Ginger herself. She was wearing a long fitted black coat and a pretty hat.

'Ginger?'

She turned to look at us. 'I ain't got no more room,' she said, sounding genuinely regretful. 'There's five of us in there tonight, and it's snug with two.'

'We don't need a room,' Maggie said. 'Though that's really kind of you.'

Ginger gave her a quick smile, but her eyes were suddenly wary. 'What do you want?'

'My name's Maggie Cameron,' said Maggie. 'I'm a detective, and these are my friends Emma and Bet. I know Ruby and Min, from the corner house.'

Ginger relaxed slightly. 'They work for you?'

'Sometimes.'

She nodded. 'I'm not looking for work.'

'That's not why we're here.' Maggie paused and Emma jumped in.

'Do you know Dr Timothy? We heard your friend Ettie went to see him.'

Ginger's face darkened. 'He's a quack, and he ain't no doctor.'

'Is Timothy his surname or his Christian name?' Emma asked.

Ginger shrugged. 'Wouldn't surprise me if it's neither,' she said. 'He ain't a nice man.' She looked at us all. 'Ettie went to see him, with a little problem, you know?'

Maggie nodded. I glanced at Emma, who gave a tiny 'I don't know' shrug.

'And while she was there, he tried to give Ettie a drink with something in it to make her sleepy.'

'She didn't drink it?'

'She spilled some of it, accidental, you know. And she was worried he was going to get cross with her. But he had a cat, and it licked it up, so she was pleased he wouldn't see the mess.'

Ginger's eyes gleamed – she was obviously enjoying telling the story. 'But then Ettie said the cat went all wobbly.' She swayed from side to side, showing us. 'And then it went to sleep, just like that.' She snapped her fingers in Emma's face, making Emma jump. 'So Ettie never drank it. She waited until Timothy was distracted then legged it.'

'You think he was up to no good?'

Ginger tutted like Maggie was an irritation. 'A bloke don't drug a woman for a good reason.'

'Fair enough.' Maggie looked amused and I thought she liked Ginger. I liked her too. She had an energy about her that I admired. 'Do you know where he lives? This Timothy? I saw him at a pharmacy near St Mary's station.'

'Near the docks, I think. Where there's them tall houses.'

Maggie nodded. 'Sounds right,' she said.

'You're not the only ones wanting to know about Timothy,' said Ginger. 'Had a policeman round earlier.'

'Silas Green?' I was interested.

'Don't know his name.' Ginger pushed her hair off her face. 'He's an idiot, though. They're all idiots, more or less, but he's one of the worst. Speaks to me like I'm nothing.'

'Maybe it wasn't Silas,' I muttered.

Ginger gave me a sideways glance. 'Why do you care?'

'I don't.'

'Sounds like you care.'

'I don't.' I was rattled.

'Did you tell him what you've told us?' Maggie asked, getting things back on track.

'Bugger that,' said Ginger, thankfully giving Maggie her attention again. 'Told him I'd never heard of the man. I ain't speaking to someone like him.'

Emma gave me a slightly triumphant look and I scowled at her.

'Well, you've been very helpful to us,' Maggie said. She held her hand out to Ginger to shake and I thought I saw her slip some money into her palm. 'You're doing a good thing here, taking in women overnight. Keep it up.'

Ginger looked quite pleased with herself.

'I will,' she said. 'Stay safe, ladies.'

# Chapter 36

## Maggie

We had arranged to do some more investigation the following day, but when I woke up I felt absolutely terrible. Full of cold and shivery. Determined not to let it slow me down, I dragged myself out of bed and got dressed, then I wrapped myself in a shawl and sat at my desk. Which was where I was later, when Emma arrived – I'd given her a spare key – and I woke with a start to find her standing in front of me, looking worried.

'Are you poorly?' she said with some concern. 'Gosh, you look awful.'

'Dank oo,' I said, through my stuffy nose. I found my handkerchief and blew loudly. 'It's just a cold.'

'You need to go back to bed,' she said. She turned as Bet came into the office. 'Doesn't she?'

'Who's going back to bed?' Bet asked. 'Oh blimey, Maggie, you look dreadful. Your nose is all red.'

'She's ill,' said Emma.

'I can see that.' Bet took a step backwards. 'Not being rude, Mags, but I don't want to catch nothing.'

'We have work to do,' I said, rubbing my aching forehead. 'We need to find out more about the doctor. I'm fine.'

'We still don't know whether Gent was really in Paris

305

when the murders happened,' Emma said firmly. 'Until we do, Timothy isn't a priority.'

'I suppose.'

'Spend today in bed and you'll be right as rain tomorrow.' She clapped her hands together as though it was all decided. 'I'll go to the police station and see what Fred knows about Gent. Coming, Bet?'

Bet shook her head. 'I'm not due at the police station today so if we're not investigating today, I might go and work with my mum again – there's more to do and the money's good.' She grinned at me. 'Way I see it, every extra penny I earn there buys me time to work with you, Maggie.'

I nodded at her, pleased. 'Indeed.'

Emma came round to where I sat and put her hand on my forehead in a motherly fashion. 'You're rather warm,' she said. 'Into bed, come on. I'll make you some tea.'

It felt quite nice to be looked after. I smiled at her.

'All right then, just this once.'

I got to my feet, slightly unsteadily.

'I'll stay for a while and get you settled,' Emma said.

'I'm going to go.' Bet blew me a kiss. 'Feel better soon, Mags.'

She hurried off down the stairs. I didn't blame her. An extra day's wages would make a difference.

Emma put her arm through mine. 'Want me to help you downstairs?'

I shook her off. 'I've got a cold, Emma, I'm not an invalid. I can manage.'

She laughed as we headed down to the living area. 'I know, I just don't like to see you this way.'

'I'll be fine after some sleep,' I said.

I went to my bedroom and got into my nightdress, slipping under the sheets with a sigh of relief. Emma was right – if I spent today in bed, I'd be better tomorrow.

She appeared at the bedroom door with some tea and put it on my bedside table.

'I'll come back later,' she said. 'Get some rest.'

To my surprise, she bent down quickly and kissed my forehead. My eyelids already heavy, I heard the front door shut, and she was gone.

I dozed on and off all day, and when I woke properly, it was getting dark and I realised I was already starting to feel much better.

I sat up in bed and thought about getting up to make something to eat, but I was so warm and cosy where I was, the idea of putting my feet on the cold floor wasn't very appealing. Then I heard a key in the lock and the front door opening – Emma, I thought, just at the perfect time.

There was a soft knock on my bedroom door.

'Maggie?'

'George?' I was shocked to hear his voice. 'Is that you?'

He opened the door a crack and stuck his head round, diligently keeping his gaze away from me. 'Emma asked me to check on you. Are you feeling better?'

'I am, actually. I was just thinking about getting up.'

'Oh, well, I'll leave you to it.' He started to withdraw.

'No, stay,' I said, surprising myself with how pleased I was to see him. 'If you don't mind, you could go through to the kitchen and make some tea, and I'll get dressed.'

'Of course.'

He closed the door behind himself, and I got out of bed, far less reluctantly than I had been feeling five minutes earlier. I got dressed in warm clothes and thick socks, and went to find George.

I found him arranging cups and a teapot on a tray. 'I thought you'd want to go upstairs,' he said.

'I hadn't seen you for so long, and yet you know me very well.'

He smiled at me. 'I have seen a glint in your eye these past weeks that I feared had been extinguished by your life with your husband.'

'Perhaps you're right,' I said. I blew my nose and he looked at me with concern.

'You go on up, and I'll follow.'

We went upstairs together and I poured the tea while George arranged a fire in the grate and lit it, and I thought once again how nice it was to be looked after.

'Emma has gone to the police station to see her husband and find out what he knows about Walter Gent's whereabouts,' George told me.

I nodded. 'Yes, she said she was planning to do that.'

'And she said she was also going to see Constable Green and find out if there is anything more to know about Dr Timothy.'

'Did she come to see you?' I asked. 'How did you know I was poorly?'

'She did come to find me, and she said you'd be glad of the company.'

'I am indeed.' I smiled at him. 'Thank you.'

'Well, we're old friends, aren't we?'

'I think we are.'

I sipped my tea.

'I saw your Bet with Green the other day,' George said casually, looking out of the window. 'They were on a night out together at Foresters, the music hall.'

'Were you on a night out at the music hall?' I said, interested.

'I was not. I was working – or at least I had been. I showed Bet the cats I carve in my woodwork.'

'Oh, heavens, I'd forgotten about those.' I laughed at the memory. 'Back then I would look out for them all over town. I'll have to start keeping an eye out again.'

'There's a lot of them.' George looked quite proud of himself. 'Anyway, I saw Bet, and I erm . . .' He paused.

'What?'

'How do you find that Green?'

I thought for a moment. 'Bet is smitten,' I said. 'Emma can't abide him.'

'And you?'

'I think I'm in between.'

George raised an eyebrow.

'Perhaps erring more towards Emma's way of thinking.'

He gave a satisfied nod. 'I do not like him myself.'

'Why not?'

'Now, that I can't tell you.' George looked a little sheepish. 'It's more a feeling than anything real.'

'I feel the same way,' I admitted.

'I told Bet to be careful.' He screwed his nose up, making him look like the little boy he had once been. 'Well, I said for her to come and find me if she needed anything.'

'You said that? That's kind.'

'I told you, Maggie. I've learned my lesson. George Lusk doesn't sit back and watch anymore.'

'Nor does Maggie Cameron.'

'Well, I suspect Maggie Cameron never did,' George said with a chuckle.

'Green has a sidekick called Constable Percival,' I told him. 'Do you know him?'

'I do. He's a piece of work 'n' all.'

'He is.' I thought for a moment. 'But Percival is all talk. He is young and mouthy, and I think easily led.'

'I know the sort.'

'From the outside it looks like he's the one in charge, but I think it's actually Green pulling the strings.'

'Interesting,' said George. 'Go on.'

'I think he winds Percival up, then watches him go.'

'I've seen that with some of the boys' mates over the years,' George said. 'It's schoolboy tactics and it ain't nice.'

'No.' I finished my tea and leaned over to pour some more. 'And there's something else.'

'Yes?'

'It's the power dynamic that bothers me.'

'How so?'

'According to Emma, Percival has worked at Leman Street for quite some time. Green hasn't been here that long. And yet he's calling the shots.'

'Behind the scenes, though. We might be wrong about that.'

'Perhaps,' I said, but I didn't think we were.

'My Alf had a mate like that for a while,' George said. 'Susannah said he acted like we should all be thankful he decided to spend time with us.'

I smiled. 'But you weren't?'

'We were not. He was polite enough, but I always felt he was after something. Green reminds me of him a bit.'

'He's desperate for recognition,' I said. 'Wants to be the one in charge.'

'Maybe it's just that he's older?' George suggested. 'He must be 30?'

'At least.' I made a face. 'Too old for Bet.'

'I think so.' George nodded. 'But we can't say anything.'

'Lord, no,' I said. 'If I know Bet, that would just encourage her to spend even more time with the man.'

'So, what shall we do?'

'I am an investigator,' I said. 'And therefore I think I shall do some investigating into Constable Green. Find out what makes him tick.'

'Will you need any help with this?' George looked hopeful.

'Almost definitely.'

'Then count me in.' He chinked his teacup against mine. 'Count me in.'

# Chapter 37

## Emma

I was later getting to the police station than I'd planned because I had made an impromptu visit to George Lusk. He was such a nice man, I thought. Kind and caring with a sharpness to his gaze that I imagined made him a good person to run the vigilance committee. He was around the same age as Maggie – in his early fifties – but he was clearly fit and well. I liked him, and it was clear Maggie did too. I had a suspicion that Maggie had been lonely before Bet and I had barrelled into her life, and that she was enjoying having us there. And I thought she'd enjoy George being a part of her life too.

But all that took time, so it was later than I'd planned when I got to Leman Street. I didn't even pretend to have an excuse for Fred this time – I simply found him in his office, where he was half-in, half-out of his coat and told him the truth.

'I wanted to see if you'd found out about Gent being in Paris when the murders happened,' I said.

Fred paused, one arm in his sleeve. 'I did.'

'And?' I went to him. 'Are you coming or going?'

'Going.'

I helped him into his coat. 'And?'

'Gent was in Paris,' he said. He turned to face me, his

expression resigned. 'I had my doubts about him from the start, so I'm not surprised.'

I began doing up his buttons.

'And what of Gent's death?' I asked, as if it were of no consequence to me whatsoever. 'Is it assumed it was an unfortunate accident?'

'It is.' As I reached Fred's top button, he put his hand on mine and squeezed my fingers. 'And I have to say, unprofessional as it may be, I'm not sorry about it. He was a man of very dubious character and I was horrified by some of the things we found in his house.'

He picked up my hand and kissed it.

'Lovely as it is to see you, Emma, I must go. Those damned journalists have another note they want to show me.'

'From the killer?' I asked.

'Apparently so.' Fred looked faintly sickened. 'It wouldn't surprise me if they're writing them themselves.'

'See you at home later?'

Fred gave me a kiss. 'You seem to be at home even less than I am.'

'Nonsense,' I said. 'Off you go.'

'Aren't you leaving too?'

'I will.' I gritted my teeth because I was about to tell a fib. 'I just want to see Bet first.'

'I've not seen her today,' Fred said. 'Is she working?'

'She is,' I lied, knowing Bet was at the tailor's all day. 'I'll track her down. Good luck with the note.'

Fred held the door open for me and I went out into the corridor. He followed, heading towards the main entrance, while I loitered, wondering if I could find Green and ask him what he knew about Timothy.

Slowly, I walked up the hallway, towards the large room I knew the constables all used. As I approached the corner,

I heard Green's voice – he was well spoken, more so than most of the other policemen, so it was easy to identify him.

'It's fine,' he was saying. 'But it just wasn't what I was expecting.'

I paused, unseen round the corner, so I could eavesdrop.

'I'm afraid you'll have to live with it for now,' said another man. Harrison. Why was Green talking to him?

'I have pulled enough strings and if I continue in this vein, questions will start to be asked.'

'I said it was fine,' said Green, sounding as if it – whatever it was – was anything but fine.

'Good.'

I peeped round the corner cautiously, just in time to see Harrison give Green a sort of affectionate punch on the upper arm. It was an oddly intimate gesture, and it surprised me.

'Everything all right, Mrs Abberline?'

Startled, I turned to see Percival behind me.

'Oh!' I said. 'Yes, I was just looking for Bet.'

Percival shrugged. 'I've not seen her.'

I saw an opportunity to find out more about Green, so I took it.

'You're back then?'

'I am.'

'How is your mother?'

'Much better, thank you.'

Percival made to walk past me and I put a hand on his arm.

'Constable Percival,' I said. 'Do you know that Bet is getting friendly with Constable Green?'

'I do.'

'I just wondered what you thought of him?'

Percival gave me a shrewd look. 'That's nice, that you're looking out for Bet.'

'We're friends.'

'Right.' He nodded. 'He's great, Constable Green. He's funny.' He began chuckling to himself. 'How he gets away with some of the stuff he says . . .' Then he caught himself. 'Yeah, he's nice.'

He sounded very much like he hadn't said everything he wanted to say.

'But?' I prompted.

'I've got a sister,' Percival said, glancing round to make sure we were alone in the corridor. 'And if she was getting friendly with Green, I'd . . .' He scratched his forehead, looking slightly sheepish. 'I'd probably tell her to steer clear.'

Well, that told me all I needed to know.

I gave Percival a long stare. 'I believe some people judge others on the company they keep, Constable Percival.'

He didn't reply, just met my gaze with a certain amount of defiance.

'I might just go and have a quick chat with Constable Green.'

'About Bet?' Percival said with concern. 'Don't tell him what I said, will you?'

'About something else entirely.'

'Right.' Percival relaxed. 'He'll be down the end. Tell him I'll be there in a while.'

'I will,' I said, with absolutely no intention of doing so.

I turned the corner – Green and Harrison were long gone – and walked along to the room shared by the constables. It was lined with tall, narrow, wooden cabinets where they stored their personal belongings, and had benches in the middle. It felt like a very male environment, and I paused for a second at the door, bracing myself. But when I pushed open the door, the only person in there was Green. He was sitting on the bench, with his jacket off.

'Mrs Abberline?' he said, looking surprised. He got to his feet. 'Are you lost?'

'No.' I stayed where I was, not wanting to be alone in the room with him in case anyone saw me and got the wrong impression. 'I wanted a quick word.'

He picked up his jacket and put it on. 'What about?'

'Timothy.'

'Ah.'

'Have you found anything out?'

'Why are you interested?'

'It's personal.'

He looked at me warily. 'Did Inspector Abberline ask you to speak to me?'

'No,' I said, shaking my head. 'Honestly, this is just me being nosy. What do you know?'

For a second, I thought he was going to brush me off, then obviously his eagerness to show off won out and he grinned.

'Quite a lot actually. I've not had a chance to speak to the inspector yet, so you're the first one who's hearing all this.'

I leaned against the doorframe and he sat down again. 'Tell me everything.'

'He's not American, for a start,' he said.

'He's not?'

'Irish. But he's lived in America for a long time – since he was a little lad.'

'And he's in London now.'

'He's been all over – or so he says. I spoke to a few people who know him, and they say he tells all sorts of stories.'

'Like what?'

'Like he was arrested for the assassination of President Lincoln.'

'What?'

'Oh it's total nonsense.' Green gave me a knowing smile. 'Just as him being friendly with Charles Dickens is nonsense, or him hobnobbing with French aristocrats.'

I was a little disappointed. 'So you think he's just a story-teller? No chance of him being the killer?'

'You're asking could he be Jack the Ripper?' Green said, a gleam in his eye.

'Oh Lord, that name isn't catching on, is it?'

'I'm afraid so. Everyone's using it.'

'It's awful.'

'It's catchy.'

'It's nasty.'

'I think that's why everyone's adopted it.'

'Urgh.' I shuddered. The whole fevered response to these killings was making me very uncomfortable, but that wasn't my concern right now. 'So could Jack the Ripper . . .' I winced. 'Could he be Timothy?'

'I think he could.' Green nodded. 'In fact, I'm becoming more convinced by the hour.'

I stared at him.

'What makes you think that?'

'He's a brute,' said Green. 'Vicious with women. Obsessed with what's underneath their skin. One woman told me his walls are lined with drawings of women's insides.'

'That doesn't mean anything, though,' I pointed out. 'If he's a medical man . . .'

'He is a medical man – of a sort,' Green said. 'And that means he knows how to cut.'

I grimaced. 'He wears a salt-and-pepper jacket,' I said.

'He does.'

'But the witnesses have reported a fairly small man, and I thought . . .' I paused. 'I heard Timothy was tall?'

Green waved his hand. 'Witnesses can get things wrong.'

317

'Do you know where he was on the nights of the killings?'

'I'm going to find out.' He leaned towards me, his elbows on his knees. 'But do you know what really convinced me?'

'What?'

'He's killed before.'

'Seriously?'

'I need to get Abberline to check with a contact in America, but apparently he killed a man in Boston.'

'A man?'

'Poisoned him, I heard. Gave him some tincture that was supposed to cure him, and it finished him off.'

'But it was a man?'

'Yes.'

'Poisoning a man accidentally is not the same as slashing a woman.'

Green bristled. 'Same result.'

'But not the same intent.'

'Does that matter?'

'I think so.'

He looked at me for a second, clearly disgruntled by my contradiction. 'If you'll excuse me, Mrs Abberline, I need to get on.'

'I think you've done well,' I said, hating myself for trying to placate him, but recognising the need to keep him friendly. 'You've found out so much in such a short time.'

'It's him,' Green said firmly. 'Mark my words. We've got him.'

I forced an admiring smile on to my face. 'I hope you're right.'

# Chapter 38

## Bet

I was tired when I finished work with Mr Segal and looking forward to collapsing into bed. 'I could sleep for a week,' I said to my mum as we headed home in the darkening twilight.

'I feel the same,' she said. 'I'm just going to have something to eat, then it's bed for me.'

'We've earned good money these last few days, though.' I looped my arm through hers. 'It's worth being tired to have that.'

'You're right.'

We walked along a short way. I couldn't help but notice the streets were emptying as darkness fell. That never happened before the murders. I tightened my grip on Mum's arm and we carried on. As we went round the corner two figures loomed out of the evening gloom and we both gasped in shock, before we realised they were policemen.

'Evening, ladies,' one said. 'Sorry to startle you.'

'Constable Percival,' I said, recognising his voice. 'And Constable Green, hello.'

'Hello there, Bet.' Silas smiled at me and I felt the now familiar flutter of excitement in my belly.

'I thought you were at the station today?' Percival said, sounding confused. 'Mrs Abberline said . . .'

'Oh I was,' I fibbed quickly, realising Emma had probably had a good reason to say so. 'Earlier.'

Beside me, my mother untangled her arm from mine and stuck her hand out to Silas.

'I'm Bet's mother, Jane,' she said. 'I've heard a lot about you.'

'Pleased to meet you.' Silas beamed at Mum and she fluttered her eyelashes at him, making me laugh. 'I've heard a lot about you, too.'

He turned to me. 'We're just about finished. Fancy a drink?'

Though two minutes earlier I'd been drooping with tiredness, suddenly I felt more awake. 'Would you mind?' I asked Mum.

'Of course not.' She smiled at me. 'Do you good to have some fun.'

'I've just got to go back to the station, so you could come with me, then we can go to the pub?' Silas said.

'I'll walk Mum back first,' I said. 'She shouldn't be on her own.'

Percival shook his head. 'Then you'd be on your own after you'd dropped her off. I'll walk your mother home, if she doesn't mind. You go with Green.'

'Are you sure? Is that all right with you, Mum?'

'Course it is.' She took Percival's arm and beamed up at him. 'It ain't far.'

'I'll see you later then, Mum.'

'No rush,' she said. 'Come on then, young man.'

She and Percival strolled away, Mum chatting away to him – she'd obviously forgotten her earlier tiredness too.

I gave Silas a sheepish smile. 'She's just excited about meeting you.'

'Likewise,' he said. 'Shall we?'

He offered me his arm and together we walked along, talking about our days.

'I saw Mrs Abberline earlier,' he said. 'She was very interested in this quack we're looking into.'

'Emma's interested in everything,' I said casually. 'I think she wants her husband's job.'

Silas chuckled as though that was an outlandish suggestion. 'I'm pretty sure Timothy is the killer.'

I stopped walking and looked at him in astonishment. 'You are? Does Inspector Abberline know?'

'I spoke to him a little while ago.'

'And what does he say?'

Silas looked a bit annoyed that I'd asked him that. 'He paid attention to my ideas.'

'So what makes you think he's the murderer?'

'Lots of things,' said Silas, starting to walk again. 'He's got a fixation with women's innards. He's killed before. He lies about everything. He was in London – in Whitechapel – on the nights of the murders.'

'Wait, he's killed before?'

He nodded. 'He poisoned a man in Boston with one of his concoctions.'

'That's different,' I said.

Silas tutted. 'It's not.' He sounded annoyed. 'Abberline thinks I've got it right.'

'It's definitely not the artist – Gent?'

'No, he was in Paris.'

'And Timothy was in London?'

'Right here.' Silas nodded.

'What else?'

'What do you mean, what else?'

We'd reached the police station and Silas paused on the steps, looking down at me.

'I mean, did he know the women? Had his path crossed with Annie or Polly? Or Elizabeth or Kate?'

'The Jack the Ripper letter said the killer was a doctor,' said Silas.

'It said people were saying he was a doctor,' I pointed out. 'Not that he was actually a doctor.'

Silas tutted. 'Timothy is a doctor,' he said firmly. 'A medical man.'

'A quack,' I said. 'With no training.'

'Who's obsessed about the internal organs of women. That in itself is enough to worry me. Maybe he's using their corpses as a learning tool. Like those chaps in Edinburgh. Burke and whatsit?'

'Hare,' I said. 'Burke and Hare. They weren't doctors – they just did the murders, then sold the corpses to surgeons to practise on.'

'Well, perhaps Timothy is saving himself the bother of finding a friendly murderer to help him get hold of some dead people,' Silas said. He smiled at me indulgently. 'It's hard to understand how these killers think. It's not something a woman can do.'

*You'd be surprised*, I thought.

'You're right,' I said, my mind racing with unanswered questions. 'Shall we go inside?'

'After you.'

I avoided the subject of the murders after that. I wasn't convinced Silas's theory stood up and he hadn't been happy when I questioned him too much. Despite that, though, I couldn't shake the memory of Kate's vicious wounds, or the way Llewellyn had suggested the killer had knowledge of women's bodies. It seemed this Timothy had that, and Silas was right – an obsession with what lay under women's skin was something to be concerned about.

These thoughts niggled me for a while as I sat in the

reception area and waited for Silas to get changed out of his police uniform. It was quiet now, though I could hear voices in the main part of the station. The old constable on duty, who I didn't know – I had a feeling he only covered the occasional night shift – was snoozing gently, his chin on his chest, and there was no one else around.

'Ready?' Silas appeared in the doorway, looking very handsome in normal clothes. He looked older out of uniform – less like a little boy playing at being a grown-up – and for a second I wondered if the age difference between us was too large. He was at least ten years older than me. But did it matter? I wasn't sure it did.

'I'm ready,' I said, with a smile.

He came over to me and with a glance at the snoring constable, he took me in his arms and kissed me thoroughly. I melted into his embrace, savouring the feeling of his bristly face against mine and the strength of his arms around me.

After a considerable length of time, we broke apart. 'Heavens,' I said, giddy with happiness. 'I think I might need a lie-down after that.'

Silas winked at me. 'I might come with you,' he said and I felt a rush of excitement and anticipation.

He took my hand and we walked to a quiet pub together. I thought we made a nice couple – we fitted together well. Silas wasn't much taller than me, though he was sturdily built, and we were both dark-haired.

Lots of the pubs nearby were less busy now, with drinkers choosing to head to safe spots before it was really dark, but the one Silas chose was quieter than most. It was near St Botolph's church.

'You know, Percival told me an interesting thing about that church,' said Silas as we approached.

'About the prostitutes?'

'Oh you know it?'

I smiled. 'Everyone knows it,' I said. 'The women can't stand still and look for business, because they'll get moved on.' I gave him an indulgent look. 'By your lot. So they walk round and round and wait for their punters to find them.'

Silas looked a bit disappointed. 'I'm new here, you know,' he said. 'I'm still learning all this.'

'I know,' I said. 'It's nice. Telling you about the sights of Whitechapel.'

'Most of the sights are where the murders happened,' Silas said. 'It's put Whitechapel on the map.'

'Hmm,' I said. Maggie had told us about that and, just like her, I wasn't pleased about the people coming to visit and gawp at the places where the victims had met their ends.

'Catherine was killed just round the corner from here,' Silas said. 'In Mitre Square.'

I knew that too, of course. In fact, part of me wanted to walk him that way – through Mitre Square – and see where she'd been found, but I didn't say so. Much as I enjoyed spending time with Silas, I didn't want to tell him about the investigations we'd been doing. Not yet, at least.

'Let's not talk about such awful things on our night out,' I said. 'What shall we have to drink?'

We found a table in the corner and sat close together, chatting, Silas making me laugh with his stories about the sleepy policemen he'd worked with in Surrey. 'Honestly, Bet, none of them would last five minutes in Whitechapel,' he said. 'We had to go to Guildford on a job once and this one copper, Ted, couldn't speak for about an hour – he was struck dumb by the big city.'

I chuckled. 'Poor Ted,' I said. 'You should invite him to visit, see how he gets on in a real big city.'

'Absolutely not,' said Silas firmly, and I laughed again.

We drank some more and talked and laughed more, and

at one point he took my hand and I felt a rush of absolute joy that I'd found him. He was so handsome – and funny – and clever. He was the perfect man for me.

'Bet,' he said, his face close to mine. 'I think you're marvellous.'

'I think the same about you.'

'I'd like you to be my girl.'

'I'd like that too.' My voice was steady but my heart was pounding. I grinned at him. 'My mum would like it as well.'

He laughed and I was chuffed I'd amused him. 'I don't reckon your mate Emma will be so pleased.'

'Really?'

'She doesn't like me.'

'Oh, rubbish, she barely knows you.' I glanced at the clock over the bar. 'I think it's time I called it a night,' I said with genuine regret. 'I'm up early for my shift at the police station.'

Silas stroked my face. 'Maybe I'll see you tomorrow?'

'Yes please,' I said.

We strolled home together through the quiet streets and, as we reached my place, he tugged my arm so we were in the shadows at the side of the street, and kissed me again, more heated this time. I felt breathless as his hand caressed my neck, then moved down to my chest.

'You're so beautiful,' he murmured, nuzzling under my ear in a way that made me dizzy. He bent his head and kissed my chest, just where the top of my dress met bare skin. He pulled it down further and I felt the chill of the night air, before he kissed me again. The cold breeze woke me from my rapture and I put my hands on Silas's shoulders.

'We should stop,' I said.

He didn't reply. Instead, his roaming hand found my breast and he squeezed gently. For a second I was tempted to give in to the tug of emotions I was feeling, but then I remembered where I was, and what my mother would say if she saw me, and I pulled away.

'No,' I said.

There was a fleeting moment as we stood there with Silas's hand on my breast and his groin pressed against mine, when I thought he wasn't going to stop. He waited a fraction too long to respond and I felt my heart beat faster, in fear this time. But then he stood up straighter, looking faintly sheepish.

'Sorry,' he said. 'I got a bit carried away there.'

He gave me his sweet boyish smile and I forgot my fear. Clearly, I'd been thinking about the murders too much.

'It's fine,' I said. 'I'll see you tomorrow.'

I gave him a kiss – just a quick one this time – to show him he'd done nothing wrong. Then I walked across the courtyard and went inside. Mum was already asleep, curled up under her bedcovers like a little girl. So quietly I went to the window and pulled back the curtain. Outside, Silas stood, waiting to check I was all right. I waved to him and he blew me a kiss, and I watched him saunter away, hands in pockets.

I felt a warm glow of joy, of lust, of attraction – whatever it was, I liked it. And as I got ready for bed, I thought I was the luckiest girl in Whitechapel to have a fella like Silas.

# Chapter 39

## Emma

Fred had sent a message saying he needed to see me and, for the first time in our marriage, I was nervous about what he wanted. The boy who'd come to the door hadn't known anything else, but I'd never been summoned before. I walked along towards the police station, wondering if something was wrong and if I should go faster and get it over with or slower and delay whatever was going to happen.

Did he know about Gent? I wondered. Or Bernard? Was he going to arrest me for murder? I imagined my own husband having to drag me to the cells, and felt my legs go weak. Should I go and fetch Maggie? Or Bet? No, the boy had told me to get there as soon as I could. I didn't want to make things worse.

I'd worked myself up into such a state that I was trembling from head to toe when I arrived at the station. Percival was on the front desk, which didn't help. He gave me a wink that made my hackles rise.

'Go on through, Mrs A,' he said. 'But I warn you, he ain't happy.'

I grimaced. 'Thank you,' I muttered, reluctantly walking down the corridor.

Fred's office door was closed – another bad sign – and I knocked quickly.

'Come,' he called.

I went inside and shut the door behind me, and he gestured for me to sit at the chair opposite his desk.

'Fred,' I began, aware that my voice was shaking.

'Emma.' He sighed. 'I have just had a very embarrassing meeting with Commissioner Harrison.'

'Oh?' I said, because I had no other words.

'He has received a letter from the prime minister.' Fred sighed, rubbing his forehead. 'Because Lord Salisbury has been in contact with Queen Victoria herself.'

I pinched my lips together and tried to keep my expression neutral.

'The queen has written to Lord Salisbury, who is, I'm sure you'll appreciate, a very busy man. He trusts in the Metropolitan Police to keep London safe while he is otherwise engaged on matters of state.'

I nodded. I was relieved I didn't appear to be about to be thrown in jail, but the mention of the queen had rattled me.

'So you can imagine how unimpressed Lord Salisbury was to receive a letter from the queen expressing her concerns about the Whitechapel murders.'

'Oh,' I said again.

'Hmm,' said Fred. He was standing behind his desk and now he put both hands down and leaned forward.

'In this letter the queen bemoans the lack of progress made by the detectives on the case. She suggests, now what were her exact words?' His face was reddening. 'She said the detective department was "not so efficient as it might be".'

'That's rather unfair,' I said. 'You're working very hard.'

Fred hit the desk with the palm of his hand, making his inkpot – and me – jump. 'Not hard enough, apparently.'

I shut my mouth again, not wanting to annoy him. I had

seen Fred's rare temper on occasion, but it had never been directed at me before.

'According to Harrison, the queen goes on to make some suggestions,' Fred said. 'She recommends lighting the courtyards, which, by the way, I'd already asked be done.'

'Hasn't it happened?'

'In some places, but not all,' Fred said with a sigh. 'It's expensive and time-consuming to add lanterns to every street in Whitechapel.'

I was beginning to hope he was angry at the situation as a whole, rather than at me specifically, though I wasn't sure why he'd summoned me if that were the case.

'What else does she suggest?'

'Nothing very practical,' said Fred. 'Finding blood-stained clothes, interviewing every single man living alone in the area, searching cattle boats and passenger boats . . .'

'Goodness,' I said. 'Everyone's a detective, as you your-self said.'

'And so are you,' Fred growled leaning forward again. 'You've been investigating this, haven't you?'

I stared at him, slack-jawed. 'Well . . .' I began.

'I asked you not to.'

'Well, you didn't actually ask me not to, you actually said you couldn't tell me what to do.'

'Have you been investigating these murders?'

I gave up any attempt at lying. 'I have. But quietly. You can be assured that no one – certainly not Harrison – knows.'

Fred gave me a long look.

'I'm fine,' I said firmly. 'Surely you can see that I'm fine? Better, in fact. The best I've been since Rose died.'

'I can see that,' Fred said. 'It's infuriating for many rea-sons – that this is what it took to make you find yourself again, that I didn't realise it could happen this way, that you are – clearly – a step ahead of me in my investigations,

329

and most of all that I can't use you in any sort of official capacity.' He rubbed his nose. 'But I can see it.'

I breathed out slowly. 'I'm sorry for not being honest, but I didn't want to worry you.'

Fred nodded. He still looked stern, despite his complimentary words. 'Shall I tell you what else the queen said?'

'Yes.' I was confused at the sudden change of direction.

'She said that she was disappointed her previous letter seems to have been disregarded and could Harrison assure her that he was looking into any medical men of ill repute.'

Suddenly I realised why Fred had asked me to come to his office. I closed my eyes briefly and then forced myself to open them again and look at him.

'Right,' I said.

'Emma?'

'Yes.'

'I gave you a pile of letters to read through, didn't I?'

'You did.'

'And in that pile of letters was there one from the queen?'

I screwed my face up. 'There was.'

'Did it mention her theory that the killer could be a medical man?'

'It did.' I took a breath.

Fred's nostrils flared. 'And did you at any time think it was worth telling me – Inspector Fred Abberline – about this? Or did you take it upon yourself to keep the content of that letter a secret, and act on it yourself?'

'Fred,' I began, but he hadn't finished.

'And the first I heard of this was when you came here with tales of this Dr Timothy?' he growled.

'Well, yes,' I said.

'When did you find the letter?'

'Before the two murders,' I admitted. 'Before Kate and Elizabeth died.'

330

Fred sat down heavily on his chair. He looked quite defeated, and I felt a rush of sympathy for him, even though he was being to my mind rather unfair and slightly pompous.

'I know you're under a lot of pressure,' I said. 'I was honestly just trying to help with the letters. I thought if I did some of the legwork, then I could pass it on to you and you'd be grateful.'

'If I'd known . . .' He rubbed his forehead again as though he had a headache building.

'You told me you were distancing yourself.'

'I did.' He nodded.

'Is Harrison angry?'

'Embarrassed, I think, more than anything else. He prides himself on his good relationships with the men at the top.'

'Will he take you off the case?'

'Fortunately, I think not.' Fred gave me a small smile. 'There's so much to it that handing it over to someone at this stage would be tricky.'

'Green's been looking into Timothy, and he said he was going to fill you in,' I said. 'Hasn't he told you anything?'

'Nothing whatsoever,' said Fred, then he groaned. 'Though he did come to speak to me yesterday, but I had just had the message from Harrison about meeting him and I was cross, so I sent him away.'

'Shame,' I said.

Fred glared at me. 'What do you know?'

'About Timothy? The evidence is shaky.'

'Tell me anyway.'

I filled him in on everything we knew about the quack and he wrote it all down.

'None of this is anything more than rumour,' he said.

'I know.' I paused. 'Except for the stuff about the man he killed. That's all fact.'

'That's not the same,' Fred said.

'Exactly!' I was triumphant. 'That's what I told Green. Accidentally killing a man with a badly made medicine isn't the same as slashing a woman.'

Fred looked at me with interest. 'You said that?'

'Yes, was that wrong?'

'No, but it's quite a new approach – to think about why a criminal acts as he does.' He gave me an approving nod that warmed my heart. 'You're ahead of the game.'

'I had a good teacher.' I was pleased that our argument – if it had been an argument – seemed to be over.

Fred drummed his fingers on the desktop. 'I'm sorry to drag you down here.'

'It's fine,' I said. 'It's a horrible situation to be in.'

I got up and went to him, and he put his arm round me and pulled me close.

'You'll get him,' I said. 'This will all be over soon.'

'I hope you're right.' He groaned again. 'Now I suppose I'd better go and speak to Green.'

'You don't like him?'

'Not much.'

'You know he's stepping out with Bet?'

'Is he?' Fred made a face. 'He's considerably older than she is.'

'I know. I'm not keen but she is smitten.'

'Hmm.' He frowned. 'Just keep an eye on her, won't you?'

'Of course. Fred? Do you think I'm getting too attached to Bet?' I swallowed. 'It had crossed my mind I was using her as a sort of . . . replacement for Rose.'

Fred sighed. 'Have you been fretting about that?'

'A little bit.'

'I think people looking out for others is the best thing about London,' Fred said. 'I imagine it's the best thing about the world. I don't think there's anything wrong with feeling protective of Bet. I feel the same over my constables.' He grimaced. 'Some of them.'

I smiled, feeling better. 'Speaking of your constables, does Green know Harrison?' I asked. 'Are they friends?'

'Not as far as I know. Why?'

'I saw them together. And Harrison did this to Green.' I punched his arm softly like Harrison had done.

'Odd,' said Fred. 'My father used to do that to me.'

'Harrison isn't Green's father, though.'

'No.' Fred looked thoughtful. 'Perhaps I'll ask him if he knew Harrison before he came to Whitechapel.'

'Good luck,' I said. 'See you at home?'

'You will.'

I gave him a quick kiss, then I went to the door.

'Emma?' Fred said.

'Yes?'

'Tell me everything from now on?'

'Of course,' I promised. 'Why wouldn't I?'

# Chapter 40

## Maggie

'I just don't think there's any real evidence,' I said, staring at the wall where we'd pinned all our information about the murders. 'Let's go through it again.'

Bet was leaning back in a chair, staring at the ceiling. 'We've been through it so many times.'

'So once more won't hurt, will it?'

Emma got up from where she was sitting and came to stand beside me. 'We know that Dr Llewellyn and the queen herself suggested the killer could be a medical man, due to his knowledge of female anatomy.'

'Indeed, and we are agreed that this is a reasonable suggestion, especially considering that Kate's kidney was removed.'

Emma made a face, but she nodded.

'We know Timothy is said to be obsessed with women's insides,' she said. 'But we have no proof of that – it's just hearsay.'

'But we do know he's killed before,' Bet added. 'Silas thinks that's important.'

Emma caught my gaze and gave a tiny roll of her eyes.

'He killed a man, not a woman, and he poisoned him, accidentally,' she said.

'But that's not hearsay,' Bet said quickly. 'It's true.'

'It's true the man died, and Timothy was implicated, but he wasn't charged,' Emma said. 'That's what Fred told me. And Fred agrees that it's a different type of crime from the murders of the women.'

'But Timothy was in Whitechapel on the days the women were murdered,' Bet pointed out.

'He was,' I said. 'That is definitely true. I checked that out myself and there were several people who saw him around.'

'Although,' Emma said, brandishing a pencil like a weapon in a way that made me wince. 'Surely if he was the killer, he'd make sure no one saw him nearby?'

'That's a good point.' I scratched my head. 'Everything sounds plausible until you dig deeper.'

'Silas is convinced Timothy is the killer.' Bet sounded a little sulky.

'I know,' I said. 'Except . . .'

'Except what?'

'Well, to be perfectly blunt, no one else has died.' I looked at both Bet and Emma. 'I'd have expected him to kill again.'

'It's not been that long,' Bet said. 'Not as long as there was between Martha and Polly.'

'Nor as long as there was between Annie, and Liz and Kate,' said Emma reluctantly. 'I think it's a bit early to say he's not killed again.'

'You're right,' I said. 'Dammit.'

Emma grinned at me. 'Timothy is clearly an unsavoury character,' she said. 'But that doesn't make him the killer, any more than it made Bernard the killer. Or Gent.'

'True,' I said.

Bet sighed. 'Everything about Timothy fits,' she said.

'We don't have any evidence.'

'Then we should find some.'

I fixed her with a stern glare. 'One of the first rules of being a detective, Bet, is to let the evidence speak for itself, not make it fit the crime.'

'Maybe Bet's too lovesick to think clearly,' said Emma.

'I'm not lovesick,' said Bet. 'And even if I was, you're so smitten with Fred that you think everything he says is true.'

'You think everything Silas says is true,' Emma said in outrage. 'And may I remind you that Fred is my husband.'

'Doesn't mean you have to agree with him about everything,' I put in, then regretted it immediately as Emma turned to glower at me instead of Bet.

'Well at least I can disagree with him without shoving him down the stairs,' she snarled. Then straightaway her expression changed. 'Oh Lord, I'm sorry – that was a terrible thing to say.'

'True, though,' I said after a moment, with a chuckle, watching relief flood Emma's face. 'Listen, let's not fight among ourselves. The real villain here is the killer.'

'We're never going to catch him,' Bet said. 'Never.'

'Does it matter?' I sat down at my desk. 'If us poking around, and the police doing their bit, and George and the vigilance committee doing theirs, and women like Ginger looking out for others, is enough to stop the murders, then does it matter if this killer never faces judgement?'

Bet and Emma both stood still, looking at me, then Emma grinned. 'It matters,' she said.

'Ah,' I groaned in frustration. 'You're right.'

We all laughed before a loud banging on the door downstairs made us jump.

'Heavens,' I said.

Bet was already halfway to the door. 'I'll go.'

'Be careful,' Emma said, going to the window to look out. 'Oh, it's fine, it's just George.'

We heard Bet open the front door, then an urgent, murmured conversation, footsteps, and George appeared. His face was drawn and pale, and he looked older than his years. In his hand was a box.

'George?' I said, getting up and going to him. 'Sit down. What's happened? You look awful.'

I steered him into the chair where Bet had been sitting and sat him down. 'Bet, could you get him a cup of tea? There's some in the pot.'

'Will do,' said Bet. She looked concerned. 'I'll be back in a jiffy.'

'George,' I said again, gently. 'Tell us what's happened.'

George looked right at me. 'I will, I'm just thinking how best to start.'

I pulled a chair closer to him and sat down and, without thinking of propriety, I took his hand.

'Start at the beginning,' I said.

'I've been getting a lot of letters, since we formed the committee, from all sorts of people. Cranks and loons – that's what Chip calls the writers.'

'Sounds about right,' said Bet, coming back into the room with a cup of tea for George. 'Get that down you, George. Tea makes everything better.'

She leaned on the back of my chair. 'So, what about these letters?'

'This one is the worst of the lot.'

'What does it say?' I asked. 'Is it in the box? Why would they send a letter in a box?'

George looked straight at me and the expression on his face made my blood run cold. 'Because it's not only a letter inside.'

'What's in there?' Emma asked quietly. 'What's in the box?'

George took a breath. 'It's a kidney.'

All three of us gasped. Bet put her fingers on my shoulder, and I reached up and patted her hand with mine, hoping to reassure her.

'Is it . . .' I swallowed. 'Is it the kidney that was taken from Kate?'

'That's what the letter says.' George put the box flat on his knee. 'But now the shock of seeing it there in my hand has passed, I'm inclined to say no. For a few reasons. Shall I open the box?'

'No,' I said, then I thought again. 'Yes.'

He slid the lid from the box and there was a folded piece of paper, alongside a small piece of kidney – instantly recognisable to anyone who'd ever made a pie, though it was smaller than those on sale at the butcher's shop. I felt my mouth fill with bile.

'What does the letter say?' Emma asked.

George took the piece of paper and unfolded it.

'Sor,' he read.

'Sor?' Bet frowned. 'What does that mean?'

'It's all written in this sort of strange Irish dialect,' George said. 'Look, he writes *"tother piece I fried and ate"* and he calls me "Mishter Lusk".'

'Mishter Lusk,' said Bet in a fairly good approximation of an Irish accent. 'Irish people don't write in an accent though?'

'Exactly.' George held the letter out so we could all read it.

It was written in red ink, just a few lines long and full of spelling errors. It threatened to send George the '*bloody knif*' the killer had used and ended with the taunt '*catch me when you can*'. Most chillingly of all, in place of an address at the top of the page, the writer had scrawled '*From Hell*'.

'It's different writing from the other letter I saw,' said

338

Emma confidently. 'The Jack the Ripper letter. It was very neatly written – I remember thinking it was strange that such a vicious killer could have such nice handwriting. This is a mess. Though the other one was written in red ink, too.'

'It feels like the writer is pretending to be uneducated,' I said thoughtfully, staring at the words on the page. 'Those spelling mistakes are odd. Why would someone spell knife that way?'

'Timothy is Irish,' said Bet. 'Perhaps this is written by someone who wants us to look at him?'

'No one knows we're looking at anyone,' I pointed out.

But George snorted. 'Come now,' he said. 'You're a striking woman, Maggie. People notice you wherever you go. And you've been on patrol with me now, three times, is it?'

'Three times,' I agreed, ignoring the surprise on the faces of Bet and Emma, who hadn't known I'd done that.

'Everyone in Whitechapel knows you, Bet. And you, Emma, are the wife of Inspector Abberline. People are bound to remember you asking questions.' He sat up a bit straighter. 'And I am the founding member of the Whitechapel Vigilance Committee.'

'You're saying everyone knows we're investigating these murders,' said Emma, sounding shocked.

'Everyone knows,' said George cheerfully, putting the lid back on the box.

'The police don't know,' Bet said.

George snorted again. 'They don't know much, do they?'

Emma grimaced. 'Fred knows. Well, he knows I'm investigating. And he knows you and I are friendly, Maggie. I kept Bet out of it.'

'Is he cross?' I asked.

'He was a bit at first.' She grinned. 'But he was less angry when I told him everything I knew about Timothy.'

'Silas tried to tell him all that but Abberline dismissed him,' Bet said, an edge to her voice.

'Fred's spoken to him now,' Emma said. 'He knows he's been working hard.'

We were getting off track. I dragged us back to the topic in hand.

'George, do you think this is Kate's kidney?'

'No,' he said with absolute certainty. 'I do not.'

'Then whose is it?'

'I think it might be from a corpse used by medical students,' he said. 'They're always larking about with the bodies. I've heard it many times.'

'Disrespectful,' muttered Bet.

'Have you taken this to Fred?' Emma asked.

'Not yet.'

'You should.' She took a breath. 'Please?'

George didn't look convinced. 'Perhaps.'

Pleased he had more colour in his cheeks now, I patted his hand and stood up, going over to the wall of information.

'A medical student would be well placed to know about the existence of a quack with an obsession with body parts,' I said.

'He would.' Bet sounded triumphant. 'So I say again, what if this is someone who thinks Timothy is the killer and wants to alert us?'

'Why wouldn't they just come to tell us?' Emma sounded less sure.

'Because they're scared?' Bet suggested.

'I suppose.'

Another banging on the front door interrupted us.

'What now?' I said with a tut.

'I'm going.' Bet darted off downstairs and was back in a flash with Ginger, who looked upset, though still with her usual air of defiance.

'Are you all right?' I asked her.

'I've heard something awful, Mrs Cameron, and I thought I should come straight to you.'

I put my hand to my mouth. 'There's not been another murder?'

'No, Lord, I hope not.'

'Then what?'

'A woman that stayed with me last night – Helen, her name was – she said she'd been to see that doctor – Timothy?'

We all exchanged glances. 'Yes?'

'He's got a place, down by the river. And he gave her some medicine for something or other. But when she was leaving, there was another man arriving, and she heard them talking.'

'What did they say?'

'She said Timothy was boasting that he had a collection of anatomy.' She said the words slowly and carefully. 'In jars.'

'Jars?' I frowned.

'What did he mean by a collection of anatomy?' Emma asked.

'Well,' said Ginger, sounding as though she was enjoying the drama of this. 'That's what I asked, and Helen said she was only listening at the door – she's ever so nosy – so she might be wrong, but she reckons in the jars are women's bits.'

'Ginger!' I said, shocked to my core. 'What on earth?'

She was unrepentant. 'That's what Helen heard,' she said. 'Timothy said he had jars with bits of women floating inside.'

'What sort of bits?' asked Emma cautiously.

'Well, Helen said he was showing off a bit and he said he had wombs,' said Ginger. She put her hands on her hips, standing up straight. Then she drooped. 'And then they walked off to the other bit of the house so she couldn't hear no more. But maybe there's other stuff, too.'

Again, I tasted bile. 'Other stuff?'

'Dunno.' Ginger shrugged. 'Kidneys? Heart?'

We all looked at the box on George's lap. He put his hand on the top, as if to stop the kidney leaping out.

'Who was the other man?' he asked Ginger.

'She never said.'

Emma screwed her nose up. 'This is all very far-fetched.'

'You're right,' Bet bounced on her toes. 'We need to go and see for ourselves.'

'Oh, Bet, I'm not sure . . .' I began.

'You said yourself we need proper evidence. This is proper evidence.'

'We need to tell Fred,' Emma said. 'The police should be investigating this – not us.'

'Oh, come on,' Bet said, throwing her hands up in the air. 'Let's just go and see what we can find out. Ginger can give us the address, can't you?'

'Well, there or thereabouts,' said Ginger.

There was a pause. I glanced at George, and he shrugged as if to say he knew what I was going to do.

'Fine,' I said. 'But we go cautiously. We don't want . . .' I trailed off. 'Well, we need to be careful.'

'Coming?' Bet asked Ginger.

'Not on your bloody life,' she said. 'I've done my bit.'

'How about you?' I said to George.

'I'll come if you want me to.'

'George, you need to take your letter to the police,' Emma said, putting her hand on his arm. 'Hoax or not, they need to know about it.'

'She's right, actually,' I said. 'Take it to Abberline – he'll know what to do with it.' I grinned at him. 'Just don't mention us, eh?'

'My lips are sealed,' he said.

'Right then,' I said, clapping my hands. 'Let's go and see this collection of anatomy, shall we?'

# Chapter 41

## Emma

I wasn't happy about going to find Timothy without letting Fred know. Partly because I knew he'd be furious if he knew where we were going without telling him, and partly because I thought Timothy was dangerous.

Though, come to think of it, we were dangerous too. Hadn't every man we'd suspected ended up dead?

So for everyone's sake, as we all trooped out of Maggie's, I took George's arm.

'When you go to see Fred to give him the box, can you give him a message from me, too?' I said in a low voice.

'Of course, love,' said George.

'Can you tell him where we're going and why?' I asked. 'But please don't tell Maggie.'

'I can't say I'm against the idea of Inspector Abberline knowing everything,' George said, knitting his brows together in worry. 'But I'm not keen on lying to my Maggie.'

I hid my smile at the way he said 'my Maggie'. 'It's not lying,' I said. 'You can tell her later.'

'You think Timothy's dangerous?'

'I do.'

George glanced over at Maggie where she stood on the pavement, talking to Ginger. 'Mind you, Maggie's no push-over,' he said with pride.

'You're right.'

I squeezed his arm gently. 'So you'll tell Fred?'

'Go on, then.'

'Thank you.' At once, I felt relieved.

'Ready for the off?' Maggie called to me.

'Absolutely. Where are we going?'

'Ginger's given me the address,' Maggie said. 'Near enough.'

Ginger gave us all a jaunty wave and sauntered off down the street. George went to Maggie and looked her, his hand on her shoulder.

'You be careful,' he said. 'This fella is dangerous.'

'You don't need to worry about me,' she said.

'No, but I do.'

They smiled at one another, and I thought how good they were for each other.

'Come on,' Bet said impatiently, breaking the moment. 'Let's go.'

Timothy lived near the Royal Mint on Glass House Street. It was quite a well-to-do part of town, close to the docks. The houses were tall and thin, like too many had been squeezed into the street.

On the corner was a pub called the Feathers. Maggie went inside to see if anyone knew exactly where Timothy lived.

As we waited, Bet put her hand on my arm.

'I'm a bit frightened,' she said. 'Silas is so convinced Timothy is the murderer. What if he is and he tries to hurt us?'

I looked at her. She suddenly seemed very young, and I felt another rush of protectiveness towards her. But whereas before I'd have pushed those feelings away, now I didn't.

'Firstly,' I said, smoothing a loose bit of hair away from her forehead. 'I do not think Timothy is the killer. Not really. But we should check – just to be sure.'

'Silas says . . .'

'I know what he says, but in this instance, I don't think he's right.' I sighed. 'Do you?'

Bet thought for a moment and then – with a certain amount of reluctance – she shook her head. 'Not really.'

'And, though he is most definitely . . . now what did the queen say? A medical man of ill repute . . .'

'The queen said that?'

'So Fred says,' I admitted.

Bet chuckled. 'Timothy definitely seems to be that – there's no doubt.'

'Indeed. But there is only one of him, and there are three of us. We – Maggie and I – we will not let anything happen to you. I promise.'

Bet stood up a bit straighter. 'And we are, after all, the wicked women of Whitechapel.'

This time I laughed. 'It's funny how I wasn't fond of that title but now I am embracing it.'

'Lord, me too,' said Bet. 'I feel I was born to be a wicked woman.'

We were both laughing now.

'Let's make sure Timothy knows who he's dealing with, shall we?'

'Absolutely.'

Maggie emerged from the pub, looking triumphant.

'It seems everyone knows Timothy,' she said. 'His is the last house on the left.'

I took a deep breath. 'Right then.' I took Bet's hand in mine and reached for Maggie's. They both clasped hands too, so we were in a circle once more. 'The wicked women of Whitechapel are back in business.'

'Perhaps for the last time,' Maggie said.

'Nonsense.' I shook my head. 'There will always be call for lady detectives.'

'Come on,' said Bet. 'Less talking and more doing.'

'Let's go.' Maggie dropped our hands and marched off, with Bet and I trotting to keep up.

'Do you think we should have a plan?' I called after her. 'We had a plan with Bernard and with Gent.'

'Neither of those went very well,' Bet said.

'He's a doctor, isn't he? Let's just say one of us is sick,' said Maggie. She stopped walking and looked at us both with an appraising eye. 'Or let's use the pregnancy thing again. Bet, you're expecting.'

'Righto,' said Bet.

'Shall I take off my shawl?' I asked, but Maggie shook her head. 'Early pregnancy,' she said. 'I have a feeling our Timothy does a good trade in sorting out women's problems.'

I was genuinely shocked. 'Really?'

'There are teas you can drink,' Maggie said, 'If it's early enough.'

'You think he sells those?'

'Well.' Maggie turned and looked at the house we were standing next to. 'Let's go and find out, shall we?'

I took Bet's hand as we walked up the path and she squeezed my fingers. The front door was only a few steps from the pavement, but shielded from the road, and passers-by, by an open porch with two white columns either side.

Maggie rang the doorbell and we heard it clanging through the house. But no one answered. There were no sounds from inside.

'Ring it again,' I urged. Maggie pulled the cord and again the bell rang. Again, no one answered.

'Oh,' I said, disappointed.

Bet stepped backwards, looking up at the house from the road.

'That window's open,' she said.

Maggie and I followed her gaze to the window over the porch.

'I can get up there.' Bet looked determined.

'Someone will see you,' I said.

'It's quiet. I can be quick.'

Two women walked past us, and we all nodded to them in greeting. They nodded back and continued on their way. As they reached the pub, they turned left and vanished from sight, leaving the street empty.

'See?' said Bet. 'I'll climb up and go through the window, then I can let you in.'

'Oh, Bet, I don't know,' I said, just as Maggie said: 'Yes, go on, worth a try.'

Bet grinned at me. She hitched her skirt up and said: 'Give me a shove on to the railings.'

Maggie bent down, linking her fingers to give Bet something to stand on. Bet put one foot on Maggie's hands, then the other on the railings and pulled herself up so she was balanced, holding on to the top of the porch.

'Careful,' I called.

Bet turned and grinned at me, then she put her arms on the roof of the porch and somehow hauled herself up. It wasn't very ladylike, but she ended up sprawled on top, just as a man came out of the Feathers and walked towards us.

'Down,' said Maggie urgently, and Bet lay as flat as she could.

'Down there,' Maggie said to me pointing in the opposite direction to where the man had come from. 'That's where you want to go. And then take the first right.'

The man was walking past us now and, to my relief, he looked at where Maggie was pointing rather than up at the porch where I could see the top of Bet's head.

'Afternoon,' he said.

'Hello!' I blurted, perhaps a little too gaily because he looked slightly taken aback and hurried along.

We watched him reach the end of the street and then Maggie looked up at Bet.

'All clear,' she said.

Bet got to her feet and pushed the sash window up carefully. Then she sat on the ledge and dropped inside. We saw her close the window behind her and disappear into the room. And then we waited.

After what seemed like forever, but couldn't have been more than a minute, we heard footsteps and the door opened an inch.

'There's no one here,' Bet said, peeking out. 'Come in.'

Maggie and I went in and I shut the door. Inside, the house was well looked after but plain. There were no pictures on the walls, and the coat rail was empty.

'Is this definitely the right place?' I whispered.

'There's no one here,' Bet said again in a normal voice, which sounded loud in the quiet hall. 'There's no need to whisper.'

Maggie picked up a letter on the table next to the door. 'It's the right place,' she said. 'This is addressed to Dr Timothy.'

'He's got a cheek calling himself doctor.'

'Don't he just?' Bet said. She pushed open the first door leading from the hallway and looked inside.

'Nothing,' she said, standing back to let Maggie and me look too. It was a lounge with plain furniture and nothing to tell us anything about the man who lived there, nor even if he lived alone or with others.

We looked round the rest of downstairs and found the same – a dining room with a large table and plain crockery in a cabinet. A kitchen with nothing personal.

'Upstairs?' Maggie asked.

'It's the same,' Bet said with a shrug. 'From what I saw, at least.'

We went up the stairs and she was right. There were three bedrooms – two on the next floor and one up at the top. Sparsely furnished, but again with no clues as to the occupants.

'Strange,' I said.

We filed back downstairs. 'There's no more to the house?' asked Maggie, furrowing her brow. 'A shed, perhaps? Or an outhouse?'

Bet walked into the kitchen and looked out the back. 'Nothing,' she said.

'It's so quiet.' I looked round the hall where we stood. 'All these drapes are soaking up any sound.' I touched a heavy curtain that hung along one wall. 'Hold on . . .'

'What is it?' Bet turned, as I pulled the curtain back, revealing a door.

'There's a cellar,' Maggie breathed. 'Of course there is. There were ventilation bricks outside.'

'And Ginger said the room had no windows,' Bet pointed out.

'She did.'

I swallowed. 'Should we go down?'

'I think so,' said Maggie.

I turned the door handle – it wasn't locked – and opened the door. In front of me was a short flight of wooden stairs with another door at the bottom, which was slightly ajar, showing a chink of light.

'Here goes,' I said.

'Wait!' Maggie said.

I turned to see her lighting a candle she'd picked up from the table. 'Take this.'

I took it from her, then holding up my skirt in case I tripped, I went carefully down. Maggie and Bet followed.

At the bottom I paused.

'Go on,' Bet whispered.

I pushed the door open and stepped into the cellar, feeling the cold, damp air wrap round me.

Stopping a few steps into the room, I blinked a couple of times, my eyes adjusting to the dim light. There were a couple of lanterns dotted round the room that gave a glow, and a weak dribble of daylight from the ventilation bricks above.

It was a largish cellar. There were wooden shelves on the walls and a long, wider surface that was clearly used as a desk. In the middle of the room was what was clearly a makeshift operating table. I felt behind me for Bet's and Maggie's hands and was grateful when they both gripped my fingers. Beyond the table was an archway, leading to another, much smaller room that was lined with shelves, and on those shelves were jars and jars of . . . well, something.

'Heavens,' I breathed.

And then, as I squinted at the archway, trying to see what the jars contained, a man appeared from the smaller room holding one of the containers.

He was just as surprised to see us as we were to see him.

We all shrieked in shock, and he yelped like a cat and dropped the jar, which shattered loudly on the stone floor.

'Who are you?' he shouted. 'Get out!'

He definitely sounded more American than Irish, I thought. He looked furious, and I was glad the operating table was between us because my legs were already shaking violently and I wasn't sure I could run away if I needed to.

Maggie took a step forwards so she was in front of me. 'Dr Timothy?' she said. Her voice was level but I could see she was also trembling from the fright he'd given us. 'We just wanted a quick word.'

Timothy's eyes were darting from side to side. We had

him cornered, I thought. Like a trapped rat. And trapped rats never reacted well.

'Who are you?' he said.

'My name is Maggie Cameron, and these are my erm, sisters, Bet and Emma. We wondered if you could help us with a small problem?'

Timothy looked completely baffled.

'Did you break into my house?' he said.

'Only slightly,' Bet said. She was edging to one side, inch by inch, as Timothy spoke. 'But the window was open.'

Timothy was still staring at Maggie.

'We've heard you can help girls who have got themselves in a bit of trouble,' said Maggie. She sounded convincing but it was clear our cover story wasn't going to work now we'd broken into Timothy's house and surprised him in his creepy cellar.

Bet took another step. 'Where are you going?' I said under my breath.

'We need to see what's in those jars.'

I nodded, following her lead and inching to my right too.

Maggie, sensing our movement, took the candle from me and held it in her left hand, throwing Bet and me into shadow. We moved again, a little further as Maggie gave a loud, theatrical sigh and burst into tears.

'It's just that we're desperate,' she sobbed. 'I don't know what to do, and someone told me you're the cleverest man in London and that you'd be able to help. It's just my Bet, you see . . .'

With Timothy's attention fixed on Maggie, Bet and I slunk through the archway behind him and into the little room. It was tiny – I thought Fred could probably touch two walls with his arms outstretched – and jars lined the shelves. A lantern was on the floor, in the corner, so I picked it up and held it close to the nearest shelf. I gasped in shock as I saw the jars there contained small parts of flesh. 'Wombs?' I whispered, almost gagging on the word. I wasn't entirely sure what a womb looked like.

'Perhaps,' said Bet in my ear. 'That's disgusting.'

Maggie was still sobbing in the main room and I lifted the lantern again to a different shelf. This one made me rear back, stumbling into Bet, who was right behind me.

'Babies,' I croaked. 'Unborn babies.'

Bet took the lantern from me and held it up herself. I averted my eyes from the light, not wanting to see them again. I felt my throat close up with tears as I remembered expecting Rose and feeling her movements inside me. She'd have looked like that back then. No little one deserved to end up in a jar to be gawped at by a twisted fake doctor.

'Maggie?' Bet shouted as she looked at the jars in horror. 'Maggie!'

'What the blazes?' said Timothy.

Maggie's sobs stopped and she appeared in the little room along with Timothy behind her.

'There's all sorts here,' I said. I pointed at Timothy, rage now overtaking my fear and disgust. 'You're a monster.'

'I'm a scientist,' he said with a sigh. 'Don't get hysterical.'

Maggie drew herself up, her shoulders back.

'Where did you get these from?'

Timothy gave her a horrible smile. 'From women.'

'Which women?'

'It doesn't matter which women,' he said. 'They're all the same inside.'

'Do you butcher their corpses yourself?' I said, trying to sound calm, though inside I felt sick with fear.

'Heavens, no,' Timothy said, as if that was a ridiculous

suggestion. 'I've a few friends in useful places. Mortuaries. Hospitals. Medical schools.'

'You're a killer,' Bet said.

'I'm not,' Timothy said mildly. 'Well, only sometimes. And usually accidentally.'

He took a step forwards and with a lurch I realised he was now standing in the archway, with Maggie, Bet and me in the small room. He was quite a tall man, and he filled the narrow entrance.

'Usually,' he said again.

My palms were sweating and I wiped my hands on my skirt.

'Did you kill Martha Turner?' Maggie said.

'I've no idea who that is,' said Timothy.

'How about Polly Nichols, or Annie Chapman?' I said.

He looked blank.

'What about Kate Eddowes or Elizabeth Stride?' Bet added.

'Listen, I don't know who these women are,' Timothy said. 'I am a doctor, not a murderer.'

'You're no doctor,' Bet growled. 'You're a quack.'

'With an unhealthy obsession with women's anatomy,' Maggie added.

'Maybe so,' Timothy said. 'But I'm not a murderer.'

I had an awful, gnawing feeling that he was telling the truth.

'Though,' Timothy went on. 'I am willing to make an exception, every now and then.'

He stepped towards us again.

'You're just trying to scare us,' Bet said. 'You're just one man. We could overpower you if you tried anything.' She looked round at Maggie and me. 'And you may not be a killer, Dr Timothy . . .' she emphasised the 'doctor' in a mocking way. 'But we've killed two men.'

'Three,' said Maggie. 'Strictly speaking.'

'Three men,' said Bet. 'Between us. And frankly I ain't bothered about adding another one to that list.'

'You're lunatics,' said Timothy. He didn't sound bothered by Bet's threats, but did I see a flash of panic in his eyes? The light was dim and it was hard to tell.

'Maybe we are lunatics,' said Bet. 'But do you want to put it to the test?' She clenched her fists. 'I can take you on.'

If I hadn't been so angry and so frightened I might have laughed at the thought of Bet pummelling this man. But as it was, I simply stood still, afraid of what he might do next.

What he did, though, was laugh.

'Oh dear,' he said. 'You're right, of course. I'm a man of advancing years, not as quick on my feet as I was. And there is indeed, only one of me. You're stronger and faster than I am.'

He turned to the shelf to his left and ran his fingers over the vials of liquid there. 'In normal circumstances, of course, that's all true.'

He picked up one bottle and shook it, holding it up.

'But I am also a scientist.' He smiled at us again. 'Do you know what this is?'

None of us answered.

'It's chloroform,' he said. 'Anaesthesia. One tiny drop of this on a handkerchief held over your mouth and nose would make you go to sleep.'

'Brilliant,' said Bet her voice dripping with sarcasm. 'Except we ain't going to let you near enough to us.'

'No,' said Timothy. He went to the shelf again and found something a little like a perfume puff, only bigger. He began unscrewing the lid of the bottle he was holding. 'But I can spray it at you and that will buy me enough time to get away.'

'Lord, you're the lunatic,' said Maggie. 'You can run but you can't hide. The police will catch you.'

'On the contrary,' Timothy said. 'I am the cleverest man in London, like you said. I've lived in Dublin, and New York, and I've been collecting specimens for years, and I've never been caught before.' He put the lid from the bottle on the side. 'Could one of you lift the lantern please, like a good girl? It's hard to see what I'm doing.'

'Get lost,' said Bet.

'Such hostility.'

Losing patience, I took the lantern from Bet's hand and shone it directly in Timothy's face. 'The police are on their way,' I said. 'They're coming right now. In fact, they could even be outside this very minute.'

Maggie and Bet both looked at me in surprise. Timothy's bravado slipped, just a little.

'You're lying,' he said.

'I'm not,' I said. 'My name is Emma Abberline and my husband is with the Whitechapel Police. I told him where we were going and why, and he is on his way.'

I cocked my head to one side.

'In fact, I think I hear something on the street. Is that horses' hooves?'

Timothy was starting to look panicky again.

'The police will come down here, and they will see your disgusting, despicable collection, and you'll be slapped in jail quicker than your chloroform can work.'

'Perhaps they'll put a plaque outside your cell saying "cleverest man in London",' mocked Bet.

Timothy held the bottle out, and I noticed his hands were trembling. He really was rattled.

'You're too late,' I said. 'Too. Late.'

But Timothy simply smiled, put the bottle to his mouth and drank the whole thing down in one go.

We all stared at him for a second and then he began to gasp for air, his breathing shallow and ragged. He dropped to his knees, clutching his chest.

'Bugger,' said Maggie. 'Bugger, bugger, bugger.'

'We need to stop him,' I said. 'Make him sick? Can we do that?'

'I think it's too late,' Maggie said.

We all looked down at Timothy, who was now twitching on the cold, stone floor. He let out a raspy breath, froth gathering round his mouth, and breathed in again. He twitched once more, his leg kicking out, his breath rattled and then he was still.

'Ohhhh bloody hell,' Bet said. 'He's gone and killed himself, the bloody coward.'

# Chapter 42

## Bet

We all looked down at the body on the floor.

'Do you think he was the murderer?' I asked.

Next to me, Emma shook her head. 'I really don't.'

'Me neither,' said Maggie.

I thought about how convinced Silas had been, and I looked at the jars around the room, with their awful contents, and then I shrugged. 'Me neither,' I said.

'Oh Lord,' said Maggie. 'Why do we keep doing this?'

'We really didn't kill this one,' Emma said. 'This was all his doing.'

'Yeah,' I said. 'But it don't look good.'

Emma's eyes widened. 'Oh blimey, Fred's coming.'

'That was true?' I said in surprise. 'I thought you were just saying that to frighten old Timothy.'

'It's true,' Emma said, almost wailing. 'I told George to tell them where we were going and why. I think they're going to be here any minute, if they're not here already.'

'And they'll find us here with a corpse at our feet,' Maggie said. 'And true though our story may be, it doesn't paint us in the best light.'

'That's definitely true,' I said.

'And if we are seen to be involved in Timothy's death,

perhaps that will cause them to start looking again at Gent's death, or even Bernard's.'

Emma was breathing quickly, her face pale. 'I'm so sorry,' she said. 'Let's work out what to do.' She tapped her fingers on her chin quickly. 'Think, Emma, think.'

She was beginning to panic. I looked at Maggie, who put her arm on Emma's shoulder.

'We're in this together,' she said, soothing her. But Emma was still frantic.

'We can leave,' she said, her voice shrill. 'We can sneak out of the house before Fred arrives. It might not be too late. Come on . . .'

Maggie shook her head. 'We can't sneak out, not this time. Because Fred knows we were coming. Us not being here makes us look just as guilty as us being here when he arrives.'

Emma's shoulders slumped. 'What shall we do?' she gasped. 'What can we do?'

I had been thinking, now I waved my hands in the air to get the others' attention.

'We can arrive,' I said.

My suggestion seemed to snap Emma out of her panic. 'What? We're already here,' she said, scratching her head. 'How can we arrive?'

'We sneak out now,' I explained, 'Assuming we're not too late, and we hide ourselves away somewhere and watch the police arrive. Then we arrive too.'

Maggie looked at me in admiration. 'This could work,' she said. 'But we need to be quick. And quiet. And we need to leave the house without being seen.'

'Is there a back door?' I asked, my mind racing. 'We could go out the back like we did with Gent.'

'There's a walled yard,' Maggie said. 'I can't remember if it was enclosed or not, though.'

'Not,' said Emma. 'It wasn't. It was open to the right – there was a sort of archway.'

'Brilliant,' said Maggie. 'Let's go. Quietly, now.'

We stepped over Timothy where he lay, bringing back memories of stepping over Gent, and headed for the stairs. Maggie led the way, treading softly then she opened the door a fraction and listened for a second. 'Nothing,' she said. 'No voices, no horses. It's all quiet.'

We all slid through the door and paused again. Still nothing. My heart was pounding in my chest as we shut the door to the cellar and pulled the curtain across.

'Tiptoes,' whispered Maggie. 'Check you're not leaving footprints.'

We made our way along the hall to the kitchen and the back door. Maggie opened the door – the key was in the lock and turned easily – then she shut it behind her and locked it again, slipping the key into her pocket. 'Go,' she said.

This time Emma led the way, darting across the courtyard, through the archway and into – to our absolute surprise – the back of the pub on the corner.

'Goodness,' she said, stopping short and causing Maggie and I to bump into her. 'I didn't expect to end up here.'

'It's fine,' said Maggie. 'Better than fine. We'll go inside, find a spot by the window and watch for the police.'

'As long as no one in the pub saw us,' I said.

'Even if they did. It won't matter,' Maggie pointed out. 'No one will ask questions about how we arrived.'

'We hope,' Emma said.

We did exactly as Maggie said. We went inside, found a window seat, and watched the street. We'd only been there a matter of minutes when a carriage pulled up and out stepped Abberline, along with Silas and Percival.

'They're here,' I said. Another two constables rode up

on horseback and clattered into the yard behind the pub, where we'd been just a few minutes before.

'We'll give them a couple of minutes,' said Maggie. 'Then we'll go.'

After a short while we all got to our feet and headed for the door to the side of the pub, furthest away from Timothy's house.

Once we were out on the pavement, I turned to the others. 'Where have we been?' I said. 'If anyone asks why it took so long to get here?'

'We can just say we had to ask round to find the exact address,' Maggie said.

'Yes.' Emma nodded. 'That's true.'

We all clasped hands again, very briefly, then let them drop, and together we walked round the corner.

The police had already got in the front door and were swarming over the house as we walked up the path.

'Fred?' Emma called. 'Fred?'

He appeared in the doorway. 'Oh, Emma, I wondered where you were. Mr Lusk told me you were on your way.'

'It took us a while to find the correct address,' said Emma. 'You got here fast.'

'Yes, well we had his address on file.' Abberline looked a little sheepish. 'He's not here, though.'

'Coward has probably got wind that you're on to him and made his escape,' said Maggie with venom.

'Possibly,' said Abberline.

'Ginger told me the worst of it was in a room with no windows,' Maggie added. She pointed to the ventilation bricks next to where we stood. 'Perhaps she meant a cellar?'

'Good thinking,' said Abberline. He turned and called into the house. 'Is there a cellar, lads?'

'We should go,' Emma said. 'Now you're here, there's nothing we can do.'

'Thank you for telling me where you were headed,' said Abberline.

'Of course.'

'And thank you all for your help on this.'

Silas came to the door. 'Inspector, we need you in the cellar,' he said.

'What is it?'

'We've found Timothy, sir. But he's dead.'

'Coward,' said Maggie again.

'Guilty,' I said.

Silas looked at me and gave me a tiny wink. 'Undoubtedly,' he said. I felt my toes curl with the thrill of his attention.

Abberline nodded, grim-faced. 'It would seem so. Lead the way, Green.'

'Let's go,' said Emma, reaching out and touching her husband's hand briefly. 'Good luck, men.'

We all walked slowly to the corner by the pub, then onwards to Maggie's office, where we spent a couple of hours sharing food and talking about anything but Timothy. I thought the horror of seeing the contents of those jars would stay with me for a long time and I wasn't ready to discuss it. It seemed the others felt the same because no one mentioned it, until Emma began to yawn.

'I really should go home,' she said.

'It's dark.' Maggie looked out of the window. 'I don't like the thought of you both walking home alone.'

'Timothy could have been the killer,' I said.

'He could have been.' Maggie sounded doubtful.

'All the evidence suggests he was,' said Emma. 'Those awful jars.' Her voice wobbled a little. 'I think I'll be seeing them in my mind's eye as long as I live.'

'Me too,' I said.

'And yet,' said Maggie.

'And yet.' Emma nodded.

'I can't understand why someone would have all those jars,' I said, shuddering at the thought.

'Perhaps it is just as simple as Ginger said,' Maggie suggested. 'Timothy was obsessed with women's insides.'

'But not obsessed enough to kill,' I said.

'He didn't have to kill,' Emma said. 'He got those samples from other places.' It was her turn to shudder in disgust. 'Just like Gent bought the information about the murders – Timothy was buying anatomy. I suppose it is true that everything has a price.'

'Lord,' said Maggie. 'All these awful men we've come across. I feel we have exposed a dark underbelly to Whitechapel.'

'It ain't a dark underbelly at all,' I said. 'It's just Whitechapel.'

'That's even worse,' she said with a sigh. 'And another reason for you not to walk home alone.'

'We could go to the police station,' Emma suggested. 'Fred will probably still be there, and if he's not, I'm sure someone will volunteer to walk us home.'

'Good idea,' I said eagerly.

Emma smiled at me. 'Green will probably be there, too.' Then she took a breath. 'You really like him, don't you?'

'I do.' My cheeks flushed. 'He's very handsome and he looks after me.'

'Do you think . . .' Emma glanced at Maggie. 'Does he feel the same about you?'

'He says so.'

She looked at me for a fraction too long and I thought she was going to say something but then she just nodded. 'Good,' she said. 'That's good.'

Outside it was cold and we both pulled our hats down over our ears and hunched down into our coats, walking quickly to the police station.

'See you tomorrow?' I asked Emma hopefully. I got the impression she was mildly irritated with me, and I wasn't sure why, but I had an inkling it was to do with Silas. Perhaps she was jealous of me spending time with him? Or perhaps our blossoming romance was reminding her of her early days with Abberline. Whatever it was, I wanted reassurance that she wasn't too annoyed.

'Of course.' She smiled at me, and I felt relieved.

She opened the police station door and there in the foyer were Silas and Abberline and a few others.

'Emma,' Abberline said with genuine delight. I wondered if Silas would be so pleased to see me in twenty years' time and then blushed at the idea of being with him for so long. I ducked my head as he looked at me, in case he could read my thoughts.

'Hello, Bet,' he said. 'What brings you here at this late hour?'

'We didn't want to walk home alone,' I said, looking up at him through my eyelashes. 'Fancy a stroll?'

'Why not?'

I was pleased.

'I was about to head home myself,' said Fred, who was wearing his overcoat and hat. 'So that was good timing.'

'Is it all right if I walk with Bet?' asked Silas.

'Go right ahead, Green.' Fred nodded. 'Good work today, everyone.'

'I need to get my coat and change my boots,' said Silas. 'Want to wait here?'

'I'll come with you,' I said, not wanting to be alone in the foyer.

'Really? I'll just be five minutes.'

I looked at the elderly constable snoring at his desk and nodded. 'I'll come.'

Everyone else went out of the front door and I followed

Silas to the constables' room. He took his coat from the stand and laid it on the bench, then he went to his locker.

'What a day,' he said. And ordinarily I'd not have paid the slightest bit of attention to how he opened his locker. But the way he stood next to it looked awkward, as though he was angling himself in a way to stop me seeing inside.

'So Timothy's dead, then?' I asked, shifting slightly on the bench so I could see better.

'Killed himself,' Silas said, taking his boots out of the cupboard. 'And let me tell you, Bet, he is no loss to anyone. What an awful man he was.'

He carried on talking, but I wasn't really listening, because as he bent to put his boots on the floor, I caught a glimpse of inside the locker. And there, on the top shelf, was a jar. I didn't have to see it properly to know without a shadow of doubt it was one of the jars from Timothy's cellar. I felt cold suddenly – as though icy rain was dripping down my spine. I tried to look again but Silas had straightened up and I could no longer see.

'He was clearly an absolute horror,' Silas was saying. He shut his locker with a bang and turned to me. 'Are you all right?'

With supreme effort, I smiled at him.

'Just tired, I think,' I said. 'I'm fine.'

# Chapter 43

## Maggie

*One week later*

Bet's mother, Jane, was waiting for us at the door, her face drawn and worried.

'Thanks for coming,' she said. She shut the door gently behind her and came out on to the street to talk to us.

'I don't want her to hear.'

I looked at Emma, who looked almost as worried as Jane.

'What's wrong?'

'She won't get out of bed,' Jane said. 'She won't talk to me. Won't eat.'

'How long's she been like this?' Emma asked.

'She was in bed all day Wednesday and Thursday, but I didn't worry so much because I was out at work, but then she just stayed there. Yesterday she wouldn't get up neither, and then I did start to worry because it's been the best part of a week now. So I took the afternoon off to come home early and check on her and she was just lying there, curled up under the blanket. And she's the same again today, but I have to go to work, and I didn't want to leave her without doing something.'

'You did the right thing, coming to find me,' I said. 'She's definitely not ill? Does she have a fever?'

'I don't think so.'

I looked at Emma, who made a face.

'You go to work, Jane,' I said. 'We'll take care of her.'

Jane looked relieved. 'Thank you.' She picked up her bag and coat, which were next to the door, and hurried away.

'Do you think it's Timothy?' Emma said when Jane was far enough away to be out of earshot. 'Those jars were awful – have they upset her so much that she doesn't want to be in the world?'

'She seemed all right, didn't she? Afterwards? How was she when you left her at the police station?'

'Fine,' said Emma thoughtfully. 'Nothing out of the ordinary. Green was going to walk her home.'

I felt a tremor of nerves. 'Do you think something happened with him?'

'Like what?' said Emma.

'Well, you know? If he took things too far.'

Her eyes widened. 'Perhaps. Oh Lord, let's go and speak to her.'

We went inside. The rooms that Bet shared with her mum were small but clean and nicely kept. There was one room for living in, and then another room to the side where the women slept. We knocked on the door.

'Bet?' I said softly. 'Are you awake?'

There was no reply.

I pushed open the door. Bet's bed was underneath the window. She was rolled up in her blanket, with only the top of her head visible.

'Bet?' I said again.

I could tell from her breathing that she was awake, but not speaking.

Emma gestured at Bet with her head and I nodded. We both went over and sat down on the edge of the bed, making Bet sigh.

'I know you're awake,' I said. 'Your mum's gone to work but she's ever so worried about you.'

'We're worried too,' Emma added. 'What's wrong, Bet?' She pulled the blanket over her head.

Emma sighed. 'Bet, we can help you, but first you have to tell us what's going on.'

Bet said something that was muffled by the blanket.

'What?' I said. 'We can't understand what you're saying.'

'I can't talk about it yet,' Bet said. 'I need to think.'

'Talk about what?' Emma asked. 'Bet, come on, we're friends.'

With some effort and wrestling of the bedclothes, Bet sat up. 'We are friends,' she said. 'And I will tell you.' Her voice cracked. 'It's just so awful, that I need to make sense of everything for myself first.'

'Is it Timothy?' I said. 'Because it might help to talk about it.'

She shook her head.

'Is it Green?' Emma said. 'Bet, did he hurt you?'

After a slight hesitation, Bet shook her head, then she looked up at the ceiling in despair. 'It's everything,' she said. 'I just need time.' She took Emma's hand. 'Could you tell Inspector Abberline that I'm ill and can't work? Just for a few days.'

'I suppose so.'

'I'm sorry,' she said. 'I really am.'

Then she lay back down and pulled the blanket over her head again.

Emma and I looked at one another in bewilderment.

'Bet?' I said, but she didn't answer, so after a few moments we left her alone and went back into the other room.

'We should give her some food,' I said. 'And something to drink.'

Emma nodded. Together we found some bread and cheese, and made tea, and I took it into the bedroom.

'I'll leave this here,' I said. 'Please eat something.'

Bet didn't acknowledge me, but I knew she'd heard.

I backed out of the room, and Emma and I went outside again.

'It's Green,' said Emma as soon as we'd shut the door behind us. 'There's no question.'

She began walking quickly along the street.

'She said not.' I followed, trying to catch up.

'She hesitated though, before she shook her head. It's Green.'

'Perhaps,' I said. 'Where are we going?'

'To see Fred. I want to know more about Constable Green.'

At the police station, Emma marched straight through the foyer. 'We're going to see Inspector Abberline,' she called to the man on the desk, without stopping, me trailing in her wake. She went on down the corridor, rapped on the door of Fred's office and went inside.

Fred was alone, writing notes. He looked surprised when we entered and then alarmed as he saw Emma's face.

'What's happened?' he said. 'Are you all right?'

'I'm fine,' she said, sitting down. 'But something's wrong with Bet.'

'Bet? Is she ill?'

I sat down too without waiting to be asked. 'We think it's something to do with Green.'

'Have they quarrelled?'

'It's much worse than that,' Emma said. 'She won't get out of bed. She won't eat. She's barely talking.'

'Odd,' said Fred with a frown. 'But not really my area of expertise, I'm afraid.'

'Tell us everything you know about Green,' Emma said. 'I know you're not keen on him. Tell us why.'

Fred put down his pen and looked at us, then he got up and went to shut his office door. 'None of this leaves this room.'

'Absolutely,' I said.

'I had a teacher at school,' he began. 'Scottish chap. He had a word he liked to use about certain boys. It's funny, I've not thought about him for twenty years or more, but this word just keeps popping into my head when I see Green.'

'What's the word?' I asked.

'Sleekit.' Fred sat back down.

I looked at Emma, who looked as confused as I felt.

'And what does it mean?'

'Sly,' said Fred. 'Cunning. Not being as he appears to be.'

'Gosh, that's exactly how I see Green,' said Emma. 'What a good word.'

'George says he uses schoolboy tactics,' I added.

'George Lusk?' Fred asked.

'That's him.'

Fred nodded in approval. 'Good man.'

I felt absurdly pleased.

'After you told me about seeing Green with Harrison, I did a bit of . . . well, nosing around, I suppose you'd call it,' Fred said to Emma.

'You saw him with Harrison?' I'd not heard about this.

'They were just talking,' she said. 'But then Harrison gave him this sort of affectionate punch on the shoulder, and it was so out of place, from an officer of his rank to a constable, that it made me think.'

Fred opened his desk drawer and took out a folder.

'This is Green's file,' he said. 'He's been a police officer for at least ten years but there's very little in it. That's surprising in itself.'

'Right,' I said, not really understanding.

'And have a look at the personal information.' Fred opened the folder and turned it round so Emma and I didn't have to read upside down.

'Silas Green, born 18th November, 1857,' I read out loud. 'And?'

'Read further down,' Fred said. 'Look at the names of his parents.'

'Father Ambrose Green,' Emma read. 'Mother Maria Green, née Harrison.'

'Harrison?' I said.

'Green is Harrison's nephew,' Fred said. 'And the emptiness of his file, and the speed in which he was transferred here from Surrey, makes me think Harrison had a hand in it.'

'You think he did something wrong, and Harrison did him a favour?' I said.

Emma hit the table with her hand. 'That makes sense of the conversation I heard,' she said. 'Green was whining about something, and Harrison said he'd done everything he could for now, or people would start asking questions.'

'I am of the opinion that Green made a mistake or got in trouble in some way in Surrey and Harrison stepped in and moved him up here,' Fred said. 'The only trouble is, I can't ask what. If Harrison got wind of me poking about in Green's past, the only person being moved on would be me.'

'You can't ask questions,' I said. 'But Emma and I could.'

There was a moment's silence, then Fred nodded slowly. He pushed the folder across the desk towards me.

'But be careful,' he said. 'Don't go to his superiors. Find

someone the same rank. There's an Edward Jones mentioned in there – find him if you can.'

'All right,' I said, gathering up the file. 'Come on, Emma. We've got a train to catch.'

We didn't reach Guildford until lunchtime and then we had to take a hansom cab from the station to the village where Green had been based. So when we emerged, dirty and tired from travelling, and went into the little police station with its attached house, I was in no mood to be messed around.

'Good afternoon,' I said. 'I wonder if you can help me? We're looking for Constable Edward Jones. Is he here?'

The police officer on the desk looked at me, then at Emma, and he shook his head. 'No.'

I took a deep breath. 'Then could you possibly tell us where we could find him?'

'No.' He sighed. 'Take a seat and I'll get someone else to help you. Lost cat, is it? Or has someone stolen your washing from the line?'

I gave him a tight smile. 'It's personal,' I said. 'And I don't have a cat.'

'We do really need to speak to Constable Jones,' said Emma.

'He's in the café across the road.' We turned to see a woman sweeping the floor. 'Don't be a coot, Hugh.' She looked at us. 'Honestly, as soon as he gets behind that desk, the power goes to his head.'

I laughed. 'So Constable Jones is . . . ?'

'Right opposite – he's on his tea break. He'll be eating fruit cake and drinking the biggest cup of tea he can.'

'Thank you,' I said.

'But not you,' Emma said to Hugh on the desk, who looked affronted.

The cleaner's laughter followed us out of the door.

Constable Jones was a rotund fellow, who was indeed eating fruit cake and drinking tea when Emma and I sat down at his table.

'I'm on my break,' he said through a mouthful of crumbs.

'We just want a quick chat,' said Emma. 'About Silas Green.'

Jones looked alarmed. 'I don't know him.'

'You do,' I said. 'There's no point in lying about it.'

'Who are you?' he said, pushing away his empty plate. 'What are you doing here?' His face paled as he looked at Emma. 'You're not his wife, are you?'

'No,' she said. 'But Green works for my husband in London. We think he might be up to no good.'

Jones rolled his eyes. 'He's in London, is he? I wondered where he'd gone. Half expected him to be in prison.'

Emma nudged me with her foot under the table.

'Is he a wrong'un?' I said.

'That's putting it mildly.' Jones looked hopefully at the counter, where a bored-looking woman stood. 'I might need another cuppa while I talk. And some more cake. This could take a while.'

'Fine,' said Emma, gesturing to the woman. 'But it had better be worth it.'

Jones sat back in his chair, his hands on his stomach. 'He came to us from Guildford,' he said. 'While ago now. Five or six years? Thought he was the cock of the walk because he'd worked in the city.'

'Sounds about right,' said Emma.

'He was really good at charming the top brass,' Jones went on. 'All smiles and helpful suggestions. And the younger coppers all loved him but he used them. Made them do stuff, then sat back while they took the blame. Reminded me of a bully I knew at school.'

I glanced at Emma as the waitress put the tea and cake in front of Jones. 'Manipulative,' she said.

'Exactly.'

'Why did he move from Guilford?' I asked.

'Well, he made out like it was his decision but I had a friend who worked there, said he got a bit rough with some women in the cells, and they moved him on.'

'Was that true?' Emma said.

'I didn't believe it at first, but then I saw the way he was with them. When he thought no one was there.'

'How was he?' Emma had gone a little pale.

'It was like he enjoyed the power,' Jones said. 'At first I just noticed little comments. He spoke to them like they were nothing.'

That was exactly what Ginger had said. I nodded.

'And then once I found a woman bleeding across her face. She said she fell, but I knew from how she reacted to Green that she wasn't telling the truth. She was scared of him.'

He took a loud slurp of tea.

'What does he do, your husband?' he asked Emma. 'What's Green up to now?'

Emma stared at him. 'He's an inspector, of course,' she said. 'Green's in the police.'

Jones spluttered his tea down the front of his tunic. 'No,' he said.

'Yes.'

'That's not right,' he said. 'He shouldn't be in the police. I thought he'd been kicked out.'

'Why?' I said. 'What made you think that?'

'Because of what he did before he left,' said Jones. He was talking as though it was all perfectly obvious. 'What happened with that woman – Maud Connor, her name was. I thought she was all right. I mean, she liked a drink, but she was harmless.'

'What happened?' Emma said.

'She was in the cells one night. Legless, she was. Barely knew her own name. We couldn't send her home like that, so we brought her in. About four o'clock in the morning, Green went to check on her. And he was gone a long time. Then he came back saying she'd gone for him and he'd had to fight her off. Like an alley cat, he said. He had a scratch down his cheek.' He looked up at Emma and me. 'Just one scratch. And Maud couldn't hardly walk when we put her in that cell. Couldn't stand up straight.'

I nodded, understanding what he was saying.

'So she was injured, was she? Maud? Badly injured?'

Jones shook his head. 'She wasn't just injured,' he said, sounding wretched. 'She was dead.'

# Chapter 44

## Bet

After Emma and Maggie left, I lay in bed for a while longer, thinking. The image of the jar in Silas's locker was imprinted on my brain and I couldn't stop seeing it.

At first, I thought I'd got muddled. Perhaps I was tired, I told myself. I was upset after such an awful day – seeing those jars in Timothy's cellar and then having the man die at our feet. I was mixing things up. Remembering things wrong.

But as I lay there, going over and over it in my head, I realised that while I had been tired and upset, I hadn't imagined it.

There was a jar in Silas's locker. And that was why he'd tried to discourage me from going into the room, and then stood in front of his cupboard the way he had done. The fact he'd done those two things made me certain I'd seen what I thought I'd seen.

What I couldn't for the life of me understand, though, was why Silas would have taken one of those gruesome jars from Timothy's cellar in the first place. Putting it on the shelf there like it was a trophy he'd won. It made no sense. It made me wonder if he was the man I thought he was.

Maybe, I thought, there was an explanation for it all.

Perhaps it was evidence? Perhaps he'd taken it on the advice of Abberline? I pushed away the voice that told me evidence wouldn't be kept in a constable's personal locker. Because what did I know? I was a cleaner, not a police officer.

What I needed, I thought, was a second opinion. I'd been so foolish to send Emma and Maggie away when I should have told them everything and listened to their thoughts on the matter.

I swung my legs out of bed, wincing a little as my bare feet hit the cold floor, and stood up. I would go to find them, I thought. And then perhaps I would speak to Silas. Surely there was a perfectly reasonable explanation for this.

I got dressed quickly and left a note for my mother in case she came home and found me gone – she'd been very worried the last day or so. I felt a flash of guilt that I'd been so unresponsive.

Then I wrapped up warm, putting a shawl over my coat because the wind was bitter, and headed out. I was disappointed, though. Maggie wasn't at her office and Emma wasn't at home either. I asked a few people if they had seen them, but they hadn't. Nor did anyone know where George was.

Defeated, I paused for a moment, thinking about going home. Then I shook my head. I had to get to the bottom of this and the only place I would find out more would be the police station.

With a new sense of purpose, I headed towards Leman Street. The station was busy when I arrived but not overly so. Inspector Abberline was walking through the foyer as I arrived.

'Ah, Bet,' he said. 'Feeling better?'

'Yes, sir.'

'Good.'

'Inspector, you don't happen to know where Emma is, do you?' I asked.

'Emma?'

'Your wife, Emma,' I said.

'Emma,' he said again. 'Hmm. No, I'm afraid I don't.' He smiled at me. 'You know what she's like, always here, there and everywhere.'

'I do,' I said wondering why he seemed to be lying about Emma's whereabouts. 'Thanks anyway.'

He wandered off.

'Oh, Inspector!' I called after him. 'What about Constable Green? Where is he?'

'Now that I do know,' he said, turning back. 'He's down at the docks, checking the boats. Queen's orders. I'm afraid he'll be there all day. Possibly tomorrow too. Now, if you'll excuse me, I really must get on.'

At a loss as to what to do next, I went to my cupboard and hung up my coat and hat, then I took a broom from the rack. There was no harm in just looking in the constables' room now, was there?

I swept along the corridor. Some policemen walked past me but took no notice. Then I casually pushed open the door to the constables' room with my behind and went in, sweeping as I went.

There was no one in there.

Quick as a flash, before I could even think about what I was doing, I pushed the broom through the door handles to stop anyone coming in while I snooped. Then I went to Silas's cupboard. It was fastened with a padlock, but that didn't stop me. I'd not learned much from my father, but I had learned how to pick a lock.

I pulled a hairpin from the nape of my neck and straightened it out. Then, carefully, I put it in the lock and twisted until I felt it click.

'Got it,' I murmured.

I pulled open the cupboard and gasped. It was empty, more or less. Silas's shoes sat in the bottom and on the shelf at the top – where the jar had been – was now just a letter in an envelope.

'Oh,' I said aloud. 'Well, that proves I was wrong, doesn't it.'

Except, I was still convinced I had been right – that I'd seen the jar in the locker. I put my hand on the shelf, almost wondering if the jar was there and I just wasn't seeing it. But no. As I pulled my hand away again, I knocked the letter on to the floor. And when I picked it up, reading the address on the front, I had an idea. I could go to Silas's house. He wasn't there – I knew that. Fred had told me he'd be busy for the rest of the day. I could get inside, have a look round, and perhaps put my mind at rest.

*Or find the jar*, that little voice in my head said.

Decision made, I put the letter in my pocket, shut the cupboard again and locked it. Then I pulled my broom from the handles and went to put it away.

Silas didn't live in Whitechapel. He lived over the border with the City of London, near Golden Lane mortuary. It was very different to Whitechapel. The roads were wider and lighter. The paving stones were more even. It felt nicer. Safer.

I walked along, trying not to think about what I was doing, or why, or that this would be the second house I'd broken into in less than a week. Needs must.

Silas's house was small and neat, built from yellow London bricks, in a row of others the same. Just as I'd done with Timothy's house, I stood back to see if there was an easy way inside. But Silas was a policeman, and he hadn't left any windows open.

Acting like I belonged there in case anyone was watching,

I went down the side of the house and round the back and breathed a sigh of relief because the back door had a window in it. Recklessly, I picked up a stone from the side of the little yard and smashed the glass. Then I wrapped my arm in my shawl, and pushed out the shards that were stubbornly clinging on, before I reached through and found the key in the lock.

'Fool,' I muttered, turning the key a little awkwardly, then opening the door. I'd have expected a policeman to have paid more attention to making his home secure. After all, there were a lot of bad people about.

Silas's house was a little like Timothy's in that there weren't many clues inside as to who lived there. But there were a few things dotted about that told me I was in the right place – a police helmet on the sideboard. A bottle of whisky in the kitchen – Silas's favourite – and a few books on the shelf. All mysteries, of course.

I went upstairs. It was small but tidy with a room either side of the top of the stairs. Silas clearly slept in the room at the front. It had a double bed and a fireplace, and a pair of trousers were slung over a chair. I opened the wardrobe, but there was nothing in there except a few shirts and another pair of trousers. The bedside table was empty, too. No jars. Nothing suspicious.

I went into the other bedroom. This one was much smaller, with a single bed and a tall wardrobe with ornate patterns at the top. I pulled at the door, but it didn't open – it was locked.

'Who locks a wardrobe?' I said out loud, pulling another hairpin from my head. A person with something to hide, that was who.

I wiggled the hairpin in the lock and felt it click into place. I took a deep breath and opened the door, reeling back as a stale, metallic smell hit me.

'What on earth?' I said, putting my hand over my mouth and nose. The wardrobe rail was empty except for one item of clothing – a heavy jacket made from a dark brownish-black tweed with flecks of white.

'Salt and pepper,' I breathed. I squeezed my eyes shut, not wanting to see what else was there, then with some effort, forced myself to open them again.

The wardrobe shelves had a selection of odd items on them that made no sense to me – a brass ring, a broken hat pin, a cigarette case, green with age and battered, a dead flower, and a folded piece of fabric.

On the bottom shelf was the jar. I reached inside and, bracing myself, took it out. I didn't want to see the contents, but I had to be sure this was one of the jars from Timothy's house. Inside was liquid, and floating in the liquid was some sort of organ. I didn't know what it was. I felt my stomach lurch and I quickly put the jar back again, in case I dropped it.

Behind the jar was a rolled piece of thick paper. I reached for that now, and unrolled it, knowing before I even opened it what it was. Sure enough it was one of Gent's horrible sketches, showing a woman in the position Annie Chapman had died in.

I breathed in, a ragged, rasping breath, wanting to look away from the picture, but somehow unable, until I forced myself to roll it back up and shove it to the back of the wardrobe where I'd found it.

Feeling weak, I steadied myself on the edge of the wardrobe door.

'Keep going, Bet,' I told myself, gripping the door so tightly that my knuckles were white through the skin. 'This is important.'

With considerable reluctance, next I took out the folded piece of fabric. It was cotton, thick with something. I

381

unfolded it with some difficulty, peeling apart the pieces, and baulked as the same metallic smell hit me. It was blood, I thought. This was a piece of clothing – a shirt, perhaps, or an apron? And it was soaked in blood.

I felt my legs begin to shake. With trembling hands, I folded the fabric up again as best I could and shoved it back inside. I slammed the wardrobe door shut, then thought for a second. What if I didn't put it all back?

I was finding it hard to breathe. I sat down heavily on the bed, desperately trying to gather my thoughts.

Silas was clearly just as obsessed with the murders as Gent had been, just as interested in Timothy's macabre jars as the quack himself had been. But this was so much more than that. So much worse that I could hardly let myself think it.

Thoughts jumbled through my mind. Silas had all these gruesome keepsakes. He had a salt-and-pepper-coloured jacket. He wasn't a tall man, he had a moustache . . . He'd even had money in his wallet when we went to the music hall. Too much money for a police constable. Could he have been the one selling information to Gent?

This was like a nightmare. Was it possible? Was Silas – the man I'd shared my feelings and my kisses with – was he the Whitechapel murderer?

My vision clouded for a second and I thought I was going to faint. Panicking, I put my head between my legs and tried to breathe normally, because the last thing I wanted to do was faint and be found by Silas out cold on his rug.

After a few minutes, I began to feel less light-headed. I sat up again, thinking about what to do. I had to tell Abberline; there was no doubt about it. But how could I possibly get him here without alerting Silas to what I had found?

I stood up and as I did so, I heard a floorboard creak on the stairs. I froze. Was there someone here? Was it Silas?

Hardly daring to breathe, I stayed as still as I could for a few seconds, listening intently. Nothing. Maybe it was my mind playing tricks on me.

Cautiously and quietly, I poked my head round the door a tiny amount, half expecting to see Silas coming up the stairs. But the house was empty.

Though, wait. Hadn't I shut the door of the room opposite? Now it was ajar. I couldn't remember if I'd heard the door close properly. I squinted at the room, trying to see any sign of movement through the gap between the door and the frame. Could he be in there? I didn't know. I just knew I had to get out of that house.

Making a split-second decision, I looked round the bedroom, hoping for a bag or something to carry my grim finds in. I got lucky with a carpet bag under the bed, so I dragged it out. It was much too big for the small items but I threw them in, averting my eyes from the jar and dropping in the rolled-up sketch, too. I'd take them to Abberline, I thought, and tell him what I'd found.

Taking a deep breath, I dashed down the stairs so fast my feet hardly touched each step. I ran through the house, and out the back door, the bag banging against my legs. And I didn't stop running until I was back across the border into Whitechapel, where I finally let myself slow down.

It was getting dark now. Weak with shock and weary from the exertions of the day, I trailed along, my senses jangling as the contents of my bag rattled. I kept startling at every noise and shying away from shadows, concentrating on putting one foot in front of the other. 'Walk, Bet,' I said aloud in time with my steps. 'Walk, Bet. Walk, Bet.'

As I reached the corner by Maggie's office, I paused

for a second, longing to see her and Emma and tell them everything, but there was no light on upstairs. I carried on, turning the corner and shrieked as a man loomed up at me out of the shadows.

'Bet?' he said, but I couldn't reply as everything went dark and I dropped to the cobbles.

# Chapter 45

## Maggie

Emma and I got back from Surrey late. We were cold and tired and reeling from what Constable Jones had told us about Green.

'Come and have a cup of tea,' I said to Emma. 'We can work out what to do.'

'There is nothing I'd like more,' she said. 'I feel all dusty and dry from the train.'

We walked along the road and up ahead, near one of the new street lamps Fred had made sure were installed, we saw a woman appear carrying a bag. She was swaying slightly on her feet as though she was drunk, or perhaps ill.

'Is that Bet?' Emma said.

As we watched, a man approached the woman, who shrieked loudly and fell to the ground.

'It is Bet,' I said. 'And George. Come on!'

We hurried over, and found George scooping Bet up into his arms.

'She fainted,' he said. 'I think I scared her. What a stupid old goat I am.'

'Bring her inside.' I felt in my pocket for my key and unlocked the door. 'She's not been well, George. This wasn't your fault.'

George carried Bet inside and into my bedroom, where he placed her gently on the bed.

'Bet?' Emma said, taking her hand. 'Bet, can you hear us?'

Bet stirred slightly, but she didn't open her eyes.

'She had a bag,' I said to George. 'Where's it gone?'

'I think she dropped it when she fainted. I'll fetch it now.'

He went off back outside and came back carrying a carpet bag I'd never seen before, which he placed on the floor beside the bedroom door.

'I just wanted to come and check you were all right,' he said, looking upset. 'I didn't mean to scare poor Bet.'

I went to him and put my hand on his arm. 'There is something going on with her,' I said. 'Something to do with Silas.' I glanced at Emma. 'I think perhaps she's found out he isn't the man she thought he was.'

George nodded. 'Better to find out now than after they walked down the aisle, eh?'

'I suppose you're right.'

'Should I get a doctor?'

I shuddered. I was a little off doctors. 'I think she probably just needs to sleep.'

Emma was sitting on the bed, unlacing Bet's boots.

'My mother said there wasn't a problem couldn't be solved by a good night's sleep.'

'Let's hope so,' I said.

'I'm going to go,' George said, edging towards the door. 'I think I'm in the way here and I'm off on patrol later anyway. Should I pop along and pass on a message to Bet's mother? Tell her that she's safe?'

'Would you?' I felt a rush of affection and gratitude towards this kind, caring man.

'Of course.' He looked at Emma. 'How about your Fred, Mrs Abberline? Shall I tell him you're here, too?'

'Yes please,' she said. 'I don't think we should leave Bet.'

'Consider it done.' George gave us a little jovial wave and headed for the door. 'I'll come back and see how Bet is tomorrow.'

He looked a bit worried, so I said: 'It really wasn't your fault that she fainted, you know.'

'Sure?'

'I'm certain.'

'Then I'll see you tomorrow.'

Emma had arranged the blankets over Bet and taken her own boots off. Now she lay down on the bed, too.

'I'm worn out too,' she said. She stroked Bet's hair in a maternal fashion. 'Poor duck. Do you think she found out about the woman in Surrey?'

'She's certainly had a shock, that's for sure.'

Emma's eyes were drooping. 'We've all had a shock.'

I sat down on the other side of the bed and started taking off my shoes, too. 'Tomorrow we'll go and see your Fred, and tell him what we know.'

'He'll know what to do,' Emma agreed. She turned on to her side. 'We'll see him tomorrow.'

I could tell from her breathing that she was already asleep. I'd have to get up and go into the other room, I thought. I was lucky I had another bedroom. But overwhelmed with tiredness, instead, I lay down too, and soon I was asleep.

I woke with a start the next morning, to see Bet sitting upright, looking confused.

'Why am I here?' she said. 'Why are you all here?'

'You fainted. George brought you here. Do you not remember?'

She looked at me, then at Emma, who was stirring, and her eyes filled with tears.

'I do remember. Oh, Maggie, it was awful.'

'What happened? Can you talk about it?'

Emma was properly awake now. She sat up, rubbing her eyes. 'How about I make some tea and we go upstairs?'

'Good idea,' I said. 'Are you feeling all right now, Bet? Can you stand?'

'I think so.' Bet got up gingerly. 'Yes, I think I'm all right. I just had a shock.' She grimaced. 'Well, a few shocks.'

She looked round the room.

'I had a bag?' She sounded panicky. 'What happened to the bag?'

'It's here.' I went over to where George had put it and picked it up.

'Good,' she said. 'Could you bring it?'

Watching her carefully in case she stumbled, I followed her upstairs, while Emma made tea and brought it up. We all sat down on the armchairs and Emma put the tea tray on the small table.

'So,' she said, pouring tea into a cup. 'What happened? Because Maggie and I have something to tell you too, and I'm afraid it's rather horrible.'

Bet looked pale but determined. 'You go first, because I'm fairly sure mine is worse.'

'All right.' Emma took a breath. 'We spoke to a chap who worked with Green in Surrey and he told us . . .' She paused and looked at me, clearly unsure how to word it.

'He killed a woman – someone who was in the cells,' I said. This was no time to hide the truth. 'But he wasn't punished. Instead, his record was wiped clean and he was moved to Whitechapel, because Harrison is his uncle.'

Bet closed her eyes briefly, nodding as if none of this was a real surprise.

'When he was trying to convince me that Timothy was the Whitechapel murderer, he told me that when some-one's killed once, they get a taste for it. That they enjoy the power it gives them. That they will always go on and kill again.' She swallowed. 'It seems like he was speaking from personal experience.'

I glanced at Emma. 'What do you mean?' I asked, unsure where she was leading. 'You surely don't mean . . . ?'

'It's easier if I show you,' Bet said.

She took the carpet bag she had been carrying when we saw her outside and opened it slowly.

'After Timothy, I was with Silas at the police station and I thought I saw one of the jars in his cupboard.'

She opened the bag and looked inside. 'I wasn't sure, though. I told myself I was mistaken.'

'Why would he take one of the jars?' said Emma in disgust.

'That's what I kept asking myself,' Bet said. 'That's why I didn't want to get out of bed. I was so shaken by it all. I was going over and over it in my head, knowing what I'd seen but doubting my own eyes. It's such a horrible thing – like a souvenir of a terrible man. I couldn't think of nothing else.'

'I'm not surprised,' I said.

'So then, yesterday, I realised I needed to know for sure. I went back to the police station but his locker was empty. Instead I went to his house.' She was speaking deliberately as though it was hard for her to say the words. 'I wanted to see . . . I needed to know.' She took a breath, reaching into the bag. 'And I found these.'

She took out a roll of paper. 'I ain't going to show you, because it's awful, but this is one of Gent's sketches. And this . . .' She lifted out a jar, just enough to show us the lid but not the contents. 'This is one of Timothy's jars.'

I leaned back against the chair, shocked. 'That awful little man,' I said. 'He clearly has a problem with women, and enjoys them being hurt. He's the very sort who should never be in the police. How dare Harrison shunt him to London to avoid him being punished?'

'He should be in jail for what he did to Maud,' Emma said. 'We need to tell Fred.'

'No, wait,' Bet said. 'There's more.'

She reached into the bag again and one by one she took out a cigarette case, a hat pin, a dead flower, and a folded piece of fabric. She picked up the bag and shook it and a brass ring fell out. She put that next to the other items.

Emma went pale. 'That's mine,' she said. 'That hat pin is mine – or at least it was. It was on the bonnet I gave to Polly.'

'Yes,' said Bet matter-of-factly. 'This ring belonged to Martha. I'm pretty sure. Lots of women her age have them. My mum used to wear one. And I think the cigarette case was Annie's – it's got initials on it, see? JC. Wasn't her husband's name John Chapman? And the flower? I think that belonged to Elizabeth.' She took another deep breath. 'And this? I think this is from Kate's apron.'

My stomach lurched as she unfolded the fabric and showed us the bloodstains.

'Bet?' I said weakly. 'This doesn't mean he's the killer. Lord knows, we've met enough men recently who are obsessed with women's pain. Perhaps Green is just one more.'

Bet looked like she wanted to cry, but she didn't. Instead, she breathed in deeply. 'Inside Silas's wardrobe I found a jacket – dark with flecks of lighter thread. Like salt and pepper.'

'No.' I couldn't quite believe what I was hearing. 'Are you saying . . . ?'

Bet lifted her chin. 'Let's consider the evidence,' she said.

'Bet, you don't have to do this.' Emma shook her head. But Bet was determined.

'Constable Green has keepsakes from all the murdered women,' she said. 'And from two of the suspects. He has a jacket that matches the one described by witnesses.' She grimaced. 'He was defensive when I asked him if he knew Gent, though I didn't make much of it at the time, and he has money. Too much money for a copper of his rank. I think he was the one selling the details of the murders.'

'George said the killer could be someone the victims trusted,' I said. 'He joked he could have been a priest.'

'Or a policeman,' said Emma.

'He weren't in his uniform, though,' Bet pointed out. 'Mind you, my dad could always spot a copper whatever they were wearing. He said they had something about them.'

Emma pinched her lips together. 'Perhaps the women thought he was going to help them, and instead he . . .' She trailed off as her voice cracked.

'The evidence is all there,' said Bet. 'I'm not picking a suspect and making the clues fit. Not this time.'

'No,' I agreed. 'You're not.'

Bet looked sickened, but she sat up straight, her jaw set with determination. 'I'm as sure as I can be that Silas Green is the Whitechapel murderer.'

I nodded slowly, and Emma did too, as the enormity of what Bet had uncovered sank in.

With slightly shaky hands, Emma reached out, took the tea tray off the table and put it down on the desk. Then she came back and arranged the items in the order of the murders – Martha, Polly, Annie, Elizabeth and Kate.

We all sat and stared at them without speaking.

And that's where we were when the police arrived.

There was a sudden pounding on the door and the sound of the lock splintering, hammering footsteps, and then two constables arrived in the room, brandishing their truncheons.

They stopped short when they saw us all together and, shocked and scared, we all stood up. I held my hand out, urging them to calm.

'What's this?' I said, trying not to sound frightened. 'I would have let you in if you'd given me a moment.'

'We're looking for Bet Palmer,' said one of the constables.

'That's me,' said Bet. 'I'm Bet Palmer.'

'You're a hard woman to find, Miss Palmer.'

'Not that hard,' Bet said, staring him in the eye. 'If you'd given me half an hour I'd have come to you. I work at the bloody police station.'

'Now now, there's no need for cheek,' he said. With a flick of his head, the constable stepped forward and took Bet's wrist roughly, making her cry out. And as quick as you like, he pulled her arms round behind her back and handcuffed her.

'What's going on?' I growled. 'What are you doing to her?'

'We've had reports that she is the Whitechapel murderer.' Harrison came into the room, looking smug. Emma and I both gasped as we saw him.

'What reports?' I said, as Bet stumbled against the bobby who'd cuffed her, and he shoved her upright. 'This is nonsense.'

'An unfortunate woman came to the police station last night, and told us everything,' said Harrison. 'She said you killed all those others, and she was frightened for her own life. Derek on the desk said she was trembling because she was so scared. She even told us we'd find you with souvenirs you'd taken from the victims, and here we are.' He looked down at the coffee table. 'Souvenirs.'

'This is not how it looks,' said Bet. 'This isn't me.'

Frantically she looked at each policeman in turn. 'This was Silas Green. He is the man responsible for these murders. I found all these items in his house, along with a salt-and-pepper-coloured jacket.'

'Did you?' Harrison said. 'And did anyone else see them there?'

'No,' Bet said. 'Well, no, I went there alone.' She turned to us. 'I heard someone on the stairs when I was there – it must have been Silas. He must have seen me and set me up.'

'How convenient.' Harrison glared at her.

'Please,' Bet begged. 'You have to believe me. I couldn't kill anyone . . .' She trailed off. 'I didn't kill those women. I promise.'

'Harrison, you must know this can't be true,' I said, hoping to appeal to his better judgement. 'Who was this woman who gave you the report?'

'She didn't give her name,' said Harrison. 'But it all checks out.'

'It was Green,' I said in exasperation.

'What, wearing a dress and a bonnet?' Harrison chuckled. 'Derek might be getting on a bit but he knows a woman when he sees one.'

I wanted to shake him by the shoulders in frustration. 'No, I'm not saying it was Green who made the report. I'm saying it was Green who told the woman – whoever she was – to report Bet.'

'Why on earth would she do that?' Harrison looked at me as if I was quite mad.

'Because she was frightened of him?' I said, trying my best to sound authoritative and make him listen to what I was saying. 'Because he probably threatened her. Because he, not Bet, is the Whitechapel murderer.'

Harrison's expression darkened. 'Constable Green is no killer.'

'He is, and you know he is. It's him you need to arrest.'

'Constable Green is taking a few days off.'

I felt cold. 'But you know where he is?' I said. 'Harrison, do you know where he is?'

He rolled his eyes.

'He's killed five women,' I said. 'Six. Six women. He's not going to stop now. You need to find him before he does it again.'

Harrison shook his head, looking at me in mock bewilderment. 'What nonsense these women come up with. Constable Paul, take Palmer down.'

I put myself in between Bet and the door.

'No!' I said. 'You can't. Bet isn't the killer – it's Green. He killed Maud Connor in Surrey and he killed all the others too.'

Without warning, Harrison hit me hard across the face, sending me sprawling on to the floor. Emma yelped in shock and Bet cried out.

'Take her away,' he said to Constable Paul. 'And Williams?' He looked at the other policeman. 'Gather up these souvenirs. It's all evidence.'

Paul gripped Bet by the shoulder and steered her towards the door. As she passed Harrison he looked her up and down. 'All this time, all this hard work, and we never thought it might be Jill the Ripper we were looking for.'

'What hard work?' Emma said in disdain. 'You've done nothing – it's Fred who's put in all the work and now you're swanning in to take the credit for arresting the wrong person. You're an idiot.'

'Careful,' Harrison said mildly. 'Or you'll be joining Miss Palmer in the cells.'

Emma gave him a hard stare. 'I'm not sure my husband would take kindly to that.'

'Well, as Inspector Abberline is currently clearing his

desk ahead of an extended leave of absence, I'm not sure he'd have anything to say at all.'

Emma's jaw dropped. I struggled to my feet, my face throbbing.

'Don't worry, Bet,' I called to her as Paul shoved her out of the room. 'We'll sort this out.'

The other constable followed Paul, clutching Bet's carpet bag, and when Harrison turned to go, I said: 'There is one thing missing from that bag of souvenirs, you know?'

'What's that?' Harrison's face twisted as he looked at me.

'The knife,' I said. 'The murder weapon.'

He looked at me. I saw a muscle next to his eye twitch.

'We'll find it,' he said.

'You can pull this whole building apart,' I said. 'And Bet's rooms, and Emma's house. You can even look in Abberline's office. But you won't find it. And do you know why?'

'Why?' Harrison was staring straight at me.

'Because he needs it. Green needs his weapon so he can kill again. And when he does, Harrison, the victim's blood will be on your hands.'

# Chapter 46

## Mary Jane

It was freezing cold and the air was full with that icy drizzle that felt like a cloud had dropped on to Whitechapel. Mary Jane's feet were wet before she'd even walked as far as the corner, and she immediately regretted leaving home at all. But she'd promised Joseph she'd meet him for a drink and she wanted to see him. She missed him, even though she was still cross with him for leaving.

They'd quarrelled when Mary Jane had started inviting girls to stay the night. Joseph said their room was too crowded with just the two of them in there, he said it wasn't seemly for him to be sharing with so many women, and that people would talk. But Mary Jane knew it was more that he wanted her to himself – he liked it better when it was only the two of them.

She wiped her damp face as she crossed the road, stopping to avoid being splashed as a horse and rider went by. Joseph, she thought, could annoy her like no one else. Except for every policeman she'd ever had the misfortune to come across. But that was a different annoyance – like having a fly buzzing round your face on a summer's day. Joseph made her rage at times. But he also made her laugh more than anyone else could. He listened to her opinions and asked what she thought about things. He told her she was beautiful, which was nice and that, but he also told her she was clever. No one had ever said that before. And he looked after her. He'd come round earlier to see her, and he'd been ever so worried about the broken pane of glass by the front door. 'I'll mend that,' he'd said. 'You'll get the wind coming in.' He'd stuffed it with some rags, to keep the warmth in, and Mary Jane had given him a kiss to say thank you, pressing herself up against him just as she knew he liked.

'Meet me later,' he'd said into her ear, his voice thick with desire. 'Ten Bells.'

So that was where she was going. She had her best dress on and no hat, so he could see her hair in all its glory. She was vain about her hair, she knew that, but it was her best feature. She patted it now, hoping it hadn't gone all flat in the rain, and hurried along quicker.

But Joseph wasn't in the Ten Bells. Mary Jane sat there for a while alone until a lad appeared at her elbow.

'Oi,' he said.

'Oi yourself.' She looked at him – he was barely out of short trousers. 'Are you old enough to be in here?'

The lad grinned. 'No,' he said. 'But no one cares much.'

'What do you want from me?'

'Got a message for you from Joseph Barnett.'

Mary Jane rolled her eyes. 'He ain't coming?'

'Nah,' said the lad. 'He said to tell you he's back at the fish market and he'll see you tomorrow.'

'At the fish market?' Mary Jane was pleased, despite being left to drink alone. Joseph had lost his job as a porter at the market when he was accused of thieving. But he said he hadn't done it and Mary Jane had believed him, and now he was working again, which meant Mary Jane wouldn't have to bring in extra money anymore.

She gave the lad the rest of her gin and ordered another

and then her friend Julia arrived so she had a couple with her, too.

'I've got a plan,' she told Julia. 'I'm going to tell Joseph, me and him should go home.'

'To Miller's Court?' said Julia, honking with laughter, Mary Jane gave her a thump, but it was affectionate.

'To Ireland,' she said. 'Back to Limerick.'

'I thought you said you ain't been there since you were a little nipper?'

Mary Jane shrugged. 'I ain't. But I feel it in my bones.'

'It rains all the time in Ireland,' said Julia, draining her drink. 'You don't want to go there.'

'It rains all the time here,' said Mary Jane. 'It's just nicer in Ireland.'

'Do you even remember it?' Julia asked.

'Not really.' Mary Jane shook her head. 'Not at all really. But it's a feeling, ain't it?'

'Homesick for somewhere you've never been,' said Julia.

Mary Jane laughed. For a moment she let herself imagine standing by the door of a cottage, green hills behind her, rosy-cheeked baby on her hip. Joseph coming home and their little lad running to meet him. 'I'm going to tell him,' she said.

'Well, make sure you say goodbye,' said Julia, slipping off her stool. 'I'll see you.'

'You don't want to stay with me tonight?' Mary Jane asked. 'You can if you want?'

'I've got a room,' Julia said. 'But thank you. Stay safe, yeah?'

She kissed Mary Jane on the cheek.

'You, too,' Mary Jane said.

With her drinking companion gone, Mary Jane decided to go home. She left some money on the bar, and went back out into the cold night. It would be the first time in ages she'd been in her room alone. She would make the most of it.

Back home, she took off her boots and her skirt, which was wet round the bottom, and put it next to the fire to dry. She put on a clean dress, and pottered around, sweeping the floor, rearranging the few bits of furniture she had, and singing to herself. She sang songs she remembered her mother singing when she was a little girl. Songs of the Irish countryside and the streets of Dublin.

And that made her think of something. She found her old battered suitcase under the bed. The one that had seen her from Cardiff to Wolverhampton to Paris and back to London. In the lining was a tiny slit, and inside Mary Jane had hidden her most precious items. Precious to her. They weren't worth nothing to anyone else. She had her wedding ring from her marriage to Owen – the chap she'd married in Wales when she was just 16. She took it out and looked at it, turning it so it shone in the candlelight. Poor Owen. Dead before he was 20 and she a widow at 18.

'That's a long time ago now,' she said out loud. It wasn't even ten years ago but it felt like another life. She dropped the ring back into the case and pulled out her mother's brooch. Her ma had always called it a Tara brooch. It was a silver hoop with swirls, and a sort of dagger through the centre and a tiny green emerald that caught the light. Mary Jane never wore it in case it got lost, but now she pinned it to her dress. A sign of the new life she planned across the Irish Sea.

When there was a knock on her door, she sighed. She wasn't expecting any visitors but perhaps it was her neighbour Prudence from upstairs.

Swishing her skirt, and still singing under her breath, Mary Jane went to the door. She couldn't see who was there without taking away the rags from the broken window, but she opened the door anyway.

Outside stood the policeman. Green. The one Mary Jane thought was the worst of the lot with his muttered asides and his roaming hands.

He grinned at her, a horrible, predatory smile.

'Hello, Ginger,' he said. 'Can I come in?'

# Chapter 47

## Bet

I had never been so uncomfortable, so cold and so absolutely scared out of my wits in my whole life. I couldn't believe I was in a cell, locked up in a room I had been cleaning just the other day, with a drunk woman called Dark Ange, who was snoring loudly in a corner, and another woman who had a lengthy argument with herself before passing out.

I'd been here for more than twelve hours now, with only a crust of bread and some watered-down beer last night. There were no blankets despite it being freezing, and there was a bucket in the corner – the opposite corner to where Dark Ange snoozed – that smelled like something had died in it. Which it might have. I was sure I'd heard mice, or rats, scratching about during the night.

I'd barely slept a wink. I was shaking with cold and fear. Where was my mother? I wondered. Did she know where I was? All those nights she'd worried about my father being banged up, and now I was the same.

And what about Emma and Maggie? Where were they? Had they found Abberline? Could they convince him that Silas was the killer? They knew as well as I did that he was the Whitechapel murderer.

Silas. My Silas.

I felt sick just thinking about it. How could I have been so stupid?

As I heard the clock on the church outside chiming six o'clock in the morning, I sat up on the pallet where I lay and went to the bars.

'Derek,' I hissed to the old boy at the custody desk. He was asleep. 'Derek!'

He started awake.

'I need to get out,' I said.

'You'll have to wait.'

'I need to see Emma Abberline,' I said. 'Can you get a message to her?'

'No.'

I wrapped my fingers round the bars, wishing I was strong enough to rip them apart. 'Derek, it's me,' I said. 'Bet. You know me.'

'I can't help you,' Derek said. 'I wish I could, but I can't.'

'I cleaned your bloody shoes,' I grunted under my breath. I felt my throat tighten with tears and I lay back down again, letting myself sob.

'Oi,' said Dark Ange from the corner. 'Shut your bloody gob.'

# Emma

Maggie and I had been up all night with Fred, who was alternating between despair and absolute fury. We'd started off at our house, but then he paced up and down, bemoaning his lack of notes and files, so Maggie had convinced him to go to her office.

'We've got everything you need,' she told him.

And so now we were back in the office with Fred

staring in astonishment at the wall where we'd pinned everything.

'You investigated all this?' he said.

I nodded, casting a slightly worried glance at Maggie. He was quick-witted, my Fred, and like she'd said herself, London's leading murder detective. He was bound to notice that the link between all our suspects – Bernard, Gent and Timothy – was that they were now all dead.

But perhaps Fred didn't notice, or maybe he didn't care, or maybe it was a bit of both, because he didn't mention it. Instead, he stared at the wall.

'There must be something we can use, to prove it was Green,' he said.

'There's no evidence against Bet,' I said.

'And very little against Green,' Maggie pointed out.

'If only Bet had left the souvenirs where they were,' Fred groaned. 'Then we might have stood a chance.'

'He'd have moved them,' Maggie said. 'He wouldn't have left them in the wardrobe, knowing Bet had already seen them. I bet he's burned his coat, by now.'

'What about Constable Jones?' I asked. 'He told us Green killed a woman in Surrey.'

'That's not a bad idea.' Fred nodded. 'I'll get a message to him, see if he's prepared to speak up.'

'Even if he does, though, it just proves Green killed Maud Connor – not the Whitechapel victims.'

'But it'll be a start.'

I went to his side. 'What about you, Fred? What about your job?'

He looked down at me. 'It'll be fine in the end,' he said. 'I've been around for long enough to know that things always come good if you wait.'

'Really?'

'Really.' He smiled at me. 'Perhaps I'll be shunted off to

another desk job for a while. Who knows? But it'll be all right.'

'I hope so.'

'Well, you're the detective in the family now,' he said. 'Are you going to give her a job, Maggie?'

Maggie chuckled. 'My reputation could be shot after all this. I might be the one who needs a job.'

'Maggie's going to train Bet,' I said. 'Bet wants to be a detective.'

'But what about you?'

'Ah, it's just a hobby for me.'

'Like knitting,' said Fred, with a small smile. But the idea of being a detective made me tingle with a little bit of excitement. I pushed it to one side for now, because we had bigger things to worry about.

'What are we going to do?' I said, thinking about Bet alone and upset in the cells. 'Can we go and see Bet?'

'I'm willing to bet Harrison has told everyone not to let us in,' Fred said. 'But you could try. Listen, I'm going to telegraph Constable Jones in Surrey, and a chap I know in Guildford – I believe he's one of the top brass now, so he could prove helpful. Shall we meet back here in an hour?'

'Absolutely,' I said. 'Shall we go, Maggie?'

'I'm right behind you.'

# Maggie

Fred was right – we weren't allowed in the main entrance. But Emma wasn't about to give up.

'We can go round the back way,' she said. We were standing at the bottom of the steps that led up to the big police station doors. 'There's an entrance round the back.'

'Won't it be locked?' I frowned. 'From the inside?'

Emma slapped her forehead. 'I'd not thought of that.'

'I'll open it.'

We both turned to see Percival coming down the stairs towards us. He gestured for us to head round the corner, so we did, and he followed.

'Something's going on,' he said in a low voice.

'Well, yes, Bet's been accused of being Jill the Ripper,' I said, my tone sarcastic.

'She didn't do it,' said Percival.

'We know.' Emma sounded exasperated. 'It was Green.'

Percival reared back in shock. 'Green?' he said. 'Silas Green?'

'Silas Green,' I said.

I expected Percival to argue but actually something odd happened. He closed his eyes briefly and nodded. Then he looked at me. 'He killed someone before, didn't he? In Surrey?'

'You knew?' I was furious suddenly. 'You knew and you didn't say anything?'

'I didn't know for sure. I just pieced bits together from things he said.' Percival looked very young and very frightened. 'I wasn't sure. But I didn't leave him alone with girls in the cells. Just in case I was right.'

'That was why you followed him round like a lapdog?' said Emma in wonder. 'You were actually being a kind of chaperone?'

'Well, no, not all the time.' Percival looked embarrassed. 'At first I really did think he was marvellous.'

'Good lad,' I said, still astonished. 'Can you let us in, then?'

'I'll go now. Give me a minute and then follow.'

He nodded at us and darted off round the corner. Emma and I stared at one another.

'Well, well, well,' I said. 'Who'd have thought?'

'He told me he had a sister who he'd tell to steer clear of Green,' she said. 'I should have asked him for more information.'

'He could have said something sooner.'

Emma looked despairing. 'At least he's helping us now. Come on, we've given him long enough to unbolt the door.'

She led me round the back to the courtyard. Whitechapel Police didn't have many horses but they had a few and the stables were at the back of the station.

'The door is round here,' she said. 'It's not used very often – just sometimes for prisoners.'

We slunk through the archway that led to the main road, and past the horses, who whinnied for attention. Emma gave one of them a cursory pat on the nose, and led me round the side of the main building.

'That's the mortuary over there,' she whispered, pointing to the whitewashed rooms tacked on to the back of the station. 'Then the cells are in the middle and there's another door right here . . .'

She stood back to let me see.

'This is where they released Polly Nichols,' she said. 'And I waited for her round the front and gave her my bonnet.'

'So it leads to the cells?'

'It does.'

'Then lead the way.'

The door was stiff and for a moment I thought Percival had let us down and it was still bolted. But with a bit of effort from both of us, we got it open. It smelled bad in that part of the police station – unwashed bodies and urine. I grimaced.

'She should be up here,' Emma said, pointing along the hallway. 'But there might be someone at the desk keeping an eye on things, so be careful.'

We crept up the corridor, and saw, to our relief, that the desk was empty. And there was Bet, sitting on the floor beside the bars of the cell, craning her neck to see further up the hallway. Another woman was asleep nearby, and a third was standing up, shouting to herself.

'Bet!' I said in a loud whisper. 'Bet!'

'Oh my goodness.' She got to her feet and reached through the bars, gripping our hands tight. 'You're here.'

'We were so worried about you,' I said. 'Are you all right? No one's hurt you?'

'I'm fine,' Bet said. 'Well, not fine, but I'm not hurt.'

In the main part of the police station, a door slammed, and voices shouted.

'Something's going on,' Bet told us. 'I don't know what, but it's something big. I'm worried it could be . . .'

I felt the blood drain from my face. 'Another murder?' I said, just as Emma said: 'He's done it again.'

'I think so.' Bet looked wretched. 'You need to find him. And stop him.'

'We need to find him,' I said, filled with rage. 'If someone else has been murdered then you're in the clear – they can't possibly accuse you when you've been locked up all night.'

'I wouldn't put anything past bloody Harrison.'

'Just you wait,' I said. 'Come on, Emma.'

'Where are we going?'

'To find out what's going on.'

Made bold with anger, I marched along the corridor and through the door into the main part of the police station, where the first person we saw was Percival.

'What's going on?' I demanded. 'Did you find out?'

He looked wretched. 'Another murder,' he said. 'Worse than ever before.' His face was pale in the dim light of the corridor. 'I said I'd go and help but they sent me away to do paperwork. Said it wasn't for me to see.'

'Lord,' Emma breathed next to me. 'We need to find Fred.'

Percival nodded. 'I wondered . . .' he began. 'I thought, perhaps . . .'

'What?' I snapped, distraught at the thought of another dead woman and unfairly taking it out on the only man nearby. 'Spit it out.'

'I was going to go and find him. Inspector Abberline, I mean.'

Emma and I both stared at him,

'You were going to do that?'

'Well, he should be here. And Harrison's got no idea what he's doing. And Green . . . well, someone needs to stop him.'

'Yes,' I said quickly. 'Yes, find Abberline.'

'I should have said something sooner,' he said, looking wretched. 'Spoken out when I had doubts.'

I felt a wave of sympathy for him. He was only young.

'Men twice your age would have done the same,' I told him. 'You're doing the right thing now. That's what's important.'

'Fred's sending a telegram to Surrey,' Emma told him. 'He'll be at the telegraph office. And if he's not there, he'll be at Maggie's office.'

I scribbled down the address, and he took it.

'I just have one tiny thing to do first,' he said. 'But it's really important and it'll only take a minute.'

'Be quick,' I said sternly.

'Yes, ma'am,' he said, which I quite liked. And off he ran.

'Perhaps he really isn't as bad as we thought,' said Emma.

'He's not found Fred yet,' I pointed out.

'He will.' Emma sounded confident.

We carried on into the foyer of the police station. It was deserted. Presumably everyone had been called to the scene of the murder.

'What should we do?' I said.

Emma shrugged. 'Wait for Percival to fetch Fred, I suppose.'

We stood around helplessly for a few minutes. I was pacing up and down. Emma sat on one of the wooden benches, her legs jiggling as she stared out of the window. And then she said: 'Oh goodness, here's trouble.'

A senior police officer was climbing the stairs to the main entrance, with Harrison by his side, and Constable Paul – the one who'd arrested poor Bet – trailing behind.

Emma got to her feet and came to my side. 'It's Jim Monroe,' she said in my ear. 'He used to work with Fred in the West End. He's a commissioner now.'

'Are you telling me young Constable Percival was making up everything he just told me? That he was lying?' Commissioner Monroe was saying to Harrison. Emma and I exchanged a glance.

'Not lying as such, no,' Harrison said, sounding both contrite and defiant all at once. 'More mistaken.'

'So your nephew Silas Green – a serving policeman – is not a suspect in the Whitechapel murder investigation?'

'Well, he, erm, I think everyone's getting a little confused . . .' Harrison said. 'If we could all just take a moment . . .'

But Monroe clearly didn't want to take a moment. 'And you are saying you did not cover up him killing a woman in the cells in Surrey and bring him to Whitechapel?'

'I thought it was for the best, sir,' Harrison said meekly. 'I could keep an eye on him here.'

'The best for whom?' Monroe bellowed, making both Emma and me jump.

Harrison simply stared at him, lost for words.

'You can hand over all your findings, then clear your desk,' Commissioner Monroe continued. 'I'll take it from here. We need to avoid the enormous scandal this clearly is. An officer of your rank using your position to hide as twisted and evil a villain as your nephew? You'll be lucky if you don't end up in jail, Harrison.'

'That was what Percival needed to do,' I breathed in amazement. 'He needed to tell Monroe everything.'

'How on earth did Percival get Monroe to listen to him?' Emma muttered.

'Sir, Percival is unreliable,' Harrison said. 'His conduct is most unsatisfactory. I've raised concerns about him in the past . . .'

Monroe glared at him. 'Percival is engaged to my stepdaughter.'

'That's how,' I said out of the corner of my mouth.

Emma grinned as Harrison squawked ineffectually and Monroe simply sighed. 'And now it is left to us to apprehend this killer before word gets out that he's one of our own. This could damage the reputation of the Metropolitan Police for decades. Has someone gone to find Abberline?'

'No sir,' said Paul. 'Not yet, we were waiting for . . .'

I stepped forward. 'Actually, I believe Constable Percival just went to find him.'

Monroe nodded in appreciation. 'That's where he dashed off to. He said he had somewhere to be.'

'I believe so.'

'And who are you?' he asked me.

Harrison gave me a look of pure hatred as I spoke. I averted my eyes from his glare.

'I'm Maggie Cameron,' I said. 'I assist the police in their investigations.'

'A lady detective?' said Monroe in delight. 'I have heard about this. Marvellous stuff. Very forward-thinking.'

'I'm Emma Abberline, sir,' said Emma, stepping forward too. 'I'm Fred's wife.'

'And are you a detective as well?'

'No,' said Emma, shaking her head. 'It's really more of a hobby.'

'Like knitting,' I said.

'Shame,' said Monroe. 'I don't wish to be rude, but I do rather have my hands full today. How can I help you, Mrs Abberline?'

Emma pulled her shoulders back. 'I'm not sure if Percival said, but our friend is currently in the cells, on the orders of Commissioner Harrison. She's been accused . . .'

'Wrongly accused,' I interrupted.

'She's been wrongly accused of being the Whitechapel murderer.'

'You have someone in the cells?' Monroe turned on Harrison, his voice booming round the foyer.

'Well, yes, sir,' Harrison said.

'A woman?'

'Yes, sir.'

'Oh good God, this just gets worse,' said Monroe. 'What on earth were you thinking?'

'All the evidence pointed to her . . .'

'Really?' Monroe's tone was icy cold. 'But while she has been locked up, there has been another murder.'

'Yes, sir.'

'So she is clearly innocent.'

'Yes, sir.'

'So let her out.'

Harrison looked at Paul. 'Could you . . .'

'No!' bellowed Monroe. 'You do it, Harrison.'

The men all walked off and Emma and I looked at one another.

'They're going to keep this quiet,' she said. 'You heard Monroe, it could damage the reputation of the Metropolitan Police for decades.

'Forever,' I said. 'No one will pay the police any heed

411

if it is revealed they covered up the Whitechapel murderer being one of their own.'

There was a pause as we both contemplated what would happen if the people of London did not allow themselves to be policed.

'So what do we do now?' Emma asked.

'Now,' I said, taking a deep breath. 'We find Green.'

# Bet

I had never seen anyone look quite so furious as Harrison did when he unlocked the cell door to let me out.

'You can go,' he said, more than a little sulkily.

'I told you it weren't me,' I said. 'But then you knew that, didn't you?'

He grabbed my wrist, twisting it so hard, I feared it might break.

'Don't give me any of that, you disgusting little . . .'

'Oi!' said Dark Ange from inside the cell. 'Leave her alone.' She picked up the remains of her watery ale and threw it over Harrison's head and I jumped back, pulling my wrist from his grip, to avoid any splatters.

'Have that,' Dark Ange said in satisfaction.

I laughed at Harrison, his face red with anger.

'Has there been another murder?' I asked him.

'I don't need to tell you anything.' He wiped a drip of ale from his nose.

Another man appeared at the end of the corridor. He was wearing the same fancy uniform as Harrison and he looked annoyed.

'What are you doing, Harrison?' he said. 'I told you to let her out, not to have a conversation about it. I want you to be out of here before Abberline comes back.' He looked at me. 'Are you Bet?'

'Yes, sir.'

'Your friends are waiting in reception.'

'Thank you, sir.' I walked along the hall, and when I reached him I said: 'I know who the murderer is, sir. It's Silas Green. He's a copper.'

He nodded. 'We know.'

'How did you work it out?'

The man straightened his collar. 'It wasn't me,' he admitted. 'It was Constable Percival.'

I was almost speechless with surprise. 'Percival? Well I never.'

'He'll be an excellent policeman one day.'

I shook my head in disbelief. 'Percival. Who'd have thought it?'

But there were more pressing concerns than Percival coming good. I fixed the policeman with a hard stare. 'What are you doing to find Green?'

'I've got extra men on their way now.'

'Right,' I said, not feeling overly reassured. 'Well, that's good.'

Feeling Harrison's eyes boring into my back, I headed off to find Emma and Maggie.

They were both in reception and I walked straight into their outstretched arms, feeling relieved and sad all at once. Relieved that I was out of that awful place, and sad that another woman had died.

'What do you know about the latest murder?' I said.

'Nothing at all yet,' said Emma. 'Oh, here's Fred.'

Abberline, looking slightly dishevelled and very stern, came into reception followed by Percival.

'Bet,' Abberline said. 'Good to see you out of the cells. Are you all right?'

413

'Yes, sir,' I said. 'But what of the latest killing? What do you know?'

Fred shook his head. 'I need to speak to Llewellyn now. But it's a nasty one, by all accounts.' He looked at the three of us all huddled together, then he came over and kissed Emma on her temple. He put his hand on Maggie's shoulder and then did the same to me. 'Take care of each other,' he said.

Percival watched him go through the doors that led to the mortuary and then he came to stand with us.

'I know who it was,' he said. He looked drawn and shocked. 'Girl called Mary Jane. I believe most folks knew her as Ginger?'

My stomach twisted. 'No,' I moaned. 'Not Ginger?'

Maggie, always so stoic and bold, burst into noisy sobs. Emma, pale but straight-backed, looked at Percival.

'Tell me what you know.'

'Word is, he went to her room. And she let him in because, well, she knew him, didn't she?'

'She didn't like him,' said Emma. 'But she'd have let him in because she was scared of him. Scared he might arrest her.'

'Well, he did a lot worse than that,' Percival said. 'He killed her.'

We all stood in silence for a moment, horrified by the news. 'Poor Ginger,' I said eventually, shaking my head. 'Poor Mary Jane. She was so young. Not much older than me.'

'It's terrible,' Emma said, her voice raspy with anger. 'He needs to be stopped. Green needs to hang for what he's done.'

'Abberline will know what to do,' I said, hoping my faith in the inspector would be proved right. 'He's back in charge now.'

'He is back, but Green could be anywhere.'

'I'll go and find out what's happening,' said Percival. 'Stay here and I'll come back.'

I had absolutely no intention of staying where we were and I was sure the others felt the same, but I nodded my head anyway. Percival scurried away and I turned to Maggie and Emma.

'Green will know they're on to him by now,' I said. 'He's bound to run.'

'They're sending men to the railway stations,' Emma said. 'I heard them talking about it. And to the docks.'

I shook my head. 'He's not stupid. He won't risk getting on a train.' A thought struck me. 'Did you come in past the stables?'

'We did.'

'Silas is a good horseman. He could get quite far on a horse.'

'Would he be so bold as to take an animal from the police stables?' Maggie looked doubtful.

'He knows those horses,' I said. 'He likes them and they trust him.'

Emma snorted. 'More fool them.'

'He would sometimes go and see them when the grooms were taking their lunch break,' I carried on. Outside the clock struck midday. 'Like now.'

We all looked at one another.

'Should we tell Fred?' Emma said. 'Or Percival?'

I shook my head. 'No time.' I tugged on her sleeve. 'Let's go.'

We all ran down the corridor, and out of the back door, which was stiff but creaked open infuriatingly slowly. In the yard, the rain was still falling and the courtyard was full of puddles. There were two horses in the stables, and a third stall that was empty, but there was no sign of Silas, nor the grooms.

'Let's wait in there,' I said, pointing to the empty stall. We can keep dry, and we'll hear him if he comes.

# Emma

We didn't have to wait long. As the rain eased, we heard cautious footsteps coming into the yard, and then a voice murmuring to one of the horses in the stall next door.

Bet stiffened. 'That's him,' she mouthed to us.

I looked at Maggie, suddenly realising we hadn't thought about what to do now he was here. More than anything, I wanted to make a run for it, to alert Fred that the man he was looking for was right here on his doorstep. But I knew that wasn't possible.

Silas was still talking to the horse. We could hear him putting on the saddle and fastening the buckles.

Through a slit in the wooden wall of the stalls I watched him leave the horse for a moment and walk across the yard to find saddle bags. Then he came back and began loading up the poor beast. I wondered where he was planning to go.

As he led the horse out of the stable, Maggie nudged Bet and kicked me. 'Now,' she said softly.

We all quietly went to the door and, as Green got up on the horse, we burst out of the stable.

'Stop!' Maggie roared. The horse startled, dancing across the cobbles as Green tried to calm it.

'I was wondering if you might show up,' Green said, laughing. 'How sweet. I'm afraid you're too late.'

'There are policemen all over the city looking for you,' I said. 'You won't get away with it.'

'You'd be surprised how incompetent the police can be.'

The horse was still nervous, lifting its feet up as though the cobbles were hot. Green leaned forward, stroking its ears.

'She's a beauty, isn't she?' he said. Then he gave a snort of laughter. 'That's what I said to Ginger, actually. She's a beauty too. Well, she was.'

I stood still, fists clenched, willing Fred to appear or one of the grooms to come back.

'So, lovely seeing you, but I have to go,' Green said. 'Oh, before I forget . . .'

He dug into the pocket of his trousers.

'You might want this.'

He dropped something on to the cobbles and Bet bent down and picked it up.

'It's a brooch,' she said, confused.

'It was Ginger's,' Green said. 'She'd pinned it on to the front of her tatty dress, bless her. But you know, my mother always said you can't make a silk purse from a sow's ear.'

Bet held the brooch at arm's length.

'Keep it,' said Green. 'I took it for you. Cut it off before I sliced her open. Thought you could put it with the other souvenirs.' He laughed again, the horrible sound echoing round the courtyard.

'You're not going to get away with this,' I said. 'Your pathetic uncle can't cover this one up. He's going to jail himself.'

'I don't care about him,' said Green. 'You're right – he is pathetic. You're all pathetic.'

'You're pathetic,' Bet spat, still holding the brooch. 'Ginger knew that. She said you were a coward and a bully. And she was right. You're a silly little man who had to hurt women to make himself feel good. You couldn't pick on anyone your own size, could you? No, it was vulnerable, scared, ill women. You're pathetic.'

'Maybe you're right,' said Green. 'But I don't care what you think. And I won't hang for these crimes. They'll let me get away and then they'll cover this up, just like my uncle covered up my mishap in Surrey. A trial would be too damaging for everyone.' He grinned down at me. 'Especially your husband.'

417

'That's not true,' I said, but even as the words left my mouth, I knew that it was. The Metropolitan Police was bigger than this. Bigger than the deaths of some women that no one really cared about. Bigger than Harrison's actions. Bigger even than Green's twisted tendencies. This whole thing would disappear – it would have to, or the police would be broken before they'd really got started.

'They'll catch you,' said Bet weakly.

'They won't.'

Green tugged on the reins, ready to make his escape. But just as he did the sun came out from behind a cloud, dazzling us all. A ray hit Ginger's brooch, still clutched in Bet's fingers, and shone a shard of green sunlight into the eyes of Green's horse, who was already skittish.

She whinnied in surprise and reared up. And Green, caught unawares by her movement, still looking at us in triumph, was thrown from her back and hit the wall behind with a sickening crunch.

He crumpled to the ground, a trickle of blood running from his ear to the cobbles below. And the horse galloped off, through the archway and out into the street.

Maggie, Bet and I all stood there for a second, staring down at Green where he lay. His eyes were open and glassy, and there was no doubt whatsoever that he was dead.

'Oh, for heaven's sake,' said Maggie. 'This is becoming a habit.'

She reached out and took my hand and I took Bet's, and together we stepped over Silas's broken body and walked out through the archway, into the sunshine.

# A Letter from Harriet Fox

Thank you so much for choosing to read *The Women in the Shadows*. I hope you enjoyed it! If you did and would like to be the first to know about my new releases, sign up to my mailing list here: https://kerrybarrett.substack.com/

I always love the research part of my writing, but I have to admit the sheer volume of books, films, documentaries and internet theories about Jack the Ripper was slightly daunting. This is also the only book I've written that's given me actual nightmares. In the end I found focusing on the people involved in the crimes, rather than the actual murders, was the way to go. And I made a conscious decision not to dive down too many rabbit holes into the background of the many, many suspects – none of whom I think were guilty.

I hope you loved *The Women in the Shadows,* and if you did I would be so grateful if you would leave a review. I always love to hear what readers thought, and it helps new readers discover my books too.

Thanks,

Harriet

@kerrybean73 (Instagram and Twitter)

@kerrybean7373 (TikTok)

https://www.facebook.com/kerrybarrettwrites

# Historical Note

Anyone with even a passing interest in Jack the Ripper will know there is a whole industry devoted to this most intriguing true-crime story. Consequently, quite early in my research I made the decision to focus only on some of the facts, and to fictionalise the rest, in order to simplify things for myself and the readers.

All the victims are, of course, real. Some of the things they say in this story are real, especially in conversations with police officers as that was all documented.

Martha, the first victim in the story, is not considered one of the 'canonical five' victims of Jack the Ripper, but I believe she was indeed murdered by the same man. I'm less sure Liz was a Ripper victim, but it would be strange to leave her out.

I have become oddly fond of all the victims. Researching their stories and reading about their families and jobs and the hard times they had suffered made me protective of them, and I am so sad that their lives ended in this way. I feel strongly that they are the people who should be centred in this story and not the murderer.

If you'd like to know more about the victims, I really recommend *The Five* by Hallie Rubenhold. She's also done a podcast on the same subject, called *Bad Women,* which is very evocative and interesting.

Inspector Fred Abberline was a real person involved in the Ripper investigation. He was well respected and liked. There is little information to be found about his wife Emma. So other than her name and the fact that she was married to the inspector, she is all fictional.

Bet is fictional and so is Maggie, though female detectives like her were a real thing in Victorian London.

Some of the police officers are real, and some – Percival and Green, for instance – are not. Dr Llewellyn was real. And lovely George Lusk was real, too. He was a very good man who worked hard to keep the streets safe.

As for the suspects, Gent and Timothy are loosely based on real suspects but the others are based on my own theories and interests. John Pizer – Leather Apron – was real.

And speaking of Johns – there were a lot of them in this story. So, for ease I have changed some of their names – Liz's ex and Kate's current partner were both called John in real life.

Similarly, Pearly Peg was actually called Pearly Poll, which is a marvellous name but which got a bit confusing with Polly Nichols. So I tweaked it, just to prevent anyone (mostly me!) getting muddled.

I would love to hear your questions, theories and stories about the Ripper murders and the victims. Please get in touch and share what you think.

x

In memory of Martha, Polly, Annie, Liz, Kate and Mary-Jane.
London 2025

Dear Reader,

We hope you enjoyed reading this book. If you did, we'd be so appreciative if you left a review. It really helps us and the author to bring more books like this to you.

Here at HQ Digital we are dedicated to publishing fiction that will keep you turning the pages into the early hours. Don't want to miss a thing? To find out more about our books, promotions, discover exclusive content and enter competitions you can keep in touch in the following ways:

### JOIN OUR COMMUNITY:

Sign up to our new email newsletter: http://smarturl.it/SignUpHQ

Read our new blog www.hqstories.co.uk

𝕏 https://twitter.com/HQStories

f www.facebook.com/HQStories

### BUDDING WRITER?

We're also looking for authors to join the HQ Digital family!

Find out more here:

https://www.hqstories.co.uk/want-to-write-for-us/

Thanks for reading, from the HQ Digital team

ONE PLACE. MANY STORIES

Bold, innovative and
empowering publishing.

FOLLOW US ON:

@HQStories